To Franc[...]

Joseph. Damiano

You have a most gracious
father. You need to be
proud of your family
& heritage. The greatest
heritage in the world

Peter d. Cimini

A Novel

The Secret Sin of Opi

Peter D. Cimini

Robert D. Reed Publishers • Bandon, OR

Robert D. Reed Publishers
P.O. Box 1992
Bandon, OR 97411
Phone: 541-347-9882; Fax: -9883
E-mail: 4bobreed@msn.com
Website: www.rdrpublishers.com

Front Cover Art by: Stephen Linde
Cover Designer: Cleone L. Reed
Book Designer: Debby Gwaltney
Copy Editor: Jessica Bryan

FSC
Mixed Sources
Product group from well-managed
forests and other controlled sources
Cert no. SW-COC-002283
www.fsc.org
© 1996 Forest Stewardship Council

ISBN: 978-1-934759-37-0

Library of Congress Control Number: 2009928231

Manufactured, Typeset, and Printed in the United States of America

CONTENTS

THIS NOVEL IS DEDICATED TO PAULINE GOLDBERG.

Pauline is that rare breed of person who has always put the interest of others before herself. She worked tirelessly for many years meeting the academic, social, and emotional needs of her students. In retirement, she continues to help children reach their potential as a dedicated volunteer. The world would be a more peaceful and gratifying place if we all lived our lives as Pauline has chosen to live hers.

In this novel, the author describes the Italian town of Opi and the surrounding area as it is today and has been for centuries. Since this is a fictional story that takes place in a real town, the author wants to make it clear that neither the current inhabitants nor their ancestors were ever involved in this tale of human captivity.

PREFACE

In the Italian province of L'Aquila in the region of Abruzzo, lies the village of Opi (pronounced "Ope"), considered to be one of a few geological curiosities around the world because of its formation and structure. The town rests on a hill of rock and cliffs in an elongated form. Opi is located in the middle of the fertile Sangrina Valley overlooking an ancient precipice in a narrow steep-sided ravine that has been shaped and eroded by flowing water for many centuries.

During the initial migration of humans to Europe around 2000 B.C., a huge cataclysm broke the Strait of Gibraltar, resulting in the Atlantic Ocean flooding Italy as well as other areas of Europe. People saved themselves by migrating and settling in mountainous regions like the Apennines, where the town of Opi is situated. Geologists have found petrified shells, fish, and other sea animals in the neighboring lower towns of Alfredena and Scontrone. But the fact that no such remains have ever been found in Opi leads scientist to believe that the town of Opi was never flooded.

The hill town of Opi is located in a vast national park in Abruzzo (Parco Nzionale d'Abruzzo). The park area has a landscape of high mountain peaks, rivers, lakes, and forests, and covers 74,000 acres in the upper Sangro valley. The central point of the park is the village of Pescasseroli in the Sangro Valley. The town of Opi is not far from Pescasseroli, and it's the starting point for the climb to the top of Monte Marsicano (2242m). A dense forest of beech and maple trees is situated at the base of the Apennine mountain range circling the park valley as well as the town of Opi. This forest is the natural habitat of the Marican brown bear, Apennines wolves, wild boars, and the chamois (an agile, goat-like antelope). Parco Nazionale d'Abruzzo is one of Europe's most important nature preserves, and it's the refuge for more than forty species of mammals; thirty types of reptiles; and more than 300 species of birds, including the golden eagle and the white-back woodpecker.

Many towns, including Opi, depended on sheep for their existence. The wool sheered from the sheep each year was bundled and shipped north to the Province of L'Aquila, where it was sorted and distributed to Rome and Tuscany. The Sangro Valley, which surrounds Opi, was such a fertile and vast area that many towns rented space there to graze their sheep during the summer months.

At the end of hostilities during World War II, the Italian political system moved to establish a republic with a central unified government. As this became a reality, the people living in the rural areas of Italy were concerned that a republic form of government would not be to their benefit. Therefore, it was not unusual for people living in small towns like Opi to be drawn to the principles of communism. The Italian Communist Party fought to have a political voice in the new government. The Italian Marxist theoretician Antonio Gramsci, who had been speaking out effectively for a number of years regarding the benefits of communism, joined with Henri Lefebvre and Ernst Fischer to lead a Marxist movement in Central Europe. This movement attracted a large audience from the Central European labor movement, the middle class, and the poor. Because of this support, communism established a minority political influence in many countries in Central Europe, including Italy, during the late 1940s and 1950s.

The house at 25 Via San Giovanni de Battista in the town of Opi— where the protagonist of this fictional story was held captive—is the house where the author's grandparents lived, and where his father and uncle were born in the late 1890s.

The stories about the Ciarletta family woven into the beginning this novel come from the author's recollections of growing up in an Italian family in the mid-twentieth century. The stories and events surrounding his grandparents, his mother and father, and his aunts and uncles were part of the traditions and culture that he experienced as a child growing up in the Bronx. The details of the Ciarletta and Sons Ice and Coal delivery business are taken from the author's family background and some actual childhood memories. As a child, the author lived in the Clason Point section of the Bronx, and the house on Beach Avenue where he was born remains there to this day.

Castellamare di Stabia is a bustling port city situated in the lower part of the Bay of Naples. The city has busy and confusing traffic on its many one-way streets. The piazza, dock area, narrow alleys, wall frescos, and wonderful biscotti shops can still be found there today.

In the Italian language, the word usually used for father is *Papa* or *Pappa*. The town of Castellamare di Stabia, from which the protagonist family in this story migrated, is located in the Naples region of Italy. In this area of Naples, the word used for father is *Pàtete*, rather than *Papa* or *Pappa*. For this reason you will find the word *Pàtete* used when the family of the protagonist refers to their Grandfather Leopold.

ACKNOWLEDGMENTS

The information in this novel concerning Islamic philosophy and the practices surrounding the death of one of the characters was graciously shared with the author by Mohamed Anwar Ali, a resident of Cairo, Egypt. Mr. Anwar Ali is a 1994 graduate of Helwan University, where he studied archaeology, art, language, history, and Ancient Egypt. He is a lecturer for the Egyptian Study Society, Denver, Colorado, and he also specializes in tours for the Denver City Museum.

The names of the various foods served when the Ciarletta family visits their son in the seminary were taken from two Italian cookbooks by Marcella Hazan: *The Classic Italian Cookbook* and *Marcella Cucina*. Ms. Hazan is the acknowledged grandmother of Italian cooking in America. She is the author of numerous Italian cookbooks and currently lives in Venice, Italy and Florida.

A good deal of information relating to the dates and events of the German occupation of Italy was obtained from the book *The Battle For Rome, The Germans, The Allies, The Partisans and the Pope* by Robert Katz.

Dr. Roscoe Brown, an inspiring teacher whose classes the author attended at New York University, went on to become President of Bronx Community College, located at the former New York University uptown campus. Dr. Brown was included in the text of this novel as a tribute to a much-admired individual and teacher.

Richard Fontana, Esq., partner of the law firm of Farrauto, Berman, and Fontanta, Yonkers, New York, and his brother, Brother George Fontana, a member of the Marist religious order, are both Italian language scholars who provided the proper Italian grammar usage for many of the Italian words used in this novel. The author is grateful to these two learned men for their willingness to share their knowledge.

A special thank you the artists: to Stephen Linde, who created the beautiful art for the cover of this novel; to Cleone L. Reed, who incorporated Stephen's art into the cover design; and to Debby Gwaltney, who not only created a beautiful design for the interior of the book but also created the profile of characters page.

I owe a debt of gratitude to Jessica Bryan, an extraordinary editor, who helped shape and fine-tune this book while respecting and maintaining my voice.

Finally, with special love, the author is indebted to his daughter, Cara Adair Cimini, a language specialist, who dissected many of the sentences in this book and guided the author toward clarity.

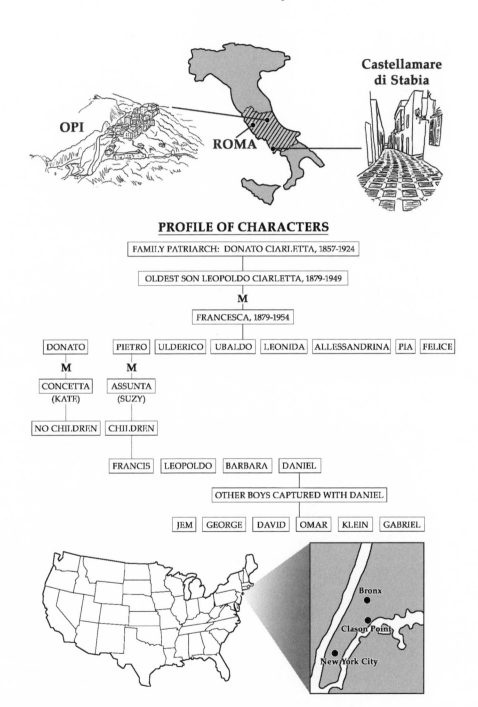

Castellamare di Stabia

OPI

ROMA

PROFILE OF CHARACTERS

FAMILY PATRIARCH: DONATO CIARLETTA, 1857-1924

OLDEST SON LEOPOLDO CIARLETTA, 1879-1949

M

FRANCESCA, 1879-1954

| DONATO | PIETRO | ULDERICO | UBALDO | LEONIDA | ALLESSANDRINA | PIA | FELICE |

M   **M**

CONCETTA (KATE)   ASSUNTA (SUZY)

NO CHILDREN   CHILDREN

| FRANCIS | LEOPOLDO | BARBARA | DANIEL |

OTHER BOYS CAPTURED WITH DANIEL

| JEM | GEORGE | DAVID | OMAR | KLEIN | GABRIEL |

Bronx

Clason Point

New York City

PROLOGUE

Thrilled to be leaving Italy after so many lonely years, Daniel Ciarletta's feet barely touched the broad marble steps of the Rome police headquarters. His *carabiniero* (police) escort—suddenly concerned that he was following rather than leading his charge—called out, "Signore, *piano, piano!* (slowly, slowly!)" Daniel stopped and waited impatiently at the bottom of the steps for his escort. As the two men proceeded toward the police car, Daniel tried to remain in stride with the police officer, but his emotions propelled his body forward, always one step ahead of the *carabiniero*.

Finally forced to stop at the door of the police car, and feeling awkward from his uncontrollable elation, Daniel entered the car, clasped his hands tightly, and reminded himself to relax. His firmly pressed hands seemed to temporarily suppress his rushing energy.

As the car moved out onto the streets of Rome, Daniel began to think about his many failed attempts to escape from his Italian prison town and the disappointment that followed each abortive attempt. Although he had been assured he was scheduled to fly home to America later that afternoon, he wondered whether something unexpected might happen. *Will today be just another cruel disappointment?* With this thought, his excitement turned to anxiety. *Something is gonna happen so I don't return to America today.* His mood quickly changed to tentative caution. He whispered to himself, *Please, Lord, don't disappoint me again. I wanna go home.*

The *carabiniero* startled Daniel from his reverie with a reminder to use his seatbelt. When Daniel and the five other men had been rescued seven days ago, the driver of the police van had to show them how to buckle up. Today he needed no assistance.

1

Daniel tried to distract himself by focusing on the streets of Rome. He saw massive old stone buildings beside contemporary contoured glass and brick structures. Buses, small cars, and scooters briskly wove through the narrow streets, and pedestrians hurried along the sidewalks. Having been isolated in a rural hill town and held captive for so many years, he was mesmerized by the many unusual street images.

After a half hour amid the frenetic rhythms of the city, the police car entered a highway, and the scenery changed to open fields, rolling hills, and farms. Daniel was all too familiar with these views, which seemed to have a calming effect, relieving some of his nervous tension. He found himself becoming more enthusiastic, allowing himself to anticipate his new life in America and being reunited with family and friends.

Daniel understood that his life and daily routine were about to change dramatically. He would be faced with new experiences, new adventures, and have to relearn simple things like the days of the week. During his many years in the Italian mountain town, the days of the week were all the same, thoroughly homogenized to the point where there was no need to know what day it was, except for Sunday. But now, each new day would be different. Daniel would need to change the mindset he had become so used to.

He suddenly asked the *carabiniero*, "What day is today?"

"Today is *Giovedi* (Thursday), *Signore*," said the police officer.

Although the days of the week had become routinely similar in his mountain prison, years were a different matter. Each spring, the new planting season meant another year had passed. At the time of his rescue, Daniel believed he was thirty-five years old, and he had been able to verify this fact during his days of debriefing with the Rome police.

As the police car entered the airport, Daniel marveled at the big sleek silver airplanes with names on their sides. This was as close as he had ever been to an actual plane. He had only seen the giant flying machines in newsreels when he was a young boy or in the sky flying over his Bronx neighborhood as they made their landing approach to LaGuardia Airport. When the police officer parked the car and

Daniel opened the door, the powerful noise of the planes leaving the ground became ear-piercing. The airport, the planes, and the noise had the effect of reassuring him that he was free—and that he was really going home to his mother and father, his sisters and brother, and, hopefully, his old friends. As the two men left the car, the police officer led Daniel to what he referred to as "the terminal."

Walking toward the building, Daniel began to think of his family, *How will they look? How will they sound? Will they accept me after all this time? Will I still feel like the son of my mother and father, and like a brother to my oldest sister Frances, brother Leopoldo, and younger sister Barbara? Or after all these years, will I feel like a stranger in my own house?* For the first time since Daniel had been rescued, he felt uncertain at the prospect of returning to his family.

At the entrance of the terminal, Daniel was startled when the glass doors suddenly opened without anyone touching them. He cautiously moved past the open doors while examining them carefully, concerned they might close as unexpectedly as they had opened. Once inside the terminal, he momentarily stopped, wide-eyed and open-mouthed; he was overwhelmed by an amazing sight. He was standing inside the entrance of the largest room he had ever seen, with a metal ceiling so high it was unimaginable. Huge windows joined together, forming a part of one high wall.

Understanding Daniel's surprised reaction, his police escort hesitated a moment, and then said, *"Avanti."* They moved quickly along the glazed tile floor. The people who rushed past them looked different than Daniel remembered. Men were wearing tight-fitting suits and colorful shirts, some without collars. The long scarves draped around their necks looked like flags billowing in the breeze as they ran to catch their flights. Women were wearing short, tight-fitting skirts, exposing their shapely legs and brazenly outlining their hips. Surprisingly, some of the women even wore pants. Walking alongside men in robes were dark-skinned women with covered heads and colorful flowing clothes draped to cover their entire body. The style of dress was drastically different from the clothing he had become used to seeing in his prison mountain town, Opi.

Daniel was intrigued by all the new sights, his eyes leaping from one amazing display to another, with no time to pause and appreciate what he was observing. He stayed close to his escort, his head bouncing from side to side, as he tried to absorb all the new thrilling scenes. Besides the huge room and interesting looking people, there were small colorful areas serving strange-looking food, a huge wall clock, large murals, bright banners, and wall signs that included words and pictures he did not understand. The room, the colors, the people—everything was exhilarating!

Continuing to move forward, Daniel became fascinated by the noise in the high ceiling room. The many private conversations seemed to mysteriously move upward, joining together and magically forming a continuous hum that returned to the ears of the harried travelers as a synchronized whisper.

Daniel and his escort arrived at a ticket counter. The *carabiniero* handed official looking papers to the woman behind the counter and they had a brief conversation. Daniel's escort turned to him, wished him well, and moved briskly into the throng of moving people.

Carrying a single canvas bag, Daniel joined the line of people who were descending a long flight of stairs. Once outside the terminal, the passengers walked toward a large airplane. Upon entering the airplane, Daniel expected to see the same silvery metal on the inside. Another surprise! He was greeted by modern upholstered seats, cream-colored walls and ceiling, light blue partitions separating sections of the plane, and a carpeted floor. An attractive, uniformed woman personally welcomed him. Another woman helped strap him into his seat. The uniformed woman cautioned him not to loosen the buckle until he was told to do so. At some point, the noise of the plane's motors changed and the plane began to slowly move backwards.

Daniel was beginning his voyage to America after so many lonely, traumatic years in Italy. The plane stopped for a few minutes and then began to move forward, maneuvering and making turns. The aircraft came to a gentle stop. After taxing to the end of the runway, Daniel felt the plane slowly pick up speed, faster and faster, bumpier and bumpier, the wings flapping and vibrating as the plane accelerated. Suddenly, the bumping stopped, and although the plane's motors were still making their unfamiliar powerful noise, there was a sudden calm. It took Daniel a few moments to release the hard grip of his hands on the arms of his chair. His eyes remained focused on the back of the seat in front of him. Eventually, he turned his head and cautiously glanced out the small window beside him. As the plane continued to climb, the objects on the ground became smaller and smaller.

Daniel's attention was now completely consumed by the views from the oblong window. He became fascinated by the shapes of the various land areas, long winding roads, the beauty of curved rivers, and the symmetry of buildings grouped in rows, circles, and lazy long curves. Suddenly, a huge body of water appeared—he could see nothing but water. Streaks of white transparent fluff began to pass his window. In a few moments, the streaks had clustered together, forming a pure white puffy carpet as far as the eye could see. Daniel's fascination with the ground now turned to the interesting shapes of the snow white clouds and the most intense blue sky he had ever seen.

A gentle tap on Daniel's arm drew his attention to a uniformed woman asking him what he would like to drink. In front of her were cans and bottles on a rolling cart. Not sure how to respond, he said, "Anything." The woman reached over the young man sitting in the aisle seat next to Daniel and made a portion of the back of the chair in front of him come down over his knees. She placed a round metal container, a clear plastic cup with ice, and a small bag of peanuts on the flat surface of what had now become his personal table. The can had a strange looking top with a metal ring. Daniel was not sure what to do, so he picked it up and looked closely at the ring. Then he turned it upside down to look at the other end. *If this was soda or juice it would be in a bottle,* he thought.

Noticing his confusion, the man seated next to Daniel said, "Hey man, you don't know how to open the soda, do you? Didja just come from Mars?"

Not knowing how to respond to the man's questions, Daniel sheepishly shrugged his shoulders. With a broad smile the young man said, "Pull the little metal circle and it'll open." Daniel gripped the circle with his finger and looked at the man. "That's right. Just pull it," said the man. When Daniel pulled on the metal circle, he heard an unfamiliar hissing sound and then a *pop* as the can opened. The two men were now smiling at each other. The liquid Daniel poured from the can was black. *It must be cola soda,* he thought. *I had this when I was a kid in America.* He immediately recognized the taste with his first sip. It was cola—and it was wonderfully cold.

After a few hours of sitting and staring out the window, his thoughts began to move from the thrill of his first plane trip to the anticipation of what was awaiting him in America. His mind was moving so fast it seemed electrified. He thought of his family, his Bronx neighborhood, the house on Beach Avenue, and his old friends: Skelly, Mitz, Dutch, Tiny, Giggy, Jack, and Joe Sal. At the thought of his old friends, he began to relax. He recalled the touch football and baseball games they played at Patterson Field and the football punting contests he had with Joe Sal, and how they often talked about trying out for their high school football team. He remembered Giggy's quick sense of humor and how easy it was for him to make others laugh. He smiled to himself as he remembered the games they had played on the street in front of his house: stoop baseball, kick the can, "Johnny on the pony" (with the help of the nearest telephone pole or fire hydrant), and "ringaliveo." Then, for the first time he thought, *Ringaliveo? What a funny name. I wonder what it means.*

Daniel remembered the time he and Skelly and Tiny had called for their friend Pete Sicilian to come out and play. Hearing them yelling outside the window, Pete quickly abandoned his chores and snuck out the back door, his mother yelling at her scampering son from behind the screen door. "Wait till you get back tonight, you mozzarella." From that afternoon forward, Daniel's friend Pete acquired the nickname "Mitz," which was short for mozzarella.

Daniel continued to reminisce about his childhood memories, his annual spring garden chores, and how he would get so angry when his father made him turn over the garden soil—when all he wanted to do was hit baseballs with his friends at Patterson field. His friends would come by and encourage him to drop his garden spade and come with them. Daniel smiled again, remembering their encouragement, "Come on, DD (which was short for his nickname "Dirty Dan"). Forget about the garden; let's hit some balls."

Oh, how he wanted to drop the spade and run off with his friends. But each year he would say the same thing, "I can't guys; my father will kill me." After they left, his fury made him violently mutilate the remaining garden soil. At night, his father, noticing his sulking son, would place his big, rough, warm, fleshy hands around Daniel's face and look admiringly into his eyes, kiss the top of his head, and with that big smile of his say, "Now, my big boy, sit and enjoy a well earned meal." It was always then that Daniel knew why he never dropped the garden spade and went off with his buddies.

Staring out the plane window for a few moments he thought, *My mom and dad always knew how to make it okay when they saw I was upset. I guess I'm pretty lucky to have such great memories of my family and friends.*

These pleasant thoughts of his youth and friends had been very important to Daniel during his forced years in Opi. The memory of his boyhood friends helped to relieve the painful sadness he felt during his confinement in Italy. During many lonely nights, he visualized their games and the pleasure he gleaned from playing with his close friends. Only he understood how important those memories became as the years dragged slowly on.

He wondered, *Do my friends still live in Clason Point? Will I be able to find my old buddies after all these years—and if I do find them, how can I make them understand how important my memories of them were in helping me to remain sane?*

So many thoughts flooded his mind that he couldn't seem to focus on any one of them. His muscles felt like they were twitching, but he couldn't detect any movement. His stomach was churning and his arms felt so light he had the feeling they could rise by themselves. The marvels he had seen since being rescued from Opi made Daniel realize he was entering a new society, a culture he would find completely changed. After being isolated for the past twenty-two years and now returning to America, he felt like an emigrant traveling to a new land. *This must have been how my grandfather felt when he left Italy to find work in America.* Daniel knew that he would be faced with building a new life for himself, just like his grandfather.

Twenty-two years previously—Daniel, then a thirteen-year-old boy—had sailed to Italy to visit his dying grandfather, Leopoldo Ciarletta. Now he was going home to America as a thirty-five-year-old man.

CHAPTER I

𝒯HE 𝒞IARLETTA 𝒯AMILY 𝒥MMIGRATES TO 𝒜MERICA

Castellamare di Stabia, a port city on the Bay of Naples, was once a vibrant economic area noted for its busy port and shipbuilding. In the latter part of the nineteenth century, Italy experienced stagnant wages, high inflation, and a dreadful economy. The economic slump had a devastating effect on the living conditions in the peaceful city of Castellamare di Stabia, as well as the general shipping industry throughout the Naples area.

Leopoldo Ciarletta, the oldest of five children, lived with his wife, Francesca, and two young children, Donato and Pietro, in Castellamare di Stabia. Young Leopoldo was unable to find steady employment, and he was desperate and mortified that he was not able to properly provide for his wife and two infant children. In the fall of 1898, Leopoldo, desperate and with no hope for the future, asked to speak with his father.

"Pátete, I can't support my family without the hope of steady work. I want to hide my face when I go home to my family each night and have to say, 'No work today.' I'm failing them and failing you. I want to go to America where work is plentiful. I'm asking for your blessing and a loan for my passage to America."

"How will your wife and children live while you are in America saving to pay me back?"

"I am asking you to allow my family to stay in the apartment you have provided and also supply my family with food. When I find work, I'll send you money each month from my American wages to repay the loan for my passage and the food you provide for my family."

Leopoldo's father was saddened by his son's desperation. "This is a very difficult request you're making. Let me consider it for the next few days and we will talk at that time."

Leopoldo's father, Donato Ciarletta was a wise and shrewd man. He had very little confidence in the Italian currency or Italy's banking system. He believed only in the stability of land and his bargaining skills. Over the years, he had not hesitated to take advantage of the difficult position of others if he felt it would improve his negotiating position on a transaction. Donato had acquired three buildings with multiple apartments and an empty parcel of land between Naples and Castellamare di Stabia. He was respected for what he had accumulated, but he was not especially liked because of his rigid business dealings. There were even rumors questioning Donato Ciarletta's honesty, but these rumors stemmed from jealousy rather than fact. As Donato was considering his son's request, he wondered if his oldest son's inability to find steady employment related in some way to his reputation in Castellamare di Stabia.

Two days later, Donato called his son to his home. He poured two glasses of wine, one for each of them, and they proceeded to raise their glasses in a toast, "*Salute.*" They enjoyed the bite the strong homemade wine made on the tip of their tongues and the warmth it provided a few moments later.

Donato began to speak in a somber tone. "Leopoldo, I've decided to loan you the money for your passage to America, as well as care for your wife and my two grandsons while you're away. There is one condition. If you can't meet your loan obligations during your first three years in America, I'll expect you to return to your family and birthplace. If you are able to pay the debt you owe during that time, then you have my blessings to make America your new home."

Leopoldo knelt in front of his father, took his hand, kissed it, and said, "*Mòlte gràzi, Pàtete.*"

"There's one more thing," continued Donato. "I've made the decision to share part of my holdings with my five children now, rather than wait till my passing. I'll make the proper arrangements in the next few days, which will give you ownership of the apartment you live in. So even though you are in America, you will legally own property in Castellamare di Stabia. In this way, you and your family will some day be able to return to your birthplace, knowing that you are the owner of a home."

Leopoldo was dumbfounded as he listened to his father's plan to transfer ownership of the living quarters to his name.

"Pàtete, your kindness is more than any child has the right to expect. I'll never forget what you have done this day." Leopoldo approached his father and embraced him with genuine love and affection.

Before boarding the boat for America in January 1899, Leopoldo Ciarletta told his wife, "I know my leaving will be hard on you and the boys, but I must take this chance so we can have a happy life in America, where our sons will be able to work and be free."

Leopoldo settled in New York City and immediately found steady work as an ice delivery man. At the turn of the century, food was preserved in ice boxes, which were usually oak cabinets divided into two sections. The top section held a square block of ice and the lower section was used to store perishable food. Home refrigeration was a technology some thirty years in the future.

Leopoldo saved a portion of his salary each week, and at the end of every month he sent money to his father. His savings were kept in a safe, secret place. He endured loneliness, a coldwater flat, indifferent Irish police, negative stories about Italians, and hostile neighbors.

However, he believed his new life in America—with all its drawbacks and discrimination—would become a better place for his children once he was economically independent.

Leopoldo's life in America over the next three years consisted of hard work and saving for the day he could bring his family to America. In April of 1903, Leopoldo sent a cable to his wife, Francesca, which included the money necessary for her and their children to sail to New York City.

Italian emigrants who left their home country for other shores had a tradition of bringing a large ball of yarn with them as they departed, leaving one end with relatives on land. Then, as the ship left the dock, the yarn would unwind from the hands of the passenger until the end of the yarn left the emigrant's hand and floated, held aloft only by the wind, until the boat was out of sight. In June 1903, Francesca Ciarletta—with her large ball of yarn, four-year-old Donato, and three-year-old Pietro—sailed from Naples to join her husband, Leopoldo, in America. They arrived in late June. The boys

11

experienced a great deal of anxiety about their new life in a strange land and a father who had now become a stranger. For Francesca, there were also mixed emotions. She was thrilled to be united with her husband, but she was homesick for her beloved Italy.

Donato, the oldest son, turned five years of age in August and was enrolled in a New York City public school that first September. During their second summer in America, Donato and his brother spent the seething hot evenings on the fire escape landing of their apartment trying to stay cool, intrigued by the comings and goings on their tenement street.

Donato experienced a good deal of discrimination and teasing from his classmates because of his limited knowledge of English. He was determined that his younger brother would be spared the same embarrassing introduction to first grade. Donato often used their time on the fire escape to help his brother learn their new language. In a high pitched voice, imitating his first grade teacher, Donato asked his younger brother the same questions he had been asked during his first year, "Peter Ciarletta. Stand at your desk and tell the class your name."

Pietro, eager to learn, stood and responded in English, "My name, Pietro Ciarletta."

"No, no," yelled Donato. "You gotta use your American name or the other boys will make fun of you. Your American name is *Peter*, and don't forget to say '*is*' before your name. Say it like this: 'My name is Peter.' That's the way they do it in America. Now try again."

Pietro, now having two things to remember, hesitated and then repeated slowly, "My name is Peter Ciarletta."

"*Bravo*, Pietro," said Donato, immediately realizing he should not have used the word *bravo*, which was a popular expression in Italy, but was not used in the same way in America. Also, out of habit, he had called his brother Pietro rather than Peter.

"Oh, listen to your brother. I make English mistakes, too," said Donato. "I'm what they call in America, *stupido*." The boys had a hearty laugh at Donato's self-deprecating humor. Then, again imitating his teacher by using his best teacher's voice and stiff manner, Donato said, "Very good, Peter, you're allowed to take your seat." Many lessons took place on the fire escape that second summer.

The following September, Pietro began his schooling. After four and five years of attending school, Donato and Pietro were able to read and write in English. In 1908, they were removed from school to work with their father. He needed their wages to help support the family.

In April 1904, a third son, Ulderico, was born, and in 1905 a fourth son was presented to a proud Leopoldo. He named his new son Ubaldo. In 1906, Leopoldo and Francesca moved into a larger apartment located on East 149th Street. Between 1906 and 1911, three girls were born: Leonida, Allessandrina, and Pia; and in 1912, Leopoldo and Francesca had their eighth and last child, another son, Felice.

One October morning in 1912, as Leopoldo and his two oldest boys were leaving for work, Leopoldo announced to his family that today would be a special day. "When I return from work tonight, I will bring my family a special surprise."

The children shouted with excitement, "What's the surprise, Pàtete, tell us now."

"No, later tonight, my children. It will be a big surprise"

After work, the three Ciarlettas reported to the paymaster of the Knickerbocker Ice Company. They were paid their half-week wages, and then Leopoldo and the boys were congratulated by a number of men in the office. A few other delivery men wished them luck. Donato and Pietro were confused.

"Is this our surprise, being paid in the middle of the week instead of Saturday?"

"My sons, your surprise has yet to come," answered their father. Leopoldo and the puzzled boys walked six blocks and entered a livery stable. Leopoldo brought them to the rear of the building and showed them a wagon with a newly-painted sign on the right front side that read, *Ciarletta & Sons Ice and Coal Delivery Company*. The surprised boys were then introduced to the two horses harnessed to the wagon, Garibaldi (named for a heroic Italian military leader) and Victor (named for the king of Italy at the turn of the century).

Leopoldo gathered both boys to his side, one under each arm, and proudly proclaimed, "This wagon and these fine horses will become the future for the Ciarletta family. We'll ride home now and show your brothers and sisters."

A new chapter in the life of the Ciarletta family was about to begin.

Sunday was a day of rest, pleasure, and their favorite food: *maccheroni* with gravy. Sundays always began with the children dressing in their only set of clean, pressed Sunday clothes and walking to the eight o'clock Mass with their parents. The family received Holy Communion, which meant fasting from the midnight hour. After church, they enjoyed a late breakfast. Then, around eleven o'clock, Francesca began to prepare her gravy for the late Sunday afternoon *maccheroni,* to be eaten as their *pranzo* (main meal).

By one o'clock, Donato's and Pietro's stomachs were quite empty, which prompted the Sunday ritual of dunking crusty bread in the cooking gravy. One at a time, they approached their mother as she was working at the stove. Each with a piece of crusty bread in their right hand, they would lovingly place their left arm around their mother's shoulder and give her a kiss on the cheek and a warm hug—hoping to distract her as they simultaneously dipped the piece of bread in the gravy. Francesca was well aware of the reason for their sudden show of affection, and she would lovingly slap their arms, and with a proud smile order them away from her gravy. She would then yell out to her husband in the sitting room, "Leopoldo, your sons are at the gravy again. Do something with these boys!" Leopoldo, obscured by Generoso Pope's *Il Progresso* Italian newspaper, would remain silent, grinning and remembering how as a young boy he had also enjoyed dipping bread into his mother's gravy.

One Sunday afternoon after the bread dipping ritual, Pietro asked his mother why she called the cooking tomatoes she prepared each Sunday *gravy.*

She looked at Pietro with a puzzled expression and responded, "Because in the Italian language, what I cook every Sunday we call *sugo,* and in English sugo is known as *gravy.* Now stop with your foolish questions."

"But, Mamma, the other boys make fun of us at school when we say we have gravy with our *maccheroni.*"

Francesca, clearly annoyed, would retort, "*Americani* make fun of what they don't understand. People in this country are able to work, but they are poor lost souls without a family history to give them comfort."

14

"Mamma, they say everyone else calls it *sauce*, everyone except Donato and me."

Francesca, now visibly angry, answered, "You tell those foolish *Americani* children that Italians call their cooked tomatoes *gravy* because it is our tradition. This gravy I make for you is not sauce, as your school friends call it. The Ciarletta gravy has been given to me by your Grandmother Caetana, who received it from her mamma, Maria Rachelle, who received it from her mamma, Anna Elena. The Ciarletta gravy is *buono* (good) because it has been made best over the centuries. You tell these *Americani* friends that our gravy has been in our family since 1740. Can their mammas say that 'bout this thing they call sauce? You children must be proud of your family's history, which your *Americani* friends don't understand. Always remember the Ciarletta gravy is much more than flavor for our *maccheroni*. You tell these children who tease you that your mamma said our gravy feeds both our stomach and our soul. That is why when you marry you'll expect your wife to make this same gravy."

Pietro, not at all surprised at his mother's fierce defense of her gravy, felt a sense of pride as he listened to his mother speaking with such passionate fervor about the most important meal for her family.

Francesca's gravy always contained canned or fresh tomatoes (depending on the season), olive oil, garlic, basil (either fresh or dried), and, depending on the economic conditions of a particular week, some type of meat for extra flavor. Other Italian families might have altered this basic gravy recipe by the addition or subtraction of a minor spice— perhaps the addition of an onion or carrot, longer or shorter cooking time, or the order of introduction of ingredients into the big dented pot in which the gravy was prepared. These minor changes might have resulted in an insignificant, understated taste difference in each family's gravy. If the truth be known, only the most discriminating palate would ever have been able to distinguish one family's gravy from another. However, every Italian family believed their mother's gravy to be special, unique in flavor, and certainly different from the gravy of every other Italian family.

Francesca was an independent, strong-willed woman, torn between devotion to her family and a passion for her homeland. This conflicted, yet confident, woman wanted to love America, but she found city living repulsive. Francesca was never able to adjust to the conditions in New York City at the beginning of the twentieth century. She disliked the close living conditions in her tenement apartment with one shared bathroom in the hallway. She found it difficult to adjust to the crowds of people, the dirty concrete streets, and the constant stale, foul-smelling air.

She would often complain, "There is not a blade of grass or distant snow-covered mountain to calm my soul." Francesca found it intolerable that she had to raise her family in a city "full of *prostitjuite* (prostitutes)." Most of all, she was unwilling to accept her neighbors' dislike of Italians and her beloved country. "If it means I must hate my country to be a patriotic American, then I must refuse this country."

Donato was especially heartbroken when his mother decided to return to Italy. Although he desperately wanted to return with her, he knew this could never be. On the fateful day in 1916 when Francesca sailed to Italy with her six American-born children, leaving behind her husband and her two oldest sons, Donato was the person on land who held the end of the yarn as the ship pulled away from the dock.

Donato and Pietro were devastated when their mother and their brothers and sisters left America. They were confused by yet another family separation. No one was able to resolve the dilemma the boys once again faced. The two older boys had to remain in America to help their father support the family, now back in Italy. Without their mother and siblings, there was gloom in the Ciarletta apartment during that first year. The once happy, spontaneous atmosphere now seemed quiet and lonely. Fortunately, the business continued to prosper. The American economy was growing, and the long hours at work for Ciarletta & Sons became a useful tonic for their loneliness.

Francesca lived in Castellamare di Stabia in the apartment that had been deeded to her husband when he left for America in 1899, and the monthly stipend he sent from America enabled her to support herself and their six children. Francesca lived in this apartment in the Ciarletta house on one of the many narrow cobblestone streets of Castellamare di Stabia for the remainder of her life, never to return to America.

CHAPTER II

THE CIARLETTA BROTHERS ADOPT THEIR NEW COUNTRY

By October 1919, Leopoldo had been in America for twenty years. At the end of a brisk working day, twenty-one year old Donato and twenty-year-old Pietro made their final ice delivery of the day. Donato placed the block of ice in the upper portion of Mrs. Giacinta's ice box and said goodnight. He left the apartment and met Pietro waiting at the top of the stairway; the boys bounced down the stairs, their work complete for the day.

Once they were in their apartment, the boys washed and helped their father prepare a hearty meal of beans with tomatoes over *maccheroni* with crusty bread and wine.

Donato noticed his father seemed somber during the evening meal. "Pàtete, d'you feel okay? You're so quiet tonight."

Leopoldo finished the wine that remained in his glass, refilled it, and then added a little wine to his sons' glasses. As he was pouring the wine, both boys noticed their father's long thin mustache quivering. They had learned that whenever he was anxious or upset he had a habit of moving his upper lip back and forth, causing his mustache to move in this odd manner. Now they were sure something was wrong. Leopoldo took a sip of wine and swallowed.

Donato once again asked politely, "Pàtete, are you worried about something? Did we do something wrong?"

Leopoldo put down his glass. "No, my sons, you have done nothing wrong. You're good boys and good workers, and for this reason I've decided that it's time for me to return to your mother and younger brothers and sisters in Italy. You're both ready to run the business without your Påtete."

Donato was not surprised to hear his father's words, because he knew returning to Italy had always been a part of his father's plan. He was uneasy, however, knowing that the time for yet another separation had arrived. Pietro, who was more adventuresome than Donato, was not at all troubled about his father's announcement. Unlike Donato, he found the idea of running the business rather appealing.

Their father continued, "It's time for me to return to Italy to begin the preparation of your younger brothers so they can join you in our business."

Donato was concerned that he might not be ready for the added responsibility, but he was unwilling to show any sign of doubt in front of his father. He knew what was expected of him. Pietro, on the other hand, quickly assured his father that he and Donato were ready and willing to do what was required to make their father's dream of economic independence for the Ciarletta family a reality.

Leopoldo told his boys that he had booked passage for Italy and would be leaving in thirty-two days. Leopoldo then repeated his final instructions, "Donato, as my oldest son, you will be the leader of the business. Pietro will be at your side to assist in all decisions. Once I have taught your brothers English and prepared them for their duties, they will be ready to come to this country and work with you. Then, at that time, the Ciarletta & Sons Ice and Coal Delivery Company will be complete."

Leopoldo repeated what he had said to them many times in the past—wanting to once again impress upon his children the reasons he had immigrated to America. He used this moment to emphasize to his sons how he struggled to live outside the clutches of the "Black Hand," the secret crime families from Sicily.

"These families, who have appointed themselves protectors, judges, and juries of our way of living in our New York Italian neighborhoods, are no better than common criminals. Above all, I expect you both to honor my name and never, for any reason, become involved with these Italian murderers and hoodlums."

The boys nervously assured their father that they understood his request in this matter and their resolve to uphold their father's most important desire.

Hoping to further assert how strongly he felt about the "Black Hand," perhaps for the last time, Leopoldo continued, "Remember, once you look to these criminals for help, there will be no escape from their favors, payments, and forced crime. I'm expecting my sons to keep this pledge, which I've so proudly honored."

The two boys understood. They had already been indoctrinated by their father in believing that work was a value unto itself. Leopoldo had constantly impressed upon them that the work he found in this new land was a source of pride, honor, and accomplishment, no matter how menial.

Leopoldo reached for his glass, took a sip of wine, and asked his sons to listen carefully to what he was about to say. He had spoken these words to them many times before, but tonight he wished to stress the purpose to which he had dedicated his life.

Leopoldo arose from his chair, finished his wine, and proclaimed, "You, my oldest male children, have the burden of honoring our family name in America and keeping the business strong for your younger brothers."

Pietro stood and said, "Pàtete, we'll make you proud of us."

With that comment, Leopoldo moved toward Pietro and gave him a forceful embrace.

He turned to Donato, who was also standing, and smiling confidently, he hugged him and said, "Remember, your Pàtete wouldn't leave you as leader if he thought you couldn't do what is needed. Let's now sleep. We've work to do tomorrow."

Donato had been quiet during his father's announcement, but later, lying in bed unable to sleep, he worried about his role as leader, thinking, *What if I am not capable of being a leader?* Donato was not as self-assured as his brother, and was more sensitive in his dealings with others. He wished he were not the older of the two. He would be more comfortable if Pietro was in the leadership role instead of it being thrust upon him simply because of the dictates of the Italian culture.

As Donato lay in bed, he thought of his mother back in Italy. He missed her terribly—he always felt safe when he was with her. *If only Mamma was here with me,"* thought Donato. *"I wouldn't have to worry.* He rolled over and eventually drifted off to sleep.

The day finally arrived for Leopoldo to leave America. At the dock, before boarding the boat, he hugged each boy, saying the same to each of them, "Make me proud of you." Then, before picking up his single, thick cardboard luggage and small duffel bag closed by rope, he reached for the hands of his two boys, held each tightly, and said,

"Remember how I have always done business. Be especially cautious of the one *che sembra pio e, che introduce il Dio nelle trattative* (who is pious and evokes God in his negotiations). He is the one not to be trusted."

Donato and Pietro waved with watery eyes as their father's boat moved away from the dock, minus the ball of twine, which was reserved only for female members of Italian families.

The two boys were silent as they rode the subway back to their apartment, until Pietro spoke. "Donato, it's only us now, you and me. We only have each other. Are you scared now that you're the leader?"

"Sort of, a little, but having you with me makes it a whole lot better."

"We're gonna be okay," said an encouraging Pietro. "C'mon, stop worrying. Working together will be fun. We'll keep the routes going and we'll be our own bosses. Remember when you used to help me learn English on the fire escape? Well, it's my time to help you. You're good at writing what needs to be ordered and planning the routes, and I'm the one who can fight if we get into trouble. Working together will be fun, and soon Pâtete will send us Ulderico, and then Ubaldo and Felice. When the five of us are finally together, we'll be the best team in New York City."

Donato responded to Pietro's reassuring words cautiously. "I hope you're right. Pietro, can I tell you something? You're the only one I can say this to, so promise you'll never tell anyone, okay?"

"Sure, I promise," said Pietro, who was now interested.

As the subway continued on its way toward Harlem, Donato—his hands together between his legs and his eyes downcast—slowly began to speak. "I feel a lot of shame about myself."

"Shame? What for? You work as hard as I do. You're a great brother. What's this shame business?"

Donato was apprehensive to speak, but he was also relieved that he had his brother to confess to. "When Pâtete told us he was leaving to go back to Italy, I wanted to go with him, to be with Mamma." Donato raised his head and looked at his brother. "Pietro, are you angry with me?"

"Donato, you're my brother and my best friend. Remember all the things we did together, just you and me. Heck, I'll never be angry with you." Pietro placed his arm around his brother's shoulder, squeezed Donato's body close to his, and said, "Castellamare di Stabia is no longer our home, Donato. New York is now our home. Hey, I have an idea. From now on, we'll stop calling ourselves Donato and

Pietro; from now on we're Danny and Pete." Pete laughed loudly, and then—in a booming voice so that everyone in the subway car could hear—he sang out, "New York! You're our home!"

Leopoldo had no qualms about leaving his two young sons in America to maintain the business, while he returned to Italy to implement the final steps of his plan to insure that the Ciarletta & Sons Ice and Coal Delivery business would be able to provide economic security for his family.

He missed his wife Francesca and the joy he received from being with his three young daughters during the three and a half years he had been in America preparing Donato and Pietro to run the business until their younger brothers were ready to immigrate to America. This was a small price to pay for the completion of his master plan.

Now back in Italy, Leopoldo taught his three sons, Ulderico, Ubaldo, and Felice, English, the customs and practices of America, and what would be required of them as ice and coal delivery workers in America. Ulderico joined his brothers in America in 1922. Ubaldo married a girl named Gerasina from Castellamare di Stabia at the age of seventeen and had two children, a girl named Annuccia, in honor of Gerasina's mother, and a boy named Leopoldo, in honor of Ubaldo's father. Ubaldo's departure to America was delayed for a year because he was required to serve in the Italian military, but eventually he immigrated to America to join his brothers in 1926.

Felice was seventeen years of age in 1930. With war on the horizon in Europe, Leopoldo once again had to adjust his plan, this time bribing officials so Felice could leave Italy in 1930, much earlier than originally anticipated. His brothers in America would have to be responsible for the preparation of their young brother.

Now that his plan was completed, Leopoldo could retire to a gentleman's way of life, respected by others in Castellamare di Stabia for what he had accomplished. He received a monthly stipend from his sons in America and lived with Francesca and his daughters in the apartment deeded to him by his deceased father. His daughters married and provided their parents with the ultimate enjoyment of grandchildren.

During this time, Danny and Pete had been making their own family plans. In 1924, they had been introduced to two sisters from Van Nest Avenue in the Bronx, Concetta and Assunta. Danny and Concetta married in 1925. Shortly thereafter, Pete and Assunta announced their intention to marry.

Assunta and Concetta had a brother, Frank, and three sisters, Anna, and twin sisters, Grace and Margaret. Grace was an independent woman, different from her sisters. She was married to Emile, who earned a modest salary. Although they had two children, Grace continued to work after the birth of her children. This was considered quite unusual for the time. With the money she earned as a telephone operator supervisor, she decorated her home with the latest modern furniture and always wore the finest clothes purchased from the Bonwit Teller department store in Manhattan.

The Ciarletta brothers gradually became more comfortable with the American culture. Donato and Pietro had already become Danny and Pete. Ulderico soon became known as Al; Ubaldo immediately became Bob; and Felice became Phil.

Pete and Danny decided to purchase a modest but substantial size house in the Clason Point section of the Bronx. Living in the same house made the two couples closer than ever. Pete and Assunta, now known as Suzy, had one child when they moved to the Bronx. They named her Frances, after Pete's mother. She was followed by a son, Leopoldo, named after his grandfather, and a second daughter named Barbara, born in 1930, and a second son born in 1933.

Danny's wife, Concetta, now known as Kate, was unable to have children. Pete and Suzy—knowing the disappointment of Kate and Danny's childless marriage—decided to name their newly-born son Daniel, to honor Danny, the oldest male in the Ciarletta family.

On Sundays, the five brothers would gather at Pete and Danny's house in the Bronx. After their main meal of *maccheroni*, the five Ciarletta brothers enjoyed playing the card game "Boss and Underboss" or traveling to visit *paesani* in the Bronx.

On one particular Sunday, immediately after their card game, Danny told his brothers he had something important he needed to ask them. He began by complimenting them first.

"Our business is doing well because of your hard work. Pàtete would be proud of us. As the oldest brother, it has been my luck to have four brothers who are willing to sacrifice for our family's common benefit."

Al was impatient and interrupted, "Danny, I hope this is not going to take too long. Claudia is expecting me to meet her at five o'clock."

Al was a handsome man who enjoyed being with women, and his brothers were quick to start joking and chastising him for interrupting Danny with this comment. "How many other girls will you be seeing after Claudia?" said Bob, his teasing causing more laughter.

Danny continued, "Y' know, I love you guys and wouldn't think of hurting you, but I have a favor to ask the four of you, and I hope it's not going to upset you. I'd like to give up my leadership role and leave the business."

The four brothers looked curiously at Danny, unable to respond immediately to his surprising revelation.

Phil was confused. "Leave the business, but why?"

"I don't have the stomach for the violence we face each day, Phil," said Danny. "There's an opening for a produce man at the Westchester Avenue Daniel Reeves food store. I know I'd be happier doing that type of work. Anyway, Pete would make a better leader than me, and the four of you can easily serve all the customers. Plus, dividing the weekly cut four ways instead of five will give you all more money to spend each week. It goes without saying that I'll still contribute to our family in Castellamare di Stabia out of the salary from my new job. Well, what do you have to say?"

The four brothers looked at Pete. They were interested to know what he had to say.

"Danny, whadda surprise, I had no idea…. I've been working with you since the fourth grade and never knew you were unhappy." Pete paused and looked at Danny while the others waited for him to continue. "Danny, I'd be honored to take your place as leader of the business. No matter what you do for work, you will always remain our wisest brother."

"Then it's settled. I'll tell the manager of Daniel Reeves that I'll start working for him a week from tomorrow. Is that okay, or is it too soon?"

Pete—immediately accepting his leadership role—responded, "Next week it is."

"Well then, the only thing left is to write a letter to Pàtete and ask for his blessing.

Pete was the first brother to rise and embrace Danny, and his embrace was the final act of approval of Danny's decision. The other three brothers each arose from their place at the table, approached Danny, and gave him a warm embrace, each saying, "Go with our blessing."

When the four brothers had finished, Danny wiped the tears from his cheeks. "Oh, look at the time," he said. "Al has to be at Claudia's by five o'clock. Let's get moving."

In Italy, Leopoldo soon received a letter from Danny explaining his decision to leave the business and assuring him that the Ciarletta Brothers Ice and Coal Delivery Company would continue to prosper under Pete's leadership. Leopoldo was not happy with his oldest son's decision. *This would not have happened if I was still in America*, he thought. *But what can I do from here. I must live with the decision of my oldest son. I will not write back, and he will know by my silence that I do not approve of his decision.*

During the next four years under Pete's leadership, the business continued to prosper, with the four brothers working as closely as ever.

Pete was a kind man who liked to laugh. He was burly, handsome, and had an air of assured self-confidence that at times caused him to extend himself beyond his ability. It was hard for Pete to distinguish between the battles he could win and those he should walk away from. His life revolved around his family and his work.

Pete's wife, Suzy, dominated the family, ultimately making the decisions. She knew how to make her husband believe he was the family leader and in complete control. Suzy was the parent who made the family function smoothly, instilling in her children the feeling that the Ciarletta family was both unique and special. Suzy was a heavy-set, round-faced, attractive woman. She was strong-willed and cunning in her dealings with others. Her life revolved around religion, family, and her Italian culture.

Suzy knew her children's every story, every injury, every heartbreak, every dream, and every fear. It was quite impossible to resist her efforts to maintain the solidarity of the family unit once she convinced each child that he or she played such an important role. When the four Ciarletta children needed to be consoled, when their egos were bruised, or when their emotions caused confusion, Suzy was the person who literally held her children and made the world a safe and pleasant place.

Frances, the oldest child, was similar to her father in temperament — she was independent, strong-willed, and the protector of her younger siblings. Frances had fair skin, green eyes, and light brown hair. Everyone agreed that she looked like the famous movie star of the period, Ingrid Bergman.

Suzy began to notice a change in her seventeen-year-old daughter. Frances seemed to be more interested in the sentiments of her friends than her cultural traditions. One day, Frances confronted her mother about the living arrangements in the Ciarletta house.

"Mother, why am I the only girl who is not allowed to use our upstairs living room when my friends call for me? My friends have to come to the back of the house to our basement door when they visit. Then we must stay in the basement living room. When I go to their houses, I call for them at their front door and we are allowed to play together and talk in their upstairs living room and kitchen."

"Have your friends told you they are upset about using our back door or playing in our basement?" said Suzy.

Frances gave her mother a typical teenage *you don't understand anything* look, and said, "Now, Mother, you don't expect my friends to actually say they are embarrassed for me. But I know they are." Frances started to cry. "Oh Mother, I just knew you wouldn't understand."

Frances was right; Suzy did not understand. She did not understand how suddenly she was unable to console her oldest daughter. Suzy did not understand how, after all these years, her smartest and oldest child could not appreciate the importance of *sempre nostrare la tua bella figura a futti* (always show your absolute best side to friend and stranger alike). *Bella figura* was such a prominent aspect of the Italian culture that it affected the physical layout of many Italian homes during that time period. In most Italian homes, daily living arrangements were organized to accommodate the need to show the best possible side to all. Italian families of the early and mid-nineteenth century would compartmentalize their home into three separate sections: the basement, the first floor living area, and the second floor bedrooms. The organization of the first floor living area and the basement were integral to the concept of *bella figura.*

The main living area on the first floor as you entered an Italian home was especially reserved for friends, guests, or visiting relatives, who would be entertained in the dining and/or living room. Family members were not permitted to use the first floor area for the activities of daily life. This rule allowed these rooms to remain in pristine condition. The upholstered furniture covered by form-fitting clear plastic allowed the visitor to admire the fabric while insuring that the upholstery remained spotless. Walls always looked freshly painted because children were never permitted to use these rooms. The visitor also had a responsibility in this ritual show of pride. A guest dare not decline the offer of their host's best food or drink— to do so would be an unforgivable insult. The final element of this compartmentalization was the conversion of the basement into the daily living quarters. The basement of many Italian homes would include a full second kitchen, an eating area, and a lounging area where the family lived, worked, studied, ate, and played.

For the first time, Suzy had to confront the idea that her children would not have the same respect for her Italian heritage and customs as past generations had so greatly valued and maintained. If a girl like Frances was unable to accept *bella figura*, a basic aspect of Italian life, Suzy was forced to accept that her other children might also act the same when they reached their teen years. Could it be that the American way of life had become a stronger influence than her maternal persuasion?

Leopoldo, the oldest son, was a quick-stepping, well-groomed boy. He was happy, well-adjusted, and a pious young man. While in the eighth grade, he informed his parents that he wanted to become a Franciscan priest and enroll in the seminary rather than go to high school in the Bronx. In Italian families there can be no greater reward than to give a son, especially the firstborn male, to God. Leopoldo was accepted as a novice and entered his ninth year of schooling at the Franciscan seminary in Callicoon, New York.

Barbara, the youngest daughter, did well in school and was a caring, loving, and happy child. She was Pete's favorite, and he affectionately called her "my princess." As a teenager, Barbara was becoming a beautiful woman, and "Daddy" was the most wonderful father a daughter could have. He was kind, loving, handsome, and daring—the kind of father every teenage girl dreams about. It was impossible for Pete not to notice the admiration in his daughter's eyes each time he arrived home from work.

Daniel, the youngest child, was a tall, stocky boy who looked much older than his age. His only interest seemed to be sports. He brought a great deal of pleasure to his parents in every way but one: Daniel was not a good student. His teachers, who were Franciscan nuns, seemed to agree that Daniel did not have the intelligence to successfully complete the work required of academic students. They advised his parents that after graduating from elementary school Daniel should attend a trade school rather than an academic high school. Suzy was unwilling to accept this conclusion—she was sure Daniel simply did not apply himself.

CHAPTER III

$\mathcal{M}$EETING $\mathcal{G}$RANDFATHER $\mathcal{L}$EOPOLDO

A telegram addressed to Pete arrived from Italy in mid-February 1947. Suzy and the children, who were eager to learn the contents of the telegram, waited impatiently for Pete's arrival from work. The children, who were looking out the windows of the front porch, saw Pete approaching, and they could hear his faint Ciarletta whistle through the closed windows.

Barbara ran to the door and yelled, "Daddy, hurry. There's a telegram from Italy."

Pete ran up the front steps—a telegram usually meant bad news. The family gathered around their father as he quickly opened the envelope. Pete silently read the words typed on thin strips of white paper attached to a half-sheet of green paper. He read the telegram aloud to his family. "Pàtete hospitalized with heart attack, stop. Fear the worst, stop. He requests to see Pietro and grandson, stop. Hurry, stop."

Suzy made the sign of the cross. The children only knew their grandfather from the stories told by their father and Uncle Danny.

Pete glanced at Suzy, and then gathered his four children in his arms and told them not to worry. He held them for a few moments, making sure to kiss each child on the forehead. He handed the telegram to his wife and said, "I'm going upstairs to rest before supper. Make sure Danny sees the telegram as soon as he gets home."

Daniel, the youngest grandson, wondered who his father would take to Italy. Would he take his older son Leopoldo, who was away at a seminary studying to be a priest, or would he be the grandson chosen to accompany his father to Italy?

Danny arrived around six-thirty, and was immediately handed the telegram. Suzy yelled to her husband that his brother had arrived. The two brothers embraced in the living room.

"Danny, as the oldest son I think you should call Italy," said Pete.

Calling another country via phone was an unusual occurrence in the 1940s. Danny waited for the call to be put through by the long-distance operator. Francesca answered the phone, and Danny's eyes became misty when he heard his mother's voice. Danny was told that his father was feeling better and would be coming home from the hospital in a few days. Francesca said her husband, still fearing he might die, wanted Pete to visit him and bring along one male grandchild.

"I understand, Mamma. Tell Pàtete we'll make arrangements for Pete to be at his bedside as soon as humanly possible." After a brief conversation, and telling his mother how much he missed her, Danny said goodbye with tears in his eyes. The family gathered around their uncle to hear what had been said. Danny explained and then looked at Pete. There was a long moment of silence.

Pete spoke directly to his wife, "Suzy, I know it will cost more having two people travel to Italy, but I can't deny my father his request." Suzy nodded, indicating she agreed. Then, looking at his youngest son, he said, "Daniel, you will come with me to Italy to visit your grandfather." Pete glanced at Suzy, who again nodded in agreement.

The following morning, Suzy began making arrangements for her husband and son's immediate departure to Italy. She learned that the Pan American Clipper plane, which had interrupted its flights across the Atlantic—from the waters off Port Washington, New York at the beginning of World War II—was planning to resume passenger service across the Atlantic on June 17, 1947, using the new Douglas DC-4, Lockheed Constellation land plane, leaving from La Guardia Airport.

This meant the only option available in February of 1947 was to travel by boat, but the cost of passage on a cruise ship was far too expensive. The only affordable alternative was to arrange passage on one of the converted troop ships that were operating as passenger liners to Europe.

Pete left work early the following day, so he and Daniel could take the elevated subway to the Bronx County courthouse and obtain their passports. Although Daniel felt terrible that his grandfather was ill, he was secretly excited to be going on a great adventure and, best of all, he would be free from school for a number of weeks, perhaps longer.

Suzy completed the passage arrangements for her husband and son. When she found out they were to land in Naples, her heart skipped a beat when she realized her secret dream could actually come true. *God works in the strangest ways,* she thought. Naples had a special religious meaning for Suzy. One of her great joys during Christmas was to display her three American Christmas nativity sets to impress upon her children the true meaning of this glorious holiday.

Over the years, Suzy had often read in magazines about the Italian *presepi* (Christmas nativity scenes) that could only be purchased in Naples. From her readings and the pictures she had seen, she had fallen in love with the *presepi* figures made by the artist Matteo Prencipe and produced by the Gramendola Company. The Neapolitans had placed the infant Jesus within the context of their everyday life in Naples during the Renaissance period.

Now that Pete was going to Naples, he could purchase a Gramendola *presepi*. The *presepi* figures could only be obtained by visiting Via San Gregario, a narrow cobblestone street crowded on both sides with workshops and display counters where every grade of *presepi* paraphernalia was made and hawked year-round.

When Pete and Daniel arrived home with their passports in hand, Suzy informed them that they would leave from the west side of Manhattan in two days and land in Italy in the city of Naples. Giggling like a school girl, she asked, "Pete do you know what that means?"

Pete gave Suzy a strange, almost comical look, and said, "Yes, it means we land in Naples. What's going on in that head of yours? I know you Suzy. When you get like this, you're up to something."

"Pete..., Naples, the *presepi* nativity..."

Pete interrupted his wife before she could finish her sentence, "Oh Suzy, c'mon, now don't start that."

Suzy would not be cut off, not now. "My dream of owning a real Neapolitan *presepi* nativity set can now come true!"

Pete was not at all happy about having to stop in Naples to go shopping, and he told his wife so.

"Pete, why would you refuse to do this for me? If it's money, I'll save it from my weekly food budget."

"Suzy, be reasonable, you already have three nativity sets. Why do you want another one?"

It was clear Pete was becoming annoyed at what he considered an unnecessary stop in a foreign country for a frivolous purchase. "Suzy, think for a minute. How am I gonna find the store? And if I do find it, how can I carry the extra packages back to America? It's crazy. Enough with this nativity business, enough."

Pete appeared to be winning the battle until Suzy, who was desperate at this point, pulled out her last and most effective argument, "Well, I just want to pay honor to the Baby Jesus, but for a few lire and a little inconvenience you're gonna take from me and the children a chance to express our devotion to God."

With this statement, the children immediately recognized that their mother had pulled victory from what only moments before appeared to be certain defeat.

Sensing she had broken through Pete's firm but good-natured exterior, Suzy continued, "Pete, in all the years we've been married, have I asked for special clothes or jewelry?" Suzy immediately answered her own question, "No." She again used the family to support her request, "Am I so terrible for wanting to bring into our home this special religious symbol for our children?"

Pete, realizing he had lost the argument, reluctantly gave in.

Before leaving, Suzy gave her husband a list of the specific figures to be purchased. Pete didn't even attempt to object to the number of Gramendola figures his wife had requested—he realized it would only result in another lost argument.

In late February, Daniel and his father boarded the bus headed to Westchester Avenue, where they passed through the turnstiles of the elevated subway going to the west side of Manhattan. Pete was apprehensive as they walked the inclined wooden plank leading to the deck of a big brown tanker that, on first sight, appeared ready for dry dock rather than a trip across the Atlantic Ocean.

Nine days later, after an uneventful voyage, they entered the Bay of Naples. "Look, Daniel, can you see the large church that's one street beyond the dock, with the columns and big cross on the steeple? I'll betcha that's a church for sailors,"

"Oh, look, Dad, over there at the park with the big statue," replied Daniel.

"In Italy, they call that a *piazza*, not a park," said his father with pride. "We don't have buildings like this in the Bronx. These buildings have probably been here for hundreds and hundreds of years."

Pete's sister, Leonida, was supposed to meet them at the dock. Daniel could tell his father was tense and anxious—he had not seen his sister Leonida for many years and was concerned he might not recognize her. The dock was crowded with people, and Pete—who was holding a current picture of her in his hand—looked at the faces of the women passing by, hoping to see a woman who resembled his sister.

After a few minutes, Pete picked up his two suitcases and told Daniel to pick up his bags. "We're gonna walk the dock. Leonida might be waiting for us in a different spot. Stay next to me and don't let anyone walk between us. I want you next to me."

Daniel followed his father's orders, although he felt it unnecessary to be so cautious. They began walking the entire length of the dock without finding Leonida. Pete, who was becoming quite concerned, was unusually short-tempered with Daniel, telling him to stay close. As they started to walk the dock one more time, they heard a voice in front of them calling, "Pietro, Pietro!" Pete moved quickly toward the sound of his name, carelessly brushing against other people as he moved. Daniel fell farther and farther behind, even though he was trying to move forward as fast as he could, while trying to keep his father in sight. Suddenly, Daniel saw his father with a woman in his arms. He was hugging her, and then he raised her off her feet while turning her in a circle. When he put her down, they were both laughing.

Pete turned to look for his son. When he saw him, he pulled Daniel close to his side and said "Daniel, this is your Aunt Leonida."

Aunt Leonida, a tall, middle-aged woman, gave the boy a long, affectionate hug. She was talking to her brother in Italian, while pointing and looking at Daniel. A number of times, she suddenly grabbed Daniel, hugged him, and kissed him, saying *"bello ragazzo"* (beautiful boy.)

The reunited brother and sister boarded a bus for Castellamare di Stabia. As the bus stopped on a busy street in the heart of Naples,

Daniel noticed a small triangular grass area in the middle of the street that was enclosed by a black metal fence. There was a person completely covered with old blankets, lying on the ground in the enclosure. There was also a child—Daniel could not tell if it was a boy or a girl because of the child's long, uncombed hair and heavy, dirty clothing. He asked his father why the person was sleeping on the ground with a young child sitting unattended beside a small wagon. Pete explained that they were gypsies and they probably did not have a home to live in.

Daniel gave his father a quizzical look. "How can people live if they don't have a house?" he said. Daniel had never realized there were people who did not have a house or apartment to live in. There were no homeless people in his 1947 Bronx neighborhood.

Daniel's father cautioned him not to go near people who looked like gypsies. "They are poor and beg for money, and they will steal anything they can." He reassured Daniel, saying "There're no gypsies in Castellamare di Stabia. They stay in large cities like Naples, or they travel by horse and wagon in the countryside."

As the bus neared Castellamare di Stabia, Leonida told Pete to get his luggage ready, because they would be leaving the bus at the next stop. "Pia and Alessandrina will be at the bus stop to meet us."

If my Italian aunts are like my American aunts, the greeting is going to take a while, thought Daniel. His family in America seemed to have an unwritten rule: hellos and goodbyes were required to last at least fifteen minutes; one hello or goodbye hug and kiss never seemed sufficient. Plus there was always an important topic to discuss when family members first greeted each other that could not wait until the person removed their coat—or a critical topic that needed to be discussed that had somehow been overlooked during the visit they had just finished. This was followed by sad expressions of how each person was going to be missed until their next meeting. Of course, this would bring on more hugs and kisses. The ritual of joy and sadness that occurred in a hallway, at a front door, on a stoop, and perhaps now at a bus stop was an integral part of Daniel's family's gatherings.

The bus stopped and Leonida led her brother and his son off the bus. They were greeted by two women, who immediately embraced Pete, crying and screeching with joy. They were Pia and Alessandrina, the two sisters Pete had not seen since they were young children.

After a few minutes, the initial round of greetings seemed to be ending, and Daniel knew he was next. He was dreading the public show of affection that was to about to come his way. He had the distinction of being the first American nephew his aunts had seen. *Zia* (Aunt) Pia was a tall, hefty woman with an attractive, round face. She gave Daniel an admiring look and then a long robust hug. Zia Alessandrina was also tall, but slender with more pointy features. She again screeched with delight as she hugged and kissed Daniel, and then wetting her fingers with saliva, she proceeded to pat down his hair in an attempt to make him look neater.

Daniel's hunch was correct—his Italian aunts were just like his American aunts when it came to greetings. They continued with many spontaneous hugs and kisses, questions about their other brothers in America, everyone's health, and inquiries about every distant relative and friend and each of their children. At times, the brisk conversation would suddenly stop, as Daniel's aunts felt the need for more spontaneous hugs, signs of affection, and screams of joy. It didn't seem to matter that this group of four adults and one boy had completely blocked the narrow sidewalk in front of the bus stop for eight to ten minutes. People passing this reunion walked in the street or behind a bench next to the sidewalk, all seeming to understand that an Italian greeting was in progress.

Eventually, they were on their way to *Nonno's* (grandfather's) apartment. They walked on narrow, winding cobblestone streets, talking and smiling with their arms around each other. They stopped at a three-story attached stone building, where a man smoking a cigarette was waiting at the front door. He was introduced as Zia Pia's husband, Rodolfo, who had been staying with Leopoldo and Francesca while Pete's sisters met him at the bus stop. Rodolfo was respectful toward Pete and seemed very solemn. When Pete and Daniel entered the Ciarletta house, they saw an elderly woman sitting at the end of a long table with matching chairs. When she saw her son, Pietro, and her grandson, Donato, she began to cry and extended her hands without getting up from her chair.

Pete quickly moved toward his mother, knelt in front of her, took her hands in his, kissed the back of her hands, and rested his head gently on her lap. She continued crying as she stroked the back of his head. Pete was visibly moved. He had not seen his mother since she left America some thirty years previously. His head lay on her lap for what seemed to be a minute or two—his body was limp and completely relaxed. He continued to speak softly as her tears of joy became sobs. Her left arm remained around her son's shoulder and she stroked the back of his head with her right hand. Pete eventually raised his head. His mother took his face in her hands and spoke for the first time, saying over and over, "*Pietro mio, Pietro mio.*" He just stared at her round, wrinkled face with moist eyes as she spoke his name.

When Pete stood, he turned, looked for Daniel, and motioned for him to approach. With his arm around his son's shoulder, he said to his mother, "*Mama, chist'é nepòtete, Donato.* (Mother, this is your grandson Donato.)"

Daniel's *Nonna* (grandmother), remaining seated, put her two hands to her cheeks, and said, "*Grazi a Dio per lasciar vedere il mio primo nipote Americano.* (Thank you, God, for allowing me to see my first American grandchild.)"

Daniel did exactly what his father had done. He knelt next to his grandmother and said, "*Nonna,*" took her outstretched hands in his, and kissed the back of her hands. She quickly removed her thick, rough hands from Daniel's, placed her arms around his shoulders, drew him toward her, and gave her grandson a warm, gentle embrace.

Through her sobs, she kept repeating, "*Mòlto gràzi* (thank you very much)." She moved Daniel's face away from her body and stared lovingly into his eyes. Now holding her grandson's hands, she said, "*Stare in piedi* (stand)." She then raised his arms, and looking at him from head to foot, she kept saying, "*Piccirì, mi piaċ assa.*" (You are pleasing to me)."

She asked that a chair be placed next to her and motioned for Daniel to sit next to her. She continued holding his left hand as she began to speak to Pete in a more desperate tone. The movement of her hand and her body language all seemed to show deep concern, and it was obvious she was talking about her husband. By now, her three daughters were behind the chair with their hands on her shoulders. Nonna Francesca arose from her chair with some assistance from Zia Pia.

Daniel's Nonna was an averaged-size woman; she walked with a *bastone* (cane) and had the posture of a much older woman. She was no longer sobbing, and Daniel was able to see for himself the independent look his Uncle Danny had often described. Uncle Danny always said that he and Pete learned to be independent from their mother, and it was through her that they were able to be successful in America.

Francesca led the way up a narrow stairway to the second floor. Her son held her by the arm while she used her *bastone* for support. When they reached the landing at the top of the steps, Francesca stopped and spoke briefly to her son while pointing toward Daniel.

Pete took Daniel's hand and said, "Since Nonno's heart attack, he has not been able to move his left arm and he can't speak as clearly as he used to, so it's important that people who visit do not act surprised or seem fearful of him."

These comments made Daniel nervous, but he said, "I understand, Dad. I'll be okay."

The family proceeded toward a closed door. Nonna opened it slowly and they quietly entered the bedroom. Leopoldo was propped up in bed, resting on two large pillows. There was a blanket at his waist. He wore a clean, pressed, long-sleeved, white shirt with a closed collar. He was also wearing a colorful tie that looked like a cross between a regular tie and a bow tie. Over his shirt he wore a black vest, fully buttoned, and on his head, a brown beret with the top pushed over to the right.

Leopoldo raised his right hand and in a soft, frail voice said, "Pietro." His son moved quickly to the bed, knelt down, kissed the back of his father's outstretched hand, and then rested his head on the bed next to his father's hip. Leopoldo used his right hand to push his son's head against his hip. Daniel could hear his father starting to sob, and his father began to tremble in rhythm with his tears. Daniel was bewildered—he had never seen his father in such an emotional state. Nonna Francesca put her right arm around Daniel's shoulders and moved his body against hers in reassurance. *"Tutt aposto* (all is well)" she whispered.

Leopoldo remained silent, continuing to hold his son's head close to his body as he gazed at him. Leopoldo's face was round but not large. He had a thick mustache that became thin at each end, and his eyes showed great strength although his gaze was also warm. As Pete arose from his knee, he leaned over and kissed his father on the forehead. Meanwhile, Rodolfo pushed a chair over so Pete could sit next to his father.

Pete turned to Daniel and motioned for him to come forward. He moved his chair so Daniel could be next to his grandfather. As

Daniel approached, Nonno Leopoldo smiled for the first time and called out his name, "Donato!" Daniel once again did exactly as his father had done. He said "Nonno," and knelt next to the bed, taking his Nonno's outstretched hand and kissing it.

Nonno raised Daniel's hand as he said, "*Viene qua* (come here)!" He used his right hand to press Daniel's face against his chest and then moved him back. While still holding Daniel's hand, and with a bright smiling face, Leopoldo said, "*Lasciarme verderti* (let me look at you)."

Daniel noticed his grandfather's eyes were like his father's, and he could see that same look of pride as Leopoldo looked at his grandson. Daniel had been hesitant about meeting his grandfather, but now felt completely at ease looking into Nonno's warm, inviting eyes.

Nonno's smile soon turned into a soft laugh as he repeated the phrase, "*Quest é na benedizzione.* (This is a blessing.)" His laugh brought new energy into the room and the others also began to smile for the first time. Leopoldo held onto his grandson's hand to keep him next to his bed.

Even if Daniel had been able to speak Italian, he would not have known what to say as he stood by his Nonno's side, but conversation for these few moments didn't seem to matter. Nonno Leopoldo playfully moved Daniel's hand back and forth, and looked admiringly at his grandson. Pete, still seated next to the bed, started a conversation, and as Leopoldo began to speak, he released Daniel's hand and began to gesture with his one movable hand. Daniel heard his Nonno mention the names of his American uncles, and he assumed that Nonno was inquiring about his other male children and the family business in America.

Daniel had not noticed, but at some point Zia Alessandrina had left the room and returned with a tray of small espresso cups and a pot of espresso coffee. Nonno seemed pleased when she poured coffee for everyone in the room, including Daniel. They all raised their cup of espresso to Nonno. With his saucer on the blankets, Leopoldo lifted his cup to everyone in the room and took a sip. Only then did the others taste their espresso. Almost immediately the room was alive with chatter. Everyone seemed much more relaxed and Nonno was smiling broadly.

Eventually, Daniel's aunts excused themselves to begin preparation of the evening meal, and Nonno Leopoldo ordered Nonna Francesca to bring a chair to the bed for Daniel. Because of Daniel's limited knowledge of Italian, he was not part of the conversation, but frequently Nonno would look at Daniel and stroke his knee softly.

Daniel's aunts and their families arrived around seven-thirty that evening; Zia Alessandrina, her husband Ruffino, and their two children were the first to visit. Soon thereafter, Zia Pia, her husband Rodolfo, and their six children arrived. Last to arrive was Zia Leonida, her husband Iseo, and their five children. Like the Ciarletta family in America, Daniel's Italian family was friendly, affectionate, and loud. There was the same need to make physical contact, and during the general conversation they continued the physical expression of hugging and kissing while laughing with each other. Daniel went through a series of cheek pinching, hugs, and kisses, as each aunt and uncle told him how handsome he was. During the introduction process, Daniel was thinking, *I'm thirteen, and yet they're still pinching my cheeks?*

Watching his aunts, uncles, and cousins interacting, Daniel couldn't help but notice how dramatically they expressed simple emotions. Although Daniel did not understand the words being used by Zio Ruffino as he conversed with Zio Rodolfo and Zio Iseo, he knew from his dramatic body language that Zio Ruffino felt strongly about whatever it was he was saying.

Pete and Leopoldo came down the stairs, with Pete on his left side holding Leopoldo around the shoulders, while Leopoldo used a bastone that he held in his right hand. He was still dressed in his formal white shirt, tie, vest, and beret. His pants were neatly pressed, and along with his vest, he was now wearing a cardigan sweater.

The family was ready for their meal. The adults were standing around the long wooden table in the first room as one entered the Ciarletta house. Nonno Leopoldo took his customary place at the head of the table and removed his beret, exposing a full head of white hair. Once Nonno was seated, the other adults took their seats. Nonna Francesca sat next to her husband. Daniel's aunts brought large platters of food to the main table and to a smaller table in the kitchen. Daniel stood behind his father's chair as Nonno Leopoldo said in a hushed but demanding voice, *"Viene qua* (Come here!)" At that command, the children stood behind the seated adults.

The adults held the hand of the person on either side of them, forming a complete connection, and the standing children did the same with each other. Daniel held the hand of Zia Pia's daughter, Angelina, to his right; on his left, he held the hand of Emilio, Zia Leonida's oldest son. Both children and adults bowed their heads in silence. Leopoldo made the sign of the cross, the adults and children did not disengage their hands as everyone listened to his prayer. Daniel understood *"Grazie a Dio"* (thanks be to God), but there were other unfamiliar words. He heard "Pietro" and "Donato," then other Italian words that he did not understand. When Nonno Leopoldo finished praying, everyone disengaged their hands and followed Nonno in making the sign of the cross. The moment the sign of the cross had been completed, everyone began talking and the kids rushed to the kitchen. Daniel stood still for a moment, not sure what to do, his father motioned for him to go to the kitchen with his cousins.

After dinner, Daniel's aunts and cousins helped clean the tables and wash the dishes while the men continued their brisk conversation, sipped wine, and enjoyed fruit and nuts. As the families were leaving to prepare for work and school the following day, Ruffino, Alessandrina's son, promised to come over the next day after school and show Daniel the town.

Daniel and his father were tired that night. While preparing for bed in one of the small, chilly second floor bedrooms, Daniel was curious about his grandfather's attire.

"Dad, when we saw Nonno in bed, I was surprised to see him so dressed up. Do people in Italy always dress that fancy when they are in bed?"

Pete grinned and said, "No, I'm sure he usually wears pajamas in bed." Pete explained that Nonno was a very proud man who felt illness was a weakness. "I think Nonno was trying to tell us that he was not seriously sick, even though he had a heart attack."

Pete thought for a moment and continued, "Your grandfather is a man who likes to be in control. It's my guess he made Nonna dress him that way because we were coming to see him. That's your grandfather, a proud man, just as I remember him when I was your age."

Before Ruffino arrived the next afternoon, Daniel's father gave him a few Italian coins and told him to use them to purchase gelato for Ruffino and himself. To be given money and encouraged to purchase ice cream was both a surprise and a treat. It was rare for the Ciarletta children to be given money to spend on treats.

When Ruffino arrived, he and Daniel said goodbye to Nonno, Nonna, and Pete. They walked all afternoon. Ruffino showed Daniel the dock area, the piazza, and the narrow, curvy cobblestone streets of his hometown. Daniel marveled at how the few automobiles on the streets were able to navigate the narrow roads at such high speeds. They seemed to be clumsy, out-of place machines amid the noisy motor scooters, donkey carts, and pedestrians that seemed to be mingling on both the sidewalks and in the streets. The two cousins enjoyed their gelato and each other. Ruffino invited Daniel to go with him on Saturday to see a local *calcio* (soccer) game. Daniel accepted the invitation with excitement.

"We'll ask Nonno and your father if it's okay for you to come with me on Saturday."

"C'mon, Ruffino, I'm thirteen. I go to games all the time without asking permission!"

"Yes, but with Nonno it is best for us to ask."

When they arrived at Nonno's house that evening, Ruffino asked Nonno and Pete if Daniel could accompany him to the Saturday *calcio* game.

When Pete found out how far the *calcio* field was from Nonno's house, he casually said to Ruffino, "I'll come along, just to be on the safe side. If you two went alone and Daniel got lost, he doesn't know enough Italian to ask directions to get back home."

Daniel was furious when he heard of his father's response. "Dad, how could I get lost? And s'pose I did! I'm old enough to take care of myself! I can find my way home by taking the same road I took going to the soccer field? I'm not a baby. You don't need to come!"

Pete felt as though he was being challenged by his youngest son in front of his parents, and he responded defensively. "Daniel, I've heard just about enough from you today. What's gotten into you? You know I don't allow you to talk back like that."

Although Daniel felt he was being treated unfairly, he realized challenging his father as he had in front of Nonno and Nonna was a tactical mistake, and he apologized to his father. Subdued, and now speaking very politely, he said, "I know you're worried 'bout me because I can't speak Italian, but how would it look if I was the only kid at the game with his father to watch him? The other kids might think I'm a baby. If I can't go alone with Ruffino, I'll just stay home. It's no big deal."

Nonna broke the tension in the room, assuring her son that the boys often went to the Saturday *calcio* games alone and that it would be safe. Nonno interrupted his wife and spoke to Pete quietly. After a few minutes of discussion between Nonno and his son, Pete turned to Daniel and said, "I have decided to let you go to the *calcio* field alone with Ruffino. But I want you to understand that I will not tolerate another disrespectful word out of your mouth while we are on this trip. Is that understood, young man?"

Daniel dropped his head repentantly and said, "Yes, Dad, I understand."

That Saturday afternoon, when Ruffino and Daniel left the house for the *calcio* field, Ruffino told Daniel, "Nonno told your Pàtete that he was too worried about you, and that no one in Castellamare di Stabia would hurt two young boys. Nonno also told your Pàtete that he should trust you more, or you would not grow up well because you were always limited."

It was then that Daniel realized his father, who could be very stubborn, was easily influenced by his own father.

Ruffino and Daniel spent a great deal of time asking questions about each other's lives. Ruffino wanted to know about America, and Daniel was curious to know what it was like living through a war. Daniel had been in Italy seven days, and in that short period of time they had become good friends. Perhaps it was because they were so interested in each other's background, perhaps it was a family thing, or maybe it was because the two cousins were so different. Ruffino was a very serious and studious boy, and Daniel had little interest in his schoolwork.

On the long walk to the *calcio* game, their conversation seemed different. Ruffino was no longer talking about America. He seemed sad and uncertain as he talked about his schooling. He was sure his parents would not be able pay for his advanced studies, and without an opportunity to attend a university he would have to become a tailor like his father. Ruffino loved science and wished one day he could become a scientist.

Daniel tried to be encouraging. "I'll betcha your school can find a university that would give you a scholarship. With your grades that should be easy."

Ruffino did not understand the word *scholarship*, so Daniel explained. Then he began comparing himself to Ruffino. "Look at the difference between us. You're six months older than me, and look how much more you know." Daniel continued trying to get Ruffino to smile. "Ruffino, you talk 'bout things I haven't even thought of. I've known you only seven days, and I've learned a lot just by listening to you. You're such a smart kid. I wish I was as smart as you." Ruffino smiled for the first time and said, "*Grazie.*"

Daniel then used the English word *mature*. Ruffino didn't know this English word, and Daniel found it difficult to translate its meaning. However, Ruffino generally understood what he was trying to say.

As the two boys walked along, Ruffino responding to Daniel's questions about the Italian Government, explained the political turmoil in his country. "Before the war, Mussolini and his Black Shirts took over Italy. The people hated the Black Shirts and the Fascista military. The young men were really mad because they'd have to serve a year in the army. Then Mussolini became *ipnotizzare* by Hitler." Ruffino was unable to translate the word *ipnotizzare* into English.

Daniel could see Ruffino's frustration, so he encouraged him to go on.

"Zio Rodolfo has been to school and knows many things," said Ruffino. "When we get home, I'll ask him about this word."

Ruffino explained that Mussolini was to blame for Italy's entrance into a war the people never wanted. "So all I've known is poverty, politicians who are thieves, fear of the Fascista, and the mean Nazis. Now another change is happening—our country has become something called a *republic.*"

Daniel, once again feeling embarrassed by his lack of knowledge, asked, "Is a republic a bad thing?"

"Oh I don't know. Some say this is what we need; others think it will not be good for the people. Zio Rodolfo is very happy that Italy has become a republic. He has read a book by a man named Machiavelli. This book says if a country is to be good, it must collect money so it can have police and an army—not to fight others, but to protect people and make sure there is justice for everyone. Zio Rodolfo told me the book says this can only happen if we have a republic."

Daniel asked, "How can a republic make all these things happen?"

"Zio Rodolfo said that the people choose the leaders, and if the leaders don't do good things, the people are allowed to choose others who will. Zio Rodolfo really believes what this person Machiavelli has written in his book, *Discorsi Sopra la Prima Deca di Tito Livio* (*Discourses on the Decade of Titus Livy*). Then there are others, like my father, who believe the poor people of our country will be forgotten, and only the people in large cities will be given justice under a republic."

Daniel, who was still confused, asked "If the Fascists were so bad to the people, why didn't the king kick them out?"

"When we get home after the *calcio* game, we'll visit with Zio Rodolfo and I'll ask him." Ruffino told Daniel that Zio Rodolfo was a smart, well-read man. "Even when I was younger, I noticed how everyone in town showed him respect because of his knowledge. So I want to go to school and learn many things, and then the people in town will respect me like they do Zio Rodolfo."

The boys arrived at the *calcio* field as the game was about to begin. After the game, on the way to Nonno's house, they stopped to speak with Zio Rodolfo. Ruffino asked him about translating the word *ipnotizzare* into English. Uncle Rodolfo went into a long explanation in Italian. He seemed to be giving Ruffino more information than just how to translate one word into English. When Zio Rodolfo finished, he seemed visibly pleased at the boy's question.

Ruffino explained to Daniel that the word *ipnotizzare* meant hypnotized—he was trying to tell Daniel that Hitler had hypnotized Mussolini. Zio Rodolfo also told Ruffino the reason he was having trouble translating the word *ipnotizzare* into English was because in the Italian language the sound of the letter *H* is only used with the letter *C* and *G*, when *"I" comes after these letters*. For example "CI" would be pronounced "chee."

Zio Rodolfo interrupted and told Ruffino to tell Daniel, "That's why his last name is correctly pronounced "Chee-ar-letta."

Ruffino asked Zio Rodolfo for help with Daniel's question. "Why didn't the king get rid of Mussolini when he treated the people so bad?"

Zio Rodolfo motioned for the boys to sit next to him—he seemed eager to explain and pleased that Daniel was interested in such a complicated question. Because of his limited English, Zio Rodolfo began speaking to Ruffino in Italian. Ruffino listened intently. There was renewed emotion in Zio Rodolfo's voice and gestures. Zio Rodolfo stopped and motioned for Ruffino to relay his words to Daniel.

"Zio Rodolfo told me that the answer to your question is a good example of why Italy needs to become a republic. When Mussolini was made prime minister by the king in 1919, the people were not happy about his leadership, but they could not legally say they didn't want Mussolini. Only the leaders could get rid of Mussolini, but they were more afraid of a communist revolution than they were of Mussolini, so he remained in power."

Ruffino looked to Zio Rodolfo for the remainder of the answer, and when Zio Rodolfo had finished speaking, Ruffino spoke to Daniel again.

"Once he was in office, Mussolini kept the people happy by making work for them. The king didn't know that Mussolini was only doing this to make himself more powerful than the king. Soon Mussolini had more influence than the king, and then he joined Hitler, thinking that together they'd win the war in Europe. If Italy had been a republic, as you are in America, the people would have been able to throw Mussolini out of office, because a republic has laws that give the people the authority to remove their leaders rather than putting that power into the hands of other politicians."

When Ruffino was finished, Zio Rodolfo arose from his chair, gave Daniel a robust hug, and said in his limited English, "Donato, I'm pleased you think such interesting thoughts."

On the day before they were to return to America, Ruffino suggested that Daniel meet him at his school at around one in the afternoon. He wanted to introduce his American cousin to his teacher and classmates. Ruffino's teacher gave him permission to make up his homework assignment for that day, so the two cousins could spend their last afternoon together.

Daniel told his father the exciting news that he had been invited to Ruffino's school.

"Walking to Ruffino's school alone is out of the question," was his father's response. "I'll take you to the school, and then you can come back with Ruffino when school is over."

Daniel assured his father he would not get lost. "Ruffino already took me to his school so I would know the way. I'm not gonna get lost, Dad. You don't need to take me. I'm thirteen," protested Daniel.

"Yes, I know, but you're a thirteen-year-old boy who doesn't speak Italian. If you go to Ruffino's school, it will be with me, not by yourself."

Daniel remembered their last disagreement on the topic of getting lost, so he politely begged his father, "Dad, I know you're worried, but a thirteen-year-old boy brought to school by his father? Do you know how embarrassing that would be for me?"

"Embarrassing? I'll tell you what's embarrassing. Me running around Castellamare di Stabia trying to find you after you've gotten yourself lost!"

Daniel's Nonno understood some English from his years in America, so it was not surprising he understood the disagreement taking place between his son and grandson.

Leopoldo interrupted and started to talk to Pete. Daniel didn't understand what they were saying, but it was obvious they were disagreeing and that Daniel was the center of their conversation. Finally, Pete agreed to allow his son to go to Ruffino's school alone.

"But here is what you must do: if you get lost, stop anyone you see on the street or go into any store and tell them you're the grandson of Leopoldo Ciarletta. Everyone knows your Nonno and where he lives. Anyone you speak with will make sure you get home safely." Daniel thanked his father very politely, and then turned to Nonno and gave him a hug.

That evening, Pete and his son were preparing for sleep in the small upstairs bedroom. Daniel had washed and changed into his pajamas, ready to get into bed. Pete asked his son to sit on the bed, "I have something I want to say."

Pete took both of his son's hands in his, and Daniel could see the serious look in his father's eyes. "It's important for you to know why I changed my mind about you going to Ruffino's school alone. Nonno told me you are no longer my little boy. You are becoming a man. Nonno reminded me that he left me and Uncle Danny alone in America and put us in charge of the business when we were about twenty. He did this because he had confidence in Uncle Danny and me, and he felt it was time for us to stand on our own. He knew we would become men sooner if he gave us this responsibility. Nonno said I should show more confidence in you. He is afraid you will never become a man if I keep protecting you. Maybe he's right. I think of you as my baby because you are my youngest child, and maybe I do protect you too much. Your Nonno is right about one thing, you're becoming a man."

Pete then immediately changed his mood and said, "But you must promise me you'll be careful and follow the road that Ruffino showed you. Promise me; I mean it. I'm very serious."

"I will, Dad. I promise I'll be very careful." In a spontaneous sudden move, Daniel jumped up from his bed and gave his father a loving, strong hug. With his head resting on his father's shoulder, Daniel whispered, "Thanks, Dad. I love you." Pete said nothing, and his eyes became moist as he simply returned his son's embrace.

Pete then took his son's face in his big, fleshy, warm hands, as he often did, kissed him on his forehead, and said, "I don't know what I would do if anything happened to you. So you make sure you are careful!"

The next morning, Daniel—energized that he was going to be on his own for an adventurous afternoon—kept busy, hoping the morning would pass quickly. The family had their usual *pranzo* meal at noon. The meal ended with Nonno sipping his digestive aid, Fernet Branca, while the others were sharing fruit. Daniel was ready to get on his way, but knew he had to stay at the table until Nonno finished his small glass of Fernet Branca. Finally, Nonno finished, and after Daniel helped clean the table, he kissed Nonno, Nonna, and his father goodbye.

After he had kissed his father and started to leave, Pete grabbed his arm and said, "Remember what I told you. Be careful! If you get lost, tell someone who you are and they will make sure you get home safely."

"I promise I'll be careful." Daniel turned and tried to get out of the house as fast as possible for fear his father might change his mind. He moved down the narrow stone sidewalk and then continued to walk straight until he got to a wider street. He knew that at this street he was to go right, and then walk three blocks to the overhead archway that connected two homes. At the archway, he made another right, and now he was on a street ascending to higher ground. Ruffino's school was on the left. Daniel enjoyed being out on his own. It made him feel like an adult, mature like Ruffino, who did this every day. A few blocks before he got to the school, he crossed the street so he would be on the same side as the school. One more block and he would be there. A few yards ahead, there was a man smoking a cigarette as he leaned against an open door. As he passed, the man nodded and said, *"Buona iurnata, ragazzo* (Good afternoon, young man)." Daniel smiled and continued toward the school.

As he entered the building, a woman seated behind a counter smiled as though she was expecting him. She got up from her chair and said, "*Avanzarsi* (come forward)."Daniel followed her down a narrow hallway to where Ruffino was waiting in front of an open door. The woman acknowledged Daniel with a bow and said, "*State buono, ragazzo* (Goodbye, young man)."

Ruffino introduced his cousin to his teacher, Professore Saltarelli, and then to his classmates as his cousin from America, New York City. The students, both boys and girls, were all sitting at their wooden desks. Ruffino went to his seat, and the teacher, speaking in English, explained to the class that the rest of the day would be spent asking Daniel questions about America. Professor Saltarelli reminded the youngsters that this time would be part of their English lesson, and they were required to ask their questions only in English.

Daniel became alarmed. Ruffino had not mentioned that he was going to have to stand at the head of the class and answer questions. Fortunately, for Daniel, there was no time to become anxious. The excited students immediately raised their hands and began to ask questions about America. As usual, one of the first questions was, "Is every person in America rich and do they live in big houses?"

After an hour and ten minutes, the clanging hand-held dismissal bell could be heard clearly throughout the school. As the two cousins left the classroom, Daniel asked, "Why didn't you tell me they would ask me questions?"

Ruffino explained it was not his idea. The teacher had suggested it during the morning. "I didn't think you would mind," said Ruffino.

"I didn't. It turned out great, but I was nervous."

Ruffino and Daniel enjoyed their last afternoon together. Daniel mentioned to Ruffino that when he returned to America he was going to study hard and be a better student, "Like you, Ruffino."

Ruffino gave Daniel a modest smile and told him he was glad Daniel had come to Italy, and that he was pleased they had become such good friends.

Daniel made Ruffino promise to visit him in America, and then with a big smile he said, "When I'm older, I'll come to visit you when you're the most important scientist in Italy." Ruffino laughed and gave Daniel an affectionate slap on the arm. They went running to the piazza to see if Ruffino's friends were there.

There was a farewell meal at Nonno's house the night before Pete and Daniel were to leave. After dinner, Pete was given directions by his brother-in-law Rodolfo to Via San Gregorio in the old part of

Naples, where Pete could purchase the *presepi* nativity set for Suzy. Rodolfo told Pete the Port`Alba Restaurant—which was where pizza was invented in 1830—was a short walk from Via San Gregorio. "You're going to be a few blocks away from the restaurant, so eat. Their pizza will be a special treat."

Pete liked the idea. He wanted his son to taste what he called, "Real pizza, not the pizza we have in America, which is full of gravy and cheese, but real Italian pizza, the way it should be made."

After the dishes had been cleaned and put away, and everyone was ready to leave, the long, sad goodbye began. Daniel's aunts thanked Pete for coming to Italy and the *per il miracolo* (the miracle) he had performed: Nonno's health had dramatically improved during their visit. Daniel said farewell to all of his cousins, telling them they were always welcome to visit him in the Bronx.

When he came to Ruffino, Daniel thanked him for their time together, and especially for his friendship. Ruffino reminded Daniel that he was serious about one day visiting New York City. He also reminded Daniel about his promise regarding schoolwork. Then, as two adolescent boys usually do when saying goodbye, they shook hands and were about to part when they both spontaneously hugged each other.

Everyone was up early the next morning. Daniel and his father were packed and ready to start their journey back to America. Nonna Francesca was calm and said very little as she placed bread, salami, olives, biscotti, and a full *caciocavallo* cheese in a box for the boat trip home. The final item to go into the box was a bottle of Zio Ruffino's homemade wine.

As Pete was fitting the food box into his suitcase, he reminded his mother not to make lunch. He had promised to treat Daniel to pizza while they were in Naples.

"The boy can't leave Naples without tasting the finest pizza in the world."

The sun was just beginning to rise as Nonno Leopoldo came down the narrow steps alone. Pete tried to climb the steps to assist his father, who had now stopped on one of the steps above his son. "Go to the table and start your breakfast. I am capable of moving down my own stairs, now go," said Nonno.

Pete, knowing it was useless to argue, slowly moved back toward the table. Leopoldo held the banister rail with his right hand, his *bastone* swinging from his right arm by its crook, as he slowly continued his descent. When he arrived safely on the stone floor, he ordered Daniel to get his sweater. A smiling, proud Nonno and his grandson proceeded arm in arm to the table for their espresso and roll.

After breakfast, Pete and Daniel said their sad farewell, hugging and kissing everyone a number of times. Nonna was concerned that her son had not taken enough food for the trip. Pete kissed his mother and assured her they had plenty of food. Pete and Daniel walked on the narrow cobblestone streets with their suitcases and bags until they arrived at the bus stop. The bus arrived almost immediately and they were on their way to Naples—and from there, America.

CHAPTER IV

𝒯ROUBLE IN

𝒩APLES

Daniel and his father arrived at the main bus terminal in Naples some time after seven in the morning. They were scheduled to board their troop steamer that afternoon at one-thirty. Pete was insistent on leaving early to allow sufficient time for the bus ride to Via San Gregorio to purchase Suzy's *presepi* nativity set. They boarded a second bus, which took them to the old section of Naples. Pete was already beginning to complain, mumbling under his breath about the extra packages he would have to carry to the boat dock.

They arrived at the Piazza San Domenico Maggiore a few minutes after nine. Daniel's father referred to his directions, and with bags in hand, father and son began walking west on the Via Benedetto Croce, looking for the San Gregorio Armeno church opposite a big red building. At this intersection they would find Via San Gregorio, the narrow cobblestone street where the vendors of Neapolitan *presepi* figures had their stores and workshops. The neighborhood was noisy and the streets dirty.

As they proceeded toward the church, Pete whispered to his son, "Daniel, stay close to me. I don't like the looks of some of these people."

"Do you think they are gypsy people, like the person we saw on the bus going to see Nonno?"

"No questions now. Just move along and make sure you stay close." Pete put his arm around his son's shoulders as he picked up his walking pace. Daniel did not protest his father's sudden anxiety.

The San Gregorio Armeno church was the home of Benedictine nuns, who lived in a convent attached to the church and presided over its various daily functions. The cloistered nuns provided a quiet haven in a rowdy neighborhood, known for its noisy vendors, stores, and street traffic. Zio Rodolfo had suggested that if they had time they might enjoy a visit to the church, which was noted for its Baroque interior and contained many frescoes by the Italian artist Luca Giordano.

Via San Gregorio was a narrow cobblestone street lined with stores, and at their entrances men were hawking the *presepi* nativity figures. Pete found a store that sold the Gramendola figures made by Matteo Prencipe. He picked out the specific figures Suzy had listed and a Neapolitan pastoral setting, which was used to display the figures, including miniature houses that arose up as though they were built on a hill. The vendor carefully wrapped the delicate, intricately made figures in paper and then in small boxes. He placed the boxes in the Neapolitan setting, which was too large for a box, and once all the small boxes were stacked in the pastoral setting, it was heavily wrapped in layered paper and taped. The package was much too bulky to carry with their suitcases and other bags. Pete spoke with the vendor for a few moments, and the vendor went to the rear of his store. Thankfully, he reappeared quickly with some pieces of rope. Using the rope, the two men managed to arrange a holder with two large loops for the large package. The vendor helped Pete slip his arm into one of the loops, and then he shifted the package so Pete could slip his other arm through the opposite loop. Finally, the package rested on Pete's back similar to a backpack.

Although they had plenty of time before boarding their boat, Daniel's father was reluctant to depend on the casual Italian bus schedules to get them to the dock on time. He asked the vendor if it was likely they could find a taxi at the Port`Alba Restaurant to take them to the boat dock. The vendor assured Pete that taxis were available at the restaurant, and if they did not immediately see a taxi, there were many people with cars and even donkey carts who would be happy to take them to the dock for a nominal fee.

Daniel and his annoyed father left the store and walked to the corner where the red building and church were located. Sensing his father's mood, Daniel did not bother to ask if he wanted to stop at the church, as his uncle had suggested. They made a left at the red building and began walking to the restaurant. Pete asked his son to reach into his side pocket and take out the directions. Pete was relieved when he realized the restaurant was only a two-block walk away. Pete reminded Daniel to walk in front of him because his vision was limited by the package on his back.

Daniel, feeling more comfortable, said, "C'mon Dad, I'm thirteen! Don't be so worried if I'm not exactly next to you each second!"

Pete stopped walking to turn and glare at his son. Daniel knew it was time to end the argument, "Okay, okay Dad. I'll walk next to you."

"No, you won't! You'll walk in *front* of me," his father growled. Daniel nodded, knowing the discussion was over.

As he walked in front of his father, Daniel was intrigued by the old city of Naples, with its beautiful Romanesque cathedrals gracefully standing next to run-down shops, old brick warehouses, and stone homes with faded painted surfaces and missing stucco—and all of this sitting atop multiple layered ancient Greek and Roman streets. Daniel was distracted by the harsh noise of the motor scooters as they zipped past small cars and slowly moving donkey carts on the congested streets. Moving on the crowded narrow sidewalks was difficult for the two Americans.

Daniel's attention was suddenly drawn away from the noise and sights when he heard his father say, "I see the Port`Alba Restaurant sign." They pushed forward, picking up their walking pace. Pete suddenly stopped and put his luggage down, but he realized they were blocking the narrow sidewalk as irritated people tried to pass them.

"Why are we stopping? We're almost at the restaurant."

Without answering his son's question, Pete said, "Let's move over to the stone wall and get our bags out of the way of this crowd."

Next to the entrance of the restaurant there was a narrow counter with a glass opening to the street and a sign that read: *take-away*. Pete was silent for a few moments as he looked at the moving cars. Although the traffic was heavy, the cars and scooters were moving rapidly, but not quickly enough for Pete.

He stood for a few moments and considered the situation. *Coming to this restaurant was not a good decision. Had I known the traffic was going to be this heavy, I would have waited at Via San Gregorio for a taxi. The cars are moving pretty good here, but what happens if we run into heavy or stopped traffic before we reach the boat? Well, we're here now. Instead of eating our pizza in the restaurant, I can get a pizza at the take-away and we can eat it at the dock, but I won't be able to carry the pizza box flat with all these bags and this damn nuisance tied to my back. Okay, I know what we'll do!*

53

Pete told Daniel to pick up his bags and walk in front of him. Soon father and son were standing at the curb in line with the take-away window. Pete told Daniel, "Here's what we're gonna do. You stay with the luggage at the curb while I go to the window and order our food. Don't move from this spot. I'm leaving the luggage with you at the curb while I order the pizza. Without the bags, I can carry the pizza box flat. Now, I'm going to be only three or four feet away from you while I'm at the window, and I don't want you to move even one inch!

"Wave if a taxi happens to come by while I'm at the window. If one stops, the driver can start loading our stuff into his car. I'm going to put in a quick order and be back in a minute. Only wave at a taxi. Don't wave for a horse and wagon or other cars, only for an official taxi. I'll be just four feet away for a minute."

"Ah, c'mon dad everything is gonna to be okay."

"Never mind, 'ah, c'mon Dad,' you just stay where you are. I'll be right back after I order the pizza." As Pete approached the take-away window, the counter man was handing another man his change, so Pete waited a moment as the man walked away. Then he stepped up to the narrow counter to place his order.

Daniel was standing at the curb next to the luggage, looking to see if there were any taxis among the swerving speeding scooters and small cars rushing by. He had been waiting for about twenty seconds when a small, older car stopped abruptly at the curb next to him. The rear door opened, and Daniel was shocked when a man reached out and pulled him into the rear of the car. Before Daniel's body was fully inside, the car swiftly pulled away from the curb. The back door, still open and hinged at the center of the automobile, slammed shut by the force of the car lurching forward, hitting the bottom of Daniel's shoes.

Daniel was so surprised that it took him a moment to get his breath. He began struggling and shouting, "Let me go! Let me out of here! What are you doing?"

The man holding Daniel had already started to tighten a rope around his hands. Daniel, looking out the rear window, could see a figure running down the middle of the street toward the speeding car. He knew it was his father. Soon the figure was out of sight, and the man next to him was tying a knot in the rope binding both his hands. Daniel continued to scream as loud as he could while kicking his legs. "You let me out of this car!"

Suddenly the man raised his right arm across his shoulder past his chin in a menacing gesture and shouted back in a deep, loud voice, "*Silenzio!*" Daniel became frightened and stopped yelling, causing the man to put his hand down without striking the boy. Then he reached across Daniel's body with his right hand, pushed the door handle down, and pushed on the door as though he was trying to open it. He mumbled something in Italian and gave Daniel a quizzical look with both hands raised. Daniel understood—he was being told the door on his side was locked. It was then that Daniel noticed all the windows in the car were rolled up.

Daniel's mind began to clear, and although he was still frightened, he shouted, "Americano, Americano. Let me out, Americano!" The hefty man completely ignored Daniel's plea. Frightened and confused, Daniel's emotions began rising to the surface, and he felt like he was about to cry. He tried not to, but he couldn't help himself. Tears began rolling down his cheeks. Now he was also embarrassed. Daniel looked away from the man and tried to wipe his face with the wrists of his bound hands. His hands had never been tied for real before—he and his friends used to pretend to bind each other's hands, but this was real. The man had fastened the rope so tight that Daniel was unable to separate his wrists. He was angry at himself for what he perceived as cowardly behavior. *I was so surprised, but I still should'a put up more of a fight,* thought Daniel. *And the crying! Why did I act like such a baby?*

He wondered how long he had been in the car. It seemed like minutes, but he couldn't be sure. Daniel had lost all sense of time. He noticed they were still in the city. The driver was speeding and passing other cars. He had to periodically slow down for traffic, but then he would continue his fast driving.

Although he had been intimidated by the man next to him, Daniel decided he needed to find the courage to be more aggressive. The car continued its rapid movement through the city streets, ignoring caution road signs, veering and zigzagging as it passed other vehicles. Soon the car was on a highway. As they sped along, Daniel could only think of how he had reacted when he was dragged into the car. *Why didn't I fight him harder and pull away? Why are they doing this? Why did they choose me? What are they planning?* Many confusing questions kept running through his mind. Then, in an instant, reality replaced his confusion. *Oh my God. I'm being kidnapped.*

For a few moments his brain stopped functioning. When his mental process returned, the first thought to enter his mind was about two radio mystery programs he had listened to in America: *The Shadow* and *Mr. Keen, Tracer of Lost Persons.* He remembered stories about kidnappings from both of these radio mysteries. Daniel's analysis regarding his predicament had to do with the events he remembered from those stories. While the car was moving on the highway, Daniel was deciding how best to act, based on what he remembered of the actions of the characters portrayed in these fictional radio dramas. He remembered the kidnapped character was portrayed as hysterical and fearful. The bad guys were sarcastic, annoyed at the hysteria, and they talked about using their guns! But he kept telling himself that the person in the story was always rescued in the end. Perhaps Daniel was trying to give himself a frame of reference for what he was experiencing—perhaps he was just trying not to cry again. In any case, his naiveté was not helpful regarding his predicament.

As the reality of his situation began to settle in, Daniel told himself to calm down and try to determine why this was happening and how he could get free. Initially it didn't make any sense. Daniel didn't think the two men knew who he was. He had never seen them with his father, so why did they take him?

He began to find it hard to breathe. He took a few deep breaths, which seemed to help. Daniel again began to assess his situation, *These men must come from Castellamare di Stabia. Like all of Ruffino's friends, they must think because I'm an American my father is rich and he will pay them money for my return. The car must have been following us in Naples, and the men were waiting for the best time to drag me into the car.*

Daniel's capture was beginning to make sense. He remembered the day he had walked to Ruffino's school and his father had said everyone in Castellamare di Stabia knew Daniel's grandfather. *So that's how they intend to do it,* thought Daniel. *They're going to call Nonno and speak with Dad.* Daniel was feeling much better now that he had figured out the motive for his kidnapping. His mind immediately skipped to his release, *Dad won't let them get away with this; he'll make sure they go to jail for what they've done.*

The man next to Daniel was acting as though he was alone in the rear seat, paying no attention to his terrified passenger. He was a large man with thick black hair. Daniel could only see the back of the head of the driver, who was chain-smoking cigarettes. The two men in the car talked very little. They exchanged a few words now and then, but there was no sustained conversation between them.

It was hard to determine just how long they had been driving, but Daniel guessed he had been in the car for about an hour. The driver entered a lane to exit the highway. It suddenly dawned on Daniel that it would be wise if he started to remember landmarks and other clues as they were driving. He wasn't quite sure how he would use this information, but it seemed like something he should be doing. The first clue appeared immediately after the car left the highway. Daniel saw a sign that read *Abbazia di Monte Cassino*. He didn't know what the sign meant, but he kept silently repeating the words on the sign so he would not forget. Soon they were traveling up a winding road, going higher and higher. *We must be going into the mountains,* thought Daniel.

The man in the back seat continued looking straight ahead, rarely looking at his captive. Daniel decided that if he could get the driver to stop the car, he might have a chance of running away. He decided to become more aggressive. He would swing his hips toward the man next to him and use his feet to kick him in the face. If he could get a solid blow to the face with his shoes, the driver might have to stop the car to help his companion. He would need to open a door, and Daniel might be able to get out of the car. *It's worth a try,* he thought.

Daniel took a deep breath and swung his hips hard to the left while trying to lift his legs. The man reacted with unusual speed, grasping Daniel's legs and pulling them upward, causing Daniel's upper body to roll off the seat and onto the floor between the front and rear seats. The man was infuriated, raising his voice and shouting in Italian, while placing his feet on Daniel's legs and tying his ankles with a second piece of rope. Daniel was completely immobilized now that his body was wedged in the narrow space between the front and back seats.

The car continued on the winding road, climbing higher and higher into the mountains. After about forty-five minutes, they came to a stop. The man in the back seat opened the locked car door on his side. He placed his arm under Daniel's left elbow, brought him to a seated position, dragged him across the floor of the car, and had him stand on the edge of the road. Daniel saw a horse drawn wagon in front of the stopped car. He was forcibly pulled forward toward the wagon, struggling to shuffle his bound feet, and then pushed into the bed of the wagon.

There was a person in a heavy coat and wool hat on the front seat of the wagon holding the reins of the horses. Daniel's wrists were fastened to the side of the wagon with rope. The driver of the wagon threw a heavy coat and two wool hats to Daniel's captor. The man put on the coat and hat, and then put the other hat on Daniel's head. He went to the driver of the car and handed him an envelope. The driver immediately pulled the car across the road, backed up, and sped away. On the back of the car, Daniel could see the word Renault and the license plate number. He kept repeating to himself, so as not to forget, the numbers and letters of the license plate: CA 261, and also the car name, the exit sign that said Monte Cassino, and the fact they had driven on a winding road going into the mountains.

The wagon started moving forward with Daniel's captor in the back of the wagon across from him. Daniel was able to clearly observe the man for the first time. He was not very tall, but he had a stocky build. The disinterested look on his face remained, as it had in the car.

Daniel yelled across to the man, "I demand that you tell me where you're taking me!"

Daniel's plea was ignored as though he had never spoken. His adrenalin was still flowing, and it was fifteen minutes or so before he noticed how much colder it was in this place than it had been in Naples. He was glad he had decided to wear his heavy jacket, the one he planned to use on the deck of the troop steamer.

The slow moving wagon was now on a road that seemed to be descending. It was a long slow ride, perhaps an hour or more. Daniel had not been concentrating on time. He was making every effort to remember all the important clues. He was confident he had all the facts memorized.

The man across from Daniel continued to stare straight ahead, not looking at his captive. As they continued on the winding road, Daniel noticed a road sign with the word *Opi* on it. He started to repeat this word, Opi—yet another clue. Then he noticed an open pasture field and a small mountain town, which seemed to be in the center of the pasture. At the end of the green pasture was a forest extending to the base of a huge mountain range, which completely surrounded the small mountain town in the center of a vast pasture. The wagon was now on a single road that had been cut through the thick forest, leading directly to the mountain town.

Ah, so this is the place they're gonna hide me until Dad comes with the ransom money, thought Daniel.

The horse drawn wagon was now on a steep single dirt road leading up to the town. At the top of the dirt road, the wagon made a sharp left onto a cobblestone road. It continued moving on the single cobblestone road, which was lined with stone houses. Off in the distance, Daniel could see a church located in the center of the highest point of the town. The cobblestone road led directly to the church and ended at its front steps. About a third of the way into the town, the wagon stopped on the left in front of a house that had the number 25 over a blue door. Daniel reminded himself that this was another important clue to remember. He had not thought much about the time of day until he noticed it was starting to get dark.

His captor removed the rope on his ankles, and holding him tightly by the arm, brought Daniel down from the bed of the wagon and moved him toward the blue door. Daniel and the man entered a dark room. Daniel's captor moved to the center of the room and pulled a string hanging from a ceiling light bulb. He untied the rope from around Daniel's sore and irritated wrists. Then, without a word, he left the room. Daniel could hear the door being locked.

The room was large and windowless. There was an upholstered chair close to the entrance, a bed, a woodstove that was hot, and a large stack of cut wood. By the bed, attached to the stone wall, was a wooden rack with pegs. There was a small rectangular table and a wooden chair in the center of the room. Daniel walked past the table toward the rear of the room. In the left corner there was a white porcelain fixture on the floor with a hole in the center. Daniel had been in Italy long enough to know this was an Italian toilet. Near the toilet was a small sink. Directly over the sink was a blue metal container that was flat where it was attached to the wall and round in front, with a faucet coming from its bottom and a pipe leading from the top of the blue container into the ceiling of the room.

There was a door on the other side of the back wall. Daniel approached the door, suspecting it would also be locked. Surprisingly, it was not. He opened the door slowly but stayed behind it for fear that someone might be on the other side. The door opened into a large room that contained two horses in stalls, a few sheep, two goats, and a mule. At the far end of the room there were black iron bars covering the entire opening and embedded in a half stone wall. The black iron bars were also firmly implanted into the concrete ceiling. These bars looked like the hand railings on the front steps of some houses in the Bronx. In the center of the stone wall there was an opening that seemed to be the way the animals would enter and exit this area. The hinged door was made from the same iron black bars. The door was at least seven feet tall, extending to the edge of the concrete ceiling. It was secured with a heavy metal lock that Daniel unsuccessfully tried to force open.

Discouraged, he returned to the warm room. He removed his coat and hat, and sat in the upholstered chair, imagining what might happen next.

Unbeknownst to Daniel, his captor, Vincenzo Sgammotta, lived above the room where Daniel had been placed. Vincenzo came into the dining room after washing in preparation for his meal. He asked his wife, "Gelsomina, have you prepared food for the boy?"

"Yes, Vincenzo, his plate is ready and sitting on the table. He's probably hungry by now."

"I will take it to him before we eat."

When Vincenzo saw the amount of food on the boy's plate, he said to his wife, "Gelsi, this is too much food for the boy's meal. He won't be able to finish all this."

"Oh, Vincenzo, it's his first night, and he probably didn't have lunch. Besides, he must be tired and confused about why he's been brought here. He'll need a good meal to make him feel better. Now go and bring the young boy his plate."

Vincenzo took the food and a metal cup half-filled with red wine out the back door and down one flight of stairs. He unlocked the gate leading to the animal stable, proceeded to the door, and entered the room. He looked around the room, glanced at Daniel, and placed the plate and cup on the rectangular table. "*Mangia,*" he said. Daniel knew what this Italian word meant.

Daniel angrily protested, "I want to see my father! The police will put you in jail for taking me if you don't bring my father! I am Americano." Without responding, the man turned and left the room the same way he had entered.

Daniel was not hungry, even though he had not eaten since breakfast at his grandfather's house. His stomach was nauseated and his head reeling. Daniel spoke out loud, as though he was talking to someone in the room. "I don't need this jerk's food. My dad will have the cops here soon enough to arrest this guy. I wouldn't be surprised if I was outta here by tomorrow morning. My dad will find me even before this guy can contact him for the ransom money."

Daniel returned to the upholstered chair, as some of the tension he had been feeling since being dragged into the car was beginning to leave his body. He knew he needed to write down the clues he had been silently repeating in his mind so he wouldn't forget. He didn't know how this information could be used, but it seemed like an important thing to do. Daniel looked for a pencil and paper, but the room was bare except for the furniture. He returned to the upholstered chair, concerned that if he could not record this information he might forget it by morning.

As time passed, the room was getting chilly, so Daniel placed some cut logs in the belly of the stove. He had an idea—using the metal poker, he took a piece of the burnt wood out of the fire and let it cool. Then using it like charcoal, he wrote the information he had memorized, *Monte Cassino, Renault, black car, CA 261, mountain road, Opi,* and the number *25,* on the bottom of the stone wall covered by the bed, which would hide the words from his captor. He felt as though he had accomplished something important, and he was proud of himself for finding a clever way of recording the words. He returned to his chair, his head still whirling. His stomach was still queasy and he did not feel like eating. *I won't touch this guy's food to show him that I'm really angry.* He put a few more logs into the stove and lay down on the bed, which was similar to the bed in Nonno's house—a thin mattress on a wooden frame.

Once Pete realized he couldn't catch up to the car, he ran back to the restaurant and began screaming, "Police! Get me the police! Somebody took my son!"

An older man behind the bar said, "Abbastanza" (enough)! I will get the police. Sit and calm yourself." The man began dialing before Pete could respond. Pete was too agitated to sit and stood next to the man who was calling. When the man had finished, he ordered one of his waiters to bring in Pete's luggage and bags. Then he said, "Please, Signore, come with me to a quiet place where you can talk to the police when they arrive."

Pete, who was now in a daze, was led to a back room where the man poured him a whiskey. "Drink this—it will calm you." The man, who was the manager of the restaurant, was more concerned about the disruption Pete's hysteria might cause his customers than he was about the fact that Pete had just lost his son. The whiskey didn't help—Pete continued pacing at the open door of the room as he waited for the police to arrive.

A police officer was escorted to the rear room by the manager. Pete hurriedly explained what had happened. After writing down his statement, the officer escorted Pete and his luggage to the police car. He drove him to the main police station and said an immediate trace would begin on license plate number CA 261.

A sergeant took a detailed statement from the distraught American. When he was finished, the officer said, "We'll have the information on the owner of the vehicle late this evening. I would suggest that you return tomorrow morning for the details."

"Tomorrow morning?" repeated Pete. "How long does it take to trace a license plate? I'm not leaving until I have the information on the car, and you better have it before tomorrow morning."

Although the sergeant was annoyed with the rude American, he tried to be diplomatic. "Mr. Ciarletta, I can see you're very upset over the loss of your son, but you must try to understand we have other cases we are working on, and we must follow certain procedures. This will take time. We'll have information for you as soon as you arrive in the morning."

Pete was unwilling to accept the sergeant's answer. "Procedures? Who the hell knows what will happen to my son by tomorrow? I want information *now*, and if you can't give it to me, then I want to see your boss!"

The desk sergeant asked Pete to sit while he went for the captain. In a few minutes, a tall man with a thin mustache dressed in a fancy dark blue uniform with golden laced shoulder epaulets, shiny brass buttons, and a peaked hat with a silver bar fastened to its front, entered the front office desk area. He greeted Pete and asked him to come with him to his office.

Once they were in the office, he offered Pete a seat directly in front of his desk. "I am Captain Sollazzo. Mr. Ciarletta, I agree that time is important in kidnapping cases. I will do everything in my power to speed this investigation along. If you return this evening after six, I guarantee we will have the most up-to-date information on the license plate number you gave us."

Pete thanked the captain and said, "I'll be here this evening." The two men shook hands, and as Pete left the police station, he meekly thanked the sergeant at the desk for his assistance.

When Pete arrived back at the police station that evening, the desk sergeant told Pete the license plate number he had given the officer earlier in the day had been reported stolen two years ago.

Pete was quite shaken by this news. "What are you going to do now?" he asked. The policemen told Pete that Captain Sollazzo wished to see him first thing in the morning. "Tomorrow! Are you people crazy? Tomorrow will be too late!"

"Mr. Ciarletta, the captain is no longer on duty, but he has rearranged his schedule to meet with you first thing in the morning."

"Tell me where the Captain lives. I want to see him now," said Pete. The desk sergeant refused to divulge the information and insisted that Pete return in the morning as requested. Pete left the station quite upset, but knowing he had taken the matter as far as he could. It was going to be a long, restless night in a hotel while he waited for positive news about Daniel.

He arrived early the next morning and informed the officer at the desk who he was and why he had come.

"Oh, yes, Mr. Ciarletta. Captain Sollazzo is waiting for you. Let me take you to his office."

When Pete entered the captain's office, he immediately said, "How will you find my son? What do you intend to do?"

The captain was sitting behind a large desk, and he offered Pete a seat. "Mr. Ciarletta, I know you are suffering, but I feel I must be candid with you. Your son was most probably taken by gypsies—and I'm sorry to tell you that gypsies don't usually request a ransom for the return of a person who, like your son, is unknown. In situations like this, they often sell their captive to the highest bidder."

Pete glared at the captain. "SELL my son? Are you telling me there is no way to get him back?"

Captain Sollazzo moved from behind his desk and sat next to Pete. "No, no, Mr. Ciarletta, I am not saying that. I might be able to find you a contact that has, shall I say, the ability to have you speak directly about your son with the Gypsy King of Naples."

Pete understood the Captain's meaning. "I am willing to show my gratitude if you could find this person for me," said Pete.

"I will make a few calls to insure that the gypsies will take no action until they speak with you." He told Pete to return to his office the following afternoon at two. "I'm sure I can be of help to you."

Pete agreed and asked Captain Sollazzo if he could provide a phone so he could make a collect call to his family in America. As he was being led to a private room, Pete asked the captain if he knew where the nearest Western Union office was located.

"Yes, I will write the address for you before your call."

As the captain was obtaining an outside line, Pete gave Captain Sollazzo his American phone number. He dialed and spoke with an operator, requesting a collect call to America, New York City: TY3-5259. After a few moments Captain Sollazzo handed the receiver to Pete.

"Your call to America has been accepted." Captain Sollazzo left the room and closed the door behind him.

"Hello, Suzy?"

"Pete, why are you calling? What's happened?"

"Suzy, I have some terrible news. Daniel has been kidnapped by gypsies."

"Oh, my God," screamed Suzy, as she fell into the chair next to the phone and began pulling at her hair. "Damn you, Pete, how could you let this happen?"

Pete quickly shouted back, "Suzy, stop! Listen to me! Get a hold of yourself. I need you to do something important."

"You need me to do something? Damn you, Pete, *you* better do something and get Daniel back."

"Suzy, I know you're upset. How do you think I feel? Now please, I need you to calm down!"

Suzy took a deep breath and said, "Tell me what you need."

"Call my brothers and tell them I need two thousand dollars by tomorrow. Wire the money to me through Western Union. Do you have a pencil?"

Suzy was ready. "Yes, give me the address."

Pete spoke slowly, "Send the money to me care of: Western Union Office, Via Pisanetti, Naples, Italy. Now repeat the address back to me."

Suzy repeated it in a low, agonized voice.

"Suzy, I must have two thousand dollars in my hands by noon tomorrow—and, Suzy, that's Italian time, not American time. Do you understand?"

"But, Pete, suppose...."

Pete interrupted his wife in anger, "Suzy, listen carefully, and no 'buts.' This must be done. I must have two thousand dollars tomorrow by noon, Italian time. Is that clear?"

"I understand," said Suzy.

Pete continued with more instructions, "When my brother Danny comes home tonight, tell him to contact the *caporegime* (street captain or soldier designation) of the Fordham Road Sicilian family. He will know how to reach this man."

Suzy gasped, "Pete, why are you doing this?"

"Suzy, do you want to see your son again?" Without waiting for a response, he continued, "I know what this means, but we have no choice. The *caporegime* will be able to arrange a meeting with the Don of the Fordham Road family. Danny must secure a loan for the ransom money we will need to get Daniel back."

There was shocked silence at the other end of the phone. Pete pleaded, "Suzy, get a hold of yourself. I need you to be strong. Don't go to pieces on me now."

"Okay, Pete, you're right," she said, with resignation in her voice.

Pete repeated his orders, understanding that she was still in shock from the horrific news.

"I know this isn't easy for you. I understand that, but when you hang up the phone, I need to know you can deliver for me. Can you do what I ask?"

Suzy, holding back tears, said, "Yes Pete, I'm okay now. Everything will get done."

Pete repeated his orders one more time so there would be no mistake. "Suzy, are you sure you understand what you have to do?"

Suzy replied, "Yes, Pete, I know what you need. Just get Daniel back."

Pete felt reassured by his wife's words, "As soon as I find out the amount of the ransom I will call you. I expect this will take two, maybe three days." Pete knew his plan was contrary to everything they believed and honored, but but there was no other way to get his child back. "Suzy, if I thought there was any other way, I wouldn't be asking Danny to get involved with the Fordham Road family, but it's the only way to get Daniel back."

Suzy, now somewhat calmer, repeated, "Okay, Pete, I understand. We'll do what needs to be done at our end."

The following afternoon, Pete met with Captain Sollazzo. He handed the captain an envelope containing five hundred American dollars. The captain looked pleased. He reached into his upper right-hand drawer and gave Pete a piece of paper with the name Janui Kwiek and a phone number.

The captain explained, "First call the Gypsy Kwiek. He has my guarantee that you plan them no harm. Then explain how you are ready to cooperate. Please understand, Mr. Ciarletta, you must be willing to show your appreciation to both the Gypsy Kwiek and the King of the Gypsies. You can be sure the generosity you have show to me will be appreciated by both of the gypsies."

"I understand what needs to be done," said Pete.

As he started to leave the office, he hesitated and turned to the captain. "Captain Sollazzo, please don't get me wrong. You've been very helpful and I'm grateful. It's just that, well, I don't understand. Why are the gypsies allowed to kidnap children?"

The captain arose from his desk and joined Pete in the middle of the room. "Mr. Ciarletta, gypsies are the direct descendants of Adam and Eve's oldest son Cain, who killed his brother Abel. For this reason they are destined to roam the earth in their caravans. They don't believe in toiling for a living, nor do they work the land. They prefer to take care of their modest needs by stealing and begging from *gadje*, the name they give to non-gypsies, people they neither understand nor like. We arrest a gypsy and put him in jail knowing there are ten others to take his place. They are a race of people who choose to live outside of society."

Pete exhaled deeply, and although he had heard the Captain's words, he was still unable to comprehend. Without saying anything, he warmly shook the hand of Captain Sollazzo and left his office.

Daniel was awakened abruptly the following morning. His captor was standing over his bed. He was angry and speaking to Daniel in Italian. It took a moment for Daniel to grasp where he was and what was happening. The only thing he could determine was that the man was angry about the food he had brought last night. Daniel was now sitting on the bed. The man took Daniel by the arm and pulled him to the table, while continuing to talk in Italian. He was pointing to the food Daniel had not eaten. Daniel tried to make him understand that he did not know what he was saying, and the man eventually calmed down.

Daniel noticed he had brought a metal cup of what looked like coffee and a roll on a plate. His captor now lowered his voice and spoke more slowly, as though that might help Daniel understand. He kept pointing to the plate of food he had left last night. Daniel surmised that his captor was upset at something to do with the food. He used the word *bottino*, which Daniel thought meant "bad." Daniel wondered if the man was angry because he had not eaten the food, or whether he was upset because the food had spoiled.

The man picked up the dinner plate and cup, and he again began speaking in Italian and pointing at the plate with the roll. Daniel understood he was being told to eat what he had been given this morning. Daniel's appetite was now stronger than his desire to be defiant, and he gladly ate the roll and drank the espresso. Having been in Italy for three weeks, Daniel was becoming accustomed to espresso. It did not seem as bitter as it had the first time he tried it at Nonno's house.

He remained alone in the room for the rest of the morning. He was pleased that he had correctly memorized the road signs, the information about the car, and Opi. The morning went by slowly. He appreciated the warmth provided by the wood-burning stove. His fear and distress slowly began turning to frustration. He hoped someone would tell him why he had been taken, and when he would be reunited with his father.

Later that day, his captor came to the room with more food. Daniel was relieved that he was not being physically mistreated. Actually, he was surprised by the way he was being treated. He expected a kidnapped victim to be bound and gagged. He was grateful to be able to walk around the room free of restraints. Daniel suspected the reason for the relatively good treatment was to demonstrate to his father that he had not been abused while waiting to be ransomed.

He spent most of the afternoon in the animal stable, hoping someone would walk by the gate so he could tell them he had been kidnapped and ask them to bring the police. But no one passed. By late afternoon, with the sun now behind the mountains, Daniel was cold and discouraged. He went back to the room and warmed himself by the stove.

That evening, his captor again brought food to Daniel, and again he protested. The man, as was the case yesterday, ignored Daniel. The following morning Daniel decided that resistance was not helping. *If I stop yelling at him and try making myself understood, he might tell me why he has taken me and when he is going to release me.*

Daniel knew a few Italian words and gestures, and he hoped that the man might know some English. Maybe he could make himself understood, and then hopefully the man would tell him when his father was coming. Daniel wished he knew more Italian, but his parents would not speak Italian around their children. They were concerned that if their young children heard both the English and Italian languages, they would become confused and not learn to speak English properly.

That afternoon, his captor entered the room with food, just as he had done the day before. Daniel began gesturing and speaking in English, and interjecting the few Italian words he thought might help: "Why *tu*, (you)? (pointing to his captor) take me (pointing to his chest) in auto (car)?" He pretended to be steering an automobile and continued, "Bring me to this casa (house)?" Daniel tapped the stone walls of the room to indicate he meant the house.

Daniel was relieved when the man responded calmly and without anger. His captor spoke Italian using many hand gestures, as though Daniel would be able to understand him. Daniel said, "*Io non capisco* (I don't understand)" a number of times, and his captor soon gave up trying to communicate verbally. He took the empty dishes, and pointing to the food he had brought to Daniel, said, "*Mangia*." Then he turned and walked to the door leading to the animal stable.

Encouraged by his captor's calmness, Daniel followed, pleading, "*Mi aiuto* (Help me)."The man continued out the door, not bothering to respond. Daniel was left standing in the open doorway, as the silent, stubborn man opened and then locked the gate leading out from the animal stable. He moved to the right and was immediately out of sight. This same procedure went on for two more days: delivery of food, Daniel asking when he was going to be released, and no response from his captor.

By the evening of the third day in his windowless cell, Daniel was getting more and more distressed. *Where's my father? Why hasn't he come for me?*

Pete was searched for weapons before he was escorted into the building to meet the King of the Gypsies. He was ushered into a dimly lit room, where a man was sitting at a small table under a light bulb hanging from a wire. The man was wearing a brightly colored, grease-stained suit with a striped open collar shirt and a fedora that was equally stained. He motioned to Pete to sit in the chair opposite him. The gypsy Janui Kwiek stood against the closed entrance door. Two other men stood at the entrance of a side door.

Django Mahai, the King of the Gypsies, was the first to speak. "So *gadjo*, you paid for my time. What is it that you want from Django?"

Pete was very careful not to irritate Django Mahai. "Sir, Captain Sallazzo will be able to vouch for my honesty in this matter. I wish to cause no trouble for you or your people. All I want is my son—and I am willing to pay for his safe return."

Django Mahai looked at Pete with a blank facial expression, and then speaking Italian with a strange accent he said, "*Gadjo*, do you think you'd be brought to me if we thought you would bring harm to me or my people?"

Pete began to apologize. He assured the gypsy leader he meant no insult, but Django quickly interrupted him. "*Gadjo*, I have no time for your groveling. If you've lost a child, it's not my people who have taken him. You can be sure of this, because we would be most pleased to exchange your child for your money."

Pete went numb, but somehow he recovered quickly enough to stammer, "Then...then other gypsy people have my son. Please tell me of other gypsies who might have him. I promise no harm to anyone. All I want is the safe return of my son."

Django's smile radiated confidence. "*Gadjo*, if you were one of us, you would know better than to ask such a foolish question. Nothing happens in Naples that I don't order or which is not immediately brought to my attention."

Django's posture eased and a smooth, sympathetic look took over his piercing eyes. "Mister, please believe me. Whoever took your child was not a gypsy."

Django Mahai stood up and told his aide, Janui Kwiek, "Take this *gadjo* back to his pickup location. We have no further use of him."

Janui Kwiek grabbed the elbow of the stunned and shaken father, but Pete broke away from him and moved toward Django Mahai, continuing to plead for information. Django Mahai turned quickly, showing a long exposed switchblade knife. The two men at the side door moved quickly to either side of the gypsy king. Pete immediately stopped his advance.

"Come forward if you want to feel my blade, *gadjo*," said Django. "If not, then leave as I have said. Now take him away."

Janui Kwiek and the two other men were having a great deal of difficulty dragging the powerful American toward the door. Losing all sense of propriety or submissiveness, Pete pulled his arm from Janui Kwiek and punched him. Then he slammed his free arm against the hand of the other man, sending his knife sliding across the stone floor. Having freed himself, he kneed the third man in the groin and quickly moved toward Django Mahai, screaming, "You dirty bastard! You have my son. Give him to me!"

The King of the Gypsies was unprepared for the suddenly crazed *gadjo*. Pete's lightning attack enabled him to get both hands around the neck of Django Mahai, but Django thrust his razor sharp blade into Pete's upper left arm, the knife going completely through Pete's arm. Django was startled, but he managed to firmly hold onto his knife—which was now embedded in the arm of his attacker. Pete was seriously cut, but he continued to hold the neck of Django, while screaming, "You're going to bring me to my son. Do you hear me? I want my child, now!"

The three other gypsies had recovered and pulled Pete away from their king. With Django still holding the knife handle and Pete being pulled off the gypsy, the blade slid out of Pete's arm, slashing more bloody tissue and skin. Pete screamed as the sharp metal ruptured its final sliver of skin, causing excruciating pain. He went limp for a few moments, and then quickly recovered by ferociously kicking his legs, trying to free himself while being dragged backward.

Janui Kwiek had his left arm around Pete's neck and his knife poised above Pete chest, as he asked the gypsy king, "Shall I end this *gadjo's* life with my knife in his heart?

"No!" said Django. "I thought this *gadjo* was just another slobbering coward, but he surprised me with his courage. He is a fearless one. Let him live for now, but remove him from me and return him as I have said. Do not bandage his wound. If he is truly as brave as he appears, he will survive. If not, let him die on his own terms out of respect for his courage. Gypsies do not needlessly kill warriors. Either way, he is no longer a threat to us. Dump him away from here and return quickly."

Pete stopped struggling when the tip of a sharp knife broke the skin of his back. "One more sound, *gadjo*, and this knife cuts you—this time all the way into your back," said Janui Kwiek. The gypsies dragged Pete to the car and thrust him into the rear seat between two men, who were each holding exposed knife blades. His battle was over.

After they dropped him off on the road, Pete made a tourniquet for his upper arm with the sleeve of his shirt to stop the bleeding and found his way back to Castellamare de Stabia, where he received medical attention. Discouraged and not sure what his next step should be, Pete went to the Naples police the following day. He met with Captain Sollazzo and informed him of his meeting with the gypsy king.

"Mr. Ciarletta, you were very fortunate to have had your life spared by the gypsies. If Django was not willing to deal for your son, you can be sure the gypsies did not kidnap him. We will now make your son's case a priority."

Pete thanked the captain and asked him to recommend the best private detective agency in Naples. The following day, he met with the head of the detective agency. A fee was negotiated for a two-month period of time. Pete called Suzy and told her to delay the ransom loan and immediately wire him money for the detective agency fee.

Daniel was awakened by his captor the morning of the fourth day, although he was usually already awake when the man brought his espresso and roll. This morning, the man also brought clothes and rubber boots with him. Without saying a word, he hung the clothes on the wall rack with the wooden pegs. He motioned for Daniel to remove what he was wearing and put on the garb he had hung on the rack and the rubber boots and wool stockings. After finishing his roll and espresso, Daniel gladly took off the clothes he had been wearing for the past four days—or had it been five?—He wasn't sure.

The garments were thick, heavy work clothes, much larger than Daniel's American clothes. The underwear was a little large, shorter, and different than what Daniel was used to wearing. He put on the heavy woolen socks and rubber boots, which easily slipped on his feet.

Soon the door leading to the animal area opened, and Daniel's captor motioned to Daniel to put on his coat and hat and come forward. The man stood directly in the open doorway. Daniel noticed that the door leading out from the animal stable was open. He quickly decided to distract the man as he approached the doorway and then move past him and run to freedom. Daniel made a hurried decision to pretend his arm was caught in his jacket as he approached the man. He was hoping the man would move to assist him with his jacket sleeve, he would then push him and bolt out the open gate.

When Daniel reached the door, he stopped, still pretending he was having difficulty with his coat sleeve. The man said, "*Avanti* (come forward)." Daniel's captor, maintaining his position at the door, did not move to help the boy with his coat. Daniel decided to act. He quickly hit the man's chest with his shoulder, but he was unable to budge him. The man wrapped his muscular arm around Daniel's neck and angrily moved him past the animals to a horse drawn wagon parked at the gate. Then he released his grip on the boy's neck and pushed him into the wagon. A second horse was tied to the rear of the wagon.

Daniel was breathing heavily, his heart was pounding, and his neck hurt. After securing the boy's wrists to the wagon, while still muttering in Italian, Daniel's captor mounted the front seat of the wagon and proceeded down the road. After a few minutes, Daniel gained his composure and was silently grateful that he had not been physically hurt by the man during his escape attempt. The wagon rolled over a dirt road until it joined the single main cobblestone road with houses on both sides.

There was a building that looked like a restaurant or bar at the joining of the dirt and cobblestone road. *This is the same way I was brought to this place,* thought Daniel. At this point, the wagon turned sharply to the right onto a dirt road going down into the valley. Daniel could see that the valley was flat pastureland surrounding the entire town. As they arrived at the pasture, the wagon continued on a dirt road, which also ran parallel to the massive rock formation upon which the town was built. Small portions of the valley had been plowed, while most of the remaining area was short green grass. Small wooden shacks were spaced at various intervals along the dirt road. The green valley extended from the hill town to the beginning of the forest, which blended into the base of a large mountain range. Daniel estimated the distance from the dirt road to the forest to be approximately a mile.

Suddenly Daniel remembered, *The ransom money! That's what this is about! My father will come to the valley, give the man the money, and I will be released!* He eagerly looked ahead, hoping to see his father or a car, but there was nothing in sight.

The wagon continued its slow saunter along the dirt road until it stopped at a large pile of what looked like animal manure. There was still no sign of Daniel's father. Daniel told himself this must be the place for the transfer and his father had not yet arrived. The wagon holding Daniel was stopped next to a strange looking metal cart on wheels. The bed of the cart looked like a long metal barrel or tub that had been cut in half lengthwise. From the wagon, Daniel could see a metal rod with spoon-like metal extensions running lengthwise in the center of the barrel like wagon. The man untied Daniel's wrists and motioned him to the ground. Daniel's captor had two pitchforks, and he handed one to Daniel, motioning for him to use the pitchfork to throw the piled material into the metal wagon.

I can't believe it. This guy is gonna make me work before my father comes, thought Daniel. Although he found this strange, he preferred it to the windowless room even if what he was shoveling was a mixture that smelled like manure.

As they were filling up the metal wagon, Daniel became aware that he was not constrained. He could easily run into the forest. His captor was big in girth and seemed to be in good physical condition, but Daniel was sure the man would be unable to keep up with his youthful legs and would tire before he reached the forest. The only problem was that the oversized rubber boots would slow Daniel down.

Since he expected his father to come at any moment, Daniel decided against an escape attempt. He resolved that if his father did not come for him today or at the latest tomorrow morning, he would try to escape either to the forest or down the dirt road. He did not intend to stay in this place beyond tomorrow morning.

When the metal wagon was full, the man attached Daniel with rope to the front seat. He also untied the horses from the front and back of the wagon and harnessed them to the front of the metal wagon. He climbed up next to Daniel and began to move the wagon forward. Although it was cold and the air was brisk, Daniel had worked up a sweat. The exercise felt good—being outside and exercising had made him feel invigorated and alive for the first time since he had been brought to this place.

The wagon moved along the parallel dirt road back toward the entrance to the village. Eventually, the man turned the horses in the direction of the forest and mountain range, stopped the wagon, and depressed a long metal handle on his left side. He snapped the reins on the backs of the horses, and as they moved the main central rod in the bed of the metal wagon started to turn. The circular movement of the spoon-like extensions began throwing the manure like substance out of the wagon and onto the ground. They continued this throughout the morning. By now Daniel knew the substance being thrown on the ground was manure, and it was being spread onto soil that looked like it had been previously planted, and also onto a portion of the green grass of the pasture.

When church bells began ringing, Daniel's captor took him to an area by one of the shacks. He attached Daniel's ankle to a leather strap device that was on the end of a thick rope tied to a stake anchored in the ground. The man laid out food and water for the boy. Tired from the continuous work and being quite hungry, Daniel enjoyed his food and then rested on the ground. He was close enough for his captor to keep him in sight. The mustached man lit a cigar and rested against a tree. Daniel was interested to see if he would close his eyes or go to sleep, but he did neither.

The rope attached to Daniel's ankle had considerable slack. Daniel began reconsidering his escape options. *If my dad doesn't get here today, and this guy does the same thing tomorrow, I'll escape tomorrow during the food break. I could slowly loosen the knot on my ankle without him seeing me and outrun him to the road leading out of town.*

Daniel carefully observed the position of his captor. The large man sat with his back against a tree, looking past Daniel toward the mountain range. Based on where his captor was sitting today, he would notice Daniel removing the ankle constraint. Daniel decided this option wasn't going to work. There was, however, another more unpleasant alternative.

The slack in the rope attached to his ankle was long enough to reach his captor. If he was brought here tomorrow, he would sit down next to a rock, which he could then use to hit the man in the head, knocking him unconscious. Then he would loosen his ankle restraint and run for the single road leading out of the valley. Daniel settled on this plan as his best opportunity to escape. *Well, let's see what happens this afternoon. If my father comes, then I'm outta here. If not, I'll escape tomorrow after hitting the man with the rock.* Daniel lay on the ground, looking at the blue sky and enjoying his rest. He was thinking of how he would explain this experience to his family and friends back home.

It seemed as though more than two hours had passed since they had stopped working. The man moved from his resting place and untied Daniel, and in a few minutes they were both back at work. The rest of the day was spent spreading the manure on the ground. Daniel was constantly looking for the car or wagon that would bring his father. When dusk came, they returned to house number 25 on the cobblestone road.

The farmer placed Daniel in the room and locked the gate to the animal stable. The room was chilly, so Daniel put wood in the stove. He took off his shirt and undershirt, which were still wet from perspiration, and hung them on the wooden pegs. He washed with cold water from the faucet over the sink, dried himself, and put on the dry undershirt and shirt he had worn when he was taken. He was disappointed and not as confident about his father rescuing him as he had been earlier in the day. He was tired and his muscles were beginning to ache as he sat in front of the wood-burning stove.

Eventually, the man arrived with food. Daniel was hungry and enjoyed the chicken and peppers, potatoes, and crusty bread, along with a small glass of wine. After finishing his meal, he lay on the bed thinking that tomorrow was the day he was either going to be rescued by his father or escape. Daniel fell asleep quickly that evening.

Daniel's captor was an Opi farmer by the name of Vincenzo Sgammotta. He was a disarmingly handsome man in his early forties with a bushy round mustache that tapered at the ends. Because he worked daily in the sun, cold, and rain, he had leathery, olive brown skin. Vincenzo wore a wide-brimmed straw hat with perspiration stains that arose from the brim toward its top centerfold. This hat covered his full head of thick jet-black hair. He had a long, thin, attractive nose that clashed with his glaring brown eyes, which spoke more words than his mouth. The physical labor performed by Vincenzo from childhood had defined his body shape. He had thick broad shoulders with arms that bulged during strenuous work and yet moved delicately when repairing equipment. Physical labor kept his body free of fat and gave him a taut muscular stomach. His broad thighs and hips seemed to be as wide as his shoulders.

It had been five days since Daniel had been brought to Opi. Vincenzo was quite frustrated that he could not make himself understood by the young boy he had brought to Opi. Vincenzo spoke of the problem caused by the language barrier during dinner with his wife and two daughters.

"It's hard to tell someone what you want them to do without the use of words. I correct the boy or yell at him in the only language I know, but we do not understand each other. What else can I do? I can see this upsets him as well."

Gelsomina, Vincenzo's wife, tried to reassure her husband. "Like many other things, it will take time," she said.

Vincenzo was not consoled by her words. He continued as though his wife had not spoken. "This business of a foreign language was not given enough thought during our planning. I have to find a way to make it clear to the boy, without using words, that I am the one in control. I don't like to be this way, but he must

76

learn to fear me if this is going to work. He must learn that trying to escape is useless. Until he learns our language, I have to treat him like an animal, break him down like a horse. I must be strict and firm, and never smile. I don't like to be feared, but I see no other way until he learns our language. If he has no fear, he will continue to challenge me."

Gelsomina once again tried to console her husband. "Poor Vincenzo, you worry too much. He is a young boy who has no way of leaving Opi. You are a powerful man, and your presence alone will be enough to make him soon know his situation is hopeless. Remember, time is on our side. Some day he will come to love Opi as we do."

Vincenzo was not quite as optimistic as his wife.

The following morning, Daniel's captor came to the room with breakfast and motioned for Daniel to get out of bed. After throwing the clothes Daniel had worked in yesterday on the bed and gesturing for Daniel to put them on, his captor left the room. When he tried getting out of bed, Daniel could hardly move. Every part of his body was stiff and aching. After breakfast, he got dressed, and soon both captor and victim were in the wagon going back to the valley.

From the bed of the wagon, Daniel asked, "Today my padre (father)? My father comes today?"

The farmer understood, and growled, "No Papa." That was all Daniel needed to hear. He knew today was the day he would escape.

When the wagon stopped, the man attached a horse to what Daniel recognized from his social studies books as a horse drawn plow. The man placed the straps from the horse over Daniel's head and around the back of his neck. His wrists were secured to the plow handles with rope. The farmer showed Daniel how to hold the handles and then gave a command and slapped the horse. As the horse moved forward, the blade of the plow slid along the top of the soil. The handles were very difficult to maneuver. Daniel was being controlled by the movement of the plowing device and was barely able to maintain his balance. He knew the plow should be digging into the soil, but it just continued bouncing along the top surface of the dirt.

The farmer caught up to Daniel, yelled a command to the horse, and pulled on the reins. Daniel's immediate thought was, *Here we go again, he's gonna start yelling in Italian and I'll have no idea what the jerk is saying.* Much to Daniel's surprise, the man talked calmly and even had what seemed to be a little grin on his lips. This was the first time in six days the man was without his usual scowl.

The farmer talked to the boy, even though he knew the boy did not understand a word he was saying. He proceeded to reposition Daniel's hands and made him understand by his demonstration how he had to lean forward so the plow blade would penetrate the soil. He positioned Daniel's elbows away from his body and started the horse moving forward. Daniel was still quite clumsy but soon the plow was digging into the top layer of the soil and moving smoothly. The plowing was going quite well by mid-morning. A large area had been plowed during the morning, covering much of the land where yesterday's manure had been dispersed. Daniel worked the land that had previously been planted, and the man plowed the pasture area, which had been covered with grass. When the church bells rang, their work stopped and both farmer and captive went to the rest area to eat as they had the day before.

Daniel decided it was time to run, and he positioned himself next to a few rocks. He could easily hide a rock in his hand next to his leg when he stood up. Daniel would wait until after they had eaten; his captor would be more relaxed, probably smoking a cigar as he had done the day before. Daniel finished his midday meal, and then sat upright with his arms clasped around his knees. The farmer began to smoke his cigar.

Daniel sat looking at the mountains, becoming more nervous with every passing minute. He kept telling himself to relax and not to rush. He would just move slowly and act as casually as possible. He was concerned he might not knock his captor out with a single blow, so he reminded himself to hit the man hard. Then Daniel had a horrible thought, *What if I hit him so hard that I kill him?* He had never considered this possibility. He whispered to himself, *Oh God, please don't let me kill him.* The thought made him very uneasy.

After a brief period of time, he told himself, *The longer I wait, the worse it's gonna get. It's now or never.*

Daniel casually scooped the rock into his right hand, remained absolutely still for few moments, and then stood up a few feet from his captor with the rock pressed against his leg, hidden from view. Daniel pretended to stretch and bend as though he were stiff, still looking at the mountains and trying to be as casual as possible. His legs felt as though they were trembling, but when he looked down, they did not seem to be moving. He told himself to be calm, but it didn't help.

I have to do it now, thought Daniel. He was sure his captor would never expect such a brazen move after his crying scene in the car.

Continuing to look at the mountains while his captor sat against a tree, Daniel slowly inched closer to the man as he continued his pretend limbering. He dared not move too close for fear his captor would become suspicious. Daniel hesitated a moment—he had never felt as nervous as he was now. *This is it,* he thought. *Do it now.* His plan was to lunge toward the man the moment he was able to see him out of the corner of his eyes. He made his slow turning move. He saw the legs of his captor out of the corner of his eye and lunged forward with the rock in his hand above his head.

The farmer, who was now up on one knee, was not surprised to see his young captive coming toward him. As Daniel's hand lunged toward the man's head, the farmer's powerful hand grasped the lower part of Daniel's arm and twisted it. The rock fell to the ground. The farmer pushed Daniel to the ground, yelling incoherently in Italian. Daniel, expecting his captor to retaliate by hitting him, tried immediately to get to his feet to defend himself. By the time Daniel got up on one knee, the man was pressing down on Daniel's shoulders. Daniel did not have the strength to rise from his knee, experiencing for the first time the strength of the farmer. The man did not physically strike Daniel, but rather spoke quickly and was quite agitated.

The man soon calmed down and Daniel did as well. His captor moved away, attempting to locate his cigar. With cigar in hand, he moved to the side of one of the shacks, farther away from his captive so Daniel would be unable to reach him a second time. As he drew some smoke from his cigar, he stopped mumbling.

Daniel tried to remain confident after the escape attempt by quietly repeating to himself, "Don't lose hope. There will be other chances to run. He can't hold me forever."

That afternoon, the farmer and the boy continued the plowing of both the prior-planted field and the grassy pasture area. The freshly plowed soil was now at least five to six times the size of the smaller, previously planted area when they had started the plowing.

The following morning, using a different horse drawn device, Daniel and the man began raking the soil and breaking clumps of plowed dirt and smoothing the surface area. As Daniel worked, he decided his next escape attempt would be either from the road or to the forest. It all depended on where he was in relation to the farmer when he was unrestrained. Daniel was confident that because of the nature of his work there would be times when he would not be bound. He reminded himself to keep alert and pick his opportunity. He no longer expected his father any time soon. Daniel was prepared to escape the first time the situation presented itself.

The church bells rang at midday and the farmer stopped working. Daniel expected to be brought to the stake and shackled as before, but instead his captor moved Daniel to the bed of the wagon. After securing Daniel to the wagon, he started off toward town. Daniel thought, *Well, I guess no more lunch in the valley. I'm gonna have to escape while I'm working.*

When they arrived at the house, his captor took Daniel from the wagon. But rather than taking him to the room where he was being held, the man guided Daniel up the rear stairs to the second floor. They entered a room similar to Daniel's grandparents' dining room, and in addition to Daniel and his captor, there were three women standing by a table set with dishes and utensils.

The older woman moved toward Daniel and gave him a warm, gracious smile. She touched his arm and said, while patting her chest, "*Sono (I am) Gelsomina Sgammotta.*" Still holding the boy's arm, she moved him a step toward his captor. Holding out her hand toward the farmer, she said, "*Questo è (this is) Vincenzo Sgammotta.*" Vincenzo's scowl remained. Gelsomina turned Daniel so that he was now facing the two young girls. Gelsomina pointed to one of the girls and said, "*Questa è Maria Antonia Sgammotta.*" Then she introduced the other girl, "*Questa è Angelina Sgammotta.*" Maria Antonia smiled warmly, but Angelina's face showed no emotion. She continued examining Daniel with her eyes as she placed the last glass on the table.

Gelsomina was a short, thin woman with an attractive, round face that appeared worn by the fatigue of hard physical labor. She was in her forties but looked much older. Her voice had a sad quality, even though she seemed happy. She wore a simple black dress that went down to her ankles. Her brown hair was combed back and somehow formed into an intricate, round bun.

Maria Antonia was an attractive, personable girl, fifteen years of age. Her facial appearance was similar to her father's. She had the same color skin except her skin was smooth and appealing. Her thin nose made her look stately, and her long light brown hair was simply tied back. Her build was like her mother's, short and thin.

Angelina, the older of the daughters, was tall and hefty, and did not look like either her mother or father. Her face was also round, and she had long, brown hair that cascaded over her shoulders and down her back. She was an attractive woman who looked much older than her seventeen years. Angelina appeared to be cautious and guarded.

After this brief introduction, Gelsomina took Daniel by the arm and brought him to a room past the dining area, which had a sink, toilet, and what looked like a metal washing tub that was built so a person had to sit in it rather than stretch out. Gelsomina gestured for Daniel to wash at the sink and then closed the door. *This must be his family*, thought Daniel. *I wonder why he brought me to his home.*

After washing and drying himself with a thin towel, he returned to the dining room. The two girls, Maria Antonia and Angelina, were carrying food to the table. Gelsomina, who was already seated, motioned for Daniel to sit next to her. Vincenzo was nowhere to be seen, and for a brief moment Daniel thought about running for the door, hoping it would be open. He heard someone coming down a flight of stairs. It was Vincenzo. Daniel quickly decided against a run for the door and followed Gelsomina's invitation. After everyone was seated, Vincenzo made the sign of the cross and said a brief prayer. Platters of food were first passed to Vincenzo, who filled his plate and passed the platters by way of the girls to Gelsomina, who, after her taking food, passed the platters to the younger girls and finally to Daniel.

The food was delicious. A brisk conversation took place throughout the meal. The kidnapped boy did not understand what was being said, nor did the family attempt to include him in their conversation. Eating in this room and the friendly reaction of the women was unexpected but pleasant. Except for the lack of verbal interaction, they seemed to be treating him like a guest rather than a hostage. Daniel wondered, *What if the women don't know Vincenzo kidnapped me? Maybe this guy told them he hired me to help him and they think he's lettin' me live downstairs.*

The meal ended with a delicious dessert, and the women began clearing the table. Vincenzo took Daniel to a small sitting room with a sofa and two upholstered chairs. As he made his way to the sofa and began to smoke a cigar, he motioned for Daniel to sit in one of the chairs. They sat silently for more than an hour. Daniel no longer heard the rattle of dishes and pots coming from the kitchen. The house was quiet. He could not imagine why he was spending the afternoon in Vincenzo's house just one day after he had tried to escape. It was as though he was being rewarded for his escape attempt. It just didn't make sense, but then he realized, *My dad, my dad, that's it. They've called my dad and they plan on handing me over to him this afternoon.* He was now bubbling with excitement. *That's why I'm in this guy's house. My dad is coming to take me home.* Daniel's spirits were soaring—he was sure today would be the day of his release.

Daniel asked again, "Father coming?" and Vincenzo answered, "No Papa."

Daniel was still not discouraged. *Vincenzo means my dad is not here yet, but he will be coming later,* Daniel reassured himself once again. *Why else would he bring me to his home to have lunch with his wife and daughters?* With his mind no longer focused on escaping, he was now anticipating seeing his dad come through the door to take him home. Looking out the window from his chair, he could see the position of the sun in the sky—it was mid-afternoon.

Gelsomina arrived at the entrance to the sitting room with neatly folded clothes over her arm. She gestured to Daniel to come to her and took him to the bathroom where he had washed before lunch. She laid the clothes on a chair, handed him a large thin towel, and pointed toward the round, deep, metal tub that was now filled with water. She made gestures indicating she wanted him to use the tub for bathing. She smiled at him, gently tapped his arm, and left the room. Daniel heard the door lock. He put his hand in the tub water, and it was warm. Not having had the opportunity to shower or bathe since being brought to Opi, Daniel gladly took off his clothes and stepped into the metal tub. Now he was positive he was going to be released. As he washed, he relished the time in the warm water, thinking of his family and friends, and how good it would be to see them once again. Much of the anxiety that had built up over the past seven days left his body, absorbed by the warm, soapy water. He stayed in the warm tub bathing, relaxing, and listening carefully for the arrival of his father.

He heard a knock on the door and Vincenzo's voice speaking in Italian. That must mean his father was here. He jumped out of the tub, dried off quickly, and dressed in the clothes Gelsomina had left for him. He left his dirty clothes on the floor. His new pants and shirt were a little large, but they were not as rough or worn as the other clothes he had used for work. This was another indication that his father was here. He put on clean socks and slipped into the rubber boots, intending to get his shoes and heavy jacket from the downstairs room before leaving with his father. He tried to open the door but found it locked. Vincenzo, having heard him at the door, opened it from the outside. Daniel quickly moved past Vincenzo and into the room where he had eaten, expecting to see his father. The room was empty.

Vincenzo led Daniel outside and down the front steps. Daniel pleaded with Vincenzo, "Father, father, padre mio." Vincenzo did not respond. Daniel looked up and down the cobblestone street, but his father was nowhere to be seen. Vincenzo brought Daniel to the lower room, unlocked the blue wooden door, and pushed Daniel into the room, locking the door behind him. Daniel was disappointed, but he told himself his father would certainly come soon; he would just have to be patient.

In the early evening, the door from the animal stable opened and Daniel's spirits jumped. He moved toward the door, yelling, "Dad, Dad!" But it was only Vincenzo with a light meal. Daniel asked him once again, "Father mio? Father mio?"

Vincenzo, now completely frustrated, looked up at the ceiling and said, "Statte zitte, nu parle semp'a papa (Please stop asking about your father)." Vincenzo slammed the plates on the table, gave Daniel an irritated look, and again said, "No Papa!" He turned and left the room.

Daniel's spirits sank lower and lower with each passing minute. *Where was his father, and why had he not come and taken him away from this place? What was the purpose of this afternoon?* Daniel sat in front of the wood-burning stove, stubbornly anticipating the unlocking of the front door and his father's arrival. Eventually, he fell asleep with moist, sad eyes.

The opening of the back door awakened Daniel from his sleep. He jumped up from the bed, still hoping to see his father. Again it was only Vincenzo with a roll and espresso. He set it on the table and left the room without saying a word. While eating his breakfast, Daniel thought only of his dad coming for him. *Why else would Vincenzo's wife have given me these nice clean clothes if Dad is not coming this morning?* Daniel rinsed his face with cold water, tucked his shirt into his trousers, and waited.

Soon, he heard the front door being unlocked. He jumped up and yelled, "Dad!" But again it was only Vincenzo. He was not dressed in his work clothes, but rather had on a clean white shirt, neat pants, and a jacket. He motioned for Daniel to get his jacket and come to him. Daniel grabbed his jacket from the wall rack and moved quickly to the door, still expecting to see his father. Vincenzo held Daniel's arm tightly and closed the door behind him.

Daniel's father was nowhere to be seen—only Gelsomina, Maria Antonia, and Angelina were standing by the door on the narrow sidewalk. Daniel resisted being moved toward the church. The Sgammotta family acted as though he was a confused little boy, ignoring his insistent demands to move down the road away from the church and out of town. Vincenzo continued to forcibly move Daniel forward. Although he was angry and frustrated, Daniel eventually stopped resisting. He was about to cry, but he somehow held back his tears.

Pete stayed in Castellamare di Stabia with his parents for five weeks, traveling to Naples twice weekly to receive updates from both the police and the private detective agency. He also had his bandage changed twice and eventually the stitches were removed. Meanwhile, Nonno was so distraught by the news of his grandson's disappearance that he suffered a relapse and was ordered back to the hospital. During their hospital visits, the conversation was always the same.

"Pietro, it is my fault that Donato is missing. If I had not been selfish in wanting to see him, he would be safe at home in America." Neither Pete nor Francesca was able to console Leopoldo.

Francesca and her daughters arranged a nine-week novena to Saint Jude, the patron saint of hopeless causes, with the pastor of their church. Each Tuesday evening for nine weeks, the church was filled with women in black dresses. Father Michele Petronio led the women in special prayers for the safe return of Donato Ciarletta. Daniel's cousins were concerned and confused about Daniel's disappearance. Ruffino was the most affected by the tragic occurrence. He and his cousins were told to say special prayers each night before going to bed for the safe return of their cousin.

At the end of the fourth week, with no promising leads, Captain Sollazzo suggested that it might be helpful to file a missing persons report in the City of Rome, just to make sure everything possible had been done. Pete agreed, and the following day he traveled to Rome and filed the report with the Rome police.

He returned to Castellamare di Stabia, booked passage home to America, and said a second goodbye to his family in Italy. Pete designated Zio Rodolfo to be his contact person with the Naples and Rome police and the private detective agency. Pete knew it would be an insult to offer money to Rodolfo for his services, so he simply expressed his undying gratitude.

When Pete entered the front door of his Beach Avenue home, his crying wife greeted him by pounding her fists on his chest and screaming, "How could you let this happen? What kind of father are you? You're s'posed to protect your children."

Pete stood motionless until Suzy stopped her flailing, and then he held her until she stopped crying. Barbara and Frances, and Danny and Kate embraced Pete with warmth and sympathy.

Kate held his arm and said, "Pete, don't mind Suzy. She didn't mean what she said. She's been frantic since she got the news. We haven't left her side since you called. She has taken Daniel's disappearance very hard and even Father Lewis couldn't help."

Danny embraced his brother a second time and said, "My God, Pete, you look terrible, but it'll be okay now that you're home with us. Everyone knows how much you care for your children, so stop blaming yourself."

It was obvious by simply looking at Pete that he had been badly shaken by the disappearance of his son. He would repeat the same mantra-like theme to anyone who would listen, "I'm responsible. I was so careful to watch him during the trip. I was only a few feet from him when he was taken. I don't know how this could have happened." Like Suzy, nothing and no one could comfort him.

CHAPTER V

A Child Becomes an Adult

The Sgammotta family continued their walk up the cobblestone street; a dejected Daniel quickly stopped his resistance, acknowledging his efforts were futile. Gelsomina and the girls were happily greeting others as the family proceeded to the church. Daniel started yelling, "*Parla inglese?* (Do you speak English?)" The people continued walking, paying no attention to him or his question. He pleaded, "*Aiuto mi*! (Help me!)" Again, there was no response to his plea. Surprisingly, Vincenzo made no attempt to muzzle his captive, nor did he seem to care that Daniel was trying to communicate with others.

The family stopped at the entrance to the church. Many people were gathered on the steps. Daniel once again tried to get their attention, but no one acknowledged his pleas or even looked at him. Daniel and the women were led into the church by Vincenzo and sat in a pew while Vincenzo stood in the doorway of the church. Daniel looked around to see if there were any other doors he might be able to reach before Vincenzo could stop him, but there was only the main entrance at the back of the church.

Daniel noticed some people in the back of the church standing in line waiting to go to confession. He had an idea: He would pretend he was going to confession, and when he got into the confessional he would tell the priest he had been kidnapped. *Priests are educated,* Daniel reasoned. *Let's hope this one speaks English.* If so, Daniel would tell him he had been kidnapped, and the priest would help him. *Even if he only knows a few words of English, I'll bet I can make him understand me.*

Daniel motioned to Gelsomina, indicating he wanted to go to confession. She understood, and under the watchful eye of Vincenzo, he moved to the confessional line. Vincenzo made no move to stop him, which made Daniel believe the priest did not speak English. He decided to stay in line, hoping he could somehow get the priest to understand he had been kidnapped. Finally, it was his turn. He entered the small partition and knelt down. Soon a small panel slid open and the priest blessed him.

Daniel whispered, "I am an *Americano*. Father, do you speak English?"

"Yes, my son, I do," the priest replied.

Oh, thank God, thought Daniel. He whispered again to the priest, "A man from this town kidnapped me.... I need your help. Call the police; have them come and arrest him. His name is Vincenzo Sgammotta—you probably know him."

There was a moment of silence. "Father, do you understand what I'm saying?"

"Yes, my son, I understand everything you have said."

Daniel's heart was now pounding with excitement. "Father, be careful. He's standing at the entrance to the church. I'll be sitting with his family by the side door."

"My son," the priest answered after a pause. "There are things that might be very difficult for you to understand this day. You must trust me when I say that in time you will take a great deal of pride in the loving assistance you will impart to the people of Opi."

Damn! He doesn't understand what I am saying, thought Daniel. "No, Father, please, try to understand my English." He said more slowly, "I am an Americano, and I have been taken from my papa. I'm what you call a hostage. Uh..., you know, taken against my will, do you understand? Father, please, try to understand. I'm a prisoner and you are the only one who can help me. You gotta bring the police so I can go home! You hafta understand."

"I assure you, my son, I understand what you are saying," replied the priest matter-of-factly. I speak English well. It is you who must understand that this was destined. Your coming to Opi was meant to be. God will bless you all your life for your presence in our humble town."

Daniel persisted, "Father, how can I make you understand? I was taken from my father about nine days ago. I am a prisoner in house number 25."

"Don't be concerned — we will talk often while you are here," said the priest. "You will someday come to love your new town." The priest then covered the screen with a sliding panel.

Daniel continued to plead, "Father, Father," but he could hear the priest already blessing the person on the other side of the confessional.

Daniel knelt there for what seemed like forever, paralyzed in his barren cubicle, until another person moved the outer curtain and gestured for him to leave.

The confessional booth was in the back of the church under the choir loft, to the left of the front entrance. Daniel moved in a daze past Vincenzo and down the center aisle with wooden pews on either side. He climbed over two people and sat next to Gelsomina. He stared at the raised stone altar, which had a burning candle on each end. The top of the altar was covered by a starched white cloth, and in the center, raised on a platform, was the shiny, metal tabernacle that held the paper thin wafers that would be consecrated and distributed during Mass. Behind the tabernacle was a large wooden cross with the figure of Jesus nailed to it. There were two statues on either side of the altar: a statue of San Giovanni Battista and one of Mary, the Mother of Jesus.

Daniel remained seated in his trance-like state, trying to understand what had just happened in the confessional, *Nothing makes any sense since I've been brought to this hell hole.* Bells rang, and a priest entered from behind the altar dressed in a green, sleeveless chasuble. Daniel was unable to focus on the Mass. He was hopelessly confused. He could only think of his situation, *Could it be the whole town is part of a plot to keep me captive? But that can't be! Why would other people be involved with this bully Vincenzo?*

The ringing of the bells during the presentation of the host jarred him out of his mental haze. Daniel then noticed the statue of the Blessed Mother. Suddenly he remembered, *During these past nine days, I have completely forgotten about prayer. How disappointed Mary and God must be with me for forgetting to pray. I'm sorry I forgot about praying, but I've been so upset. Please forgive me.*

He spent the remainder of the Mass praying to Mary to help him in this, the greatest crisis of his young life. Daniel had learned his special devotion to the Blessed Mother from the example of his Mother and his Aunt Kate.

When the Mass concluded, he followed Gelsomina and her daughters out of the church. Many people stood on the steps, engaging in conversation in the bright morning sun. He was standing near Vincenzo and his family, who seemed to be more interested in conversing with others than in him. Daniel was not being restrained, nor was Vincenzo paying attention to his captive.

Daniel noticed that the houses surrounding the church were not attached. There was an alley to the right of the church between two houses, which led to a low stone wall. Beyond the wall was the solid rock formation and freedom. If he was able to reach the stone wall, he could easily jump over it and run down the mountain and out of the town. Daniel slowly moved a half-step away from Vincenzo in the direction of the alley and stopped. Vincenzo didn't seem to notice. Daniel slowly started to inch his way in the direction of the alley. He stopped again, now pretending he was looking at the church bell tower. He was trying to see how far he could separate himself from Vincenzo before beginning to run. Vincenzo—who was still engrossed in conversation—had not noticed that Daniel had moved about two feet away from him. The beginning of the alley was approximately twenty yards away. Daniel felt he could reach it easily without being caught. The element of surprise was on his side.

After a few seconds, Daniel decided to do it. He took a deep breath and bolted for the alley, running as fast as he could. Almost immediately, he was at the entrance to the alley, with the open hill only yards away. His heart was pounding and his adrenalin flowing. *This is it, I am going to make it*, he thought as he ran through the alley. At the end of the alley, and in front of the low stone wall, there was a narrow dirt road. He was about to leap over the wall with his hands on the ledge of the stone barrier, and with one leg in the air, when he noticed the village on this side was also a sheer, strait drop hundreds of feet to the ground. He halted his forward momentum by dragging his back leg while maintaining his grip on the ledge.

Straddling the stone wall—and with one leg still on the dirt road side and the other hanging on the precipice side—he boosted himself backwards onto the flat dirt road. He could see the houses were built very close to the edge of the stone formation. It was impossible to scale down because of the mountain's sheer angle.

As he picked himself up, he inspected the cuts and bruises on one leg and both hands and the hole in his pant leg. Vincenzo, who was now standing in front of Daniel holding his arm, brought him back to the edge of the hill and made him look right and left so he could see the entire side of the town was a steep drop. Grasping him tightly by the arm, Vincenzo pushed him back up the alley between the houses.

Daniel was upset at yet another missed opportunity to escape, and he jerked his arm out of Vincenzo's hand and shouted, "Stop pushing me!"

Vincenzo was unable to understand Daniel's words, but he clearly comprehended the meaning of his emotions. He glared at Daniel, grasped his arm once again, and led him out of the alley. The people on the church steps were now looking at Daniel. He mused gloomily, *Well whaddya you know; now they decide to look at me.*

Vincenzo moved Daniel past the front of the church and continued to the other side of the road, walking into an alley between two houses. This side of the town had a mesh wire fence between the edge of the mountain and the dirt road. Vincenzo once again made Daniel look right and left. This side was also a sheer drop. Vincenzo, still talking rapidly in Italian, marched Daniel down the main cobblestone street, which was approximately 150 yards long, and past the house where he had been keeping Daniel captive. They arrived at the point in the cobblestone road where it bent sharply to the right, gradually descending down the dirt road to the pasture and farm area.

At this bend in the road, Daniel saw two older men in a small two-seat, horse drawn wagon. Directly behind them was the town bar. Daniel had seen men sitting in a wagon on the three days Vincenzo had taken him to the pasture area, but had thought nothing of it. Vincenzo, still talking in Italian, pointed to the men in the wagon and then back at Daniel, and then he pointed to the dirt road leading to the pasture. As Vincenzo was talking, the two men in the wagon raised their rifles and placed the butt handle of their weapons on their thighs. Daniel grasped the meaning of Vincenzo's gesturing—the two men were stationed on the road to insure that Daniel could not escape from the only road leading out of town. Vincenzo marched Daniel back toward the church, stopped in front of the blue door with number 25 over it, pushed Daniel into the lower room, and locked the door.

Daniel sat in front of the woodstove, angry with Vincenzo, Opi, the people, and the priest. He reviewed in his mind how the priest had responded to him in the confessional, *He spoke English, and I asked him twice if he understood what I was saying. He said, "Yes my son, I have told you I speak English." If he understood English, why did he refuse to help me?*

Daniel thought about the other things the priest had said, *People will appreciate my charity? I'll feel proud? Your kidnapping was destined? God will bless you all your life? You'll come to love Opi? What's wrong with that priest? Nothing makes any sense. From the way he talked, you'd think he knew I was a prisoner. It sounded like Vincenzo said something to him about me.*

Daniel then spoke out loud, as though to firmly disagree with his own conclusion, "But that's really crazy. Why would the guy kidnap me and then tell the town priest? That's just too weird."

After receiving his lunch in the windowless room, he spent the rest of the afternoon trying to understand what had happened that morning. He was now convinced that ransom money was not part of Vincenzo's plan. *Well, if not ransom, why am I here?* he thought. Although he found it hard to believe, he eventually concluded that the entire town knew he had been kidnapped, even the priest. He was slowly accepting the most deranged possibility—the whole town was in on his kidnapping, or at least approved of what Vincenzo had done.

Daniel also reassessed his ability to escape. It would be impossible to escape from the town. His only option would have to be from the valley area. He would wait for his first chance to run to the forest at the base of the mountain range. Daniel reassured himself that Vincenzo would not be able to catch him. Once he was in the forest—and unable to use the one road leading to and from Opi—the first thing Vincenzo would try to do would be to block the road and recapture him. He would have to run to the right, find an opening or a different road out of the forest and then get help from the police.

Daniel was now convinced of what had seemed implausible earlier: Vincenzo had captured him to work on his farm. Still, the strangest part was that other people in the town knew what Vincenzo had done—and their refusal to help meant they condoned his actions.

Later that afternoon, without consciously understanding his own thought process, he began to wonder if he had been too hard on himself regarding what he initially considered cowardly behavior when he was first captured. Sitting in front of the stove he began to think about what had happened to him, *I was just standing on the sidewalk and my father was a few feet away. Who would have thought someone would drive up in a car, pull me in, and speed away? Why am I blaming myself? There's really nothing I could have done.*

As he considered the past nine or ten days in Opi, alone and frightened, he thought, *I never imagined I'd become someone's prisoner. It's no wonder I got scared. I was just so surprised! Maybe being surprised is different than being a coward.*

Comfortable in front of the warm wood-burning stove, his reasoning process began to evolve from hopelessness to self-assurance. If he was going to be successful in a future escape attempt, he was going to need more confidence. *I'm a pretty strong kid. I play lots of sports. I'm pretty fast, so it should be easy for me to escape to the forest,* he told himself.

He was beginning to gain more confidence in his ability to escape and find his way back to the Bronx. He seemed to be thinking more clearly. For the first time, he was able to contemplate his past actions as more theatrical than real. It was as though the only script he had to follow came from movies and mystery radio dramas.

With this tiny glimpse of new understanding, he thought, *I was so sure my dad would somehow know I was being held in this stupid little town in the middle of nowhere, and he would blast his way into Opi, beat up Vincenzo, and take me home. Oh boy, how dumb was that! Sure, that's how it's done in the movies and on the radio. Boy I wish this was a movie—but this is for real.*

He considered his "brilliant" detective work, *I was so proud of myself because I could remember the signs and the name of the car and, just like in the movies, I found a clever way to write the information on the wall. How could I have been so stupid?*

His next thought would have been funny, except for the seriousness of his situation, *How could I think I was getting back at Vincenzo by not eating his food?*

He began to consider the events of that first day in the valley, *I had actually convinced myself that I would not try to escape because my dad was going to come and get me, when really I was scared and not really sure what to do. I was more scared about what would happen if I did try to escape than about getting out of this place.*

Becoming more agitated, Daniel began to pace back and forth, talking out loud in the empty room, "Y'know, maybe I'm not such a creepy little kid. I guess when you don't know what's happenin' it can really give you the jitters. How many guys my age get kidnapped? Yeah, so what if I'm scared, maybe that's okay too. Maybe the way I've been acting since I've been here has not been so dumb. Maybe I had to experience all this crap to begin to understand it better."

Daniel was feeling more optimistic, and he walked around the room with a new bounce in his step. In the past two hours of emphatic mental concentration, Daniel had managed to become more accepting of his actions since being brought to Opi.

He did not completely understand why his experiences became so clear to him that afternoon. Perhaps it was the new routine over the past two days—being in Vincenzo's house, eating with the family, his wife being kind, a new set of decent clothes, and enjoying a hot bath—or was it almost falling to his death over the stone wall. Something had happened to spur this new positive attitude, and Daniel was grateful for whatever it was.

One thing was now clear: Whatever the reason, the whole town was conspiring to hold him prisoner, because they knew what Vincenzo had done. Once again, Daniel began talking out loud to the empty room, as though that would make the situation clearer, "But why would people kidnap a kid just to work on their farm? Stealing a person to work seems so mean. People used do this hundreds of years ago, but not today. If they had planned to trade my freedom for money, that I could understand, but keeping me just to work makes no sense. There has to be another reason."

He was determined to find out why.

His afternoon of filtering information was surprisingly satisfying. It made him feel more mature. The exact number of days since his capture was no longer so important. He had been in Opi long enough that somebody should be able to tell him why he had been taken, and, more importantly, when he was going to be released.

Daniel was ready for sleep. He placed a few logs in the wood-burning stove and adjusted the damper so the fire would burn slowly through the night.

He slipped into bed under the covers, ready for sleep, but he lay there for over an hour tossing and turning, his mind churning with many questions, *Is it enough to just feel better? I feel great now, but how will I feel when I run to the forest? These new feelings...are they real, or am I just making this up, thinking that I'm more mature? Oh, damn, I don't know. Am I going nuts?*

He sat up in be, and pushed the blankets down around his hips. He angrily spoke out loud, although there was no one there to listen, "Stop it. You're thinking crazy! Already you're beginning to get scared again. Don't you feel good? Don't you feel like you've learned something today? Okay, so maybe I won't be Superman tomorrow, but I'll get stronger each day, and you watch, one of these days I'll escape!" He lay back and covered himself once again.

Daniel wished his mother and father and even Ruffino were with him. He would feel proud explaining to them what he had learned. His mother—who was always encouraging him to do better in school—would be especially proud of him. He was pleased that he had learned something new, by himself and without anyone's help.

Yesterday, he had been depending on his father to come to Opi, rescue him, and beat up Vincenzo. Tomorrow would be a new day in his life. He would depend on his abilities, on his own cunning and skill to gain his freedom.

The next morning, Vincenzo brought Daniel his usual breakfast, the clothes Daniel had been wearing when he was brought to Opi, and the work clothes he used last week. All of the clothes had been washed. Vincenzo motioned for Daniel to dress in the work clothes. Daniel had decided he would run to the woods at the base of the mountain range the first time he was unrestrained. When he dressed, he put on the shoes he had worn when he was kidnapped. He would be able to run faster in his shoes than in the rubber boots. He hoped Vincenzo would not notice and make him change.

Shortly after Daniel was dressed, Vincenzo entered the room. He directed Daniel past the animals and motioned him into the rear of the wagon. Vincenzo began to move the wagon without securing Daniel to the railing, causing Daniel to think of escape. *Could Vincenzo have forgotten to tie me to the wagon?* He might not have to escape to the forest if he remained unrestrained. Daniel decided to wait until the wagon arrived at the place where the dirt road met the valley. Like last week, he was sitting in the back of the wagon with his feet dangling over the end. Now that he was not bound to the side of the wagon, he could simply slide off the wagon as it moved without Vincenzo noticing, hide in the brush until Vincenzo was down the road, and then run on the road away from the valley. Daniel's excitement level began to rise.

After passing the men stationed on the cobblestone road, the wagon made a sharp right and began descending the dirt road to the valley. Daniel turned his head to determine the best place to slide and run. That's when he noticed two men in a horse drawn wagon with rifles at the spot where the dirt road met the valley. Now he understood why he had not been tied to the wagon. The momentary excitement passed and he resigned himself to his original plan. *No problem*, he said to himself. *I'll run to the forest the first chance I get. Vincenzo didn't notice I was wearing my shoes—he'll never be able to catch me.*

When they arrived at the farm, Vincenzo parked the wagon besides three wooden shacks next to the land they had worked the previous week. He motioned Daniel into the smallest of the three buildings, which contained large barrels that looked like big straw baskets. He directed Daniel to move one barrel outside as he moved the other. The containers were filled with dried, wrinkled green beans. The containers were marked *piselli* (peas). Vincenzo attached one of the horses to a device that looked like it would make a trench in the soil.

Daniel was standing about ten feet from Vincenzo, unconstrained, when he decided to make his move. He began running as fast as he could toward the forest area at the base of the mountain. He was moving fast in his shoes, not bothering to look over his shoulder to see how close behind him Vincenzo was. He just kept running. He must have run the length of a football field, yet he was still a good distance away from the forest and his freedom, when he heard the galloping of a horse behind him. He tried to run even faster. Suddenly, he felt something sharp and biting around his arms, bringing them against his sides and forcing him to trip, fall, and tumble along the ground. Coming to a stop, he arose to his feet, looked up, and saw Vincenzo on a horse holding a pole that had a wire loop attached at its end. The loop was now wrapped around Daniel's chest.

As Vincenzo walked Daniel back to the shack, he was once again rambling in Italian as though Daniel was able to understand him. Daniel didn't bother responding—he just walked alongside the horse with the wire loop still around his arms and chest.

When they returned to the shacks, Vincenzo released Daniel from his wire tether and prepared him for work. Vincenzo bound Daniel's wrists to the horse drawn farm device. With Daniel's hands on the farm machinery, Vincenzo snapped the reins on the back of the horse, and the metal blade began to make a furrow in the newly plowed soil. Vincenzo, walking behind Daniel, dropped dried *piselli* in the newly made furrow. At their midday break, Vincenzo stayed a sufficient distance from Daniel to avoid another escape attempt. They continued planting for the rest of the day.

As the sun was getting low on the horizon, they stopped work and were returning to town. Vincenzo stopped the wagon at the bend in the dirt road leading to the village, where two men sat in a wagon holding rifles. He again spoke to Daniel in Italian, while pointing and gesturing to the two men. Vincenzo was able to make Daniel understand that these men were stationed in this position to prevent any further escape attempts.

When they rode through town, Daniel saw two other men in a small wagon in the center of the road. They were obviously controlling the access in and out of town. Daniel was now aware that the town of Opi was sealed tight, his theory now confirmed beyond any doubt: Vincenzo was not acting alone—the entire town was working with him. Escape was not going to be as easy as Daniel had originally thought.

That evening, sitting in his room, Daniel reviewed his situation. Ransom would have been his best chance for release, but that no longer appeared to be an option. Escape from the town was impossible. His only way out of Opi would have to be from the valley farm area. He had to remain alert each time he was in the valley—his escape depended on being ready at the opportune moment.

CHAPTER VI

$\mathcal{F}$IRST $\mathcal{Y}$EAR IN $\mathcal{C}$APTIVITY

Five weeks had passed since Daniel's last escape attempt, and he began to think of other alternatives, *What would Vincenzo do if I refused to go to work? Would he beat me? Leave me in this room? Deprive me of food? What's the use of doing something like that, when working makes the day pass quicker, and working in the valley is better then staying in this lousy room?*

Daniel decided there was no possible benefit to refusing work, except perhaps to irritate Vincenzo. The forced work, although at times boring, was not tiring to the point of exhaustion.

On Sunday mornings after Mass, all the people of Opi spent a leisurely hour or so socializing. After a few months of captivity, Daniel was allowed to sit by himself away from Vincenzo, and he was even allowed to move about freely. Vincenzo felt confident that Daniel understood there was no way for him to escape from the town proper. Daniel was limited in how far he could stroll, but the freedom to walk alone or sit in a specific area, even for this short period of time, was enjoyable.

On Saturday afternoons, he was brought to the Sgammotta living quarters for his main meal, a rest period, and his weekly bath. On Saturdays, Gelsomina encouraged Daniel to help her prepare for the following day's bread-making.

After about a month of this new routine, Daniel noticed something strange about the population of Opi. There seemed to be the normal number of older men and women that he would have expected to live in a town this size. There also seemed to be the normal number of middle-aged women like Gelsomina, and the normal number of young women like Angelina and Maria Antonia. However, he saw very few middle-aged men such as Vincenzo and no young men in their late teens and twenties. This seemed strange, even for a small town like Opi. Equally odd was the fact that he had seen only two other boys his age, and only a few small children. He never saw anyone use the soccer field across from the cemetery. There were no lines marked on the field and the rusty broken goals had no nets. He surmised that the young men must be away at high school and college. He suspected the elementary school was so far away that even the young children lived at their school. He also concluded that since there were only young women in Opi, they must not be permitted to attend school. Daniel expected the young men would return during the summer. This was an interesting passing observation, but he had more things to worry about than the make-up of the people in his prison village. It was his plan to be far away from Opi when the boys and children came back from school.

After early morning Mass and socializing, Daniel and the Sgammotta family had a light breakfast in the upper apartment. He would remain in their apartment for the Sunday main meal and spend the remainder of the afternoon relaxing with the family. They often listened to the radio in the late afternoon. He wished he could understand Italian; by now he was hungry for news from the outside world, even Italian news. He was surprised but very pleased that Vincenzo was allowing him this free unrestricted time in their apartment—being in rooms with windows was in itself a pleasure. He enjoyed the pleasant family atmosphere on Sundays.

Daniel realized that in order to find out why he had been brought to Opi, he was going to have to learn Italian. He figured that if he found out why he had been kidnapped, he would also find out when he would be set free.

The only other person in Opi who spoke English was the priest. Daniel would often ask Father Mascia why he was being held in Opi, but the priest would only respond with general platitudes about Daniel's service to God and the people.

Daniel began listening carefully to Vincenzo when they were working, and he made a point of repeating Italian words having to do with their farming tasks. Vincenzo seemed as interested in teaching Daniel Italian as Daniel was in learning. The Italian words used for communicating the farm chores came quite easily.

Daniel estimated that he had been in Opi for three months. It was May and the air was still cool and crisp, which was usual for May in the mountains. One Saturday afternoon, Daniel was able to make Gelsomina understand that he wanted to learn Italian. Thereafter, when the dishes had been cleaned and stored—and prior to his bath—he received Italian lessons in the dining room. Vincenzo was pleased at Daniel's eagerness to learn Italian. The more Italian Daniel knew the easier farm operations would be. However, Daniel's purpose was not social or work-related—he was eager to understand what was being said on the radio and hopefully learn something about his incarceration.

Leopoldo Ciarletta was a seminarian in his fifth year of religious studies at the Franciscan Holy Name Province Seminary in Callicoon, New York. It had become a family tradition for the Ciarletta and Gallo clans to make their annual fall trip to Callicoon to visit the pride of their family, the future priest Leopoldo.

In May of 1947, Suzy surprised her husband by informing him that she wanted to make the annual family excursion to see her son Leopoldo now, rather than at the usual time in the fall.

Pete—who was brooding about the lack of information from Italy regarding Daniel—questioned her change in plans. "Suzy, it's May. We usually go in the fall when we can pick apples off the trees. Why make the trip now?"

Suzy was adamant in her desire to visit her son earlier this year.

Pete's spirit had been dealt such a severe blow by the disappearance of his son that he did not have the energy or inclination to mount a counter-argument to his wife's unusual request. He shrugged his shoulders and said, "Well if that's what you want, we'll go."

Suzy always enjoyed visiting Leopoldo, especially in the seminary's rural, tranquil setting. However, this trip was for another equally important reason: She wanted to meet with Father Benedict Dudley, the Provincial Director of the Franciscan Seminary in Callicoon.

Father Dudley was a six-foot-three, influential Franciscan priest with a powerful baritone voice and a dominating personality. He was the type of person who could draw everyone's attention simply by entering a room. He had been pastor of the main Franciscan church at the order's headquarters on 33rd Street in New York City, Chaplain of the New York Giants Football team, and a very successful fundraiser for the Franciscans. Early in 1946, Father Dudley had suffered a heart attack. In August 1946, he was assigned the post of Director at the Callicoon seminary to reduce his workload and expose him to the clean, fresh air of upstate New York.

Suzy made arrangements with her sisters and Pete's brothers to visit Leopoldo, on the last Sunday in May. A caravan of seven 1930s black Buicks, Chryslers, and Chevrolets full of happy, rowdy aunts, uncles, and cousins arrived in Callicoon with their picnic feast. It was always a happy occasion for Leopoldo, the other seminarians, and the friars.

The Ciarlettas and Gallos were convinced that the seminarians were underfed, and this was their way of temporarily remedying this problem. Upon their arrival, blankets were spread on the front lawn of the seminary. Sterno cans were lit under large, aluminum, deep platters containing Suzy's *lasagna verdi al forno* (Baked Lasagne with a Bolognese Meat Sauce); Aunt Diane's *Ravioli Verdi D'Agnello Alla Pesarese Col Sugo Di Peperoni Glalli* (Green Ravioli Pesaro-Style stuffed with Lamb and Sauce with Yellow Peppers); Aunt Margaret's *Gnocchi Verdi* (Spinach and Ricotta Potato Gnocchi); and Aunt Gerasina's *Calamari Ripieni* (Stuffed Whole Squid, Braised with Onions, Tomatoes, Chili Pepper, and White Wine). Each dish was accompanied by *prosciutto* (spiced, smoked, cured ham), *salami, cheese, crusty bread, red wine,* and, finally, Aunt Kate's *cream puffs* and Aunt Grace's *sfogliatelle* desserts. The seminarians and friars waited all year for this Italian feast—which came much earlier in 1947.

While the food was being warmed, Suzy spoke with her son in private, "Leopoldo, while I'm here, I need to speak with Father Dudley. Go and tell him I need to see him privately. I only need a few minutes of his time, but make sure you tell him it's extremely important that I see him today."

Leopoldo saw the urgency in his mother's expression and heard the deep desire in her voice. "I know he likes to stop by and greet parents whenever they visit," he told her. "So I think he will see you. But since you want to speak with him privately, I'd better go to his office and check with Brother Tom, his secretary. Mom, can I tell him what this is about? Does it have anything to do with my studies here at the seminary?"

"Oh, no, my sweetheart," said Suzy. "It has nothing to do with you. I just want to talk to him about Daniel's disappearance."

Leopoldo hurried off to the main building, and when he returned to the picnic, the seminarians and friars were enjoying the food and his young cousins were playing softball. Suzy saw Leopoldo approaching and hurried to him.

"Father Dudley will see you now. I'll take you to his office."

Suzy and her son walked across the open grass area to the main building, which was built in the Gothic style. They entered through large, elaborately carved, oak doors and proceeded down a darkened hallway. The sound of their leather soles striking the stone floor echoed loudly. Leopoldo and Suzy entered the director's office. A friar typing at a small desk arose and welcomed them.

Suzy asked Brother Tom, "What are you doing here working when there is delicious food waiting for you outside? Go eat!"

Brother Tom assured her that when he finished the letter he was typing he intended to join the picnic. He knocked on the clouded glass portion of the director's door, paused for a few moments, and then opened the door. "Go right in, Mrs. Ciarletta," he said "Father Dudley is expecting you."

As Leopoldo was leaving, Brother Tom told him, "I'll join everyone as soon as I finish this last letter. Make sure they don't eat all the lasagna. Save me some if you can."

As Suzy entered the room, a large figure of a man in a dark brown monk's habit, with the traditional Franciscan capuche hood resting on his shoulder, greeted her with a broad smile and shook her hand warmly. "Mrs. Ciarletta, I am so pleased to meet you. Please sit down. Would you like Brother Tom to get you something cool to drink?"

"No, thank you, Father, or should I greet you as Director?" said Suzy, sitting stiffly in her chair.

Father Dudley smiled. "Father will be just fine. Mrs. Ciarletta, how may I be of assistance to you?"

Suzy was prepared—she had rehearsed what she was about to say numerous times. "My husband's father, who lives in Italy, became seriously ill last February. He requested my husband visit him and bring his grandson, my son Daniel. They were scheduled to land in Naples, and I asked him to buy me a Neapolitan *presepi* nativity scene, which can only be bought in Naples. My youngest son

Daniel disappeared immediately after my husband had purchased the nativity set. I believe my son's disappearance is my punishment for being a sinful woman. Since I am the sinful one, I know God will not listen to my prayers. My only hope for my son's return is to ask you to have the friars and the seminarians pray for the safe return of my Daniel."

Father Dudley looked lovingly at the odd expression on Suzy's face, which was a mixture of hope and grief. "Mrs. Ciarletta, may I ask you a personal question?"

"Well, of course," said Suzy.

Father Dudley prefaced his question by saying, "Please understand, I will consider your answer to my question as though this was the sacrament of confession."

"I understand. By all means ask your question."

"Why do you believe you are a sinful woman?"

Suzy dropped her eyes, removed a tissue from her pocketbook, and held it in her hand. Raising her head and looking directly at Father Dudley, she said, "Since childhood, I have always had a special devotion to the Blessed Mother. I only prayed to the mother of Jesus, never praying to the Almighty Lord. Father, you know better than anyone, the Almighty talks to us through his divine messages. God's message to me was clear. Since I had chosen to ignore him in my prayers, and so that I would understand His displeasure, He had the disappearance of my youngest son take place immediately after the purchase of the *presepi* nativity scene, which honors the birth of His son, Jesus. As you know, God has a way of making things obvious to sinners." Suzy pressed the tissue to her nostrils and once again dropped her eyes.

"My dear, good woman, I have been a priest for twenty-eight years, and in all that time, my faith has grown for one reason and one reason only: I know that our Lord is loving and forgiving. He is not a God of vengeance who decides to punish people by taking away someone they love. Mrs. Ciarletta, you must drive this false thought from your mind."

Suzy used the tissue to wipe away her tears and then answered him in a low, trembling voice, "Father, I respect your learned views of religion, but that is not why I came to see you. I have not come here today to be consoled. I am here because I have the greatest respect for you as a powerful man of God. All I ask is that you grant my request to have your Franciscan Friars and the young men under your guidance pray for the return of my Daniel. I beg you. Please say you will grant my request."

Father Dudley could hear the pain in her voice, and he realized she was not yet prepared to listen to his reasoning or be consoled. "Mrs. Ciarletta, you have my priestly vow that I—and every member of our Franciscan community here in Callicoon—will pray for the speedy and safe return of your son Daniel. I will also send out a notice this evening to our Franciscan prayer network around the world requesting special prayers for your son."

Suzy, who was now sobbing heavily, dropped to her knees in front of Father Dudley, kissed the back of his hand, and said, "Father, that is so much more than I ever hoped to receive. How will I ever be able to thank you? God bless you. God bless you!"

Father Dudley assisted Suzy up from her knees and encouraged her to stay and tell him more about Daniel's disappearance.

"No, I have taken too much of your time already," she said. "You have honored me by your vow. I will ask nothing further from you."

Father Dudley thought it best to accept Suzy's answer, but he made a mental note to contact the pastor of Suzy's church and have a friar pick up this discussion at a later date.

Daniel was not sure why, but he still clung to the notion that finding the reason for his captivity would somehow be useful. He soon learned enough Italian to hold simple conversations, and when he was able to make himself understood, he asked Vincenzo why he had been brought to Opi and when he would be allowed to leave.

Vincenzo's response never varied, "In time, it will all be explained."

Daniel protested that his answer was not sufficient, but Vincenzo simply shrugged his shoulders and said, "This is how it will be." Daniel's continued badgering only brought silence. He tried to get some answers from Gelsomina, but she always deferred to Vincenzo. "You must speak with Vincenzo. It's not my place to answer your questions."

Obtaining information from the two daughters during the time they trimmed his hair was also impossible. "Oh no, Donato. You must speak with papa for that answer," was their standard response.

One morning in early June, as Vincenzo and Daniel were proceeding to the valley for their day's work, they were greeted by many sheep, maybe a hundred or more, grazing on the grass of the valley.

"Where did the sheep come from?" asked Daniel. Vincenzo said they had been grazing in Foggia for the winter, but they were brought back from southern Italy each spring for grazing in the valley—in time for the two-day feast of the patron saint of Opi, San Giovanni de Battista, which would be held in two weeks.

On the morning of the first day of the feast, Daniel's breakfast was brought to his room while he was still sleeping. It was clear from the noise outside his door, and the fact that he had been allowed to sleep late, that preparation for the feast day had begun. He assumed he would remain in his room during the day. Around mid-morning, Gelsomina entered the lower room by the front door. She told Daniel that it was the annual day of celebration of the Feast of San Giovanni de Battista. There would be a high Mass at eleven that morning, and Daniel was welcome to attend with the family. He quickly agreed— anything to get out of his dreary room. On their way to Mass, Daniel could see the decorated houses, tables and chairs on the road, and food being prepared on the narrow sidewalks.

After high Mass, Vincenzo said to Daniel, "I want you to enjoy these two special days, so I'm going to let you stay outside until just before dusk, but I want you to know that the men will be in their wagons guarding the entrance to the town."

Daniel did not look up—he just kept walking, thinking, *Well, aren't you a kind kidnapper!* Oh how he wished he could express his sarcasm openly!

As they continued their walk up the main road, Vincenzo explained the various events of the two feast days. Daniel missed some of the words but understood most of what Vincenzo had said.

"Donato, I hope you accept my kindness and will not cause a disturbance." Daniel understood that Vincenzo was referring to him trying to escape. Daniel did not acknowledge Vincenzo—he was not about to say something in his limited Italian that might give Vincenzo the impression he was grateful. Daniel was determined never to say *grazie* to his captor.

When Vincenzo finished talking with Daniel, he left to join the conversation with family and friends. No one seemed to be paying any particular attention to Daniel. It had been almost four months since he had been so free of restrictions or others watching him. A tingling energy began to surge through his body as the realization of his limited freedom took hold. He stood in place a few more moments, feeling insecure. *Why do I feel so scared?* he wondered. *Isn't this what I've been hoping for—a time when I could walk around without somebody giving me orders and watching where I go? So why am I standing here unable to move and feeling so funny?*

Three minutes passed before Daniel allowed himself to move. Then he started to walk slowly and cautiously, placing one foot in front of the other before stopping and looking to see if he was being followed. No one was paying any attention to him. He was feeling better but still moving slowly. He walked to the lower part of town and the road leading to freedom. He kept looking over his shoulder to see if someone was following him. The town was bustling with activity, and Daniel seemed to be anonymous as he strolled along the cobblestone street. He soon became more comfortable, and after about forty minutes he was feeling buoyant and happy as he moved about freely.

For the first time, he had an opportunity to closely observe the area. Looking past some shade trees growing behind homes, he could see the deep, green valley and the small, neat cemetery. He noticed the beauty of the untrimmed edge of the thick forest beyond the valley, with the morning haze rising, ready to disappear against the solid stone of the snowcapped mountain range that completely circled his prison town.

Perhaps it was the emotion of the moment or the brief taste of freedom, but suddenly Opi seemed beautiful. He smiled to himself as he walked.

Eventually, he came upon the guards in their wagon at the road leading out of town. In an instant, the dark image of his reality returned, deflating his spirit once again. He stood looking at the two men in the wagon thinking, *I've got to find a way out of this miserable place.*

He soon became more disciplined as he walked leisurely. These two days might present his long-awaited opportunity to escape, and he became more analytical as he sauntered along the cobblestone street. The people were beginning to celebrate, and with too much wine someone might get careless. He intended to stay especially alert for an opportunity to run.

Daniel heard music on the main street. A small band was leading a parade of eight men carrying the statue of San Giovanni de Battista, which had been taken from the church and was now on a platform draped with a colorful silk cloth. Along the way, people were pinning *lire* (Italian paper money) to the garment covering the statue, as well as the platform skirt. Townspeople walked behind the statue. At various times during the parade, the band would stop playing. During these intervals, a small group of older women in long black dresses, walking directly behind the statue, recited a litany of prayers. The male leaders of the town followed the praying women. The parade continued to move slowly until, at the end of the cobblestone road, the procession turned and continued back to the church for the purpose of returning the statue to its pedestal.

The people spent the rest of the day eating, rejoicing, singing, dancing, and playing games. Daniel noticed a teenage boy he had not seen before. This seemed to bring the number to either five or six teenage boys, all of whom Daniel assumed were held out of school to help their fathers with the farming chores. Daniel was surprised that more teenagers were not attending this celebration. *Surely they would be home for the summer vacation,* he thought. It was odd that they were still away at school, but he assumed the Italian school holiday must come later in the summer. Also, the absence of young children was very obvious. Daniel expected to see many more children running around and playing on such a festive day. He had, by now, also concluded that the absence of young men was due to the fact they were still serving in the Italian army, even though the war had been over for almost three years. He suspected the countries that had the war fought on their soil needed men to remain in the army longer than was usual in order to help rehabilitate the damage caused by war

Daniel received sweet bread from some of the people, but still they seemed unwilling to engage him in conversation except for a polite hello or a pleasant nod. He knew they had seen him in church and during the socializing time after Mass on Sunday, yet the townspeople were careful to avoid him.

Daniel had never been behind the church, so he decided to see what was there. He walked up the street toward the church, while looking at the various tables on the narrow sidewalk holding homemade food, crafts, colorful pots, and metal trinkets. When he reached the church, he turned to see if Vincenzo had followed him. He was still quite surprised that he was not being restricted. He walked behind the church and saw a small stone piazza area that extended back to a low stone wall similar to the wall behind many of the houses. He peered over the wall and saw the steep drop down the mountain. This spot was the highest elevation of Opi.

Daniel waited until late afternoon to walk down by the bar in the area leading out of town. His hope was that by this hour the men in the wagon would have had too much to drink. His plan was to pretend he was interested in the horses pulling their wagon. He would pretend to be examining the horses, stroking their backs, and inching his way toward the side of their cart. He was also counting on the people in the bar to have drunk too much and be slow to react when he made a run for the dirt road leading to the pasture area.

He casually approached the two men sitting in the wagon with their rifles. He had learned the Italian word for "hello," so smiling broadly he waved at the men and shouted, *"Pronto!"*

As Daniel approached the wagon, the two men stood and shouted, "Stop! Come no closer." Daniel shrugged his shoulders, lifted his hands in anger, and turned to go back up the street, once again experiencing the anguish of failure.

Daniel's daily chores presented a bit of irony. He often remembered how angry he had been in America when it was time for him to turn over the soil in his backyard garden in the Bronx. He much preferred playing baseball with his friends. Now, for the past seven months, he had been helping to maintain a large farm. Vincenzo and Daniel worked many acres, and the land produced a wide variety of vegetables, root crops, wheat, barley, and fruits. Much more food was grown on Vincenzo's farm than could be sold at market, cold-stored, preserved, or eaten by one family.

Vincenzo sold a portion of the crops he and Daniel grew at the market in Pescasseroli, a town five kilometers southeast of Opi. Early each Saturday, beginning in mid-July, Daniel would be awakened just before sunrise. Vincenzo would take him to the farm area to load his wagon with the ripe produce they had grown. After the wagon was loaded, Daniel would be taken back to 25 *Via San Giovanni de*

Battista and locked in his room. When he awoke from his "second sleep" on market Saturdays, he would spend a leisurely morning talking with Gelsomina and her daughters, and helping them with minor chores before the late afternoon main meal.

The first Saturday he helped Vincenzo load the wagon for market, he noticed the guards were on duty in their wagons at the top of the road leading out of town and at the end of the dirt road leading to the valley. Daniel wondered if these men were stationed at these spots twenty-four hours a day, or if they arose early for their guard duty only on market Saturdays. By early fall, he had noticed these guards were always different men, usually older men, so he assumed there was some sort of planned rotation schedule. During his first farming season, Daniel often wondered, *Are all these men on guard duty to prevent one boy from leaving? Did Vincenzo pay them money or perhaps share some of the surplus food from the farm with them for their time? This must be how he uses the excess crops grown on the farm.*

Daniel also noticed other men loading their wagons. He knew there were other farms in the valley, but the distance between farms prevented any close observation or socializing. The only signs of recognition they gave each other were nods as they passed on the dirt road that ran parallel to the elevated town. The few young boys he had seen in town seemed to be helping their fathers with the farm work. These boys looked to be about Daniel's age, and by now he concluded that some families held boys out of school to help their parents raise crops. This would be similar to his father's generation, when his dad and uncle left school in the fourth grade to help their father in the business. Daniel concluded that Vincenzo had no male children, and the reason he was kidnapped was to help the sonless Vincenzo with his farm work. The only part of his confinement Daniel could still not comprehend was why an entire town, including the priest, would cooperate with one man's selfish and immoral act.

Toward the end of the growing season that first year, Daniel had begun to fall into a pattern of acceptance. He knew this was not a good sign, but he didn't seem to have any recourse. Although he kept alert for escape opportunities, the men with the rifles and the location of the town were successful in preventing him from gaining his freedom. The best possibility was still the forest, but Vincenzo either worked close to him, or when both horses were being used, he constrained Daniel in some fashion.

It was now October and the end of the growing season. The sheep were no longer grazing—they had recently disappeared as quickly as they had appeared last spring. Vincenzo and Daniel spent two days cutting and using pieces of the chaff to tie the wheat into upright bundles. On the afternoon of the second day, they loaded their wagon and hauled the bales of wheat to the dirt road parallel to the town.

That evening, after placing Daniel in his room, Vincenzo explained, "There will be no work for two days, so you will remain in your room. These days will be used for turning the wheat grown on the various farms into flour. A rented combine truck will arrive tomorrow to process the wheat into flour. Your meals will be brought to you by Gelsomina."

By the middle of November, Daniel had been in Opi for almost eight months. This was a particularly difficult period. He had given up the idea of being rescued by his father. During this time, he found he was able to converse very simply with Vincenzo and Gelsomina in Italian. When he asked why he was being held, they would repeat the same meaningless comment, "In time, in time," as though there was some magical moment when his questions would be answered. The secrecy was infuriating. He was confident he was making himself understood; they simply refused to answer. He was unable to have Vincenzo clarify whether "in time" meant he would find out why he was being held or if this meant his release. The confusion and uncertainty of his situation was almost as frustrating and depressing as his loneliness.

Before he learned to converse in Italian, eating with the Sgammotta family on weekends was monotonous. The food was good, and he enjoyed being in rooms with windows, but the conversation had no meaning. In those early days, his only diversion was to observe the family interaction. Vincenzo was the obvious master of the house. Gelsomina was affectionate but very deferential to her husband in all matters. Angelina, a tall woman with a rough demeanor, seemed to be the more independent of the two daughters. She tended to be contrary but very aware of how far she could take a disagreement with both her mother and father. Maria Antonia, the other daughter, was personable and very much the obedient daughter, close to her mother and ready to fulfill Vincenzo's every order without any sign of disagreement or protest.

As time passed and Daniel became more fluent in Italian, he found their conversation and interaction, when compared with his family, different in tone and theme. There was an obvious strong family bond, but there was not the loud, joyous expression of emotions and feelings so common in Daniel's American family. He eventually concluded the difference had more to do with cultural upbringing and the traditions of this small rural town than with personality differences. They could spend the better part of a meal talking calmly about the other people in Opi as though they were members of their family. Daniel eventually came to understand that, at some level, the people of Opi felt as though they were all part of a single family unit.

At mealtime, they often spoke of their church bell with great pride and affection. The Opi bell was an Agnone bell. The town of Agnone in Abruzzo is famous for bell-making. To own an Agnone bell was a symbol of pride. The people of Opi felt their bell had a distinctive tone, unlike any other church bell. They took great pleasure in assuring each other of this fact. The church bell not only served to announce the time of religious services but it also rang to announce daily vespers, which Daniel learned was the time of religious services, identifying the seven canonical hours—periods of the day set apart for prayer and devotion. The bell also rang daily to announce the time to recite the *Angelus* in memory of the Annunciation. The bell informed the people when it was time to rise in the morning, work, and eat, as well as the time to come in from the fields. The bell announced births and deaths, and other special occasions. Their bell was the keeper of their time and the recorder of their social order. They were literally in love with their bell and the sound it made.

In the fall, Daniel worked at stowing food for the coming cold months. Edible items such as seed potatoes, peas, and beans were carefully placed in large straw barrels, which allowed air to circulate. Small seeds were dried, segregated, and placed on flat surfaces.

Daniel's chores from December to late March primarily involved cheese and wine-making. The cheese came from sheep and goat milk, and the wine from red grapes. Daniel was surprised at the amount of wine they made—it was far too much to be used by one family. Other families from town would take away a good deal of the wine. Daniel assumed this was another way Vincenzo and the other farmers earned money for their families.

Another major chore during the winter months was chopping wood for winter heat. Vincenzo and the other men used mules to collect wood from the forest and mountain areas before the winter snows. Mules with large canvas bags hung over their sides were tied to each other and taken to the forest to transport the wood collected by the men back to town. Daniel noticed that on these trips into the forest the men carried rifles and side arms. He wondered why the men were so heavily armed on these wood-gathering trips. Vincenzo told Daniel the guns were needed for protection against the bears and other wild animals that inhabited the forest.

Daniel's job was to chop the wood for use in the wood-burning stoves that provided heat for the numerous houses in Opi. Wood for the Sgammotta house was stored outside Daniel's room in the area where the animals were housed.

Daniel attempted to remain positive during the winter. He reminded himself that the Sgammotta family treated him better than he would have expected, considering he was their hostage. He had all the wood he needed to stay warm; he was given warm clothes; and he was also fed better than he would have expected. Saturday afternoons and Sundays were spent with the family in their apartment. On these days, Gelsomina, Vincenzo, and the girls often treated him as though he were a member of their family. Vincenzo did not talk much, but Daniel could tell that he tried in his own way to treat him with kindness. But no matter how Vincenzo tried to manipulate Daniel's thinking, the separation from family and friends and his normal life continued to cast a terrible cloud of inconsolable despondency over his daily routine. It was a mournful sorrow so deep that tears never appeared. The constant sadness became such a heavy burden that by early spring it had consumed his personality. If only he had someone to share his burden with—if only he had someone to speak with who understood what he was experiencing, perhaps then his constant depression would not be so overpowering.

As the days folded into weeks and then months, he found himself becoming fond of Gelsomina. He thought this odd—and for the first five or six months of his captivity, he refused to allow himself to become friendly with her. How could he possibly be fond of a person who was a part of the nightmare that had become his life? For some reason, whether it was desperation, weariness, or just plain boredom, his hostility toward Gelsomina faded as he gradually learned he was not as lonely when he worked with her. She was very maternal and indulgent with him, and to a certain extent she supplied some of the emotional connection he had lost by being separated so long from his mother.

The daughters, although shy around Daniel, did try to make life easier for him. They usually tried to hide their token acts of kindness from their parents. As Daniel became somewhat fluent in speaking and then reading Italian, he would often discover books and newspapers in his room when he came back from his work in the fields. Along with the reading material, Daniel might find small bags of cookies and other sweets. There were even a few occasions when he would return to his room and discover a small glass jar containing a sweet liqueur that had been left for him.

The Sgammotta daughters gave Daniel a haircut every six weeks or so. This took place in the sitting room. Vincenzo and Gelsomina were always in the next room, and the door to the sitting room remained open. During this time, the girls would quietly ask how he enjoyed the book or sweets, but they spoke low enough so their parents could not hear. Daniel did not respond or show any sign that he heard the girls—he was unwilling to show appreciation to any member of the Sgammotta family because he felt it would only justify the injustice of his imprisonment. Their questions stopped after a period of time, but the reading material and sweets continued.

Daniel found it self-serving that the family tried to make his life in Opi bearable. He was pleased that he was not being abused, but he was never able to resolve the fact that the family members acted as though they had a just claim to keep him as their slave. He was being held against his will and made to work for no compensation other than shelter, food, and clothing. Yet the family acted indignant when Daniel refused to show gratitude for the way he was being treated. If they wanted to justify their actions, they were going to have to accomplish it without his help. He was not about to relinquish the very little power that remained his.

Daniel's worst week was during his first Christmas in captivity. Although the Sgammotta family made an effort to acknowledge this holiday for him, they could not take away the pain of his physical and emotional separation from his family. They took him to Midnight

Mass, with the usual Christmas pageantry and carols, and he became very emotional and teary-eyed when the choir sang "Silent Night." They even gave him a small gift on Christmas morning and shared a festive meal with him that afternoon. He took what was offered, but he again refused to say "*grazie*" or show his appreciation in any way.

Christmas had always been a very special time for Daniel, so special that he felt totally abandoned during his first Christmas in Opi. He had so many wonderful memories from his Bronx home that being away that first Christmas was the saddest time of his life. Daniel thought of his family and wondered how they were spending their holiday this year without him. He hoped they had not forgotten him. He spent Christmas day recalling the family traditions: the big meal after Midnight Mass, staying awake the entire night, the smell of the tree in the living room, the gifts, the relatives and friends that visited on Christmas day, and the happy time the Ciarletta family enjoyed. Nothing the Sgammotta family did could ever replace what they had taken from him.

CHAPTER VII

$\mathcal{M}$EETING WITH $\mathcal{F}$ATHER $\mathcal{M}$ASCIA

The weather continued its warming pattern. Soon Daniel and Vincenzo would be going to the valley for a second year of farming. Daniel was feeling sullen and angry, because he realized he had been in Opi for a year. As these feelings continued, he found himself spiraling into deep depression, losing all interest and desire for life. Spontaneity had left him many months ago and simple chores that used to be a comforting diversion were now drudgery. He was having difficulty sleeping. He felt hopeless and no longer optimistic about returning to America any time soon. His mental state so clouded that he had long ago stopped scheming about ways to escape.

The second Sunday in March began as every Sunday had for the past year. Daniel, in his clean pressed clothes, went to early Mass with the Sgammotta family. After Mass, Vincenzo told Daniel to remain in church because Father Gerado Mascia wanted to speak with him.

Father Mascia looked to be in his late thirties. He was a small, thin man with crisp, square, facial features, but his appearance was deceiving. He had the energy of three men and could lift his own weight. He was noted for his energetic stride, and he was proud to show everyone his ability to break the shells of nuts by smashing them with the fist of one hand.

As Daniel waited in one of the pews, he noticed other teenage boys sitting in the other pews. They were the few other Opi teenage boys he had seen helping their fathers with farming during the past year. Daniel thought, *Oh no, don't tell me I'm gonna have to sit through a religion class with these other Opi kids.*

Daniel crossed his arms over his chest, threw his head back, and slouched in the pew. He was in no mood to listen to what the priest had to say, unless it was about when he was going home!

The priest came out of the sacristy wearing his usual flowing black garment. He asked all the boys to come to the first pew. When they were seated, he said, "My purpose this morning is to explain to you why you were brought to Opi."

This simple, sentence jarred Daniel from his rebellious lethargy, and he was suddenly filled with new vitality. A thought that seemed too good to be true entered his mind as he and the others looked at each other, *Is it possible I'm not alone?* There was noticeable new energy in the church as all seven boys stared at Father Mascia.

"When I was assigned to Opi six years ago," Father Mascia began. "I studied the history of the people and the unique geological formation of this town. The book I read referred to the Opici tribe that settled on this precipice, which stood like a monument overlooking the rich valley pasture area of the Sangro. Living on the mountain gave the people a natural fortification against floods and conquerors, as well as the advantage of a fertile valley. These features made the natural elevation ideal for the settlers. With the construction of a road to the mountain, the Opici tribe had access to and from the valley for farming and grazing their animals."

Father Mascia began to tell the young hostages about the importance of sheep to small towns in the Abruzzo region of Italy. "Opi has for centuries depended on its central sheep herd, which at times amounted to fifty thousand or more. The sheep belonged to the people of Opi. Seven families owned grazing land in the valley, and also winter grazing land in the southern part of Italy. These families were responsible for the hiring of young men from Opi to act as shepherds, mule skinners, and guards. It was the responsibility of these young Opi men to care for the sheep as they grazed in the valley from May to October. During the winter months, the hired shepherds would take the full herd to grazing land in southern Italy."

Daniel was getting more frustrated by the moment with this talk of sheep. He was only interested in why he had been brought to Opi, *Why is he talking about the history of the town and sheep when he said he was gonna tell us why we were brought here?*

Father Mascia continued, "The sheep were taken from Opi through ancient mountain *animale carreggiata* (animal roadways). Many towns in the region depended on sheep for their existence, and they all used these same roads. The people of Opi survived on the revenue from the sale of the wool, as well as meat and cheese from the sheep."

One of the boys interrupted the priest, "Excuse me, Father, why are you telling us about sheep, when you said you were going to tell us why we were brought to this town?"

Father Mascia responded, "My son, it's important for you to know the history of Opi so you'll be able to understand the reason why you were destined to save the town and its people from losing their heritage and culture. My explanation of this history will help you accept your presence in our beautiful town."

The seven youngsters looked at the priest with furrowed brows and quizzical expressions. They were confused and disheartened by the priest's answer.

The priest continued as though he had never been interrupted, "But this happy, comfortable life would change forever when Italy entered World War II." As Father Mascia talked about the war, the youngsters could see and feel a change in his presentation. He no longer talked with pride in his words—his voice became mournful and his posture that of a defeated man.

"The German command decided to make a major stand, which included the Sangro Valley. Our beautiful, peaceful valley surrounded by mountains became a battlefield. We were unable to understand how a valley so peaceful could be shattered by war. Our personal war was given a name by the German military: the Battle of the Sangro Line. The Axis powers decided to defend and hold a stretch of land through the Sangro Valley, forty-five miles wide and extending to the Adriatic Sea, with the hope of preventing the Allies from reaching Rome. In August of 1943, the Germans began establishing their forces with two divisions, one placed in the town of San Angelo del Pesco, twenty-eight kilometers inland from the Adriatic Sea, and another division of solders in Alfredena, twenty kilometers southeast of Opi. They also employed army garrisons in the towns of Capracotta, Castle del Giudice, Cianni, and Martano."

Daniel could no longer suppress his anger. "Father, please, you said you would tell us why we are here. I'd like to know about that, not about the war," he said to the priest.

Another boy spoke up and supported Daniel, "Yeah, we wanna know why we're here." A few other boys added their voices in unison, "C'mon, why are we being held here against our will?"

The priest quickly responded in an angry tone of voice, "Young men, remember this is a church. You are being very disrespectful, and I will not tolerate your rudeness in the house of the Lord!"

After a full year of captivity, isolation from reality, and the dread of the unknown, each captive boy's sense of moral outrage at being held unjustly against his will had been so severely compromised that the seven prisoners were intimidated into silence by Father Mascia's self-righteous eruption and pompous anger. Without understanding the relevance of their reaction to the priest's reprimand, the confined youngsters allowed themselves to be transported to an alarming state of terror and panic—a feeling so intense that they suddenly expected their very lives were in danger.

After an indignant pause and a deep exhale, Father Mascia continued, "Boys, please, knowing this history is the only way for you to appreciate your contribution to our town."

Father Mascia went on to explain more about what happened during the war, "Because of Opi's location high in the center of the Sangro Valley, the town was taken over by the German Command and Communication operation for this major battle. The Germans desecrated the church you are now sitting in. The Church of Our Lady of the Assumption became the headquarters of command operations for the Battle of the Sangro Line. Because of this, our town was in danger of complete destruction by Allied bombing.

"In late September, prior to the expected shelling and bombing, the women and children were sent to caves in the mountains to the east and west of Opi for their protection. The men, as well as boys as young as nine and ten years of age, were forced to remain in Opi to be used by the Germans for work details. The older men were forced to do daily chores, which freed the German soldiers to establish and strengthen their communication center against attack. The older men were also forced to slaughter sheep for food, prepare daily meals, gather and chop wood, and often attend to the general needs of the Germans. This created a great deal of resentment. The men of Opi were not comfortable fulfilling tasks normally performed by women. But does one have a choice when looking down the barrel of a rifle?"

Father then returned to the topic of the sheep, and the anger of the boys once again began to rise. However, they were not yet ready to confront the pious priest.

"In October, the Germans would not allow the shepherds, muleskinners, and guards to leave their work details so they could move the herd to Foggia and Frosinone for the winter. The governing council pleaded with the German commander, explaining that if the sheep didn't have grass for grazing, they would die during the winter. The German commander would not listen to reason, and in October of 1943 the people of Opi were forced to sell all but seventy-five sheep for less than their real value. The sheep that remained were kept alive by housing a few in the animal shelters of people's homes. These sheep would be used to start a new herd once the war was over."

Much to the continuing frustration of the oppressed boys, Father Mascia's talk now moved back to the specific details of the battle. The frustration of the boys began to show in their facial expressions and continuous movement. Father Mascia did not seem to notice their agitated behavior.

At that point, one of the captives found the courage to interrupt the priest. "Father, I don't mean to be disrespectful, but when will you tell us why we are here?"

Father asked the seven youngsters to be patient, and none of the seven felt confident enough at that moment to further challenge him. He continued, still oblivious to the feelings of the seven boys. "In November of 1943, the British Eighth Army reached the Sangro Valley. The Allied forces decided to concentrate their bombing on the towns of San Angelo del Pesco and Alfredena, which were located in the center of the German and Italian defensive line rather than Opi, as had been expected. We believe the prayers of the townspeople saved us from destruction. Only two bombs were dropped on Opi—one hit the side of the mountain and caused no damage and the other hit a house across the street from 27 Via Giovanni de Battista, killing four people. You can still see the empty space at this location."

Father Mascia finally became aware of the restive posture and fidgety behavior of his audience. He paused and said, "I will not go into the details of this great battle this morning. I will save that for another time."

The priest became visibly emotional as he described the end of the battle. "The Germans — realizing they were about to be defeated — prepared to leave Opi on December 20, 1943, taking all the youngsters and able-bodied men with them as work prisoners. Nine young men refused to leave town and were shot by a firing squad. Only the old and some of the middle-aged men, who had acted infirm and feeble when the Germans first arrived, were left to bury the nine dead brothers and sons. Their wives, mothers, and young children, who were in the caves, were not present to grieve for their heroic fallen sons and fathers.

"Immediately after the Germans left, word was sent to the women and children in the Capracatto, Gioia De Marsi, and Il Parco Maxionale mountains that it was safe for them to come home. When the women and children returned to Opi in late February of 1944, we were all saddened when we learned of the many deaths of the children was due to the disease that spread among the people in the caves."

The priest ended this part of his long-winded talk by saying, "Now that you understand our history, you will be better able to accept your value to our town."

Father Mascia explained how the people began to assess their ability to go on with their lives without income from the sheep herds, and the men and boys, who had not yet returned from their slavery at the hands of the Germans. The people feared their lives would never be the same, but they had no choice but to go on living."

At this point, one of the captive boys again interrupted Father Mascia, "It's beginning to sound as though we were brought here so the people of Opi could — as you say — go on living. If that's the case, why don't you just tell us the truth and forget the details."

Father Mascia seemed truly surprised by the young man's statement, "I thought you would want to know how the people tried to survive, and how we had no choice but to bring the seven of you to Opi."

One of the boys who spoke Italian with a British accent, politely replied, "Well, Father, speaking for myself, it doesn't much matter why I was captured and brought here. All that really matters is when am I going to be released."

"I'm unable to answer your question at this time," said Father Mascia. "I do want you all to know that the people of Opi had no choice. They would not have survived without you. It's important that you understand our hopelessness, so that some day you will be proud of how you saved many desperate people and their culture. Not everyone has the opportunity to be a hero to so many who had experienced such pain and loss. Perhaps I've misjudged the time needed for your hearts to be open to our problems. I'll try to be as brief as possible, and maybe later you will be interested in more details."

"Yes, Father, maybe later. But now tell us why we have been forced to live in your town," said one of the other boys.

"As you wish. I'll only explain what I feel is important for you to know. The Governing Council of Opi planned to use the remainder of the money from the sale of the sheep herd to feed the people until the men taken by the Germans as work prisoners returned. The older men were limited in their physical ability, so only small community gardens were prepared in the spring and summer of 1944. The money from the sale of the sheep, along with gardens, fruit trees, and our grapes for wine, helped feed the families during that first year of rationing. The older people, who were unable to work the gardens, looked after the remaining sheep, as well as our few goats and mules. They also helped with minor chores to maintain the town's various functions. The people learned to trap and kill small animals. This meat, along with a few vegetables, a little sheep, and goat cheese— and by purchasing small amounts of flour and oil—enabled the people to survive that year."

Father Mascia talked about the end of the war and the anticipation for a new beginning with the expected return of the Opi men. "November 16, 1945 was a great day—the first young man returned: Patrizio Ursitti. He came walking up Via San Giovanni de Battista. He was gaunt and dirty with ragged and torn clothes, and he walked with a limp. But there was a bright smile on his face now that he was home. Word quickly spread that Patrizio had returned and his journey of horror was over. Everyone came out to greet him.

"Patrizio told the people about his time with the Germans. He had been quickly separated from the other young men of Opi. He confirmed that the men and boys were treated poorly and forced to do hard physical labor at the point of a rifle. There was barely enough food to sustain them, and some of the younger prisoners died in the arms of their fathers. They were forced to steal whatever clothes and rags they could find to stay warm during the winter. Taking boots off dead soldiers to replace their worn-out shoes was a common practice."

Next, Father Mascia discussed the events of the winter of 1945 in Opi. "With each passing day, hope was being replaced by the sad reality that the husbands and sons of Opi might never return. Many women would be unable to experience the final act of burying their loved ones in our beloved Opi soil."

At this point, a dark-skinned boy with an unusual way of speaking Italian stood and angrily interrupted Father Mascia. "Why do you continue to tell us about things that have no meaning for us? You told us you would explain why we have been illegally brought to this town, and I demand to hear the reason!"

The priest was clearly caught off-guard by the boy's aggressive confrontation. The other hostages were also surprised. The priest did not respond angrily as he had done earlier, but rather pleaded with him as though apologizing.

"These facts are necessary so you will be able to better understand and accept your role in Opi."

Instead of consoling the incarcerated youngster, the priest's statement only served to anger the boy further, and he became outwardly furious at Father Mascia's statement. "Since I am being held in your town illegally, I will *never* accept your role for me! Why do you think you can make me accept the criminal acts of your people?"

The young priest, still flustered by the boy's confrontational tone, hesitantly stated his reason for continuing. "I assure you this information can only be a comfort to you." The captive, who in a few minutes would be identified as an Egyptian boy named Omar, sat down with a look of resignation, realizing that the priest was incapable of understanding the perspective of the seven boys.

The priest gave a deep sigh and continued, "In the Italian culture, it is not considered proper or acceptable for women to be assigned the type of labor needed to expand the farming or the herding of the sheep. These tasks are only allowed to be accomplished by men. Patrizio successfully took the now eighty-nine sheep to the southern pasture fields for another winter and returned in late May with only one sheep lost."

At this point, the reason the boys had been kidnapped was becoming clear. The priest continued to use his "history lesson" as a rationalization for the illegal detention of the seven hostages.

"At that time, the people believed it would take ten to twelve years to increase the herd to the point where it could once again support the families of the town. However, in the fall of 1945, the governing council informed the people there was only enough money to sustain the population for one more winter—and with each passing day the people were losing hope that their men and boys had survived their labor imprisonment.

"The governing council, now desperate for solutions, proposed the idea of adopting Italian war orphans. Adopting children would solve the problem of the town's future, as well as provide some comfort to the families who had lost children in the caves. However, this was not a practical solution. We were told the adopted teenage boys would be required by the government to attend school until they were sixteen years of age. They would, therefore, be unable to help in the expansion of the land into farms for three or four years. Then, when they became sixteen, orphans, like other children in Italy, must be free to choose their own vocation. For these reasons, this solution was not considered further.

"The council called a meeting of the entire population in early December, 1945—I recall it was just prior to Christmas—to discuss their two-part plan for the continuation of the town. Vincenzo Sgammotta, who was President of the Governing Council, reminded the people that Italy was expected to become a republic through the newly adopted election process of 1946. The expected formation of the government into a republic had increased the growth and popularity of the Italian Communist Party. The council proposed that Opi be run as a model communist experiment, with everyone sharing in the labors of the entire community, while rejecting the atheist philosophy that was part of the world communist movement."

Father Mascia walked to the corner of the altar entrance, picked up a small wooden chair, and brought it up to the front of the pew. He sat down before continuing. The difficulty of telling the story seemed to have drained the life energy out of the thin but strong young priest. Once seated, he proceeded to describe the second part of the plan.

"The seven land-owning families recruited seven families from neighboring towns who were willing to farm Opi land as tenant farmers for the spring of 1946. Fifty percent of the food grown would be taken by the tenant farmers, and the other fifty percent would be given to the town to be communally shared by all residents in true communist fashion. The plan was implemented but the results were disastrous. The accounting of the percentage of crops going to the people of Opi could not be accurately verified. The people received far less food than they had expected and were once again on the verge of starvation. The lease to the thieving tenant farmers was not renewed for the spring of 1947.

"The despondent people demanded answers from their leaders. The governing council called an emergency meeting of the people to discuss what seemed to be a hopeless situation. Many of the people of Opi were beginning to believe that abandoning the hill town would soon become a necessity. Their culture, their homes, and their very existence would dramatically change. Many people did not know how or where they could rebuild their lives."

As Father Mascia spoke, the seven boys were each mentally finishing his long rant.

"The council told the people what many had been thinking. The end of Opi as a town was now before them. They would meet as a council and return to the people in a few days."

Father Mascia's thin face expressed despair as he summarized the situation in a proverb. *"La prima parola della guerra è pronunciata dal cannone, ma l'ultima è sempre disse dal pane* (The first word of war is given by cannons, but bread always has the last word.)"

The priest continued with a doubtful tone in his voice, "In four days, the council returned as promised. At that time, Vincenzo stood before the gathered community and said, *'Opians,* my brothers and sisters, as your leaders it's our responsibility to present a plan to save our way of life. We have decided to offer you the only answer we could think of to solve our problem. However, we must consider this carefully and all must agree before we move forward, because this alternative is a distasteful one.'"

Father Mascia had finally arrived at the explanation of why the seven prisoners had spent the past year in Opi, and repeated what Vincenzo had said that day. "'We have asked seven families if they would be willing to convert their seven gardens into seven town farms, which would be able to feed all our people. We have recruited seven of our strongest middle-aged men, some of whom are members of our governing council, to *conscript* seven foreign young men. These seven Opi men, with the help of those *conscripted,* will be responsible for converting our now-existing seven gardens into farms. The seven Opi men willing to take on this responsibility will be paid for their service in extra sheep for their families when the herd has regained its full size. They will also receive a substantial percentage of the revenue that is earned by selling the extra crops at the Saturday market in Pescasseroli.'"

The word *conscript*—a word Daniel had never heard before—was instantly defined for him. The priest continued by repeating, in essence, what Vincenzo had said. "'A portion of the money earned by the sale of the products in Pescasseroli would provide some extra income to help pay for basic town functions, and hopefully in a few years the farms would raise enough extra crops to sell wholesale to distributors. Father Mascia conveniently failed to mention that this expected earned income would result from the labor of the seven captives.'"

Father Mascia's long ramble now centered on justification. "After much debate as to the merits and moral correctness of the plan, the people looked to me for guidance. Many individuals shouted out to me, 'Priest, tell us what is just in this matter. What should we do?'"

"I knew the people were unsure and needed the proper guidance to go forward with this plan. In that moment, I knew through Divine inspiration what was right. I spoke to the people of what was in my heart. I explained that in seminary I had been taught of the suffering our people endured through the centuries by the actions of the non-believers—how they murdered God's people and stole our children to expand their power.

"To make my point, I told the people of Opi the true story of the capturing of the great Christian monument, the Hogia Sophia Byzantine church built in 537 A.D. in Constantinople. This church was a holy monument, a landmark of medieval Christianity, which contained sacred artifacts, pieces of wood from the actual cross Christ was crucified on, the lance that pierced Christ's side, the crown of thorns, and some Christ's own blood. I explained that Hagia Sophia was the seat of the Orthodox Patriarch, the counterpart to Roman Catholicism's Pope.

"In the fifteenth century, the city of Constantinople was surrounded by territories controlled by the Ottomans. After a seven-week siege, the Turks launched a final assault on Constantinople. The terrified citizens flocked to the Hagia Sophia church, expecting that its sacred walls and holy artifacts would protect them. Instead, the Ottoman Turks battered through the great wooden and bronze doors, destroying tombs and desecrating sacred icons. Screaming wives were taken from their murdered husbands and their children were chained and taken away to be sold into slavery.

"I told the assembled people of Opi that ever since the fifteenth century our children have been taken from us. I reminded them that we had all witnessed the taking of our children by the heathen Nazi devils.

"Then I told them how I prayed to God to stop the destruction, but when our men and boys did not return, I understood that He was not listening to my prayers. I stood before the people that evening and told them it was finally time for God's people to stand up and say, 'Enough! It is just and right for our culture and our lives to survive through the children of others.' I blessed the people and the seven men, and said, 'Go to the cities and bring to Opi our *Angels*. What God has not given, man will take.' The seven families went into the cities and each brought back a young, foreign male to assist them in expanding the current gardens into working farms. You seven young men were to become our Angels, taken to correct the wrongs done to our people for these many centuries."

The priest then discussed the role of the elders of Opi. "The plan also involved the elders of our town. Those unable to do physical work would act as protectors, to be posted on the road to prevent our Angels from leaving the town."

Father Mascia did not have to explain how the mountain acted as a natural barrier in preventing any escape attempt from the town proper. "You have no doubt noticed when you are working in the valley that there are men stationed on the valley road in their wagons to make sure you do not leave your duties. Someday we truly believe there will be no need for these protectors to be stationed on the roads. We believe you—our Angels—will come to love our humble town as we do."

What Father Mascia had been explaining in his convoluted and detailed manner was now quite clear. He had made a point to assure the boys that the decision had not been acted on lightly, as though the boys should somehow appreciate the difficult effort the people put into their decision.

The priest continued by referring to an essential aspect of Italian culture—the type of work considered appropriate for men and women. "You might be asking yourselves why the women of Opi weren't expected to turn the gardens into farms. My sons, it is not culturally acceptable for women to do the work of men. This would result in a devastating loss of pride for our men."

Then, with a tone of finality in his voice, Father Mascia stated the town's rationalization for the decision to kidnap seven boys. "The Germans had taken and killed forty-three young men and boys from Opi. It was, therefore, proper justice for the victims of such an atrocity to conscript, house, clothe, and feed a very small fraction of that number. These young men would, by their labor, save the lives of so many."

It took a few moments for the absurdity of his statement to register with the young boys. Father Mascia had sanctioned the immoral act of kidnapping seven foreign-born boys because of the murder of forty-two men and boys during a war on Italian soil.

The priest then explained the decision of the people of Opi to offer their kindness to the boys. "The hope of the people is that in time you will come to love our small town as we do. Starting today, Sundays until dusk will be a free day for you, our seven Angels. The people want to show their appreciation. But remember, if you forget to return to your homes by dusk, *escorts* will be there to remind you."

The young priest—finally acknowledging the frustration growing in the seven hostages—asked them to be more attentive. "What I'm about to say is important for your safety and your future, so please hear me well.

"The placement of the town, the forest, and the mountains form a natural barrier that prevents anyone from wandering off. Humans would be unable to survive in the forest because of the bears, wild boars, and wolves that inhabit this vast wooded area at the base of the mountain range—and if by some magic the animals did not kill you, you would be forced to roam the dense, uninhabited forest until you starved or froze to death. I ask you to look closely at the forest the next time you are in the valley. If you do, you will see only one road coming from the mountain and through the forest, leading directly to Opi. There are no other roads leading in or out, only a circular dense forest that follows the base of the mountain range. To protect you from certain death—in the event you are foolish enough to threaten your own survival by trying to leave by the forest—each family member was given an extra horse to prevent your suicide."

Father explained the duties of men he referred to as "escorts." "Finally, the council thought it would be wise to assign escorts to keep an eye on you during your free Sundays. These are men who do not have the endurance to do physical farm work"

During the priest's lengthy "homily," the word *kidnapping* was never used. In fact, the priest's explanation of their abduction and captivity sounded as though it was an unpleasant but nevertheless justifiable act, given the hardship the war had brought to the people of Opi.

Father Mascia added one final comment, as though to convince himself of the justice of what had been done to the seven innocent boys. "Some people were reluctant to accept this survival plan until it was agreed that the families responsible for an Angel would act with kindness and help their Angel feel like a part of their new Opi family as quickly as possible."

Father Mascia then made the sign of the cross over the boys and disappeared into the sacristy. The seven boys silently stared at each other, unable to speak.

Although each hostage had correctly speculated the reason they were being held against their will, hearing the actual words spoken for the first time had a dramatic impact. By the words he had used, Father Mascia had made their abduction and captivity sound legal. Daniel understood for the first time how people who believe they are basically good need to methodically arrange their immoral choices to pacify their conscience.

Finally, one of the boys spoke in Italian with a Welsh accent, "I don't know about the rest of you lads, but I, for one, am happy to finally know why I was brought here, and it feels good to know I'm not alone."

At that comment, the others smiled for the first time since they had entered church. The Welsh boy added, "I'm Jem Adair, and I come from Wales, England."

Another boy jumped up and shouted, "I'm from Harrogate, in Yorkshire! My name is George Buttermere."

By now, the boys were all standing, shaking hands with each other, and introducing themselves. In addition to Jem and George, there were Omar El-Mokhtar from El-Arish, Egypt; Gabriel de Corvo from Braga, Portugal; David Houptmann from Zurich, Switzerland; Klein Wien from Linz, Austria—and Daniel Ciarletta from the Bronx, New York City.

CHAPTER VIII

$\mathcal{P}$ETE $\mathcal{C}$IARLETTA $\mathcal{R}$ETURNS TO $\mathcal{I}$TALY

Daniel had been missing for thirteen months. Pete was furious and irritated at the lack of communication from Castellamare di Stabia over the past month, and he could wait no longer. He placed a long distance call to his brother-in-law. Rodolfo explained he had not heard from the police or the private detective agencies for over a month, so he agreed to visit both agencies the next day, assuring Pete he would call him during America's evening time.

The following evening, Pete waited by the phone and picked up the receiver the minute it rang. "Hello, Pete, this is Rodolfo. I have bad news. The Naples police have closed Daniel's case, and the detective agency told me that all their leads have been dead ends. Like the police, they have taken their man off Daniel's case."

Pete was infuriated by the news, and he questioned Rodolfo further, "Why wasn't I kept informed?"

"Pete, since I didn't hear, I thought they were still working on the case. I was surprised myself by the news," said an embarrassed Rodolfo.

"Is there anything that can be done to keep the police and the detective agency working on it?"

"I asked the police and the detective agency that same question," said Rodolfo. "They went over the reports with me, and I'm sorry to say there's nothing more that can be done."

Pete was outraged that Rodolfo had not maintained constant contact on his son's case, but somehow he was able to remain relatively calm. Pete diverted his anger by inquiring about his parents, which would turn out to be Pete's last rational course of action.

"Your father seems to have lost his determination. Your sisters are worried because he easily accepts the decisions of others, which as you know, is not like your father. He still blames himself for Donato's disappearance. Francesca is healthy, but also worried. She, unlike some others, hasn't lost hope—she continues her prayer vigils for Daniel."

Pete was exasperated by Rodolfo's comments and unable to further control his anger. "Damn it, Rodolfo, you tell whoever those 'others' are to go to hell because I haven't lost hope, and I'm gonna bring him home."

Pete slammed down the receiver without saying goodbye and repeated to himself out loud a comment made by Rodolfo during their phone conversation, *I'm sorry to say there's nothing more that can be done. That's bullshit.* Pete remained seated, red-faced, and staring straight ahead for at least ten minutes. He told himself, *Yeah, well I'm gonna show that bastard there's plenty more that can be done. When I bring Daniel home, he's gonna be the first to know.*

That evening, Pete talked with his brother Danny. "I've decided to return to Italy and find Daniel. I need to raise money to bring him home, and I want to sell my half interest in the house. I know you don't have the cash to purchase my half, but do you think you could get a second mortgage and buy me out?"

"I'll try, Pete. Without much cash to put down, it doesn't look that great, but let me find out where I stand with the bank. Maybe they'll let me work something out. Have you tried raising money from the business?"

Pete responded as though he had already considered this option. "Nah, we're trying to get financing for conversion to oil heat trucks. If I added more to that loan, the whole deal might fall through."

Danny visited his bank on the corner of Westchester and Soundview Avenue the following day during his lunch hour, and the loan officer told him he would be unable to refinance the home mortgage based on his salary and the amount he had to put down. That evening, he gave Pete the news. "I'm sorry, Pete, but they won't let me refinance. We'll have to sell the house."

"I hope you and Kate understand that I have to do this," said Pete.

"Pete, I know better than to try to talk you out of it. The truth is I'd probably do the same thing."

"I feel badly for you and Kate, but this is my last chance of getting my son back."

"C'mon, Pete, stop the feeling badly crap. Sell the house, take all the money, and bring Daniel home. I can afford to rent, and you'll need the extra money for Suzy's rent. Remember, Daniel may be your flesh and blood, but he's also like a son to me and Kate."

"I love you, my brother," said Pete, as he and Danny embraced. "Only you understand. We have been together since childhood, and we will remain together until the good Lord takes one of us."

The house on Beach Avenue was sold in late August 1948, and Suzy and Kate found a two-family house for rent on Bolton Avenue in Clason Point. Both women decided that living together in the same building, although in separate apartments, was the best way to maintain family life as they had known it. Pete was set to travel to Italy immediately after the Labor Day holiday. Kate and Danny moved into the first floor apartment the last week in August. Suzy and Pete, and their two daughters, moved into the larger second-floor apartment. Frances, who was engaged to be married, planned to live on White Plains Road after her marriage in March of that year.

In addition to selling the house, moving, and planning for Pete's trip to Italy, the four brothers were also in the middle of making plans for the gradual transition of their ice and coal delivery business to an oil delivery business. The ice and coal delivery service was beginning to lose customers because of the rapid conversion from coal for home heating to oil burning furnaces. Also, refrigerators had become more affordable for middle-class Americans. These newly affordable conveniences for the average American family forced the Ciarletta Brother's business into a period of modification.   The only question remaining was financing. The four brothers were planning a partial restructuring of their business for October of 1948. They would sell one ice and coal truck, purchase an oil delivery truck, and obtain a wholesale heating oil contract. In this way, they would be able to service all their existing customers through the winter of 1948-1949, those who had converted to oil and refrigeration, and those still using coal and ice.

With the full support of his brothers, Pete was due to leave for Italy in early September of 1948. The day before he was to leave, the four brothers finalized their procedures for converting the business. In the process of moving from Beach Avenue—and thinking only of his trip and the plans he would employ to find Daniel—Pete had failed to finalize the bank loan for the purchase of the oil delivery truck.

The brothers met to discuss their plans, and as usual, Pete began the meeting. "My brothers, I've had other things on my mind, and I never got around to completing the final details of our bank loan for the truck. Al, you being the next oldest, I want you to go to the bank and get the best interest rate you can, sign the deal, and get the truck."

"Pete, I'd be honored to take this burden off your shoulders."

Pete then looked at Bob and Phil. "Phil, I want you to be responsible for selling the old Chevy truck. Bob, you negotiate the wholesale contract for purchase of the heating oil."

The three men embraced Pete and wished him well. They encouraged him to put all his energy into finding Daniel and not to worry about the business. They would make sure that all his plans were carried out. "Hold things together until I get back," said Pete when the meeting was over.

Once in Italy, Pete found the Italian bureaucracy almost impossible to overcome. He fought, bullied, pushed, and bribed until he had copies of both the Naples and Rome police reports and the detective agency documents regarding Daniel's case. With these official papers in hand, he went to Rome, found the best detective agencies money could buy, and gave them all the information he had acquired since March 1947 and a recent picture of Daniel. The agency planned on producing thousands of reward notices with a picture of Daniel for placement in and around Rome, as well as placing a missing child reward advertisements in various town, city and local newspapers with Daniel's picture. Pete duplicated these efforts with a Naples detective agency. Then he traveled to Sicily, made contact with the head of the Sicilian crime families, and hired them to inquire about his son. He returned to Naples, met with the head of the Camorra, the emerging Naples crime family, and also hired them to help him search for his son.

During this time, Pete lived with his parents in Castellamare di Stabia, calling the detectives and others involved frequently to determine the progress being made. Leopoldo did not protest when he found out Pete had visited Sicily and contracted with the newly organized Camorra crime family of Naples. Leopoldo seemed convinced that he was responsible for Pete's desperate state of mind.

Both his parents and the rest of the family noticed how Pete had changed from the friendly, laughing, confident person they had always known, to a suspicious, nervous, and dour man. Leopoldo, who had the most influence over his son, spoke with him. "Pietro, you have changed since Daniel has disappeared. I feel as though I have lost both a grandson and a son."

"Don't ever say you have lost a grandson because I'm gonna find him."

"Pietro, I'll not scold you for the way you've just spoken because I know you're in pain. I only remind you there comes a time when you must accept the burdens you've received. There are things that even my brave son has no control over."

"Påtete, Daniel will be found— I'm gonna bring him home with me."

Francesca approached her son and warmly embraced him. She had tears in her eyes as she said, "Oh, my son, what you have suffered, it is no doubt you are a changed man. Pietro, go home to your family in America. They also need your attention. Leave Daniel in the hands of the Lord. If he is still alive, then only God can bring him back to you, not the police, the fancy detectives, or those villains."

Pete knew what he was about to say would deeply hurt his mother, but soon even this simple rational reasoning would abandon his consciousness. His anger and hurt were about to become so intense that it would completely dominate and guide his every thought and emotion.

"Mamma, God is no longer a part of me. From childhood, I followed your example of faith and obeyed what my father taught me. I never cheated our customers, and I never turned to the Black Hand, even during hard times in America's Great Depression. I went to church with my family, even though it was not expected of me. So how does God respond to my good deeds? He takes away my child. No Mamma, God has chosen to turn his back on me, so I choose to turn my back on Him."

Francesca did not respond. She simply embraced her son with the understanding that he was not ready to accept the loss of his youngest child.

Pete remained in Italy for two months, checking his sources twice weekly and reviewing interim reports. At the end of six weeks, both detective agencies informed Pete they had found no leads and would be closing Daniel's case. Pete then visited the Camorra and received a similar report. He traveled to Sicily the next day, only to be given more bad news. Pete was completely despondent and broken in spirit, but he was not yet able to emotionally give his son to God—as suggested by his mother. Nonetheless, he finally agreed there was no more he could do in Italy. He followed his parents' advice and sailed back to America in December 1948, twenty-two months after Daniel's disappearance.

The entire extended family visited Pete and Suzy on the first Sunday after Pete's return. Pete was unusually quiet during the meal. While having their espresso, the three brothers—who were excited about sharing their good news with Pete—began to talk about the business arrangements they had made while he was in Italy.

Al was proud of their accomplishments, and he began the progress report. "Pete, I think you'll be pleased with what we've been able to do. I got us a bank loan for the oil truck from Chemical Bank on Gun Hill Road at the interest rate we discussed before you left. Mack Trucks gave us a good deal on one of last year's models, and the oil deliveries so far are working out."

Bob, who was impatient to explain to Pete the good news about the oil contract, interrupted Al. "I negotiated a two-year contract with the Schildwachter Oil Wholesalers on Pugsley Creek, and the contract came in two cents lower per gallon than we expected."

Then Bob, with a big smile, placed his arm on Phil's shoulder, and while messing Phil's neatly combed hair said, "Guess what? Our baby brother gotta great price for the Chevy, a hundred and fifty dollars more than we expected." Everyone except Pete was laughing at Bob's playfulness.

Pete's reaction was subdued. "Let's wait until we finish our meal before we talk business," he said. The brothers were disappointed but accepted his response.

They finished their coffee, and the women began to clear the table for the "Boss and Underboss" card game. Pete suggested, "Before the game, let's go down to Danny's apartment to discuss the business changes in more detail."

The five brothers descended the stairs to Danny's apartment, ready to share with Pete this new exciting phase of their business.

Pete looked casually at the bank loan agreement and then looked up at Al. He hesitated a moment, and then in a soft tone, which was unusual for Pete, said, "After all we have been through. After all Danny and I did for you. My younger brother stabs me in the back."

The four brothers were caught off guard by Pete's comment. Danny was about to speak, but Al interrupted. "Stab you in the back? Pete, what the hell are you talking about? For Chrissakes, when you left for Italy you told me 'sign the deal and get the truck.' I was following your orders. How can you say I stabbed you in the back? Damn it, Pete, whaddya talking about? "

"You've always been this way, Al," said Pete. You'll never change. You've never pulled your weight from the first day you came from Italy. All you think about is women. If you worked like the rest of us, we might not be facing what you've presented to me today—and behind my back while I was out of the country."

Al was furious at Pete's inaccurate, irrational comments, but he chose not to respond. He was afraid he would say something hurtful to his older brother. He sat back in his chair and lit a cigarette. Bob and Phil, respectfully appealing to their older brother, came to Al's defense. Both brothers assured Pete that they too understood that he had given Al the authority to finalize the loan, buy the truck, and start servicing customers. The solidarity of the brothers only served to make Pete more uncompromising and defiant.

Phil asked, "Pete, what did you expect from Al?"

Pete seemed calmer when speaking to his youngest brother. "He was to present me with the cost of the loan, the make of truck, and its cost. I also expected wholesale prices from various distributors, not a negotiated contract and the bids you got on the sale of the truck, and I did not expect you to start serving our customers before I got back."

Phil pleaded with his brother. "But, Pete, all of that had been done. We had the costs of the various trucks before you left. Al got the best deal on the Mack; Bob took the best price offered on the wholesale oil; and you told me to sell the old Chevy. It was mid-October and the customers were calling to have their oil delivered."

Pete, now equally irritated at Phil, said, "Well, you were wrong if you thought all of that was settled." There was a short period of silence as Pete's overwhelmed and confused brothers just looked at each other.

Al broke the silence, "Pete, you are my older brother, and I don't want to be disrespectful. But I can't just sit here and let you accuse me of not workin' as hard as my other brothers and being the cause of our business restructuring that's….Pete, please, I'm trying be calm and show you the respect that comes with your position. How can you hurt me like this? We're brothers."

Danny felt it was time to mediate the situation. The words could not be taken back, but he believed the situation was resolvable if he could only find a way to penetrate the unexpected anger that seemed to have saturated Pete's entire body. "Pete, please tell us what Al did, what we all did, to make you so angry. We need to understand how you have been wronged. I want to understand what has happened. No one in this room would ever deliberately hurt you, but something has been done or said to make you feel betrayed. All we want is to understand and then make things right. I know this matter can be resolved. Did we somehow misunderstand or accidently hurt your feelings? If you would only explain your side of it, I'm sure we can fix this. We are all Ciarlettas from the same flesh and blood."

Pete arose from the table, and without directly answering Danny's question, he spoke directly to Al, "I wish you well, but if you can't accept your faults, I want nothing further to do with you." Pete then turned to Phil and Bob. "It would seem you agree with Al, so you both are free to leave me and join Al. For myself, I'll take the one remaining ice and coal truck as my share of the business and continue to service the ice and coal customers."

"Wait, Pete. It doesn't have to be this way. Please tell us what's wrong. This has to be a simple misunderstanding," said Danny, who was completely bewildered by the conversation.

Pete looked at his older brother, Danny. "I told you when you left the business that you'd always be my wise brother, and I believe that with all my heart. But in this matter I'm afraid there is no simple misunderstanding. This has been willful and planned."

Pete went over to Danny, kissed him on the cheek, and without another word went directly upstairs. Danny followed Pete up the stairs and tried unsuccessfully to reason with him. The three brothers silently followed Danny to the upstairs apartment.

The three brothers instructed their wives to round up the children—they would be leaving at once. The three wives, alarmed and confused, could tell something disturbing had happened at the meeting, and they called for the playing children. The brothers retrieved their coats and went to the kitchen to say goodbye to Suzy and her sisters. They told the women that Pete had dissolved his business partnership with his brothers. The Ciarletta wives kissed and hugged the Gallo sisters in silence. The Ciarletta brothers left the Bolton Avenue apartment, and Al left without acknowledging Pete. Bob and Phil silently shook hands with Pete, their stoic and impenetrable brother.

CHAPTER IX

𝒯HE 𝒜NGEL CLUB OF 𝒪PI

After leaving the church, Daniel and the other boys immediately became boisterous. They had seen each other's faces around town, each believing the others were Italian Opi teenagers who were helping their fathers with farming chores. The seven boys were full of renewed energy, each understanding for the first time in a year the glorious feeling of no longer being alone. The atmosphere was magical. Looking into the eyes of another person who had been experiencing and feeling the same bizarre emotions was breathtaking. They wanted to touch each other and hold on, both physically and emotionally. Each hostage had an unconscious fear that the others might disappear. If that were to happen, who would be able to understand them? Who would be able to reassure them that they were not losing their minds? Each boy had suddenly found others able to verify that his personal hell was not somehow his fault, others who were able to support and vouch for his often-confusing reality. The boys had met each other just ten minutes ago, yet they felt as though they were old friends. They were bound not by the familiarity of time, but by the similarity of their unique experience.

It was Sunday morning. Usually, each boy would be with their Opi family preparing for the Sunday meal. But the boys had no thought of food—which in and of itself was miraculous—all they wanted was each other. After leaving the church, thoroughly enjoying their freedom and wandering about town, the first thing the seven strangers discussed was how Father Mascia had used his long lecture to justify their kidnapping.

Jem was the first to comment. "The thing that got me is that he actually sounded as though he believed the bullshit he was giving us."

Gabriel added, "Did you ever think he was going to stop talking about those damn sheep, like I cared about their lousy sheep."

Daniel agreed by saying, "Yeah, he used his little talk to cover his butt."

Klein asked Daniel, "Cover his butt? What do you mean when you say 'cover a butt?'"

The other boys also did not understand Daniel's unusual American phrase.

Daniel explained that in American, *butt* was a slang word for *ass*. "Now let me see, how to explain this...when a guy says, 'He was covering his butt,' he means the person is making up excuses and lying to convince the other person that he was right to do what he did."

The other boys thought the American phrase was awkward, but they had their first joyous laugh when Gabriel started jumping around with both hands on the cheeks of his ass, yelling 'Oh look at how I'm covering my butt.'"

It's unimaginable how glorious it feels to laugh a hardy "belly" laugh, when one has not even smiled in over a year.

As they strolled along, enjoying the brisk, sunny Sunday and each other, they became more serious. They agreed the long talk by Father Mascia was simply an attempt to rationalize what the town had done to them.

Omar was the first to speak on this subject. "I'm disappointed in myself, and also the six of you, for not objecting and telling your holy man that he was wrong to excuse himself and his people for what they have done to us. If I had had the courage to confront the holy man, I would now feel proud of myself."

At first, the boys were annoyed at Omar's statement and there was momentary silence. Omar made them feel uncomfortable for being so flippant about Father Mascia's talk, now that the priest was not available to be confronted. The seven boys had no understanding that they were about to experience the first of many group learning experiences.

A boy by the name of David broke the silence, "Uh... I... guess we did let him have his own way. It's not like he was right and we were wrong. It was the other way around, and none of us, except for Omar, a little, tried to stop him."

A stocky, rough-looking boy named Gabriel added his opinion to the conversation. "You know, I don't know why I got so scared when he yelled at us about being disrespectful in a church, but he really scared the hell out of me."

The other boys, who had spoken so brashly about Father Mascia after leaving the church, soon found themselves agreeing with Omar.

"I wonder what he would have done had I stood up and told him he was just covering his butt," said Daniel. This brought on laughter once again, and some of the mild tension that had built over the past few moments dissipated.

The boys did not fully comprehend the psychological dynamics surrounding their failure to confront Father Mascia, considering their long period of captivity. They did not have an understanding of the unusual courage it would have taken to confront the priest in the church, given the isolation and suppression they had experienced over the past year. Although it might have been true that Father Mascia was trying to justify their kidnapping and although nothing would have changed, they now agreed that they probably would have felt a greater sense of personal pride had they either individually or as a group found the courage to confront the priest more forcefully.

They continued strolling about town, comparing experiences, and making each other laugh. It felt wonderful to walk freely and share their loneliness. Their Italian vocabulary did not contain words to express the weight that had been lifted from them. They all spoke reasonably good Italian by this time and were able to converse easily. The rest of the afternoon was spent walking and nervously asking each other about their backgrounds, and how their Opi families had been treating them. They were having such a joyous day, teasing each other as teenage boys are inclined to do. They joked about their seven escorts, who walked at a distance and never let the seven boys out of their sight. They strolled, talked, and laughed all afternoon, with never a thought of returning to their rooms. They wanted this newfound feeling of togetherness to last forever.

By late afternoon, Jem, who lived with a family in one of the detached houses by the church, said, "I'm hungry. Let's go to my family's house. I'll get my 'mum' to make us sandwiches and we can eat them on the church steps."

"Would she make sandwiches for all of us?" questioned Gabriel.

Jem replied with confidence, "Oh, not to worry. I can get her to do most anything I want. She loves the way I tease her." It was easy to laugh with Jem, who spoke Italian with a strong, guttural Welsh accent, which seemed so in conflict with the flowing, rhythmic beauty of the Italian language. They all laughed, except for a boy named George, when they heard Jem call the wife of his Opi captor "mum." Daniel, as early as that first day, secretly admired Jem for the way he dealt with his captivity, always with a smile and able to make jokes.

Jem told the others his name was James George Adair. In the United Kingdom, Jem is short for James. He was slender, not very tall, and had blond hair and a high forehead. His thin hair seemed to come to a point in the center of his forehead, and his bodily movements and overwhelming cheerful temperament made him stand out from the others. Jem had a positive, good-natured attitude, which was in keeping with his pleasant nervous energy. He gave the impression of being in constant motion.

His parents had met at a youth hostel in San Francisco. His mother, Cara, was "a Yank," who came from a small town called Newington next to Hartford, the capitol city of the state of Connecticut. They started their married life in Sheffield, England. Then, with a friend, the two families bought a non-working farm in Llwydcoed, Wales, called Ty Rhos Farm. During the ensuing years, the boys never learned how to properly pronounce the name of the Welsh town where Jem had lived.

Jem's father was an engineer who was involved in building and construction. He had accepted a one-year contract for a reconstruction project in a bombed-out area in Salerno, a town on the Mediterranean, south of Naples. Jem's entire family moved to Salerno for the year. Jem and his sister attended an English-speaking religious school sponsored by the Marist Brothers, a French religious order. One April day, on his way home from school, Jem was walking alongside a series of stone row houses. As he passed an open door, a man pushed him into the house. He was kept there, gagged and tied to a chair, and then late that evening he was transferred to a car and brought to Opi.

George Buttermere was quite different from Jem, except for the similar way they spoke Italian with their Welsh and British accents.

George was calm and reserved, tall for his age and quite slim. He had a long, thin nose to go with his long, thin face. George was verbally and physically reserved. He walked, sat, ate, and talked all within a similar controlled manner. He was most concerned not to be a burden in any way to his new friends. George was raised in Harrogate in Yorkshire, England. Harrogate was a spa town for the wealthy.

George's mother and father were hotel workers. They had met while working at the St. George Hotel in Harrogate and were married within a year. He told the other boys that although he did not remember ever seeing his parents hugging or kissing "like these Italians," he knew they loved each other and were happy together. Harrogate eventually lost its attraction as a spa town when England began to see war as inevitable. George's father was drafted into the army, and his mother continued working in Harrogate.

When the war ended, there was little opportunity for employment in the hotel industry in England, and George's parents secured permanent positions in 1947 in a hotel in Lugano, Switzerland, a lake resort town just over the Italian border. The family crossed the English Channel by ferry to France, and from Paris they went on to Rome for a one-week holiday. At the end of their week-long vacation, the Buttermere family was waiting at the Termini Station for their morning train to Lugano.

They had just finished a light breakfast, when George visited the men's room before the departure of their train. As he entered the toilet area, an old man sitting on a chair holding his leg pleaded, "Fall hurt foot, help, help." George helped the badly limping old man out of the bathroom.

The man directed George toward a near exit door, saying, "My brother, my brother." There was a car parked on the street outside a rear exit door. As George and the old man moved toward the car, another man jumped out of the car and opened the front and rear doors. Then the two of them helped the limping man into the front passenger seat. The younger man—who George assumed was the man's brother—took money from his pocket and extended it as he moved aggressively toward George, but George gestured that he did not want money. He was trying to move away from the man and, in so doing, he was moving toward the rear door of the car, when he was pushed into the back seat, followed by the man who had been holding the money. The old man with the fake injury had moved to the driver's side of the car, and as the rear door of the car closed, they sped away from Termini Station and drove to Opi.

Daniel, the only Angel from across the Atlantic, was a little heavy. He appeared to still have some baby fat on his young body, even at the age of fourteen. Daniel was unsure of himself and had little confidence in his mental ability. He had brown hair, a round face, and a pleasant smile. Daniel tended to be quiet, preferring to listen to his new friends, who he felt were more knowledgeable than he.

David Hauptmann was and looked to be the oldest of the boys. He was very mature for his age, especially when compared to the others, but he never acted as though he was superior. David was very likeable. Although he was the oldest, he was not physically larger than the others. He was slight in build and had a serious, determined face, primarily due to his piercing dark eyes. David Hauptmann was sixteen and a half when he was brought to Opi.

David's parents were German Jews, who left Germany in 1932 when he was sixteen months old. They resettled in Zurich, Switzerland. His father, Isaac, was a watchmaker and Jewish scholar. In the winter of 1947, David's father went to Rome to study the history of the Roman Ghetto, Tiber Island, and the main Roman synagogue. He brought David with him, hoping the experience would acquaint him with his Jewish heritage. The Jews had experienced persecution in the sixteenth century when Pope Paul IV forced all Italian Jews to live within a walled enclosure, an area that is now the center of the present-day ghetto. Via del Portico d' Ottavia, the district's main street, leads to Rome's central synagogue with Ponte Babricio (Babricio Bridge) linking the ghetto with Tiber Island, which David explained still remains a center for healing.

During the last two days of their stay, David's father intended to finish his review of the synagogue's historical collection. On the second day in the synagogue, David was bored, and he convinced his father to allow him to explore the ghetto one last time while his father completed his work.

David was strolling toward the ghetto along via del Portico d' Ottavia, when he passed a car that appeared to have a flat tire. A man lying on the ground by the jacked-up rear tire called to David, asking David to reach into the open trunk and hand him a lug wrench. As David reached into the trunk toward the tool, he was grasped by two hands that came out of a hole in the wall separating the rear seat from the trunk. Someone dragged him into the trunk of the car, and the trunk lid was immediately slammed shut. He felt the jack being banged out from under the car, and in the next moment the car was moving. David ended his tale by commenting, "Next stop, Opi."

Omar El-Mokhtar, an Egyptian, was the tallest of the boys. He had a broad nose and high cheekbones. His dark eyes seemed heavy, as though they were weighted down. He moved in a stoic manner and showed little joy or grief. He always seemed to be under complete control both physically and mentally. As he had demonstrated in the church, Omar was brutally honest regarding his feelings and easily expressed his thoughts. Omar was quite intelligent. He spoke modern Arabic and was of the Islamic faith. He proudly explained to the others that Modern Arabic is different from classical Arabic, and for this reason the Egyptian dialect varies greatly from that of other Arabic speaking nations.

El-Arish, a resort city on the Mediterranean between Sheesha and Sinai, was the Capitol of the North Sinai Governorate. El-Arish was a historic military route at one time, but now it was a restful holiday retreat on the Mediterranean, noted for the fact it is the only beach area in Egypt with palm trees. Omar had relatives in Paris, which has a large Muslim population and very good schools. France allowed students the freedom to practice their religious traditions while attending school. His parents wanted Omar to finish his schooling in France, and he was on his way to Paris when he was kidnapped. Omar chose not to reveal as much as the others about the particulars of his capture, but simply stated, "I was traveling through Rome, bound for Paris, and like you, I too was deceived by two men to enter their automobile and then taken to Opi." None of the other boys chose to question Omar further on the details of his capture.

Gabriel de Corvo had olive brown skin like many of the people in Opi, and thick, dark, curly hair. Gabriel was rough in manner and speech, although his Italian was better than the other Angels. He was a handsome fourteen-year-old, in a very rough sort of way. His facial features were jagged, and some might have described them as too large, but Gabriel's features seemed to blend well with the shape of his body. He had a muscular torso with large upper arms and a thick, firm chest that complimented his slim waist. Gabriel was very friendly and outgoing. He always seemed ready and willing to accept any dare or challenge.

Gabriel had lived in Braga, Portugal, a city in northern Portugal noted for its beauty and its attractive square bordered by flowers, restaurants, and enticing shops. Portugal's oldest cathedral is located in Braga and was the pride of the community. Gabriel's father was a surgeon in Braga. At the end of the war, he was asked by the Portuguese government to visit Italy and train Italian doctors on the care of large body wounds, which was his specialty.

Doctor de Corvo took his family to Italy for the training conference. Gabriel was the youngest of five children. The de Corvo family was staying at a hotel in the Adriatic Sea town of Pescara, where the medical conference was being held. One day, as he and his brothers and sisters were sightseeing in Pescara, Gabriel became distracted by a street magician and eventually realized his siblings had moved on. As he walked on a broad boulevard trying to find his way back to the hotel, Gabriel passed two men. One was seated in a car and the other was leaning against the car's front door. He told the men he was lost and gave them the name of his hotel. They motioned for him to get in the car and indicated they would drive him to his hotel. When he realized he was being taken out of town, he tried to stop the car, but he was restrained.

Klein Wien was shy and reserved. He was good-natured and easy to talk to, and also tease. He had wavy, light blond hair and fair skin. Klein was very handsome, but in quite the opposite way of Gabriel. Klein's facial appearance was smooth and elegant, and his features were petite and sensitive. He had a moderate build and appeared to be on the verge of quickly growing. Klein had a very interesting accent. He loved wintertime in Opi because of the snow-capped mountains surrounding the town—it reminded him of his home in the Oberösterreich region of northern Austria.

Klein had lived in the city of Linz, the state capitol, and his father was head of the water department for the city of Linz and responsible for the purity of the city water. His father was an important member of the community, and his mother was a grade school teacher in Linz. Klein was an only child. He and his family had been on a holiday in Italy, visiting Venice, Bologna, Florence, and Siena.

In Siena, they attended *Il Palio*, the Siena Palio horse race, which is held in the main Piazza del Campo. Klein and his parents, and many other spectators, were standing haphazardly around the dirt racetrack in the piazza, shoulder to shoulder, jumping and cheering for the various horses and jockeys. During the last lap of the race, Klein felt himself being moved by the boisterous crowd. Because of the loud screaming around him, he could not be heard by his parents, who were focused on the finish of the race. During the mass confusion, three men moved Klein toward one of the small streets leading into the piazza. There was so much excitement and movement in the crowd that no one heard Klein calling for help. His calls just blended with the cheering spectators.

Once they were on the narrow street off the piazza, the three men rapidly pulled him a short distance and into the waiting truck that would bring him to Opi. Klein was the last of the seven Angels brought to Opi. Daniel was the first to arrive; five of them came in the late winter or spring of 1947; and Klein arrived in July of that year.

Klein spoke of his feelings about his parents. "Do you guys worry about your parents like I do? I can't get that day out of my mind. It was bad enough that I was taken, but my parents must feel terrible, thinking they were responsible for not watching me more closely."

Jem commented, "Klein, you can't think like that or you'll really drive yourself crazy. You can't blame yourself because these Italian clowns kidnapped you. Look, you have enough to feel bad about without giving yourself more headaches. Blaming yourself doesn't make any sense."

Gabriel added, "Hey, Klein, what Jem is saying, feeling bad about your parents, I think he means you got enough to worry about being a prisoner, without brooding about your parents."

Omar offered his opinion. "I agree that you should not accept responsibility for being taken. But you have reason to be concerned about the effect your disappearance has had on your parents." Omar, like Klein, had often thought about the effect his disappearance was having on his family.

Daniel said in an understated tone, "Klein, I'm glad you mentioned how you feel about your parents. I have to admit that I have been so wrapped up in my thoughts about being here and thinking of ways to escape that I never thought about how my mom and dad must feel about me being missing."

"Hey, Dan, don't you start now," said David. "The guys are right. We have more than our share of problems. Let's think of only one thing: how we're going to get out of this town. We'll have plenty of time later to feel guilty."

The boys spent the rest of the afternoon and evening on the church steps, eating their sandwiches and talking about their families and how they must be coping. Although it was difficult being held captive and consumed by their situation, Klein and Omar taught the others the need to be more sensitive regarding their family members.

As darkness approached, and the boys were about to go back to their rooms, Jem said, "Oh, wait, before you guys go. Did any of your Opi families set you up with girls from town?"

The other six boys looked at Jem in disbelief.

David was the first to speak. "You've got to be kidding. Are you telling us that your family gets you dates with girls?"

"No no, this isn't dating. About six months ago—that's right—it was late October, I knew enough Italian to hold a limited conversation. One Saturday afternoon, Caterina, the wife of the bloke I farm with, asked me if I wanted to meet a nice girl. My Italian was really bad then, so I had to ask her again because I was thinking I must have heard wrong. I couldn't believe she wanted to set me up. Well, I heard right. She told me that she had spoken with the parents of a family that live a few houses away. Now listen to this."

Jem flashed an impish grin and nudged David with his elbow. "The father was willing to let me *court* his daughter as long as Caterina or Orsolo was present. Now I know that meant he was trying to marry her off, so I told Caterina, 'Sure I would love to meet a girl.' I was thinkin' that a young girl, even if she wasn't that great lookin', was better than sitting with Orsolo. Sure enough, the next Saturday the girl came to visit. Her name is Marisa, and would you believe it, she looks pretty good! After two weeks, I was tryin' to figure out a way to be with Marisa alone, but no luck. No way could I shake Caterina or Orsolo. We couldn't go anywhere alone, and one of them was always in the next room in clear view. Have any of your Opi families tried to fix you up with one of the local girls?"

The six others agreed that none of their families had, nor had they even hinted at such an arrangement. The boys were now interested and wanted to hear more, so Jem continued his tantalizing discussion.

"Well, as I said, Marisa was better than Orsolo, but the problem was that after six or seven months I'm starting to get a little excited when she comes by. I wanted to do more than talk, if you know what I mean. But there was nothin' I could do about it. They wouldn't let us alone for a minute. My only hope is that someday Caterina and

Orsolo will get tired of hanging around and maybe we'll have some time alone."

"I wouldn't count on that—unless you marry her," said Gabriel.

"Wooh, I don't plan on marryin' any Italian girl from this town, no matter how horny I get."

At that point the escorts approached and informed the boys that it was time for them to return to their rooms. Before breaking up, they shook hands and agreed they would be looking forward to next Sunday.

Evenings were the most difficult time for Daniel. He would usually sit in front of his wood-burning stove, alone and lonely, thinking of his home and family in America. But tonight his spirits were high—he had not felt this kind of joy in thirteen months. As he warmed himself in front of the stove, he kept thinking of Father Mascia's lecture earlier in the day. All these months wondering why he was being held in Opi, and there it was, explained in fifteen minutes. But tonight he was not alone—he was once again part of a group. Their names were not Skelly, Dutch, Tiny, Mitz, Giggy, Jack, or Joe Sal, but that was okay. He would teach his new friends how to play stoop baseball, and he guessed they would teach him how to play soccer.

CHAPTER X

$\mathcal{L}$IFE IN $\mathcal{O}$PI

By the third free Sunday, the seven boys were still learning about each other. It was April, and the second year of work in the valley had begun. Vincenzo and Daniel followed the same procedures as the previous year. Daniel was familiar with many of the tasks and the work was easier, now that he was able to communicate in Italian. Time passed quickly as Daniel waited enthusiastically for each Sunday to arrive.

The month of May, although brisk and breezy in the mountains, brought with it the warmth of the bright spring sun, which helped to remove the memory of their first harsh mountain winter. By the middle of May, the seven boys had become much more comfortable with each other.

The conversation had begun to move from exploring their different backgrounds to inquiring about the feelings they had experienced during the past year. Their conversations were becoming more and more intriguing. Their fifteen months of confusion, loneliness, and depression began to take form in words, rather than lonely thoughts.

On one bright May Sunday, Gabriel candidly expressed his feelings over the past year, "For me, it was worse than being in solitary confinement in jail. Sure, I was out in the air and was kept busy, but let me tell ya, I was scared and felt sad all the time. After I learned a little Italian and still couldn't get any answers from Tiziano or Rosa, I began losing hope of ever being released. Not only that, but Tiziano is such a mean pain in the ass. After each of my escape attempts, he got even meaner, yelling, pushing, and slapping me around. After my first escape attempt, I got a hell of a beating and no food for...I think...a day or two."

Gabriel then moved his conversation to a frightening thought. "I keep thinking about something real scary. What if we can't find a way out of here, say in two or three more years. Is it possible that we could, you know, go crazy, lose our minds?"

George offered his opinion. "I don't think that could happen, Gabe. There are people who get sent to jail for years and years. Have ya ever heard of them going mad after being in a jail for five or ten years? I don't think so."

"Yeah, George, I'll bet you're right; a lot of people spend years in jail. They wouldn't let'em out if they were nuts."

Klein quickly changed the subject back to the possibility of escape and the others did not seem to mind. Klein was surprised to hear that Gabriel had tried more than once to escape. "I wish I had tried to escape. I never figured out a way to do it. I would sit in front of the stove staring at the flames. I couldn't even think clearly—sometimes I couldn't move. Just like you, Gabe, I was really lonely and scared. Then when I was working in the valley, I always seemed to be...the only word I can think of is *numb*. Is that the word when you feel you don't have enough energy to move or think?" The other boys thought he was right.

David encouraged Klein to continue. "Well, this will seem really strange, but things I saw seemed cloudy and I thought of nothing but my home. I can't even remember what I did in the valley during those first five or six months. Until I met you guys, the past year has been a dream, a real bad dream. I kept asking myself, 'Is this actually happening to me?'"

Jem chided Klein, "C'mon, mate, you gotta snap out of it. Y'need to try and have some laughs, give your family a hard time every once in a while. If not, let me tell ya, you're really gonna be miserable."

Jem, as was his way, quickly took over the conversation. "The second week in this lousy excuse for a town, I said to myself, *I'm gonna make my time here easy. I'm gonna have as much fun as I can.* Right off, I started teasing Caterina, even before I knew Italian, and I found out that she loved my kidding around. The best part was to see how mad it made Orsolo. Once I saw that, I teased her more."

David interrupted Jem. "Yeah, Jem, but getting to know you, kidding comes easy. I couldn't be like you. I'm more like Klein. In the beginning, I was so confused and scared that it took me about a month before I even felt comfortable getting angry with Jacopo, never mind trying to escape. Then another month passed before I could get up enough nerve to make my first escape attempt."

Daniel was now smiling from ear to ear. "What a relief to hear you guys talk like this. When I was first captured, I was so scared and unsure of myself. I was convinced that I was a coward. Then after a few failed escape attempts, I felt like a real loser. Now that I hear you guys were also afraid and couldn't escape, I feel a whole lot better."

Omar sat silently during these early discussions, unwilling to share. It was July before he was ready to discuss how he felt after being kidnapped. One Sunday, he began expressing his rage at the injustice he was forced to endure. Omar was unaware of the gradual but radical change he would soon begin to experience in Opi.

On the first Sunday in August 1948, Jem told the boys about a plan he had to escape. He had noticed metal bars embedded in a concrete slab that was sitting in about ten inches of dirt and not cemented to the concrete floor of the animal shelter.

"Using a steel bar and a spoon I'll take from one of my meals, I'll dig a hole under the concrete slab deep enough so I can squeeze my body under it on my stomach. I'll use my hands to grab the dirt on the other side of the gate and shimmy my body out onto the road. I haven't figured out the details yet, but once I do, I plan on giving this a go."

Gabriel asked Jem, "As you're digging the hole, how are you gonna hide the hole and what are you gonna to do with the dirt you dig up? You can't leave it in a pile for Orsolo to see."

"That's what I have you guys for. I need some ideas."

"S'pose you do manage to get your body under the gate, then what?" said Daniel. "The 'protectors' ain't gonna let you walk past them and out of town."

"I know it's a long shot, Dan, but here's what I'm thinking. I could leave the hole early in the morning when its still pitch black. It's August; the moon won't be bright, and I'm hoping at that time of night the old men will be half asleep. I'll quietly walk down the dirt road in back of the houses till I get to the cobblestone road. Then I'll crawl up to the wagon, staying as close to the wall as possible. I'll go slow and careful, and just keep inching my way until they notice me. When that happens, I'll jump up and make a run for it. You know, it's also possible that if I'm quiet and lucky, I could even get past the wagon if they're sleeping.

"Yeah, or you might get shot in the back as you are running from the wagon," said George.

"I'm not gonna worry about that. Look, I think this is a good idea—my first worry is hiding the dirt and then how to hide the hole. C'mon, guys, I need some ideas. How am I gonna hide the hole?"

The more the boys brainstormed ideas about how to escape, the more excited they became. The ideas were flowing, and after an hour or so the plan was set. Each boy would go back to his stable and find a narrow piece of scrap wood long enough to fit into a pant leg. If he had to use a piece that was longer than his leg, he would extend it beyond his belt and cover it with his shirt. Then, moving slowly and trying not limp because of the wood inside their pants, each boy would return to Jem's room using the unpaved animal road behind the houses, being careful not to return as a group. More than one limping boy at a time might look suspicious.

Within a half hour, six pieces of wood were quickly hidden behind the stack of hay bales in Jem's animal shelter. Before the others left, they cautioned Jem to dig the dirt around the hole so the wood strips covering the excavation would also be below the surface. In that way, loose dirt would cover the wood and the ground around the hole would appear level.

Starting the next evening, Jem began to dig his hole, placing the dirt in animal water buckets. When he finished the time-consuming digging, he used the surplus stones that were in each of the stables to fill in the small hole. He then rested the strips of wood securely on the stones and covered the wood with part of the dirt he had just removed. Finally, he spread hay over the dirt to camouflage its fresh appearance.

When he was done digging each night, he would evenly distribute any surplus dirt on the concrete floor of the animal shelter and also cover it with hay. Every evening that week, Jem dug the soil from under the concrete. He continued to work late in the evening after Orsolo had gone to bed, in spite of his raw, blistered hands.

After about two hours of work on the fifth night, Jem was able to wedge his body under the concrete slab with the embedded railings and shimmy his body forward until his right hand could grasp the dirt on the other side. He pulled himself free of the gate, took a deep breath, and rested a moment.

After a few minutes, he began quietly walking down the dirt road used by the animals leading to the entrance of town. He estimated three more hours of darkness. At the corner of the last house, he peeked at the cobblestone road exiting the town. As expected, he saw two protectors with their rifles in a wagon. He hoped darkness and boredom would cause the guards to be sleepy and unable to detect his presence until he was able to get to the road leading out of town. Once in the valley, he would run until he could find someone to direct him to the police.

Lizard-like, he slowly moved on his stomach alongside the stone wall, inching toward the two men. After about an hour of slow, patient effort, he was approximately ten yards from the wagon, and the two protectors were still unaware of his presence. He would lie absolutely still after each inch of movement, afraid to breathe too heavily. His bloody hands and scraped knees were throbbing with pain, as he continued to move closer. He would inch his body forward and then stop and sneak a peek at the men in the wagon. He was close enough to them to notice any hint of reaction to his movement. He was sure that if they detected him he could jump up and make a run for it. If luck was on his side, he might be able to crawl up to or even past the wagon without being noticed in the darkness.

So far his plan was working perfectly. He was confident he was going to make it. He would wait a moment before inching forward to make sure his last movement had not startled the guards. After a moment of absolute stillness, he slowly reached forward with one hand, fingers tenderly gripping the soil, while at the same time he wiggled his stomach and pushed the soil ever so gently with the toes of his shoes, moving a few inches closer. He maintained, absolute stillness for a moment, and then glanced at the protectors, who still had not moved. He waited a moment and began his slow snake-like movement forward one more time. He was now only ten to fifteen feet from the wagon. Again, he reached forward with his right hand to silently grip the soil with his fingers. But this time his hand hit pebbles rather than soil, making a sudden noise, and he could see movement from the men in the wagon. Without the slightest hesitation, he arose to his feet and began to run past the wagon. He heard three gun shots, and then a sharp, biting, stinging pain engulfed his lower legs, bringing both feet together and causing him to fall.

It was odd, but at this moment the thought that entered Jem's mind was, *So this is what it feels like to be shot in the legs.*

As he looked up, he saw the end of a rifle pointed at his face and a second man holding the handle of a long leather whip that was wrapped around his lower legs. He had not been shot, but rather taken down by the leather whip, which caused two deep cuts in his lower legs.

Two days later, with bandages on his legs, hands, and knees, Jem watched Orsolo Monteverdi, the husband of his Opi family, and three other older men dig a trench the length of the concrete stable floor. They constructed a two-sided wooden frame that formed a mold into which concrete was poured, oozing under the existing slab, while also making contact with the existing animal shelter concrete floor.

For the seven boys it was yet another disappointment to contend with, but being together and being a part of Jem's plan seemed to ease the pain of what they saw as one more failure.

The second farming season for the boys was beginning to come to an end. It was now late September 1948. All the crops had been harvested except for some root plants that would soon be dug, cleaned, and prepared for market. Other crops would be dried and stored for use during the winter.

On the first Saturday in October, the farmers knew they had approximately four weeks remaining to sell their fall crop at the market in Pescasseroli. The morning sun had not yet risen, when Gabriel was wakened by the sound of Tiziano Vecellio, the man he farmed with. Tiziano, in his usual unpleasant voice, cried out, "Rise, Gabriel. It's time for us to load the wagon for market."

Gabriel knew if he hesitated, Tiziano would pull off his warm covers and drag him from his bed. Tiziano, in his late forties, was one of the men who had escaped the German work group during their occupation of Opi. He achieved this by acting as a cripple, using a crutch and pretending he did not have the proper use of one arm and leg. Tiziano's son was among the group of young men who had faced the firing squad rather than go with the Germans as work prisoners. Gabriel jumped out of bed, grabbed his work clothes, and dressed in front of the smoldering woodstove.

Soon Tiziano and his captive were on their way to the valley to load the wagon with crops. After loading, Tiziano returned Gabriel to his room just as the sun began to rise. Gabriel stoked the fire and added more logs to the belly of the stove. He undressed, returned to his warm covers, and was soon back to sleep—knowing he had a long, free Saturday morning to sleep, stay warm, and relax.

Rosa Vecellio, Tiziano's wife, usually brought his breakfast on Saturday morning at around half past eight. She was deliberately quiet so as not to wake Gabriel if he was still sleeping. This morning, Gabriel was awakened at around nine o'clock by a sweet, lyrical voice saying, "Gabriel, it is time for you to get up. I have your breakfast." As Gabriel slowly opened his eyes, he was surprised to see Tiziano's only daughter, Theresa. He sat up quickly and said, "Theresa, what are you doing here? You're not allowed in my room alone!"

"Oh, Gabriel, you're such a foolish young man. Stop telling me where I should and should not be. Now get out of bed. I have your breakfast."

Gabriel hesitated, knowing he was only wearing a pullover shirt and underwear. Theresa smiled and said, "Gabriel, I'm a thirty-seven-year-old woman. I have seen men in their underwear before. Now stop being childish, get out of bed, and come to the table. I want to talk with you."

Theresa moved to the stove and added more logs, as Gabriel jumped from his bed and quickly dressed. She was waiting for him at the table.

"You better not stay here," said Gabriel. "What if Tiziano finds out? He'll go crazy!"

"Why are you concerned? Tiziano is at market and won't be back until later in the

afternoon. Besides, I want to talk with you."

Gabriel was aware that in Opi *papa* was the respectful name to be used when speaking of one's father, and he asked Theresa, "Why do you call Tiziano by his first name rather than *papa*?"

"A father is called *papa* by his children out of respect. I have no respect for Tiziano."

As he ate his breakfast, Gabriel was surprised to hear Theresa talking so candidly about her father. This was very unusual for an Opi woman. "You sound like you're really mad at him."

Theresa had been smiling, lively, and happy when she entered Gabriel's room a few minutes before, but now she had a fierce scowl on her face and her warm, green eyes had turned as cold as the

October chill. "Mad! I hate the drunken, abusive pig. That's why I talk about him with such disrespect."

A sheepish smile crossed Gabriel's face because of the way she was talking about her father. "Look, Theresa, I don't really care how you talk about Tiziano," he said. "It's just that I can't believe a woman from Opi would speak like that about her father. I can't stand him, but you're his daughter."

"He is the kind of man who thinks nothing of hitting his wife and daughter. Mamma had to live with that drunken pig for too many years, and like a foolish woman, I also put up with him for too many years. Lord only knows why I waited so long before I made him stop."

"Wow, and I thought I was the only one he hit, but he hits you and Rosa? How did you get him to stop?"

Theresa flipped her head to take the hair away from her eyes. "I was twenty-two the last time he hit me. When he finished, I lifted my battered face, looked Tiziano in the eye, and told him, 'The next time you strike me or Mamma, I will wait for the first night you come home in your drunken stupor, and that is when I will put a knife through your heart.'"

Gabriel smiled nervously. "Oh God no, you really said that to him? What'd he say?"

"You can be sure he was surprised to hear these words from his daughter."

"Do you think Tiziano thought you would really do it?"

"Oh, yes, he knew his daughter very well. Gabriel, you must understand, I take no pride in threatening one of my own family. I'm sorry to say, but my own flesh and blood is a *crudele* (abusive) man. Oh yes, Tiziano knew I meant what I said."

"Did he ever hit you or Rosa again?"

"Is he alive and walking?" asked Theresa. "No, the coward knew he had hit us both for the last time." Gabriel was surprised that Theresa used the word *coward* in reference to her father. "Why do you call him a coward? I've never seen him afraid," he asked her.

Theresa rolled her eyes as if she was becoming frustrated with Gabriel's questions. "Gabriel, I came to this room to speak with you about something very important to me and, I hope, also to you. That man is not part of what I have to say. So, I will answer this one last question, and then no more Tiziano. This will be the last time I speak of him today.

"So you want to know why my father is a coward. I call him a coward because only a coward hits women and children who are not able to defend themselves. Only a coward uses the excuse of watching his son murdered by the Germans to get drunk. Only a cowardly, greedy man would bring to me, his only unmarried daughter, men willing to pay him to marry me. Men who pay money to marry a woman are just like him—ugly drunkards who only want someone to feed them. Then, when their bellies are full, they make themselves feel brave by slapping their wives. My brother, he was brave. He chose to die rather than be a slave to the Nazi dogs. Tiziano begged at the feet of the Germans to save his cowardly, miserable life. Gabriel, your questions have spoiled my mood. I woke up this morning happy, knowing I was prepared to speak with you, but now talking about Tiziano has made me angry. No more about this devil."

"Okay, Theresa, okay. No more Tiziano. But what if your mother found you here alone with me?"

Theresa stood and walked over to the warm wood-burning stove, clasped her arms around herself as though trying to shake the chill from her body, and said, "Aha, Gabriel, I hope you have not destroyed my mood."

Theresa put a few more logs in the wood-burning stove and stared for a time at the red and yellow jumping flames.

Gabriel began to notice for the first time her well-groomed hair and colorful dress, which was cut square in front and showed the skin of her upper chest and the top of her cleavage. The women of Opi did not usually wear such revealing dresses.

Theresa eventually returned to Gabriel at the table. The scowl on her face was gone, but her smile and the warmth of her green eyes had not yet returned. Theresa had facial features that matched her long legs, broad hips, thin waist, and exciting breasts. She was an appealing, long boned, mature woman.

Theresa asked Gabriel, "What is your age, eighteen, nineteen?"

"Oh no, I turned sixteen last month."

"Sixteen? No, you are fooling with me—a muscular man like you with such broad arms and shoulders? I have never seen a man as big and strong as you claim to be only sixteen years."

"Yeah, I am pretty big for my age," said Gabriel, feeling smug.

Theresa was now prepared to explain the reason for her visit. "Gabriel, I'm a thirty-seven-year-old, unmarried woman. At my age,

I don't wish to waste time with small talk, nor do I have the patience to pretend to be someone I'm not. You're very handsome and strong, and you seem like a sweet, gentle man. I'm a vital woman who has warm, passionate blood running through my veins. I want a passionate, gentle man to lie next to me in bed, and I believe you are that man."

Gabriel's eyes grew wide and his sheepish grin immediately returned.

"Gabriel, I can make your hard life here in Opi seem like warm sunshine when you are with me, and I believe you can arouse in me passions that I've only dreamed about. Together we can make both of our dreary lives bright and happy, even if only for short periods of time."

Although Gabriel was only sixteen, he clearly understood what Theresa was suggesting. He had never had sexual intercourse with a girl in Portugal. He had kissed girls and tried to touch their breasts, only to be rebuked. Gabriel had never even seen a naked woman. Now this older, attractive woman wanted to have sex with him. He could not believe what he was hearing.

His disbelief did not interfere with his arousal, yet he was uncertain. He had no experience with women, and was uncertain about how to respond to a grown woman like Theresa. *I'm not sure I'd know what to do,* he thought.

Theresa detected Gabriel's apprehension, and said, "Gabriel, I know my words have taken you by surprise, and if you are doubtful about us being together, remove that thought from your mind."

Theresa slowly took Gabriel's hands in hers and placed the palm of his left hand on her chest above her breasts. Her green eyes had regained their warmth and they showered Gabriel with silent passion. She spoke slowly and in a low tone. "I will show you things you never imagined. I will teach you how our human bodies can make us feel like we can touch the stars and the moon."

Still holding Gabriel's hand on her chest, Theresa leaned forward, forcing the fleshy part of Gabriel's hand to press deeply into her skin. She gently pressed her lips against his for a moment and then leaned back. Gabriel's powerful, compelling urges were boiling, his penis growing erect and hard.

Gabriel was very excited, but still restrained by the thought of Tiziano and Theresa's mother. "What if Tiziano caught us, or even your mother?" he said.

Theresa calmly replied, "As for my mother, she knows I'm here. She wants this happiness for me as much as I do, so be not concerned. As for Tiziano, you know he is at the market every Saturday until one in the afternoon. Every Monday, he attends the meeting of the governing council, and when they finish speaking business, they open their wine and stay at their meeting until late in the night. When he comes home, he can hardly find his bed, let alone find us, so Monday night will be only for you and me. Each Wednesday night he goes to the bar in town. Again he returns late and is unable to find his bed — we often find him in the morning, sleeping in a chair. There are times when he is unable to even reach the chair, and we find him sprawled on the floor. So, my dear Gabriel, for now we have three times a week to relieve our tension and boredom. You can trust me when I say we will not be disturbed, and I can promise heaven for both of us three times a week. For a young man like yourself, you must admit this sounds inviting, no?"

"Yeah, but Theresa, wait a minute. What happens, you know, if you have a baby? I'm afraid Tiziano would actually kill me if I gave you a baby."

Gabriel, Gabriel, I did not think you would put me through all of this — first having to answer all your questions about Tiziano, and now you have fears about things that have already broken my heart. This miserable town has destroyed all my hopes for a real life."

"Theresa, this time it's not the people in Opi — it's Tiziano. You know what he's like. I'm not joking, I think he might kill me if you had a baby and he found out it was from me."

Theresa released her hold on Gabriel's hand, which was resting on her bare upper chest. She slouched in her chair, and her facial expression became sorrowful and no longer tantalizing.

"I s'pose talk of a *bambino* was to be expected. It's just that most Italian men who have a chance to be with a woman don't think of a *bambino*. They think only of their pleasure. But not my Gabriel, no, he inquires about the result of our pleasure. I can see that it's necessary to explain," said Theresa.

"In 1923, I was a twelve-year-old girl living in Opi. I had a terrible pain in my body for two days. Dattore Tatti told my parents he could not help me, and that I should be taken to the hospital in Pecasseroli. I will never forget the long, bumpy ride in the wagon with such pain at each bump. I remember thinking it would take so long to get to the hospital that I would surely die. I thought, *Oh why did I have to live in Opi where there was no hospital, so far away from everything.* That's why I call Opi a miserable town."

When we finally got to the hospital, the doctor said I had appendicitis, and that if I had waited longer, yes I would have died. I did not know it was appendicitis, but after the doctor removed my appendix, he told me the horrible news. My appendix had broken, and I will always remember the two words he used, *gangrene* and *gangrenous.*

The doctor said that when my appendix had broken it died, and since this death stayed in my body so long, the gangrenous material caused an infection that went to the place in a women's body where a bambino grows, and even though he took the dead appendix out of my body, the infection damaged forever this place. My female eggs could no longer get inside the place that grows the bambino. He then told me that I would never be able to be a mamma. How horrible, my life as a woman, over at twelve years old."

Since Gabriel's father was a doctor, he knew a little about the body and how it works. He understood the part about the appendix, but he did not realize a ruptured appendix could make a woman sterile. Trying to be sympathetic, he said, "Why did you feel your life was over. So what if you can't have children, you are still a beautiful woman."

"Gabriel, you're young and not Italian, so you don't understand. There are two types of Italian men. There is one kind of man, a family man, who is willing to marry a woman who can provide him with children. This will satisfy his need to be a papa. Then there is the other kind of man, a selfish man, who only wants a woman to give him pleasure and cook his food. This type of man does not want the responsibility of having children, he is unable to love others. He seeks only his own pleasures. This is the only kind of man who would marry a woman who can never be a mamma. Even at the young age of twelve, I knew a loving family man would never accept me as a wife. So I decided I would rather be a lonely woman than marry a selfish man, and I was right—look at what Tiziano has become.

"We are very much the same, you and I, Gabriel. We are both prisoners in this place. Can you now understand why our union together, even if only a few hours a week, can bring some joy into our lives."

Theresa arose from her chair, took Gabriel's hands, and walked him slowly toward the bed. She sat him down and slowly unbuttoned his shirt. Gabriel couldn't take his eyes off her smiling face, as his body screamed with excitement far beyond any titillation he had ever known. Theresa slowly and deliberately removed his top shirt and then his undershirt, slowly stroking his arms and chest, and gently kissing him. She unbuckled his belt and said, "You do the rest so I can remove my dress."

Gabriel was unable to remove his eyes from Theresa, as he fumbled trying to remove his pants. Theresa, who was now standing before him in her plain cotton brassiere and underwear, was the most exciting sight Gabriel had ever seen. Her smooth olive skin, her firm breasts trying to burst from their support, her underwear, and the delicious jewel he imagined it covered, her round hips and long, thin legs had plunged Gabriel into a trance-like state.

She sat next to him, held his cheeks in her hands, and gave him a long, soft kiss. Theresa's full lips warmed Gabriel's entire body. Bending and slithering her body slowly and smoothly toward the pillow, she moved under the covers, patted the mattress with the palm of her left hand, and said, "Gabriel, this spot is for you. Come next to me. I need you."

Theresa was accurate in everything she had said. Using few words, she was able to teach Gabriel many ways to please and sensually arouse a woman that were also quite pleasing for him. She and Gabriel touched the stars and the moon twice that Saturday morning.

The first week in November, the farmers and their captives went through the procedure of clearing the land of dead vegetation, and then they cleaned, oiled, sharpened, and stored their tools for the winter. The remainder of the month was taken up with wine-making.

December again brought the gathering of wood for the coming winter months. The mules were tied together and taken to the beech tree forest surrounding the mountain range. The heavily armed men were prepared to protect themselves from the killer bears and wild boars as they loaded fallen beech wood into the canvas bags hanging from the sides of the mules. More wood was tied in bundles and rested on the blankets covering the backs of the mules. Some of the dead trees were carefully chopped down, chopped into smaller pieces, and also loaded onto the back of the mules. Five days of wood collecting provided sufficient wood for each Opi family for the coming winter. Chopping wood was one of the major December tasks for the seven boys, along with the other able-bodied men of Opi.

It was now the second Christmas in Opi for the boys. The holiday was celebrated by the preparation for religious rituals rather than festive activities. This Christmas was much easier for six of the boys, as they shared the various Christmas customs of their individual homelands. Omar talked about his Islamic holidays that fell during a different calendar period.

January was devoted to the making and curing of cheese made from sheep and goat milk. February was usually the coldest month in the mountains, and most of the work that needed to be done was accomplished indoors.

On a cold February Sunday in 1949, the young boys met at their usual gathering place, the empty, bombed plot of land on the main cobblestone road. After that first October Saturday, Gabriel had told the other boys about his weekly encounters with Theresa. Even now, four months into the affair, the boys enviously waited to hear about his latest fun in bed with Theresa. They were living vicariously through Gabriel's experiences. Even Omar, who had a religious objection to the affair, listened attentively. Due to the cold, strong wind this Sunday, the boys decided to go to David's room for some warmth.

The seven boys were warming themselves on the floor around the wood-burning stove, and Klein was talking about his wish to get to the snow-covered mountains with a pair of skis.

Omar changed the subject by directing a statement to Gabriel. "Although my religious beliefs force me to disagree with your decision to be with Theresa since you are not married, I do not condemn you. If I had not met my six dear friends and never left my Islamic surroundings, I might have been more judging of your actions. I am learning a great deal from the six of you, and I am a more compassionate human being for knowing you."

Omar was the most serious and intense of the seven captives. He was approximately the same age as the others, and although the seven boys had quickly bonded, Omar initially was not as friendly as the others. However, after a few months of being together on Sundays, he gradually became more comfortable and was very much an integral part of the "Angel Club of Opi."

David continued the discussion, saying, "What I find interesting is how different we are even though we have been living the same life for two years.

Klein asked David to give some examples of what he meant.

"Well, there's one example right there. You're the one who is first to question what people are saying and the things you see. You are always interested in the differences in our cultures and our personalities."

"I'll give you another example," said George. "I don't understand how Dan and Jem can possibly enjoy the company of the wives in their Opi families."

Daniel was the first to respond, "I don't know about Jem, but it took me almost a year of telling myself that I shouldn't like Gelsomina. I would lie in bed at night and think, 'How is it possible for me to enjoy working with a woman who is part of the plot to keep me a prisoner?' Then, at some point, I stopped fighting with myself and decided that if being around her made my life in Opi happier, what the hell, I'd be stupid not to use her. At some point after I was brought here, I said to myself, *I'm not going to say no to any pleasure that happens to come along, even if they are pleasures that I don't understand.*"

George than asked, "What about you, Jem?"

"It sounds like it was a lot easier for me than it was for Dan. Orsolo is such a grouch, but Caterina was just the opposite. I enjoyed being around her. You know how I love to be a tease—well, she enjoys it. When I learned a few more Italian words, I could really make her laugh. I guess she likes to laugh, and no wonder, living with 'Mr. Sour Face.' I wouldn't be surprised if she had never laughed before I was brought here. In the beginning, when I first made Caterina laugh, Orsolo didn't know what to make of it. Then later I could see it made him mad as hell, so that made me want to make her laugh even more."

Jem picked up on the question started by Dave, "And how about Gabe, and the way he enjoys breaking Tiziano's balls every chance he gets, even when he knows he is going to get smacked around for being the ball breaker he is?"

"Yeah, he smacks me around a little, but Theresa is right. He's a coward."

David added, "Boy, I hope he doesn't find out about you and Theresa. No telling what he would do to you."

Gabriel shrugged his shoulders. "The way I look at it, I have him in a corner. If he found out Theresa and I were doing it, what could he do? He can't kick me out of town. He can't kill me or break my knees. If he did, he wouldn't have anyone to help him on the farm. We have a saying in Portugal, '*Aquele que faz a sopa demasiado quente, tem que come-la!* (He who makes the soup too hot has to drink it.)' He brought me here. He is the one who locks me in his house. If he hadn't brought me to Opi, Theresa and I wouldn't be fooling around. Theresa has him so scared that if she came near him with a knife he would probably crap in his pants."

David continued on the theme of individuality. "Omar amazes me. He is so defiant when Nicoangelo tries to take him to church." He turned to Omar and said, "You don't give an inch, no matter what he says or does. Me, I gave up long ago trying to explain my Jewish background. They just can't understand how I can believe in God and not believe that Jesus is the Son of God. More than anything, I go with them to church just to break the monotony of my daily routine."

Omar smiled broadly and said, "And I, my friend, don't understand why you are surprised. I'm only acting as any Egyptian would if they were in a similar situation."

The seven boys were continually surprised at how differently they saw the similar things so relevant to their daily lives. Being bound together by common experiences and isolated in the same environment, they assumed they would react in a similar fashion to their intangible surroundings.

The boys offered each other a social and emotional support system, and it was a resource they learned to value. This sustenance not only helped them endure their captivity, it also made them feel valued as human beings—valued for something more than their ability to perform farm labor. They felt a sense of belonging to a social network that was outside of their strange, unusual existence in Opi.

The seven boys received no formal education beyond what they had received up to 1947. They were fortunate to have this one day a week to be together and learn from each other. In the beginning, they didn't fully comprehend just how important Sundays would become in their lives. As the years continued to drag on, they learned to value the weekly meeting of "The Angel Club of Opi" above all else.

CHAPTER XI

DANNY TRIES TO REUNITE THE BROTHERS

Since the split of the Ciarletta brothers' business, Danny had made numerous efforts to repair the damage caused by Pete's unreasonable and bewildering reaction to the restructuring plans. He decided to make one final attempt at reconciliation between Pete and his three younger brothers. In May 1950, Danny met with Al, Bob, and Phil. After a cheerful greeting and a glass of wine, Danny explained the purpose of his visit.

"I'm here to ask if you would be willing to let Pete rejoin the business."

Al was the first to speak. "Why isn't Pete here talking for himself? Did Pete ask you to come here today?"

"No, this is your oldest brother speaking, and it's my idea. Pete knows nothing about this visit."

Al continued, "Danny, Pete was wrong when he accused me of not doing my share of the work. If it was anyone other than my older brother who said that about me, I don't know what I would have done. Pete hurt me deeply that day, but he's my brother and I love him. My hope is that, in time, when he comes to accept Daniel's disappearance, he'll tell me he's sorry for what he said. So if you're asking me will I stand in the way by asking for an apology before agreeing, no I won't. I know he is not ready for that, but this fact doesn't make him right."

With these words Danny knew the largest hurdle in unifying the brothers had been overcome. Danny arose from his chair, approached Al, hugged him firmly, and said, "Al, you're a great man and a cherished brother."

Danny turned to Bob and Phil. "Let's hear from you two."

Bob spoke first. "I've always loved and respected Pete, but when Daniel disappeared, he changed. What a burden the man has to bear, and I have nothing but sympathy for my brother. I would not stand in the way of his returning to the business. I only hope that someday he'll become the Pete we all once knew. Let me also say I'm a practical man. We could use another hand who knows our business the way Pete does. I wouldn't even mind if he came back as leader. Look, Danny, to tell'ya the truth, business is booming, and we've been dividing the leadership responsibilities among the three of us. I think we could use his help, and as the second oldest brother—even after what happened—why not let him take his rightful place as the head of the business."

Danny reached over and squeezed Bob's hand. "You're not only a good brother, but also a wise one."

Danny now looked at Phil with renewed confidence. "Well, my youngest brother, let me hear from you."

Phil responded in a similar fashion. "Danny, I remember when I came to America as a young boy. I wanted to work right away and make money, but you refused—you made me go to school and learn English. Pete would slip me money on the side during those years while I was living with Bob and Al. I'm obligated to all of you for my life in this country, and also to Pete for his kindness. And how can I forget how Pete protected us during those dangerous days on the streets of the Bronx. I'll not object to him leading us once again. And there's another thing. I know he's too proud to ever admit it, but I think it would be good medicine for him to come back as leader. So I say, let's make it happen."

Danny smiled broadly and tapped Phil's hand. "My baby brother doesn't forget the deeds of his older brother. Bob and Phil mentioned leadership. Al, are you willing to accept Pete's leadership?"

"Danny, if Pete's willing to accept the fact that ice, coal, and sawdust are things of the past and agrees that heating oil is the future for our business, yeah, I'd gladly accept his leadership. He was a hell of a leader in the early years, and there's no reason why he can't do it now."

Al hesitated for a moment, reached for his wine, and finished what remained in his glass. With a more serious tone in his voice, he said, "Bob, Phil, there is one thing you must be prepared for. If Pete comes back, and if at any time he says one word, just one word, about me not pulling my weight, then older brother or not, I'm telling him to stick it and either he goes or I go. That means you two will be forced to make a choice: Pete or me. I'll tell you now, I won't stand for that crap a second time and that's final. They'll be no talkin', no negotiatin', no misunderstandin', and no telling me he's not the same man we once knew. No nothin'. One bad word about me from Pete, and I'll look at you two—and you'll have to say "goodbye Al" or "goodbye Pete," right then and there. It's gonna be as simple as that. I'll expect your answer: me or Pete."

Bob and Phil looked at each other and Bob spoke first. "Well, Phil, for me the choice is pretty easy. Pete walked out on us so I gotta stick with Al."

Phil also agreed. "God, it would be a hell of a thing telling my oldest brother I don't want him, but you're right, Bob, we would have to stand with Al."

Danny, understanding the risk, was not about to let anything scuttle the deal. He was pleased with the attitude of his brothers and understood their positions.

"All right, now that I know where you guys stand," said Danny. "I'll speak to Pete and arrange a meeting. Here's what I have in mind. Give me coupl'a weeks to talk with him about hooking back up with the business. I'll tell him I came here today and talked to the three of you about him rejoining the business, and the fact that business is booming. I'll make sure he understands it's strictly heating oil delivery, and that you want him back handling the leadership responsibilities.

"Danny, there's one thing that doesn't square with me," interrupted Al. "It's not that we want him back as leader, but that we agreed to take him back as leader."

Danny was disturbed by Al's clarification. "Is it that important for you to be so picky with the words?"

"Yeah, Danny, it feels important to me."

"Okay, I'll make it work your way."

Danny explained the remainder of his plan. "In the meantime, Suzy and Kate will invite the whole family for Easter Sunday like it used to be on Beach Avenue—the five brothers, our families, everyone together again, like before…before we lost Daniel."

It was still difficult to speak of his namesake and favorite nephew. He fought back the lump in his throat and continued, "Remembering the good times should put everyone in a good mood. After the meal, the five of us will go to my apartment, and based on what you've said today, I expect Ciarletta and Sons will be complete once again. We can then walk up to Pete's apartment in agreement. Suzy and Kate will make sure the table is cleared and the cards and gallon of wine are set up for our Boss and Underboss card game."

"Danny, you're the only one who can pull this off," said Al. "Pete respects you more than anyone else in this world; only you can make it work for all of us." The men warmly embraced and Danny returned to Clason Point by bus.

Danny spent the following weeks talking with Pete about meeting with his three younger brothers, and how they all agreed that he could be an asset to the business in these good times. Danny stressed the need for Pete's guidance and leadership. Danny understood his younger brother better than anyone—he knew appealing to Pete's old swagger would be very seductive.

"Your brothers need your leadership. The business needs you."

"For you, Danny, I'm willing to listen to what they have to say, but I'm not sure that our history will allow us to be as we were in the past," said Pete.

"Ah, Pete, forget history," Danny pleaded. "Your brothers have forgotten, and they want you back. That's all the damn history you need to know."

Danny stopped with that statement. His strategy was not to push too hard now, but rather to let the three brothers express themselves as they had in Al's apartment. Danny felt that once Pete was welcomed back as leader, the issue of pride and honor, which were important elements for Pete, would allow him to return with his dignity intact.

Danny, Pete, and their families went to early Mass on Easter Sunday at Holy Cross Church. When they returned, Suzy and Kate began to prepare for the arrival of the family. There was a feeling of excitement as the preparations proceeded. Danny and Pete put extra leaves in the dining room table, which now extended from wall to wall in the small apartment. Danny assured Suzy there would be enough room for everybody. The wives had been praying that today would be the day the families would be reunited. Suzy and Kate were determined to make their preparations have the same feel as the old days on Beach Avenue: antipasti, a pasta dish covered with Ciarletta gravy, and roasted chicken with sausage stuffing, vegetables, nuts, and fruit, topped off with espresso and Aunt Kate's cream puffs.

Suzy knew Daniel had been missing for three years and two months, because she kept a calendar hidden in a clothes drawer of her bedroom dresser. If Daniel could not be with her, perhaps her husband might return to her today. This was an intention Suzy felt she could pray for.

Danny, on the other hand, was banking on this festive occasion to get Pete in the proper mood for their after-dinner meeting with the brothers. Their approaches might have been different, but their objective was the same — return Pete to the family through the business.

Everyone arrived, the greetings were festive, and the food was placed on the extended table. The adults were in the dining room, the children in the kitchen. Danny observed Pete closely. Pete greeted his brothers politely, almost shyly, and his brothers, not sure what to expect, were subdued but smiling broadly. Pete had not spoken to them since the breakup of the business two and a half years ago. Danny was overjoyed at the low key but cordial reception Pete gave his brothers. He had every expectation that Pete would become more engaged and cheerful as the dinner progressed.

The meal was savory, the company joyful, and everyone was recalling the good days of the past on Beach Avenue. They had been cautioned, prior to the visit, not to mention Daniel's name. Danny continued to observe the demeanor of his brother. Pete seemed to be enjoying himself and took part in the conversation. Danny could not have been more pleased. Pete was seated at one end of the table with Suzy on his left, followed by her sisters and their husbands. Danny was seated next to Pete on his right, followed by Kate and the other brothers and their wives. This was how it used to be on Beach Avenue. The dinner concluded, the plates were removed, and nuts and fruit were brought to the table. As in the past, Kate and Suzy were in the kitchen preparing espresso and the cream puffs. The happy guests were at the table engaged in conversation and genial banter as they enjoyed the nuts and fruit, anticipating their espresso. The children had gone outside to play.

Grace, Suzy's twin sister, with her back to the open kitchen door, turned her head and with a broad smile and in a jovial tone, yelled out to the kitchen, "Hey, Suzy, don't eat all the cream puffs, okay? Remember, to save some for us!"

Pete suddenly stood up from his place at the head of the table. Staring at Grace, he shouted, "I've had enough of your uppity, better than anyone else manner. If you want cream puffs, why aren't you in the kitchen helping your two sisters? You have always thought yourself better than anyone else, with your important job, fancy clothes, fancy apartment, always too good for this family. Well, that ends as of now! You have eaten my food for the last time. Emile, take your wife out of my home, and, Grace, know that you're not welcome back in my house."

Suzy and Kate stood frozen at the counter as they heard the outburst coming from the dining room. Grace, after an initial moment of disbelief, ran from the living room in tears to the bedroom to get her jacket, which was lying among all the coats on Suzy and Pete's bed. The others at the table sat in silence not sure what to do. Emile, choosing not to confront Pete, slowly arose from his seat to attend to his wife. Suzy was now in the living room, trying not to show anger as she attempted to convince her husband that the playful comment was a harmless joke. She begged him to go to Grace and apologize.

Pete sat in silence, his rigid body told his wife he was refusing her appeal. Suzy, knowing Pete better than anyone, accepted that the damage was beyond repair. Although she was furious, she did not allow her anger to become apparent. Instead she calmly looked at Pete, making sure he was looking directly at her, and rather sympathetically said, "My husband is lost. His life no longer holds any meaning. He has destroyed himself and now his family. Pete, I hope you can hear what I am saying. You have left me and entered a different place. God have mercy on your tormented soul."

With that, Suzy turned and slowly walked into the kitchen.

Danny moved to the hallway and begged Grace to stay until he had a chance to speak with Pete. "Grace, this has been a terrible misunderstanding. Let me speak with Pete. Once he understands you were just teasing, I'm sure he'll apologize."

"Danny, you know I would do anything for you. I love you like you were my own family, but I'm afraid Pete is in no mood to listen to reason. I know he's suffering because of Daniel, but it's clear he will not listen to reason, not even from you. Besides, I'm too embarrassed and hurt by what he said to go back to his dining room. I'm afraid Pete will never be the same now that Daniel is gone forever."

Danny heard the words spoken out loud for the first time— *Daniel is gone forever*—the words he had been denying since 1947. He put his arms around Grace and Emile and began to cry. Grace's tears soon followed.

After a moment, Danny composed himself. He knew it was time to get Pete ready for the meeting with his brothers. When he returned to the silent dining room, Suzy's sisters were in the kitchen trying to console her and Kate. Pete's body was taut and wooden, as he sat sipping his wine and glaring straight ahead. Al, Bob, and Phil were making small talk with their wives as they waited for Danny to return, unsure what to do or say.

As Danny moved toward Pete, he stood up and said, "My brothers, maybe it's best you and your wives also leave."

Danny countered his brother's request. "No, they can't leave. We're still going to have our business meeting."

Pete spoke directly to Danny. "No, Danny, I am not interested— it can never be the same." Next he turned to his younger brothers and said, "Whatever you wanted to say to me today won't change our past. You made your decision years ago by your actions. You'll now have to live with that decision and get along without me."

"No, Pete, you're upset. You don't mean what you're saying," said Danny.

"I know you mean well, Danny, but my mind is made up. There can be no going back to the past. This matter is closed forever."

The three brothers and their wives arose from the table without speaking and walked to the kitchen to say good-by to the Gallo sisters. Then they went to Danny and gave him a warm embrace. Al turned away without looking at Pete, and Bob and Phil said goodbye to Pete without shaking hands. Pete nodded his head in their direction. The three brothers and their families left the apartment without another word.

CHAPTER XII

𝒯HE 𝓔DUCATION OF THE 𝓐NGELS

In April 1950, the seven Angels were back in the valley to begin their fourth year of forced farming. With the recent warmer weather, the hostages had been spending their Sundays outside, strolling around the small town and sitting together in the empty lot that had been bombed during the war. Klein was especially pleased to be outdoors on Sundays, referring to the air of Opi as "delicious Italian mountain air."

On this Sunday, after their first week in the fields, the conversation turned to one of their favorite subjects—America. After three years, Daniel was used to the many questions about his homeland, an experience which had begun with his Italian cousins in Castellamare di Stabia. He was happy to talk about his American life to his fellow captives, who seemed so interested, because it made him, for that moment, less homesick. Daniel noticed that his friends were disappointed when he attempted to clarify the many misconceptions about his country. Daniel came to understand how important American culture and practices were for non-American youngsters.

As the Angels strolled toward the church to sit in the sun, George asked Daniel, "You often talk about the business your father owns. Is he an American capitalist?"

Daniel's lack of knowledge about world events became evident once again when he had to ask, "What's a capitalist?"

Gabriel said, "Now, Dan, stop bullshitting us. Everybody knows about American capitalists and the wealth they have accumulated. C'mon, you don't have to feel bad because your father is a capitalist. Hell, it ain't nothin' you did."

Daniel felt embarrassed that here was yet another unfamiliar word. "Honest, guys, I never heard that word. In America, we refer to people who own a business as *businessmen*. My family isn't wealthy—we own a house in a regular neighborhood, not a mansion somewhere."

Omar tried to clarify the word for Daniel. "I believe the word *capitalist*, in Europe and my part of the world, is used to describe American businessmen who abuse their workers by paying them very small wages and treating them like slaves. Tell us—is this a correct description of an American *businessman*?"

"From what I know, that ain't right. America doesn't have slaves. We had a civil war to end that," replied Daniel.

Omar immediately interrupted him. "Your people may no longer own slaves in America, but is it not true that in some parts of your land, the American Negro is not allowed to go to school, cannot drink from the same water spouts as his white brothers, and cannot gather with whites? The thing that most angers people in my part of the world is that Americans boast about their democracy but try to hide the fact that not all their people are truly equal."

Daniel, feeling defensive, responded, "In the southern part of America, yeah, some of the things you said are true. Maybe there are some people in America who don't like Negroes, but there are plenty of others who are okay with Negroes and work with them. But one thing you said is wrong—Negro kids are allowed to go to school, even in what we call the South. They just go to their own schools."

Daniel thought for a moment and had to retreat a bit in his argument. "You know, Omar, I guess I have to agree in part with what you're saying. I once had a teacher who told us that Negro schools in some southern states of America aren't as good as the white schools in those same states." Daniel felt his face grow red with embarrassment. "Look, Omar, I love America, but I don't know why Negroes are treated badly. I just don't know why."

"Could that be part of the problem?" said Omar. "You don't know why the American Negro is not equal to the American white citizen." Daniel gave Omar a confused look but didn't respond to his question.

Daniel, who was now feeling more embarrassed than defensive, said, "Well, I guess I should know, but I don't. I lived in a neighborhood with all white kids. I don't know any Negro kids. For all I know, maybe the whites did keep them out of my neighborhood. I just never thought about why no black kids lived there. Maybe white people made it happen that way, I don't know. Omar, if what you say is true, then I guess I just don't know why."

"I have come to know you have a good heart, Dan, so I am not blaming you. I feel that many people in countries with a white population have been conditioned by the wealthy class to leave their eyes closed so they can continue with their greed to gather more wealth, which gives them more power. The British came to my country, inhabited our land, and told us how to live. They justified their crime of plundering by saying that Egyptian people needed to be civilized and they tried to teach us their ways. Yet in British history books it is written that Egypt was the beginning of civilization for mankind. So how could we be uncivilized? They sent well-meaning holy men to our country to give us their God and his teachings. They did the same thing in Africa and in the Middle East. The British entered countries they believed were inhabited by people who were inferior to them, thinking that if they gave us their God and their ways we would become civilized. Our people tried to explain that we want the God we have and that our different ways do not make us uncivilized, they just make us different. They chose not to listen, and because of this many innocent people died—both the British and my countrymen."

Omar then turned the discussion back to American history. "Dan, did not the founding fathers of your country proclaim that all men are created equal with inalienable rights? As they were writing this down in their Constitution documents, they owned black slaves from Africa. Is this not proof that your country's founders chose to accept black men and women as creatures who were not equal to them, creatures who they did not see as human beings? Why was this?"

Without hesitating, Omar answered his own question. "It happened because if black men and women were less than human, then it would be acceptable to use them to make their owners wealthy. Even among us here in Opi, is it not true that there are no Italian boys as captives, only foreigners? It's my belief that when we were captured if they dragged a boy into a car and he spoke Italian, they stopped and let him out. The people of Opi, like the British and Americans, feel justified in enslaving others who in their minds are different and therefore inferior."

It was clear that Omar was well schooled on the topic of black versus white, as well as the topic of slavery. He finished by saying, "In Modern Arabic, the word 'abd' refers to the designation of a person as a slave, and it's often used when referring to dark-skinned people. It's disruptive to all cultures that people in many countries decide that a person who has dark skin can easily be considered the property of another person and can be sold and traded like cattle or tools."

The boys were quiet when Omar finished. His intensity had made Daniel and the others uncomfortable. They had learned to respect Omar's mind and his worldliness, and none of them disagreed with him.

Gabriel had been waiting to enter the conversation, and he broke the momentary silence by explaining how America is perceived in Portugal. "I don't know history like Omar, so I don't know much about black people in America. When my family talks about America, they get angry because Americans brag about how great their government is and how they think every country in the world should be a democracy like theirs. Then the next day you read about how America is supporting a dictator because he promises to help them. My father would always say, 'If a dictator helps America, then he is called a *good* dictator.' Most citizens of Portugal think Americans have a great land, but they think the American government is phony!"

The discussion of slavery always had a special meaning for the seven hostages. They were living examples of the subject. They had a personal understanding of the emotional side of slavery, minus the physical abuse or disfigurement that is so often a part of the master-slave relationship.

David talked about slavery and how it might apply to the seven of them. "Y'know, Omar has reminded me of something I've often wondered. Why do some people find it so easy to beat and mutilate a slave, but at the same time they're kind and generous to friends and even strangers? People who act like that must not see dark-skinned people as humans—possibly they see them as animals. Why else would people so easily mutilate a dark-skinned person and then be kind to others who have white skin? Think of the way animals are treated. Aren't they often made to do things by causing them pain? I wonder if the people of Opi see us as animals. Do you think they expect us to one day become trained like their other animals? They don't always hit us, but we're all in pain just by being held here. I think they know that. Are we being slowly trained? We oughta think 'bout this and remember to keep telling each other we're good people—we're human beings—and no matter how long they hold us, we can't let them make us feel like we're not persons."

There was silence once again after David had spoken, as though an important, critical decision had been commonly made in silence.

Daniel broke the silence by saying in a thoughtful manner, "I know one thing....when I get back home, I'm gonna understand how the black people in America feel. Since I've been in Opi, the one thing I've learned is what it feels like not to have any control."

David immediately interrupted. "Dan, that's the word, *control*! We have no control over things. You're right, that's what bugs me—I have no choices."

Omar once again added to the conversation by introducing a concept he had been pondering. "Have you noticed whenever we talk about our Opi families, we refer to them as *your* Vincenzo or *my* Nicoangelo. The way we use the word *your* or *my* before our Opi family's name is how you might expect a pet animal to speak about his owner if the animal could talk. I think it shows, in some way, that Dave's thought needs to be always remembered."

The boys discussed many topics during their free Sundays together. Daniel had never experienced the effects of war, except for some rationing, and he was most interested in learning about living conditions during wartime. He would often ask Jem and George to tell stories of their experiences during World War II. Jem was a good storyteller, but his World War II stories always seemed to end with the same theme: The British people were pleased to have American help in fighting Hitler, but if America hadn't entered the war, the British people would have eventually beaten Germany. Daniel, who lacked an understanding of the historical specifics of the war in Europe, never disputed Jem's conclusion, but the other European boys were usually quick to challenge Jem.

Gabriel would often say, "Jem, you're crazy. Without the Americans, the Germans would've kicked your asses!"

George would then come to Jem's defense, "Gabe, Jem and I may have been kids during the war, but we were there. I'm not saying we didn't appreciate the help we received from the Americans, but for sure we would've eventually beaten the Germans on our own."

David entered the conversation by supporting Gabriel's point of view. "In Switzerland we heard that because of the constant bombing and the buzz bombs, the poor British people were close to the breaking point."

"Poor British people, my ass," Jem replied sarcastically. "That may be what you heard, but George and I lived in the war. Let me tell you, the bombing only made us more stubborn and determined to eventually kill that bastard Hitler."

Jem continued, explaining how he and his friends had responded to the German bombing. "The morning after an air raid alert, we would leave early for school so we could explore the buildings and houses that had been destroyed the night before by a direct hit from a bomb. I remember how the rubble would be all wet from the fire hoses that had put out the fires. The real fun was to grab a piece of broken wood or a piece of destroyed pipe and walk through the broken walls, piles of bricks, with broken glass all around, looking for things that weren't broken up. One time I remember seeing a white sink that had been knocked loose from its base but had not been broken. It was just lying on the floor. Using a piece of broken pipe, I began smashing that sink until it was in small pieces like everything else around it. We had a lot of fun breaking up everything before and after school."

"Why was that fun?" asked Omar.

Jem hesitated, shrugged his shoulders, and said, "I dunno. I guess it was just fun."

He recalled his behavior and was able to tell the others about it, but he was unable to answer Omar's penetrating question. Although he was now years away from his childhood war experience, he also silently wondered what he and his friends found enjoyable about destroying things that had survived the vast, wanton destruction of the night bombing.

George then asked Jem, "Hey, did you and your blokes go looking for odd pieces of shrapnel after the bombings? I once found a piece of shrapnel that looked just like a bird. One time when my dad was home on leave, he told me that he heard about a lad in London who found a piece of shrapnel that looked just like one of the German bombers."

Klein was curious about the stories he had heard regarding the treatment of Jews by Hitler during the war. "Is it true that Germany had camps where they killed Jewish people?"

Daniel was the least familiar with the events surrounding the Holocaust, so he encouraged David to explain what he had been told. When David was finished telling the stories that had been told to him by his parents, the boys were both intrigued and horrified. They had come to know David as someone who did not exaggerate or lie, and for this reason the boys accepted David's explanation, even though the atrocities sounded unbelievable.

David had a confused look on his face when he finished, and he asked the other boys a question. "Hey guys, can I talk to you about something that has been bothering me?"

"Sure, why not?" said Jem. The others nodded in agreement.

"After my first year or so here in Opi, I began to wonder if the history of my people had anything to do with how I think and feel here in Opi, especially at night. When I am lying in bed unable to sleep, I often think of the long history of my people, who were in and out of captivity for generations. I wondered if this history has made me more accepting of my time on this mountain. I listen to you guys talk about how angry you are at being held prisoner, yet I'm not sure I feel the same. There are so many questions that have bothered me since I was brought here: Is it because I'm Jewish that I feel differently than you? Do I easily accept my time in Opi because of my ancestors? Was I chosen to join you in Opi because I am a Jew?" Is it possible that some Jew must always be held a prisoner somewhere in this world? I don't believe these things are true, yet that's all I seem to think about."

The others were surprised at the confusion of their friend. They were unable to understand the dilemma David had expressed, because the idea of accepting their life in Opi was contradictory to everything they knew and felt. Yet it seemed that David perceived his incarceration differently. They all used different words, but their responses were similar, clear, and definite. David's captivity was an egregious evil act, and for him to consider his imprisonment as preordained was not only offensive, it was beyond their understanding.

Klein was especially disturbed that David would even consider such questions; unfortunately, he did not have the legal, philosophical, or religious comprehension to respond more effectively, so he answered David the only way he knew how. "We were all in the wrong place at the wrong time, David. It's as simple as that. If you think because you're Jewish that makes it okay for these Italians to hold you prisoner, that's nuts." Still David wondered, and the limited knowledge and preparation for such a complicated question did not allow the other captives to be of much help to him.

One Sunday in the spring of 1951, soon after they had started their fifth year of farming, the boys had built their usual fire on a brisk day in the empty, bombed-out lot. Klein was making *palatschinken* pancakes on his improvised grill with ingredients contributed by the other boys. These pancakes are regarded as the national dish of Austria, and Klein was proud of the fact that they were invented in his home city of Linz.

As they were enjoying their pancake snack, Daniel brought up a topic that had been troubling him. "Guys, is it just me, or do you also think the people in Opi act as though we are lepers?"

George was the first to respond to Daniel's observation. "I think I know what you mean. I've noticed how the people don't wanna look at me. They act like I'm some sort of invisible ghost."

Omar added, "I think the people of Opi are uncomfortable when they see me. It might be the color of my skin and my different heritage that makes them so uneasy."

The others assured Omar they all experienced similar treatment. The captives concluded this behavior was the result of the heavy guilt that stirred within the people each time they saw one of their Angels.

Over the years, the boys discussed many topics and would often have lively discussions as they ate their delicious pancakes.

The weather in Opi from early spring to early fall was always invigorating, and the people spent Sundays during this time of year strolling, socializing, and visiting each others' homes. The seven boys spent their Sundays in the empty lot on Via San Giovanni de Battista. This place became their unofficial hangout. During the first few years, when the residents of Opi passed the empty lot, they were inclined to ignore the presence of the captives, looking straight ahead, pretending they were deep in conversation, and always walking with a hurried step.

Then, in the fall of 1950, a change in the routine occurred when a group of young girls passed the boys. The hurried step was no longer evident—the girls moved slowly, smiling and giggling, and their behavior encouraged the boys to ask the girls to join them. Early on, the invitation was never accepted, although it did not prevent the girls from frequently walking up and down Via San Giovanni de Battista and passing the empty lot. After a while, Gabriel and Jem refused to accept "no" to their invitation, and they would pursue the girls down the road.

"Oh, we are not permitted to be with you. Our fathers would not approve," said the girls.

By the end of the fifth year, the girls, presumably no longer bound by their fathers' orders, stopped to talk—first on walks along the road and eventually sitting down and chatting with the boys in the empty lot. By the end of the sixth year, the boys and girls were allowed to walk together for longer and longer periods of time. They were now on their way to becoming young men and women, and with the social restrictions now greatly eased, Marisa, Jem's unofficial but still guarded girlfriend, would bring female friends to visit. The escorts now had the dual role of being prison guards and chaperones. This unique supervision prevented hand holding, arms around waists, cheek kissing, and many other things on the minds of the boys—and perhaps on the minds of some of the girls. The escorts would order a girl back to her family if they noticed any physical contact that seemed even slightly provocative.

By the summer of 1956, the seven boys had blossomed from teenagers into young men. Jem and Daniel were now twenty-two years old. Jem remained slender and had grown to over six feet tall. His thin blond hair had darkened. Daniel's teenage body fat had changed into firm muscle. He had grown in confidence and personal maturity, but he was still somewhat reticent.

Gabriel, George, and Klein were twenty-three. Gabriel was a muscular man with an outgoing, pleasant personality. George had changed very little in physical appearance and personality. In 1947, he was a quiet, cautious teenager, and now in 1956 he was a quiet, cautious young man.

Klein, who was a handsome teenager when he first arrived in Opi, was now a strikingly handsome figure of a man with delicate facial features and thick, golden blond hair. Klein's personality remained reserved, but his six Opi brothers had helped him grow emotionally.

Omar was twenty-four. He was almost as tall as Jem and had a slender, strong body and a sensitive, intuitive personality.

David, the oldest, was twenty-five. He often seemed awkward because of his large-framed body. David was mature for his age and wielded a considerable amount of influence among his fellow prisoners.

They had arrived in Opi as young adolescents and were now young mature adults. Going through their formative years with only each other, and dealing with the many physical and emotional changes during this period, had been a difficult process.

August always brought the most pleasant weather in the mountains. One mild, sunny Sunday, as they sat in the empty, bombed-out lot, Daniel turned the conversation to the subject of his virginity. "I often wonder if I was free and back home, would I be married? I was always a little shy around girls, and given my strict Catholic schooling with the priest and nuns always saying how sinful it is to have sex until you are married, I betcha I would be just as I am now, never knowing what it is like to have sex with a woman."

Jem said, "The mistake you're makin' is if you were home and had the chance to be around American girls, talkin' to them, going to dances, or whatever you American blokes do to meet girls, you might not be as shy as you think."

"Oh, I don't know...knowing the way I am, well, I just don't know."

The subject made George nervous, and he asked Daniel, "What happens when you see a girl and you get excited? It seems as though all I think about is being with a girl, and when Gabe tells us about his time with Theresa, I get, uh... now don't laugh, okay? But you know what I mean....It starts getting a little hard just by listening to him talk about her."

George, who was now blushing, continued, "I'll tell you, Dan, I don't know how I'm going to make it if we are here a coupl'a more years. You say if you were home you probably wouldn't be having sex. What would you do? You know what I mean, how would you control yourself?"

The question had been asked, and Daniel wished he had never brought up the subject. He was embarrassed, but he had to say something. With a self-conscious grin on his face, Daniel said, "Ah hell, George, why did you have to ask me that?"

"Sorry, Dan, I didn't mean to put you on the spot. It was just... well...I guess I'm glad someone finally talked about it. Forget it; just forget I said anything. I probably said more than I should have."

David entered the two-way conversation. "Look, Dan, what makes you think you're the only one with these feelings? David looked at Gabe and with a wide grin said, "Except for you know who."

David continued, "It would be good for all of us if someone had the guts to talk about it. How about it, Dan? Maybe you could help the rest of us."

Gabriel jumped into the conversation. "Hey, Dan, I'm not embarrassed to talk about Theresa and me. It's okay. C'mon, if you can't talk with us after all these years, who the hell can you talk to?"

Daniel felt much more comfortable, now that his friends seemed so supportive and encouraging, and he decided to continue. "Well, as a Catholic, it's...oh, it's...well, you know, doing it with yourself is a real bad sin. So, I go to confession to Father Mascia. He tells me not to do it again, but in my gut I know that in a week or so—some night in bed when I'm feeling miserable and lonely—the urge gets so strong that I can't help myself. All I know is the relief is unbelievable. Just before it happens, a tingle starts in my ankles and travels up through my whole body, and when it happens, I shake all over. I can't believe Father Mascia really expects me never to do it. I don't know about him, but it's something I have no control over."

"You're being too tough on yourself, Dan. I do it, too. It is part of human nature," said Omar. Daniel was pleased that Omar had entered the conversation. He had been interested in asking Omar a question for a long time. "I hope you don't get mad if I ask you this, Omar, but does *your* holy man say it's a sin to do it?"

"No, Dan, he doesn't."

"God, you're so lucky."

"Good show, Dan," said George. "It was first-rate that you were able to talk about it. I feel a whole lot better. I didn't know what to say or how to say it, so I didn't wanna bring up the subject, but thanks to you I'm not feeling so, so, what's the word?"

"Strange? Embarrassed?" said David.

The boys, who were now clearly men, were forced to sort out their manhood with no adult guidance, no experience to fall back on, and no one who had been through the difficult process of leaving one stage of life to enter the next. Although Gabriel was enjoying sex with a much older woman, even he was often confused. Perhaps, at some level, he was even more confused than his celibate companions. They had no way of halting the process, nor did they have any access to adult counseling. They had only each other to learn from. Their physical and psychological growth presented them with manhood, and the only way they were able to confront this natural process was through trial and error, and talking with each other about their successes and frequent failures.

Maturity was a frequent and important topic. They felt a certain strength and resolve, even though they had no way of understanding the enormous intricacy of going from childhood to manhood. They were now men, and they felt normal and whole in spite of their abnormal life. They had not been defeated; in fact, they were now even more determined that someday, somehow, they would have normal lives.

When the seven boys became men, something also happened to the makeup of the group. They knew beyond any doubt they were as one. They had complete trust in each other. They could not lie to one another—truth somehow had become hallowed, sacred, and they intuitively knew this bond would remain, even in freedom.

However, one question continually seemed to surface, although they had difficulty articulating its existence. How were they able to maintain their sanity? They used words such as madness, insaneness, saneness, mental balance, crazy, and going nuts. Omar used the phrase soundness of mind. One thing was clear: they knew they were sane, but the issue of insanity lurked as a dark cloud somewhere in their consciousness.

One cold, windswept Sunday afternoon in the winter of 1956, the seven captives were enjoying the warmth of the woodstove in Klein's room, when George returned to the question of his fear of eventually going crazy.

"I'm frightened that if we can't escape this town soon we will all lose our minds—and I think I'll be the first to experience what it means to go crazy. I'm afraid I won't be me anymore."

Gabriel responded abruptly, forcing George to momentarily stop his train of thought.

"Why do you always have to look at our life in this place as hopeless? You talk like we are doomed. Why don't you try to laugh more, and try keeping the good thoughts in your head, rather than always thinking the worst?"

"My way of life has been taken from me, my heritage, my friends and family, the plans my parents had for me," said George. "I don't know about the rest of you, but I've gradually come to understand the harm of being forced to live an unnatural life. Six days a week, I'm surrounded by a place and people who make me uncomfortable. Thank God I have you guys on Sundays. If you think I don't smile often enough, God only knows what I'd be like if I was here alone."

"George, George, I feel the same as you," said Omar. "I have been taken from my natural life, but right after being taken in Italy I decided it was necessary for me to hold hope in my body. If not, I felt I would soon die."

The conversation ended uncomfortably, when George said, "Yeah you're right. It's just so hard for me."

By the time they went to the valley in the early spring of 1956, the boys had formed a bond of friendship that was unbreakable. George and Jem were able to understand the Egyptian's dislike for their country, and Omar felt no personal bitterness toward Jem and George because of where they had been born. David and Omar talked frequently about their cultural and religious differences without the animosity that might be expected. Daniel was not detested because he was born in a country viewed by the others as the world's "bully." The six boys were not jealous of Gabriel because of his desirable liaison; rather, they were pleased for him. Klein was supported by the others, growing at his own pace, and eventually becoming confident and self-assured. Was it the nature of the boys that made them so tolerant and understanding, or was it the circumstance of their captivity that shaped their unbreakable bond?

Jem had a saying that always sounded comical in Italian because of his strong Welsh accent. "*Siamo compagni per la vita.* (We are mates for life.)" They promised they would always be there for each other, always and forever.

The summer of 1956 passed uneventfully and in late October, the mountain air was clear and brisk. The captives and a group of four girls were strolling and talking about customs in their various countries, when one of the girls, Giovanna Fincantieri, slipped a piece of folded paper in Klein's jacket pocket.

Klein felt a hand going into his pocket—startled, he looked at Giovanna. She simply blinked her eyes and separated herself from Klein before he could question her actions, moving forward to join two other girls. Dusk soon arrived, and the young men and women returned to their individual homes and rooms.

Once he was alone, the first thing Klein did was unfold the paper Giovanna had passed to him earlier in the afternoon. Written in pencil on lined paper, was her personal message to him:

"Klein, I would like to know you better. I hope you don't think me foolish, but I would be willing to come to your stable area. I am able to leave my house on Wednesdays and Fridays after dinner, and I would like to visit you on those evenings. My parents will not know I will be with you, and I can stay for only an hour and fifteen minutes. If you also would like to know me, then I will come to your gated animal shelter, so we can talk together. I will pass your meeting place next Sunday at four in the afternoon. If you prefer me not to come by your shelter, do not look up as I pass. If you would like my company, wave your hand when you see me pass. Make sure you do not go to the road to speak with me. I prefer to draw no attention of the men who follow you on Sundays."

Klein read the note one more time, making sure he was reading the Italian correctly.

Giovanna Fincantieri was a petite young woman of nineteen, but she could easily pass for a much younger adolescent. She combed her hair back and tied it together just above her shoulders. In Opi, a woman's hair was either straight or curly, and tied in the back, made into a bun, or hung casually over her shoulders. A coiffed hairdo was unknown in the rural mountain town. Giovanna was a rather average young Opi teenager, in both appearance and intelligence. She had delicate round hips and shoulders, smooth olive skin, and round facial features. She was a pleasant but undistinguished young girl, that is, until she spoke. Her light, tender voice was able to turn the lovely Italian language into lyrical song. When Giovanna spoke, everyone was delighted, not so much for what she said, but how the sounds of her words made listeners feel as though they were hearing beautiful romantic music.

Giovanna had become infatuated with the handsome, blond-haired Austrian boy, who possessed a kind of shyness that made her feel comfortable. Although Giovanna was troubled by her out-of-character assertiveness—initiating a personal relationship with a young man—she nevertheless was willing to risk the embarrassment of rejection. Were her actions a rescue fantasy, a need to mature, a grandiose scheme to defy her papa, or simply an unrecognized desire to defy the cultural laws of Opi? In the end, none of these questions mattered. She felt only the sensual excitement of being with the beautiful blond stranger, an infatuation with a young man trapped behind an iron gate.

Klein did not feel comfortable mentioning the note and the fact that Giovanna would be passing the empty lot at four this Sunday. The other captives decided to walk to the piazza behind the church that afternoon, and Klein said he would meet them there later.

Gabriel began to tease Klein without knowing how accurate he was. "Klein is going to secretly meet a girl, and he doesn't want us to steal her."

"Aha, c'mon, you guys, you know there's no girl. I had a hard week, and I just want to sit for a while in the sun and relax. I'll meet you at the piazza later."

"Oh, poor Klein, he had such a hard week he needs a nap," Jem said humorously, messing Klein's hair. The six boys went off, enjoying their little laugh at Klein's expense.

On schedule, Giovanna passed by the empty lot. Klein smiled and briskly waved. Giovanna smiled back and continued walking without breaking her stride.

Wednesday arrived, and Klein finished his dinner quickly and waited by the gate. Giovanna arrived at seven o'clock, as promised. She immediately told Klein, "It is not in my nature to be the one to speak first, but in this situation with you being held here in Opi, I decided to be the one to act. I don't want you to think of my conduct as being overly bold, because that is not my nature."

Klein was standing close to Giovanna but still separated by the locked gate. "I'm pleased you gave me the note. I'm very happy that you're here," he said in his usual shy, low-key manner.

The nervousness of their first meeting soon passed, and they became more comfortable as they talked quietly. Two weeks passed with four wonderful, satisfying seventy-five minutes for the young boy and girl.

On the fifth night, Klein accidentally brushed against Giovanna's arm as she passed him a few cookies. Klein held on to her hand and then reached for the other. They both slowly moved their faces close to the opening between the bars.

Klein whispered, "I long for the touch of your lips on mine."

Their faces came closer as they looked into each other's eyes. Finally, with cheeks pressed hard against the cold metal bars, their lips gently met.

Klein was the first to speak. "I am so excited that you have entered my life. I hope I will be able to continue seeing you, even if only for two nights and with bars between us. My life has been without happiness for so long. I still think I'm dreaming that you want to be here with me."

Before leaving for the evening, Giovanna asked, "Do you believe all events have a purpose, Klein?"

"I don't understand what you mean."

"Is it possible that the purpose you were brought to Opi was for us to meet?"

"No," he replied in a firm, assured manner. "I cannot believe I was made to live this life so I could find someone as beautiful as you. How could the result of my miserable existence become you? No, our relationship has nothing to do with the people of this town." Klein gently kissed Giovanna good night and reminded her that he would be waiting for her visit on Friday. A blushing Giovanna hurried away.

Klein and Giovanna had been meeting twice weekly for more than three months. Despite their unusual circumstances, the young couple had fallen in love.

One evening during their twice a week masquerade, Klein asked Giovanna a probing question: "What did you and your friends think when the seven of us were brought to Opi?"

Giovanna had often thought about the inevitability of this question. Her response was a mixture of confusion and disillusionment. "I love and admire my papa, and I am greatly influenced by him. I was ten years old when you and the others were brought to our town. Papa said you were foreigners who were going to keep us from starving so we could stay in our house in Opi. He also told me, as did my friends' papas, that you foreigners could not be trusted and might even be dangerous. But he assured me the men assigned to guard you on Sundays were armed to protect the people of Opi. In the beginning, we were frightened by your presence in our town. But as the years passed and we were able to see your friendly nature, we became more at ease. When we began talking with you, we were confused by our parents' warnings. I'm very sad to say that my papa's story of your presence in Opi was the first time that I had any reason to question his judgment. My friends and I are disappointed with our parents, but you must understand, Italian girls are taught not to disagree with their papas."

Klein was a young man in love with a lovely girl, and he unconsciously accepted Giovanna's pragmatic response rather than challenging the obedient Italian young woman. He calmly tried to reason with her, "I understand your devotion to your parents, but what has been done to us is not only unjust, it's evil."

"Klein, I know you are unhappy about being held in Opi, but evil is such a harsh, damning word, to be saved only for men like Hitler and Mussolini."

He was still cautious, and unwilling to be confrontational for fear of damaging the recent joy that had entered his life, so he tried to be diplomatic while attempting to convince Giovanna of the tragic harm that was being done. "Do you believe that evil only looks like a man with a square little mustache or a man known as *Il Duce*? Evil can look like anyone and be anyone. Before I was brought to Opi, I also believed that evil only came from deranged, unbalanced people. But now I understand that evil can also come from people who are so terrified and confused by the unknown that they lose the sound judgment they once had and soon find reasons to justify their deeds."

Giovanna had lived a sheltered life, and his words forced her to consider a reality about her parents that she had been avoiding. The parents she admired so deeply, the two people she had put her trust in, the papa and mamma who until recently she considered infallible, were part of a deliberate conspiracy that had devastated the lives of seven innocent young men. Giovanna, although flustered, was also deeply in love. Was this unlikely young man becoming more important to her than her parents and the values she had inherited from them?

After a long pause—during which Klein became concerned that he had inadvertently demonized Giovanna's father—she finally responded. "Klein, you are the one suffering, so how can I dispute what you say. Please try to understand that my love is very deep for my parents, yet I'm saddened by the iron bars between us. You have become more important to my life than my parents or my town. I don't know what will become of us, but I want you to know I visit you not to try to undo what has been done, but because you make my heart joyful."

One day in January 1957, Jem and Orsolo had been chopping wood for most of the afternoon. Orsolo ordered the work to stop and told Jem, "Go to your room and clean yourself properly and rest. I will bring your dinner at the regular time. Sometime after dinner, I will bring you to the upstairs dining room to meet with Mr. Pelaccio and Marisa.

Pleased at any opportunity for a break in the routine, Jem asked, "What's the occasion?"

"Mr. Pelaccio wants to speak with you."

"What about?"

"He didn't say. He simply asked permission to visit my house for the purpose of speaking directly to you. For your sake, I hope you have not taken advantage of that poor girl."

"Stop worrying; I never touched her."

After dinner, Leardo Pelaccio and his daughter Marisa were warmly welcomed by Orsolo, who opened a special bottle of wine. Caterina served *strufoli*, which are pea-sized sweet pastry piled in the form of a pyramid and covered with honey and sweet red and white sprinkles. After a few friendly toasts, Leardo graciously thanked Orsolo and his wife Caterina for their hospitality, and especially for chaperoning his daughter Marisa during her visits with Jem.

"I hope that your daughter has not been violated in any way," said Orsolo.

"Oh no, no, my friend. I come here tonight to discuss with the young man his intentions toward my daughter."

Orsolo, now relieved, said, "Let me go to his room and bring him to you."

"I would be most grateful," said a confident Leardo.

A few minutes later, Jem and Orsolo were in the living room. Orsolo did not offer Jem any wine, but Caterina had a plate of *strufoli* waiting for him.

Leardo wasted no time in addressing Jem directly. "We are here, young man, to find out your intentions toward my daughter. You have been allowed to court her for a very long time, much longer than I would have agreed to, but out of respect for my daughter's wishes I have waited. Now I refuse to wait any longer. I wish to know what your intentions are toward my daughter."

Relieved the question had finally been put to him, but also knowing his answer would surely mean the end of their pleasant time together, Jem responded directly to Mr. Pelaccio rather than Marisa, knowing this was culturally correct. He chose formal words that he hoped would ease his rejection for Marisa, while making his point about being a captive.

"As a father, you have every right to be proud of your daughter, Marisa. She's a wonderful, faithful, and beautiful woman, and she has been a comfort to me during her visits while I have been held here in Opi. If I had been able to court Marisa in a normal way, I think my feelings might be different, but under these conditions I cannot offer marriage to Marisa."

Mr. Pelaccio's body stiffened and resentment seemed to come over him. He asked Jem to clarify his statement. "Young man, what are you referring to when you say 'in a normal way' and 'under these conditions?' Has not my daughter made the effort to come to this house? Have not my dear friends Mr. and Mrs. Monteverdi been capable chaperones? You will have to explain what you mean because I do not understand."

After all these years, Jem should have been prepared for Mr. Pelaccio's irritable demand for clarification. In that moment, Jem thought, *I don't think these people will ever understand.*

Jem quickly came back to the question. "Mr. Pelaccio, I'm referring to the fact that my six friends and I and are being held in this town against our will. We are prisoners. If I was a free man, I believe things would be much different between Marisa and me."

Mr. Pelaccio, who was now red-faced and defensive, said, "Young man, I can only understand from your comments that you have taken advantage of my daughter's good nature by not informing her sooner that you had no intention of staying in Opi and marrying her."

Jem lost what little calm he possessed. "Take advantage of your daughter? You arranged for Marisa to meet me." He quickly reconsidered his angry statement because of Marisa and softened his tone.

"Mr. Pelaccio, I truly appreciated the opportunity to spend time with Marisa. She's such a wonderful woman, and I have enjoyed her company. Marisa is a daughter you should be very proud of."

Now back on the attack, Jem continued, "The people of Opi kidnapped me, brought me to Opi, and have been holding me prisoner. Why would I want to stay in a place where I am not free to make choices? Now, all of a sudden, you expect me to choose your beautiful daughter in marriage. Can't you see how impossible that would be for me considering that I live in a prison?"

Mr. Pelaccio was visibly shaken by what he considered brash and rude comments from the young foreigner. He stood up and spoke directly to Orsolo and Caterina. "My dear friends, I feel sorry for you because you must take responsibility for this ungrateful and disrespectful foreigner. If I'd known of this man's vulgarity, I would never have allowed Marisa to be introduced to him."

With these words, Leardo took Marisa, who was now crying, by the arm and left the house. Marisa was the only source of comfort Jem had to depend on, but now she was gone. For all the independence, humor, and flippancy Jem displayed in public, he needed a crutch to sustain his swagger—and now his support was lost forever.

Rosa immediately went into the kitchen. Orsolo was furious. He escorted Jem roughly to his room. After opening the door, he pushed Jem into the room and began shouting. "You have damaged my relationship with my friend and neighbor. How am I to greet Leardo when I see him next? What can I say to him except to apologize for the rude behavior of a foreigner, a foreigner I welcomed into my home?"

His reality was so deluded that Orsolo actually believed he was the injured one.

Jem was furious at Orsolo's comments, and he no longer cared how Orsolo might respond. "You bastard; you finally spoke the truth. All this bullshit about how I will come to love Opi and live at peace in your wonderful town was one big bucket of horse crap. You finally said what you and the other people in Opi have always believed: the seven of us are foreigners to be used simply for your own benefit."

Orsolo, now red-faced with indignation, could no longer contain his resentment. He punched Jem with a closed fist, striking him hard on the side of his head and throwing his body against the stone wall of the room.

Jem cupped his hand around his pounding temples and with sarcasm in his voice said, "Good night," as Orsolo stormed out of the room.

By the fall of 1958, back in New York, Danny was the only person Pete had not alienated. Danny regularly visited his other brothers and always encouraged Pete to come with him. Pete refused, remaining moody and inflexible, especially when it came to his three brothers. However, it was not only his three younger brothers that he rejected. Pete no longer had the desire to socialize with anyone.

Danny was unable to watch the continuing self-destruction of his dearest brother, so he decided he had to leave New York, the only home he had ever known. He told his wife, "Kate, there is nothing left for us in the Bronx but misery. I can no longer stay here and watch my brother slowly killing himself. Leaving Suzy will be difficult, but watching the hatred and bitterness that comes from my brother is making me ill."

On a Saturday afternoon in mid-December, Danny trudged up the stairs to Pete's apartment. Suzy and Kate had traveled to New Jersey to see their sister, Anna, and brother, Frank, for the Christmas season. Danny did not want to tell Pete of his plans with Suzy present—it would be too painful to watch the disappointment on her face. Danny quickly came to the point.

"Pete, since the disappearance of Daniel, you've become a stranger. The brother I came to America with was a happy, wonderful man, a helpful brother, and once a great leader. The brother I now see is a man who finds fault with everyone. I fear you won't accept this, but the people you have wronged are waiting for you to say you're sorry. They understand your torment. All you have to do is ask them to let you back into their lives, but I can see you are still not ready, and, for now, I can no longer stand by and watch the slow destruction of my dearest brother. Pete, it's too painful for me to stay in the Bronx with you. If some day God allows you to heal, I promise I will come back. But until then, understand that Kate and I have to leave, not out of anger toward you, but because I can no longer live with a brother who has let so much anger and sadness consume his life. Kate and I have decided to move to Miami, Florida. The husband of our niece, Rita, has a job waiting for me at the A&P grocery store in Coral Gables, Florida. My job starts the day after the New Year holiday. I will miss you and Suzy but we must make this move."

Pete listened attentively to his dearest brother. He stood and walked a few paces to the nearest window. With his back toward Danny, he was silent as he gazed at the street in front of his apartment. Waiting patiently for a reaction, Danny remained seated and lit a cigarette. Pete continued to stand in silence, glaring at the street below. Danny flicked the ash from his cigarette.

Pete slowly turned and finally spoke. "You're the one I grew up with in Italy, the one I went to school with in America. We helped our father build a business; we ran that business; and we trained our younger brothers. You're the one person I thought understood the harm that has been done to me. I never expected you to abandon me. You say you can't stay and be with me. Then do what you feel is right for you, but before you go, know that I have injured no one. I am the one who has been injured!"

Danny squashed the lit end of his cigarette in the ashtray and approached Pete with tears streaming down his face. He hugged Pete, realizing this was his final private good-bye. Pete's arms remained at his sides. Danny turned and left the apartment.

Immediately after a shattered Christmas holiday for the families of the two brothers, Danny and Kate left New York for Miami, Florida.

CHAPTER XIII

$\mathcal{P}$LANNING $\mathcal{T}$HEIR $\mathcal{G}$ROUP $\mathcal{E}$SCAPE

The one constant thought that occupied the mind of each captive was how to escape. After being brought to Opi, each boy, except for Klein, had attempted to escape to the forest without success. During the first year, the six hostages had tried to escape numerous times, each believing he was alone and trapped in Opi.

After that first year, when they were together, each boy agreed that whoever managed to get free would expose the evil conspiracy taking place in Opi. During their free Sundays, the boys were always looking for new faces or people they thought might be strangers. But this never happened, and it proved not to be accidental or a matter of bad luck. Eventually, the boys presumed that any work needing an outsider was completed on weekdays while they were in the fields. After two years of never seeing any newcomers on Sundays, they concluded that the people had somehow planned for this detail, although in this rural area there were probably very few strangers or visitors who might be "passing by," even during the pleasant summer months.

On a March Sunday in 1959, just prior to beginning their twelfth year of farming, the boys once again found themselves discussing the topic of escaping. In frustration, David stopped the conversation. "I'm tired of listening to how we almost made it. Let's stop re-hashing all our failures. We only wind up feeling sorry for ourselves. Aren't you guys tired of listening to the same old depressing stories?"

Gabriel was quite irritated. "Why are you being so bitchy? Hell we've done our best."

"I'm bitchy because all I hear is moaning and complaining about how unlucky we've been."

Gabriel angrily responded, "Okay, if you don't want to hear me complaining then tell me what you do wanna hear."

"Well, rather than complaining, we could start by trying to figure out why these Italians keep stopping us from getting outta here. They've made their plans to stop us—so where's our plan? Why don't we do something together instead of each of us trying to run alone when we think we see an opening?"

George was annoyed with David's comments. "Damn it, David, we've been talking about escape since 1948. What the hell makes you think we can all of a sudden come up with a plan that's gonna get us out of this blasted place? My hopes have been raised so many damn times I don't know if I'm ready for another let-down."

David sympathized with George and agreed that another disappointment would be painful. "George, I feel lousy, too, and I get angry when I think about how these peasant farmers have been able to stop us from escaping. But does that mean we shouldn't try?"

Daniel added, "Y'know David, I understand what George is saying. I feel like one more disappointment is gonna break me, but you did mention something we've never talked about—and that is planning an escape together. Maybe we should at least talk about it. Whaddya think, George? Who knows; maybe we can figure out what we could've done differently."

Omar added, "We could each describe our escape attempts. This might show what they always do to stop us. That might tell us more about their planning and how they operate. Maybe our mistake has been trying our escape attempts only when we think we can make it, rather than, as David is saying, making a plan. At least David's idea of involving all of us is something we haven't tried. If nothing else, it might give us new hope."

George was still not convinced. "Yeah, that's just what I mean. I get full of hope, and then the next day, guess what, I'm still here."

The six young men looked sympathetically at George. He frowned and squirmed with his head down, and remained silent. The others understood exactly what George was feeling—the anguish and disillusionment that might follow another failed attempt would ravage their minds and bodies. It had never been said, but lurking behind their hesitation to try another escape was the constant fear that the next serious letdown might be the one to extinguish their desire to go on living.

Finally George broke the silence. "As Dan and Omar were talking, I was thinking of what I said. Have I given up on ever leaving this place? Is it possible that I'm ready to accept this miserable life? Are the people of Opi right when they tell me that I should be happy about staying here the rest of my life?"

Omar tried to give clarity to George's dilemma. "Repeated failure, over time, can destroy the soul. When this happens, people accept what is safe rather than risk the results of more torment. You're not wrong to feel this way, George. It's not necessary to be a prisoner to feel this way. It can happen to people who are living a normal life. I believe if we never find our way out of our prison existence, some of us might give up our spirit. We must never feel ashamed."

George was about to continue, but he hesitated and inhaled deeply. He sat silently for what seemed like an eternity. None of the others spoke. It was as though they didn't want to interrupt George's thought process. Then, with a robust, animated surge of energy—as though he had suddenly found a hidden treasure of courage—he said with great force, *"Blimy*, let's go for it. What the *blooming* hell; whatever it takes; let's be a team and beat these Italian farmers! Omar is right—if nothing else at least we will have something to live for!"

Jem jumped up and yelled, not in Italian, but in his guttural Welsh English, "Hip hip hurray! Hip hip hurray! Hip hip hurray!" The young men smiled at his enthusiasm, but Daniel was laughing and wide-eyed with astonishment as he repeated Jem's phrase, "Hip hip hurray!" You guys actually say that? I thought they only said those things in English war movies."

Jem's pride was dented by Daniel's lack of understanding of British culture, and he said with firm certainty, "Ah, you *Yanks* will never understand. How many times do I have to tell ya, I'm Welsh? I come from Wales, not England? Wales and England are two different places."

Jem was feeling much better for having had the opportunity to demonstrate the fierce loyalty he felt toward his homeland. He looked at David and said in a buoyant, confident manner, "Okay, David, you're now the leader of our *group escape attempt.*"

"Hold on," said David. "I only suggested an idea. Before we decide on a leader or anything else, let's first decide if we're gonna do this."

Their energetic discussions went on for the next three Sundays. Even the passing girls couldn't distract the captives from their focus. The first and unanimous decision was the elimination of the forest as an escape destination. They often saw large bears, boars, and wolves roaming the fringe of the forest, they correctly assumed the accounts of not surviving in the forest were valid.

They decided the next step was for each of them to describe, in as much detail as possible, the events of their escape attempts. Each attempt was then analyzed to determine why it failed. George volunteered to take detailed notes, which, when they were finished, amounted to thirty-four individual escape attempts over the past twelve years. Looking at the results, the overwhelming reasons for failure were that they were either outnumbered or did not possess resources comparable to those of their jailers.

As the discussions progressed, David, who had initially been reluctant to take charge, was now becoming the de facto leader because of his piercing, precise questioning. As the planning went forward, the group looked to David more and more.

They finally decided their best chance would be to rush the protectors at the entrance of town, but they had to somehow take some of the protectors and escorts out of the equation.

"C'mon David, how about some good ideas?" said George.

"How about you guys come up with some ideas?" responded David.

After a brief silence, Klein spoke up. "We've gotta find a way to get close to the protectors. How can we make them trust us?"

Daniel had a flash of inspiration and quickly responded, "Wait a second; why would they have to trust all of us? I think one or two would not make them as worried as if all seven of us showed up."

"Go on, Dan. It sounds like you have something in mind. Let's hear what you're thinking," said Omar.

"Well, let's say two of us try to get them to trust us—and really, that's what we're talking about, trust. That isn't gonna happen in a few days or even a few weeks. Somehow we have to get them to see a few of us as their friends, not as their hostages. For that to happen, they'll have to get used to seeing a few of us hanging around the entrance of town. Then we'll have to figure a way to get them to start talking with us."

"That's going to be a tough one?" said Jem. "Does anyone have any ideas?"

David was pleased with the progress of the conversation. "Klein, Dan, you may have hit on something. Whaddya think of this?" David looked directly at Daniel and Gabriel. "I think you two would be perfect for the job. Gabe is familiar with horses, so he knows what questions to ask. Remember horses are important to the men in Opi, so it's my guess they would be interested in talking about their animals. And Dan, like the rest of us, the people of Opi are interested in hearing stories about America. I bet they're dying to ask questions about America; you could talk about your home and your father's business."

Jem interrupted David. "Remember, Dan, he's a capitalist." The boys enjoyed a good laugh at Daniel's expense, which was a good indication they were feeling spirited once again.

David continued brainstorming, "Then there are cowboys, New York City, American movies.... There is plenty of stuff to keep them interested."

Klein thought this was a perfect plan, but he asked Daniel and Gabriel pointedly, "How do you guys feel about this idea? Won't it be more dangerous for you than for the rest of us?"

Gabriel, the adventurous one, spoke first. "Sounds good to me. I'm ready."

Daniel followed, more out of loyalty than bravery. "Well, David, I can't argue with what you say, so it sounds okay to me. I'm in."

"Are we all in agreement?" asked David. They all nodded. David, still asserting his quasi-leadership, added, "Does anyone have anything else they wanna say?"

They looked at each other with a new sense of excitement. There was nothing more to say.

"Then it's settled. We rush them at the entrance of town. Now we need to come up with a plan and practice every detail."

There was nothing but smiles on the faces of the young men. Omar was right when he said at least they would have something to live for, an action to revive their spirits.

Gabriel stood up and said, "Well, Dan, what the hell are we waiting for? Let's go to the front of the town and get started."

"Get started with what?" asked Daniel.

"I don't know, probably nothing, but didn't you say they need to get used to seeing us? Well, let's go down there and have them start getting used to seeing us."

"Yeah, okay uh...yeah, I guess you're right, let's start." Daniel jumped up with an enthusiastic smile on his face, put his arm around Gabriel, and said to the others, "See you guys in an hour or so, and while we're gone, get to work on a plan. No goofing off when we're not around."

David's calm, encouraging command of the situation filled the boys with confidence. There was a new sense of hope as the planning process began and the belief that they would be able to execute whatever they needed.

Daniel and Gabriel decided not to be too assertive during the first two Sunday afternoons. When they arrived at the entrance of town, they kept their distance, only waving and saying, *"buon giorno."* They sat against a stone wall simply having a conversation and not paying any attention to the protectors. They soon left, waving to them, saying, *"buona sera."* They followed a similar procedure six Sunday afternoons at different times, each Sunday finding a different place to sit, or examining some stones or other things that made them look busy and interested in what they were doing. One Sunday, they were close enough for Gabriel to initiate verbal contact. "That's a nice looking horse you have. How old is that beauty?"

Surprisingly, one protector answered. They instinctively knew that was enough for today, and they pretended to continue their leisurely conversation. When they left, they waved and again said *"buona sera."* The phrases *good afternoon* and *good night* were now a permanent part of their act.

Two months passed. Although Daniel and Gabriel were eager to speed up the process, they had to remind each other to go slowly. Spending so many years in Opi had taught the captives that familiarity, patience, natural flow, and tranquility were an important part of the people's existence. The citizens of Opi were distrustful of anyone who didn't have similar qualities. They were also a proud people. Scorn seemed to be more robust than their history of hardship and calamity. Perhaps for this reason they acted as though "outsiders" would only disturb their perception of established order.

Two months into the little charade on their cobblestone stage, Daniel and Gabriel, although closer than they had been the first Sunday, decided to continue moving slowly, maintaining their distance, but now they shouted, "Hi fellas. How you feeling today?"

The men in the wagon responded with a nod of the head, but no other reaction. By now Gabriel and Daniel needed to do more than just pretend to talk. They devised games to play. With little pieces of wood, they pretended they were playing "pitching pennies" against a stone wall, a game Daniel had played back in the Bronx, and box ball, a modified game of handball in which participants remain in a designated area. They acted as though they were having a good time and making gestures as each won or lost. After an hour or so, they would cheerfully say *buona sera* and be on their way.

The following month, they invented different play activities that incorporated a part of the landscape at the entrance of town. From this position, they were able to hold a conversation with the men without having to shout. The men seemed to enjoy conversing. Perhaps it made their boring time on duty more pleasant. Daniel and Gabriel had to fight the urge to move closer, but their plan was working so well that they decided to continue their protracted but casual sham.

They knew they had made progress when one afternoon the protectors seemed disappointed when the boys went to play a game rather than continue their conversation.

After the boys said *buona sera* and began walking up the street, Gabriel whispered to Daniel, "Let them come to us. I think we got them hooked."

The two boys continued to be visible, but they made an effort to be disinterested in the two men. They would act surprised and be very apologetic when they got too close and were cautioned to stay back. This little "cat-and-mouse" game was being played out well by Daniel and Gabriel. Time was necessary, and the seven young men had become disciplined in the matter of time and understood its importance. Being a part of Opi had taught the boys the value of remaining patient.

When living intimately with captivity, the simple passage of time takes on special meaning in terms of learning how to wait. Captives have time in abundance. The young men grew physically and, to a more limited extent, emotionally. Time passes and people change, but somehow place and physical circumstances remain constant, and the captive learns the meaning of patience. With such an abundant amount of time in a slowly changing environment, agitation can be very unsettling.

In late May, the air was brisk in the mountainous region, and the top of the Apennine Mountains were still pure white with a heavy coat of snow. Gabriel and Daniel had made significant progress in establishing a trusting relationship with the men in the wagon. They knew the various men by name, and when Gabriel was permitted to stroke and talk to their horse, they knew they had the full confidence of the protectors. One sunny but windy May Sunday, Daniel and Gabriel said *"buona sera"* to the two protectors and proceeded to join their friends in the empty lot on Via San Giovanni de Battista.

When they arrived, Gabriel enthusiastically told his brothers, "Our job is done, guys." Gabriel, holding his hands straight out in a cupped fashion, said, "We've got them right here in the palms of our hands. They're no longer worried when I stroke and talk to their horses."

Daniel and Gabriel felt the following Sunday was the best time to escape via the road to the valley. Daniel made one final cautious statement. "I'm still worried about our escorts. They seem to be as relaxed as the protectors but the minute you five appear I know they're going to fall back into their 'on-guard' role. I hate to bring this up, but even if everything goes as planned, there's gonna be shooting. Is everybody ready for that?"

Gabriel disagreed with Daniel. "C'mon, Dan, I think you're wrong. Remember, if one of us gets killed or even wounded, they've lost a worker. Sure, they'll do everything to stop us, but killing us, nah, that'll be their last option, and that's why we have the advantage. Like we said, their hesitation is gonna work to our benefit."

George made a request. "David, let's go over the plan one more time to make sure we all know our places."

Purely out of habit, the seven young men huddled closer and checked the street before the plan was reviewed. David began giving instructions, "Danny and Gabe will go to the entrance of town about a half hour after the church bell rings at the five o'clock hour and do whatever it is they do down there. Once the church bell rings at six o'clock, announcing dinner, the bar will clear out. When the five of us see that the street is clear, we'll start to move. We can't wait too long or our families will get suspicious. So the minute the street is clear, we gotta move.

"Gabe and Dan, your timing is gonna make this work. After the six o'clock bell rings, you'll wait till the men from the bar are off the street and hopefully in their houses. You two can only entertain the protectors for a coupl'a extra minutes by pretending to say g'night. This is going to be a bit unusual, because you've made a habit of leaving the area when the six o'clock bell rings. Dan, try to time it so that you're in the middle of a story when the bell is rung and pretend you need the extra minute to finish. You'll have to talk to them long enough to give us time to get down the street after the men are in their houses.

When the five of us come in sight of Dan and Gabe's escorts, Gabe has to be talkin' to the horse on the right side of the wagon, as you're lookin' at it—and Dan needs to be talkin' to the protector on the left side of the wagon, opposite Gabe."

David finished his review with the last and most important part of the plan. "Remember, Dan, you have to somehow time this as best you can. Gabe will try to help, but we need an extra forty-five seconds. We have been timing the clearing of the street in that part of town and we hafta have the extra time.

"Gabe will have the stolen fork in his sleeve. He will be talking to the horse on the left, stroking its neck. Dan, you'll be telling your little story to the protectors and tryin' to get them laughin'. As we approach the exit of town, we know our escorts will be about twenty yards behind us. We'll walk down the center of the main cobblestone road, shoulder to shoulder. Omar will be in the center, and Klein and I will be on his right—with George and Jem on his left. Now, this is the moment we gotta be ready. Omar will give the signal to move. His attention will be focused on Dan and Gabe's escorts. The second he sees them, Omar will shout, 'Hey Gabe.' At that moment, we will all move at the same time. Klein and I on the right will start running toward the wagon, remembering to separate ourselves and weave. We don't wanna be running together or in a straight line when the shooting starts. George and Jem will do the same on the left, and Omar will streak down the center.

"The greeting Omar yells to Gabe will be Gabe's clue to jab the fork into the neck of the horse. The horse should rear up, causing the wagon to jerk, hopefully throwing the protectors out of the wagon. If not, they'll at least be distracted long enough for Daniel and Gabe to wrestle with their rifles so they can't fire at the five of us as we're running toward them. Dan, being next to his protector when the horse rears up, should have no problem wrestling with the rifle, so Dan's protector should not be a problem. Gabe's protector will be our biggest worry. After Gabe jabs the fork in the horse's neck, he will have to dash a few feet and try to wrestle with the rifle of his man. Hopefully, Gabe's man will be startled long enough for Gabe to reach him before he can shoot anyone."

David discussed their unsettling concern, "We probably don't have to worry about our escorts. They're usually twenty yards behind us. It's Gabe and Dan's escorts that'll be our biggest problem. When the horse rears up, hopefully Gabe and Dan's escorts will run toward the wagon rather than shooting at us. If they don't shoot, we are in good shape, because we'll be down the dirt road and into the valley by the time they reach the wagon. If they start shooting, we've separated and we're weaving, so they can't hit all five of us. Let's hope we all make it past the wagon, but if not, at least one of us should. So if any firing starts, some of us may get hit. Does everyone understand?

"Again, if anyone feels it's too risky and chooses not to to be part of this, remember what we decided. No one will be judged, and whoever gets free will bring back the authorities for those of us who don't make it out. So think about it this week, and if some of you are not comfortable, it's okay. Dan and Gabe have already said they're not backing out. Does everybody understand his part? Any questions?"

They all nodded in agreement and quietly dispersed to their homes for the evening. The excited young men went about their daily chores, and Monday and Tuesday passed quickly. Monday and Wednesday evenings, Gabe and Theresa comforted each other. Gabe said nothing about the plan to her.

Giovanna visited with Klein at the usual seven o'clock hour. She placed her hands through the black metal bars and grasped Klein's hands, and they tenderly kissed their unusual kiss with cheeks pressed hard against the cold metal bars. Klein had not previously mentioned the escape attempt to Giovanna.

Klein was concerned and worried, and he had to tell her. "Giovanna, I have something important I need to say."

"Klein, what has happened?"

He had no fear of Giovanna divulging the plan to escape on Sunday, because they had agreed a year ago that if Klein ever escaped or was released, he vowed to return to Opi, marry Giovanna, and take her back to Austria to live.

"Giovanna, we have been working on an escape plan for many months. There is some danger involved. It is not likely, but there is always the possibility that one or more of us might be wounded or even killed."

Giovanna frowned, making her dimples more pronounced. She was about to interrupt when Klein said, "No, Giovanna, let me finish. I'm gonna tell the other guys about us next Sunday before the escape attempt."

Giovanna was surprised that Klein was about to reveal their secret. "Klein, we said we would keep our relationship secret so my parent's won't know."

"Please let me finish—this is important to me." Giovanna lowered her head. "If by some freak chance I happen to get killed, I plan to ask my brothers to return to Opi and take you to my parents. I believe they would be happy to know we loved each other and planned to marry, and I know they would want very much to meet you."

Giovanna began to cry. She turned her head and looked down at the ground—she was unable to look at Klein.

"No, no, Giovanna. It's very unlikely someone will get killed."

Through her tears, Giovanna said, "Oh, Klein, I cannot think of life without you. Do you have to be part of this?

"Yes, I must."

"But if you are gonna tell them about us, if they knew we were planning to marry, they would understand if you asked not to be part of the escape."

"Giovanna, it's not that simple. I have a bond with these men. I can't abandon them now. It's the same as with us. I love you and would never abandon you. I also love these men. Please don't ask me to turn my back on them now."

"Yes, Klein, I should've known better than to ask you to do such a thing. I guess this is why I love you so deeply. If you are…oh I can't even say the word. If something happens, I will do as you ask."

The remainder of the hour was grim for both lovers. Giovanna asked about the escape plan, but Klein felt it better that she not know any details so that after their escape she could not be implicated in any way.

Sunday arrived and the young men met as usual. Gabriel had his fork and was anxious to start.

"Is there anyone who chooses not to go? said David. "If so, now is the time to speak up." There was silence as the boys looked at each other. David hesitated a moment longer and then said, "Okay, then today is the day." They clasped their hands together.

"Let's go to my room," said Daniel. "I've got a good fire going in the stove."

Once the seven young men were comfortable, Klein interrupted the enthusiastic nervous energy floating throughout the room by saying, "I have something important to discuss with you before we attempt our escape."

Klein explained the relationship he had been having with Giovanna. The others initially congratulated him, and they were quite surprised that he and Giovanna could keep such a secret for so long in the small town. Klein then told them he needed a favor. He explained his wish to have Giovanna brought to Austria to meet his parents if he were killed. He told them he had discussed this with Giovanna and that she had agreed to follow his wishes and travel to Austria with the other captives to meet his parents if he were killed.

Gabriel interrupted Klein. "She knows of today's escape?"

"Well, yes, of course. I had to tell her what to do in case I am killed."

There was a moment of silence. The others went numb from the impact of Klein's statement, but then they burst with sudden rage.

Jem jumped up and shouted, "Have your lost your mind, telling her? She's one of them!"

"Stop shouting! They can hear you upstairs," said David. Then he turned to Klein and said, "Do you realize what you have done? We can't go now. You've really screwed this up."

George, in an unusual display of anger, said, "Okay, so you fell for a girl, but what in the bloody hell made you tell her we were planning on escaping? She's from Opi. Did you think you'd come before her family? Klein, I can't believe you did this!" Disgustedly George turned away from Klein and sat down.

"You should have discussed this with us before you spoke to Giovanna. I am afraid David is right. We can't chance this now. It's too risky," said Daniel.

Red-faced, veins bulging, and with rage in his eyes, Gabriel stood face to face with Klein and said, "You ass! You dumb ass! I should stick this fork in your stupid neck. That dumb horse has more brains than you. God, you're an idiot." Gabe hurled the fork against the stone wall nearest the stove. "Shit, all the weeks and months of kissing their sorry asses, and for what? Nothing! It's over. God damn you, Klein!"

Klein had never taken such verbal abuse in his life; he was completely unprepared for the antagonistic outburst from his friends. In Klein's mind, telling Giovanna was perfectly safe. He knew she would not tell. He never for one moment considered this to be a problem. He now began to doubt himself. *What have I done? Was I wrong?* He no longer knew what was right or wrong—all he knew was that the people he depended on most, the people he trusted most, had lost faith in him.

Omar, who had been silent throughout the past few chaotic minutes, spoke quietly, "Klein, are you sure in your heart that Giovanna is not just an infatuation that has consumed you because of your many years in this mountain prison? If that's the case, there's no cause for shame. It would be quite normal. I am sure any of us in the same situation would have acted as you did. So, please, answer this question only if you are positive. It is most important when answering that you have no doubt. Klein, do you understand my meaning?"

Klein was sitting against the stone wall of Daniel's room with his knees up and his arms folded tightly across his chest. He was frightened and devastated because he had disappointed his brothers. "Yes, yes, Omar...ask whatever you want and I'll do whatever you say."

Omar was annoyed that Klein was unable to focus on his question, so he spoke more firmly, "Doing what I say is not what I asked. Klein, get hold of yourself. I need you to listen and understand me. There can be absolutely no doubt on your part. You need to be absolutely sure of your answer. Is Giovanna the woman you love, the woman you would sacrifice your life for?"

Klein was about to answer, but Omar continued. "Or is Giovanna the woman who has made these years tolerable for you?"

"Omar, I feel so badly that I upset everyone. I...."

"No, no, no," said a frustrated and now angry Omar. "Again, that is not what I asked. Klein, you must stop being worried about how we feel and listen to me carefully. I am going to say this one more time, and I expect you to clear your mind and listen closely."

Klein had never seen Omar so disturbed and intense, and it forced him back to the reality of his situation. The attention of the other five men was now drawn to Omar—they were also surprised, never having seen Omar so provoked, so out of character.

Klein stopped his self-doubt and looked into Omar's eyes. "Yes, Omar, I'm okay now. Just tell me what you want to know."

I will ask one more time," Omar said. "Disregard how you are now feeling and focus on answering my question. Is Giovanna an infatuation that any man might desire, or is she the woman you want to live with the rest of your life? You must think clearly and answer honestly, because this is very important."

Klein responded without hesitation, "Giovanna is the love of my life. I want to spend the rest of my life with her."

Omar calmly asked Klein one last question. "Now, Klein, this next question is also very important, so listen carefully. You must be absolutely sure of your answer. Remember our lives depend on your clear and doubtless answer. If you are not one hundred percent positive, beyond any doubt, we must know. Do you understand—one hundred percent positive?"

Omar waited for a response. Klein was still too intimidated to be annoyed, and he responded simply, "Yes, Omar. I understand."

Omar continued, "Is Giovanna simply infatuated with her handsome friend or—please listen carefully—are you positive she also wishes to spend the rest of her life with you as your wife?"

Klein responded with confident assurance, "Yes, I know this with every bone and muscle in my body. We've made our plans. She has agreed to marry me in the church in Opi, and then she will come with me to Austria, where we expect to live our lives. I know this to be true beyond any other truth. Omar, we have talked about our love and how our relationship affects her parents, so I know she's loyal to me and our plan for life in Austria."

Omar turned to the other five men. "My brothers, I believe we have nothing to worry about. True love cannot be manipulated. We know the kind of man Klein is. If he believes in Giovanna, then she will not forsake him for her family or for Opi. I believe love to be the strongest bond between humans. If it exists—and I can see in Klein's eyes that it does—then I am confident we have nothing to fear."

There was a long period of silence, as Klein nervously scanned the faces of his friends and waited for a response.

Gabriel squatted in front of Klein, grabbed his shoulders, and said, "Klein, I was out of line when I called you an idiot and said I should have jammed the fork in your neck. I was hot with anger, I didn't mean what I said. I was wrong about everything. Buddy, d'ye forgive me?"

Klein nodded his head without looking up.

Jem, George, Daniel, and David approached Klein one at a time, shook his hand, and apologized.

Omar looked around and said, "Can we agree that we will still have our 'meeting' with the men at the entrance to Opi later today?"

"This new twist makes me a little nervous, but I guess I'm in," said George.

"Wait," said David. "You guess you're in? That's not good enough for me. If you have any doubt, don't go. No one will think badly of you."

George spoke without any hesitation. "No, it was just as I said. I'm going. Omar's right about Klein. You guys know me by now; it's just me, always being so damn worried about things. I want more than anything to be with the six of you all the way."

The men were re-energized and smiling.

David approached Klein. "If something happens to you and we get free, we will make sure Giovanna meets your parents. Now stop worrying; you're not going to die."

This statement released the piled up negative feelings that Klein had been holding back, and he broke down and sobbed as he sat on the floor near the warm stove. His friends gathered around and comforted him. The seven, once again, were as one.

The five o'clock church bell finally rang. Gabriel and Daniel waited about a half hour and left the group to prepare for their role in the escape. The other five sat and waited for the six o'clock church bell to announce dinner. The bell rang on schedule, and men leaving the bar could be seen walking up Via San Giovanni de Battista to return to their homes as they did every Sunday. The street finally cleared. The captives took their places and moved quickly and silently down the street shoulder to shoulder.

The moment Omar caught a glimpse of Daniel and Gabriel's escorts, he cried out in a loud voice, "Hi, Gabe."

The five immediately broke their formation and began to run. The horse bucked and whinnied, the wagon bounced, and the protectors were thrown back but remained in their seats.

Daniel, who had been next to his protector on the right, was wrestling with him for the rifle. Gabriel, who was at the head of the horse, took a moment to get to the second protector. In that moment, the protector fired his rifle three times in the air. When the captives started running, Gabriel's and Daniel's escorts ran toward the running hostages and started firing their pistols. George was hit in the shoulder and fell in front of the horse. David was hit in the upper thigh; as he grabbed for his injured leg, he stumbled to the ground. Omar stopped to help Gabriel, who had lost control of his protector. Klein and Jem dashed past the wagon and made a sharp right to the dirt road and freedom, but they were suddenly faced with two men in a wagon who had moved halfway up the dirt road. Their rifles were cocked and aimed, and they issued a command to stop or die.

The three shots fired in the air, just prior to Gabriel trying to wrestle the rifle away from his assigned protector, signaled trouble on the cobblestone road to the two men who were stationed at the bottom of the dirt road. The escape plan had worked as designed, except for the fact that the prisoners did not know there were men stationed on the lower road, even on Sundays, just as they were during the week. Klein and Jem once again chose to live as prisoners rather than die—they obeyed the command to stop and slowly walked back to the cobblestone road.

George and David were treated by *Dottoe* Tatti (Doctor Tatti). George had been sedated with chloroform, and the bullet was removed from the muscle directly under his shoulder bone. Fortunately for David, the bullet had passed through the fleshy part of his upper right thigh. David was returned to his room from the *Dattoe's* office after three days, George after five.

The seven young men were quarantined in their rooms for the next six Sundays. In June, they were allowed to be together once again on Sundays. Time had healed George's shoulder and David's leg faster than it healed the disappointment of their aborted escape attempt.

Daniel was now twenty-five years old and going through the worst depression of his long confinement. He felt as though his entire life had been taken from him. He no longer envisioned a life outside of the town that held him prisoner. The memories of his Bronx home were distant and badly faded, and he no longer had any hope of going home again. Resignation dominated his state of mind, and he lay in bed at night questioning God and trying to accept Opi as the only life he would ever know as an adult. Daniel was convinced that the people of Opi never had any intention of freeing their captives. They couldn't risk their crime becoming public. He reasoned that when the captives were no longer of any use to the people they would be killed. He chose not to share these thoughts with his six Opi brothers. *Why burden them with my depressing conclusion,* he thought. However, he often wondered if they felt the same way.

In November 1959, the young men were completing their thirteenth year in the valley. George and David had fully recovered from their gunshot wounds.

The next twenty-six months passed slowly. The seven men chose never to discuss what had now become obvious to them. Daniel's assumption was correct—the others had also arrived at a similar conclusion: The people of Opi could not afford to ever release their seven captives.

January 1962, and another lonely Christmas had come and gone. It would soon be sixteen years of isolation in Opi for the hostages. In three months, they would be going to the valley for another year of farming. Jem and Daniel were now twenty-eight; Gabriel, George, and Klein were twenty-nine; Omar was thirty; and David was thirty-one.

On the next to the last Sunday in January, the weather in the mountains was approaching its coldest of the season. Fortunately, the bright sun helped keep the young men warm as they walked for a while. Then they sat in their empty lot around a warm fire enjoying the last rays of the sun before it slipped behind the western mountains.

Omar began to talk about an important decision he had made. "My brothers, what I am about to say affects me directly, but since we have become linked in so many ways over these past fifteen years, I know my decision will also affect you. My brothers, I have decided that today I will walk past the guards on the lone road leading out of town. I understand this will most likely result in my death. I know the men in the wagon will do everything in their power to stop me. I am determined to either leave Opi or be killed. However, if a decision by Allah causes me to be successful in leaving, the first thing I will do is expose the people of Opi and have you freed."

George was the first to respond to Omar's startling statements. "Omar, how can you calmly sit there and tell us you are going to commit suicide? Do you realize what you're saying?"

Omar responded in a half angry, half clarifying tone, "Yes, George, I fully understand the possible results of my intended actions."

A startled and irritated Daniel said, "Why did you wait until today to tell us? How long have you been thinking of this? Don't you think we should have been told before today?"

"My dear friends, I have made a personal decision, which I will not change, so why should I burden you when there is nothing you can say or do to change my mind? Telling you earlier would only have led to unnecessary and useless debate and concern."

The magnitude of such an important decision finally registered with David. "How long have you been thinking about such a crazy idea? What did you do, wake up this morning and decide you wanted to die? Don't you think you should have said something before now? I just don't understand why after all this time you are doing this now!"

Jem got everyone's attention by raising his voice. "Okay, everyone, stop for a minute and take a deep breath. I want to hear more from Omar."

Omar did not speak immediately—he was staring ahead at the mountain range. Finally he said, "This has been on my mind for about a year. The reason I chose to wait was I knew this act would also affect each of you. Please don't think badly of me, but I cannot face more years of isolation."

David asked a follow-up question. "What made you decide to leave by the road leading out of town?"

"I thought about trying to escape to the forest, but the odds have always been against that. We have all tried the forest numerous times without success. I have decided to force their hand on the town road. I would rather die from a bullet than experience the agony of hunger or being mangled by a bear or boars, and then having my remains eaten by wolves. I know the protectors will do everything in their power to stop me from leaving. They can't take the chance of having their history exposed to the world.

I assure you, I fully understand that my actions will most probably end in my death, and I know my death will affect all of you. The comfort you provided on our Sundays together will remain within my soul. Brothers, please try to understand, I simply can no longer continue living this life. As each of you can appreciate, it is a great misfortune to have your heart, mind, and soul in one place and your body in another. So I ask you to please accept my death with understanding and without any suffering on your part."

Jem said with a tinge of bitter sarcasm, "Without any suffering on our part? Well, it's awfully nice of you to tell us we don't have to feel anything."

David felt Jem was being a bit harsh, so he picked up the conversation as soon as Jem had finished. "Omar, don't be upset with us. It's just that we never expected this."

"Omar, I probably know the answer to this question, but I want to hear it from you," said Gabriel. "Are you absolutely certain this is what you want to do? Do you have any doubt, any doubt at all?"

Omar responded to Jem first, "My friend, I'm not angry that you have spoken so forcefully. I know it is selfish of me to tell you this without any warning." Then looking at Gabriel, he continued, "I have thought about this often and carefully, and I am positive this is right for me."

Jem said, "Wait. Let's talk about this for a minute. Why can't we try to distract the protectors? That might improve your chances of success. There must be something we can do."

Before any of the others could add to Jem's suggestion, Omar interrupted, "Jem, thank you for your expression of help, but under no circumstances do I wish for any of you to assist me in this. I could not find peace if I thought my actions might endanger any of you. This is my decision and I must fulfill it alone."

George had been willing to accept the permanency of his mountain prison thirty-two months ago. He had felt escape was a useless effort, and he was one of the two wounded in the 1959 escape attempt, but now he was unwilling to accept Omar's rejection of assistance. "There you go, being pig-headed as usual, turning down our offer of help because of danger to us," he said. "It's very hard for us to just sit here knowing you're about to die."

Omar looked at George with loving affection and responded to his plea. "George, please don't be angry with me, not now. I love you and my other brothers as I love my family in Egypt. Perhaps, if I explain what the prophet Mohamed has taught, you will be better able to accept why I need to do this alone.

"If I am killed during my attempt to leave, I will enter a state in conformity with my faith and the actions in my life. Before being kidnapped, I lived a life according to the teachings of the Prophet

217

Mohamed. The Prophet teaches that Allah is a just God, and he will account for my sufferings these past years in Italy and understand that I was unable to fully practice the rituals of my Islamic faith. If I die, I am confident that Allah will be pleased with how I have lived my life. Therefore, the place in the earth where I will ask you to place my body will become comfortable, and in that place there will be a sense of brightness. For those who have not pleased Allah through their deeds on earth, their place under the earth will be cramped, and they will feel as though they are being crushed, and they will experience darkness."

Omar then asked for their help. "If I die today, please bury me according to my religious beliefs. Take my body back to my room; clean it as best you can with soap and water; and be especially attentive to the parts of my body where the bullets enter. Then wrap my body in clean strips of seamless cloth. If I were back in Egypt, the cloth would be linen, but I know here in Opi this will be impossible. Please do not be concerned. Allah knows how I have been living and will understand. I would ask you to go to your Opi families and request clean strips of seamless cloth so you will be able to cover all the skin on my body. Tie the cloth at the top of my head and the bottom of my feet."

David reached for Omar's hand and held it gently, "Omar, I promise we will find a way to wrap your body as you have said— leave that part to us."

"Thank you my brothers. I know you will be successful."

Omar explained how his burial plot should be constructed. "Bury my body before twenty-four hours has passed. The hole in the earth should be long and wide enough to place my body flat on my back, making sure no part of my body is bent. You can lay my body directly on the dirt or on any kind of platform if that is easier. It is very important that I not be placed in any type of box. Finally place me in the hole so that I am facing Mecca. If you bury me in a hole by the cemetery, my head should be closest to the town. This will ensure that my head is looking toward Mecca. At the end of the world, I will be called from where I lie, and I will be together with Allah in heaven. At that time, Allah will give everyone an accounting of how they lived their lives on earth. There will be no need for a judge. Allah and each individual will be able to see both the good and the bad deeds each person has done while on this earth."

Omar described heaven to his six Christian brothers. "There are different levels in heaven, with Allah at the top. The level directly below Allah is saved for the prophets and messengers. This place of honor, close to Allah, assures the holy ones of contentment for eternity. The next level is for those people who were given great wisdom and knowledge, and used this gift to help their brothers and sisters while they were on earth. If Allah gives a person the gift of great wisdom but they do not use that gift to help others, that person will be banished, never to have contact with Allah.

Another high level in heaven is for the poor and the sickly, those who have suffered here on earth, yet still lived their lives trying to be kind and helpful to others. Allah will reward them for their suffering. Others, whether they were rich or healthy or only average, they, too, will be assigned a level in heaven depending on the good deeds they performed while on this earth. Merciful Allah even provides a level in heaven for those who have done an equal number of good and bad deeds. However, they must first serve a period of purification, during which they are unable to see Allah. After this period of time, which is decided by Allah, they will join Allah in heaven, but at a lower level. Finally, Allah in his justice will send those who were unjust, greedy, or chose not to do good deeds for others to hell. These poor souls will never be allowed to be with Allah, their creator. So, dear friends, I hope you can understand the contentment I desire and the reason I have decided to leave you this day."

After Omar's explanation, his six brothers had a much clearer understanding of why Omar had come to such a fatal decision. They also knew Omar did not use words carelessly just to endear himself to others. Only now was it slowly registering with them, the extent of Omar's sacrifice over the past year in delaying his decision until today. Jem sat quietly with his head down, embarrassed at his earlier outburst. Omar made a point of reaching across to Jem and touching him gently on the wrist, but Jem was unable to raise his head.

Daniel placed his arm lovingly on Omar's shoulder and looked directly into his deep, dark eyes. "You were more worried about how we would feel than you were about your own happiness. Now I understand how much you love us."

The men huddled closer together, sitting on their stones in the empty lot in front of their warm fire. The sun was beginning its descent in the west. George had learned to express his emotions in a way he could not have if he had remained within his British culture, and he told Omar what they were all feeling. "You have been a good and wise friend. We're going to miss you terribly. If you are killed, I hope Allah will allow you to give us some of the peace you are going to find in death. If that can happen, the rest of our years will be much easier."

"I hope that your Allah allows you to stay spiritually connected to us," added David. "Just think how nice it will be if we can feel you with us every Sunday."

Omar made one final request, speaking without any doubt that some day they would be free men. "If I am killed, and when you are finally freed, I wish for you to tell my family where my remains are located. I believe they would want to bring me back to Egypt."

The six men agreed, each silently doubting the possibility of freedom. Omar stood up and each brother gave him a warm embrace. Without a further word being spoken, he walked toward the cobblestone road, made a left, and slowly walked down the street leading out of town. The others sat in silence, which was soon broken by three sounds: first, the voice of an Italian yelling three separate times, "Arresto" (Stop), then scuffling, more shouting, and finally the sound of a single rifle shot, followed by deadly silence. The six men ran to the entrance of the town. Some people rushed from their houses or stood in front of their open front doors. Others moved excitedly toward the sound of the rifle shot. When the six brothers arrived, Omar was lying motionless on the ground about five feet beyond the wagon. His shirt was spattered with blood and both of his eyes were tightly closed as if he had died with all his outrage resolved. It was obvious that Omar had faced death with defiance.

The protectors were standing around Omar when the captives arrived. People who had been in the bar were now standing by the cart. There was total silence, as the two protectors looked at the six other hostages with confusion and bewilderment.

Gabriel, immediately followed by Jem, rushed the two men and started punching, knocking them down. The rest of the captives instinctively rushed forward to protect Gabriel and Jem from the other people. The brief melee was quickly brought to order. The angry captives glared at the crowd as they circled Omar's body. Both protectors assured the crowd they were fine and did not want anyone to take further action. Without a word, the six men gently lifted their dead friend and carried him back to his room.

As the six men slowly walked up Via San Giovanni de Battista, many people were on the street watching as Omar's body was being carried up the middle of the cobblestone road. They seemed as flustered as the protectors had been.

The six men placed Omar's lifeless body on his bed. George and Daniel fashioned a platform out of scrap wood and then washed the platform thoroughly. David washed Omar's body. Gabriel, George, and Klein went to the various families requesting clean cotton material for wrapping Omar's body, and the families were generous with their offerings. After covering Omar's body as he had directed, the six hostages proceeded to the valley and explained to the men in the wagons that they intended to dig a grave. The protectors from the top and lower roads led the six men to the valley with the seven escorts following behind.

A large hole was carefully dug outside the iron fence of the cemetery. This vigorous digging enabled them to deflect some of the anger caused by the needless death of a close friend and their feelings about the selfish attitude of their captors, who were unable to understand the complexity of what they had done. The following day, the six prisoners told their captors they were going to bury Omar and would not work on the farms. Each family agreed. After breakfast, the families let them out of their rooms to bury Omar.

Omar's clean, wrapped body was carried to the grave on the wooden platform. No one else was on the road or the narrow sidewalk as the men proceeded down the main cobblestone road carrying their dead friend. The people of Opi chose to watch this solemn parade from behind their window curtains. Omar's farming family followed, along with members of the governing council. At the gravesite, the captives lowered the wooden platform holding Omar's body into the grave using ropes Daniel had borrowed from Vincenzo. As they covered Omar with dirt, the townspeople left without saying a word. The only people remaining were four protectors with rifles in two wagons, the seven escorts, Vincenzo, the head of the governing council, and Nicoangelo, the husband of Omar's Opi family. The escorts had handguns at their waists, clear for all to see. They maintained a distance from the gravesite, where the six brothers stood.

The captives spent some time softly talking about Omar, how they felt about him, and what he meant to them. By now, all the hostages had come to accept the most annoying habit of the people of Opi—never saying a word or communicating a feeling or thought when there was a serious problem or crisis involving an Angel. The hostages were never able to determine if this trait was the way the people of Opi normally responded or if their silence came from their profound guilt. In this particular case, their silence was probably wise. The six hostages were in no mood to listen to anything the people of Opi might want to say. Even their sympathy would have been disingenuous and probably serve only to further anger the hostages.

During the following week, Klein convinced his Opi farming partner to allow him to bring to his room an unusually shaped stone that had been on their farm for many years. Under the supervision of his Opi family, Klein crudely chiseled the letters *Omar* on one side of the stone. The following Sunday the six captives were permitted to place the stone at the head of Omar's grave.

By the fall of 1965, the six remaining captives were approaching their nineteenth year in Opi. Jem was handsome, blond-haired, slim, and muscular. His positive attitude was not quite as forceful as it had been when he was first brought to Opi, but he was still far from total resignation. Jem had learned to look at his life with a new perspective. He was not a beaten man, although he now possessed a similar level of conflict as the others because of his forced stay in Opi.

Daniel had learned that his personal and mental growth occurred in a limited and distorted context of time and environment. He had been able to change and grow during this period of time with little choice or control over how he lived his life. Without schooling, travel, tutors, or the advantage of a wise mentor, the boy from the Bronx— who had often been overly quiet because he was concerned that what he had to say might bore others—was now confident in his ability to contribute. This change was due in large part to his six special friends and the luxury of uncluttered time. Daniel's self-confidence was an unexpected gift from his forced stay in Opi.

Gabriel, a healthy-looking, muscular man, remained involved with Theresa. Their mutually satisfying sexual relationship had become the scandal of Opi. Theresa was now fifty-six years of age and still physically vital. She expected her life with Gabriel would continue as it was for as long as he remained in Opi. Theresa understood that someday he would leave, and she would be left with only his memory and her lonely life. She might survive without his touch, but she could not endure a broken heart.

The relationship between Theresa and the foreigner had become common knowledge. Tiziano was powerless to intercede. He would have to live with the disgrace and shame of being a father who was too weak to control his only daughter. For an Italian father, this was a particularly devastating stigma. Because of this Theresa never had to use a knife to gain her revenge—Gabriel's continued presence was much more effective.

George had been tall and slender when he arrived in Opi, and he had changed very little physically over the years. The farming tasks that had made the other boys muscular and firm did not have the same effect on George. However, during his years in Opi, his internal change was radical. He had gradually learned to shed his "stiff" British demeanor, and he was surprised to find that he had a natural, intuitive skill to console or intervene successfully when the other captives found themselves in an emotional crisis. However, George was going through a personal emotional crisis that he was unable to admit to himself and the other captives.

Klein was still strikingly attractive and deeply in love with Giovanna. Although Giovanna no longer had to sneak out at night to meet him, she had accepted the severe restrictions on their time together. Many years ago, they had vowed to live their unmarried celibate life, satisfied, for now, to be with each other on Saturdays under the close chaperoning eye of Klein's Opi family, and on Sundays with the other captives and the few other women who had remained unmarried, all under the watchful eye of the escorts. Giovanna opted to accept the dual role of unmarried companion and loving daughter until the day Klein was free.

Throughout their years in Opi, David had become a pillar of strength for the six prisoners, who credited him with making the stress of their personal conflict more controllable. David was somehow able to convince the others that their survival depended on keeping alive a slim belief that freedom was a possibility. His brothers helped him deal with his Jewish heritage and his life of captivity, but he still harbored doubt.

The six brothers had been living with tension for some nineteen years. Separation from family, friends, and society for such a long period caused a great deal of internal stress. They had no name for their feelings—they just knew that at times things became so difficult that they felt threatened by everybody and everything.

During a peaceful conversation one Sunday in the winter of 1966, Gabriel was feeling particularly defensive about his relationship with Theresa, and he responded inappropriately to a simple statement by Daniel.

"So, you think I don't have anxious thoughts? You talk as though I'm able to think straight. Let me tell you, my teeth clench the same as yours. I pace, I bite my nails, and my mouth is always dry like yours. Do you think you're the only ones with butterflies in your stomach? Sometimes my heart beats so fast it scares the shit out of me."

Tension between the young men was as high as it had ever been. Each of the five boys was pleased when David entered the heated conversation between Daniel and Gabriel. "You guys mentioned everything except how we tend to rub our hands together nervously. How could you two have forgotten our favorite habit?"

This mild bit of "inside" humor forced Gabriel and Daniel to smile at each other, and Gabriel gave Daniel a gentle, affectionate slap on the shoulder.

The others were laughing, except for George, who unexpectedly jumped up and shouted, "Stop it, stop it, stop it. How can you jerks laugh at the fact that we've all gone crazy? Are you so scared that you won't face the fact that we've lost our minds? David, you sit there making fun of us for rubbing our hands together, you of all people. I thought you, more than any of us understood, but I see that even you're afraid to admit you're nuts like the rest of us."

Daniel, who was seated next to George, jumped up and said, "George, tell me what's happened. What's wrong?"

George moved away from Daniel, who was attempting to make physical contact with him, and shouted, "Stay away from me." George's back hit the stone wall. He vigorously moved his head right and left, and his glassy eyes were wide and full of fear. George's posture became that of a trapped animal. He shouted again at Daniel, who was moving very cautiously toward him, "I warn you, stay away from me. I want nothing to do with you or your friends. You are all stupid and don't even know you've gone crazy. Stay away! I'm warning you."

The other men remained seated, feeling that their active involvement might make things worse. Meanwhile, Daniel continued his calm, slow advance toward George. He tried to be tranquil and reassuring. Speaking in a whisper, he said, "George everything is going to be okay, you're fine. George, it's me, Dan. I'm your friend, your very special friend....

"No, you're not my friend. You're as crazy as I am. Now get away from me, do you hear, get away from me."

Daniel continued his calm, soft, encouraging dialogue as he touched George's arm. George immediately pulled his arm away and started to run toward the door. Daniel dove at him and tackled him. Daniel's full body was on top of George, and he grasped George's arms and held them close to his body so that George was unable to swing.

Daniel quietly whispered in George's ear, "You're safe now, George. I won't let anything happen to you. No one can hurt you. You're with your brothers. We love you. We are your friends; we'll never leave you. You're safe with us."

George slowly stopped struggling and eventually became still. Daniel remained on top of him, continuing to whisper comforting words. George began to sob. Daniel slowly moved off George, sat him up, and firmly embraced his distraught friend.

The others slowly circled George and Daniel, each man making some type of physical contact with George. After a period of time, George's enormous tension gradually seeped from his body, and his eyes lost their frenzied stare. Daniel slowly released his hug. George reached out to touch each of his friends, although he kept his head down, unwilling to make eye contact.

The six men sat silently in physical contact with George until he was able to regain his composure. The six hostages spent the rest of the afternoon talking frankly about their feelings. George was silent and embarrassed, but he listening intently. They agreed to be more open with each other regarding their day-to-day feelings and emotions, especially their loneliness and sadness. They also agreed to be more alert to each other's mood. As dusk arrived, they volunteered to escort George back to his room.

George refused their offer, saying, "My outburst is over, and I prefer that each of you understand and accept me as though I am now stable and well. I have been enough of a burden for today."

The following Sunday, the six men continued their discussion of the previous week. They concluded that they had a better understanding of their distress and apprehension, which was caused by so many things they were unable to control. They knew they had to accept their situation as a permanent part of their lives.

David continued to expand on his discussion from last week. "We'll probably never get used to it, but we need to remind each other that these feeling are never going away. We're still gonna fidget and feel tight, have sleep problems, wake up sweating, and, of course, Dan's crazy dream will still be part of his nights. The point I'm trying to make is we need to remember that any one of us could at any time have the same experience as George had last week. It's a miracle that it took this long to happen. Let's remember we are all in this until the day our misery ends. George did us a favor by reminding us of that."

CHAPTER XIV

PETE RECEIVES A MEDICAL EVALUATION

In the spring of 1961, Pete was fifty-nine years of age, and he could no longer endure the physical demands of his construction job. He obtained employment as a night janitor at New York Life Insurance Company in Manhattan. Although the work was not as physically demanding, Pete still felt tired from morning to night.

One evening, after approximately a year at his night job, Pete fainted. He was taken by ambulance to the nearest hospital, where he was diagnosed with low blood pressure. The doctors informed Suzy and the children that a new medical procedure, the implantation of a pacemaker, would correct Pete's problem and give him many more productive years. The fact that the doctors proposed placing a metal device in his body was more than enough reason for Pete to decline treatment and demand immediate release from the hospital, refusing to listen to the pleas of his wife and children.

Then, very gradually, something began happening to Pete's speech. He developed a stutter, which grew steadily worse. Talking was becoming more difficult, and he was having trouble forming words. His mind seemed clear; he was able to function normally in all his daily tasks; and he continued to read his paperback detective novels. But by 1963, Pete was unable to form words in any understandable context. Barbara, his daughter, was puzzled by this development and took him to a number of specialists, including: neurological, eye, ear, nose, throat, and lungs. The specialists were unable to find a reason for his inability to speak. One specialist thought it unlikely, but he did speculate that Pete's speech problem could be caused by his chronically poor blood circulation. The doctor suspected that with less blood going to his brain, Pete's cells could be dying from lack of oxygen.

Barbara decided to make an appointment with Dr. Gorman at New York's Cornell Medical Center. Dr. Gorman had been recommended by the neurological specialists. After a series of further tests, some of which Pete had not previously received, Dr. Gorman, like the other specialists, could find no physical cause for Pete's inability to speak.

He told Barbara, "Mrs. Rives, your father's voice mechanism is perfectly normal. I have found nothing to suggest why he is unable to speak. From everything I can see, and from the reports of the other specialists, there is no reason why your father should not be able to speak. To make your father's condition even more baffling, I'm absolutely convinced his poor circulation has no bearing on his problem. He has responded favorably to tests that would have shown the loss of brain cells.

"Can you recall any trauma that might have occurred around the time you first noticed the stuttering?" said Dr. Gorman.

Barbara thought for a moment, and said, "He did work very hard physically for many years in construction. But no, he hasn't had an accident or injury."

The doctor looked confused. "No, hard physical labor in and of itself wouldn't be the cause for speech loss. Tell me, when he was in construction work, did he ever have an accident that caused him to miss time on the job?"

Barbara thought for a few moments and then told the doctor she couldn't think of any such accident.

"Do you know of any mental or emotional problems that might have occurred at the onset of his speech problems?" said the doctor.

"No, there were no mental problems when his stuttering began."

"You say that as though he had mental problems prior to his stuttering."

"Well, the only serious emotional problem he ever had was the disappearance of my younger brother."

"How long was your brother missing?"

"Oh, he was never found. The case has been closed for many years, and we're sure he is dead by now. My brother was thirteen when he disappeared during a trip to Italy with my father, but that was almost twenty years ago."

"Can you tell me the circumstances of your brother's disappearance?"

Barbara told the doctor everything she knew about Daniel's disappearance.

"After your brother was given up for dead, was there any noticeable behavior change in your father?"

"When you say behavior, do you mean did he start drinking or other things like that?"

"Well, yes, that's the type of behavior change I am referring to — any change that you would consider out of character for your father."

What immediately came to Barbara's mind was how her father had alienated his family. She explained in some detail her father's irrational behavior directed toward his brothers, Aunt Grace, and other family members and friends.

Doctor Gorman leaned forward at his desk with a serious look on his face. "Mrs. Rives, I have a theory about what might be causing your father's inability to speak."

"You do?" said Barbara.

"It's very possible that the cause is psychological in nature."

"What do you mean by psychological?"

"Your father may be suffering from what we call 'mutism.' There are two types of mutism. 'Akinetic mutism' is a condition caused by a lesion in the third ventricle, which makes people unable to utter a vocal sound. This is also known as 'abulia.' My tests show conclusively that abulia is not a factor for your father. The second type of mutism is called 'selective mutism,' and I believe this could be the problem in your father's case. This is a neuropsychological disorder that is often confused with depression. But I don't think that is the case with your father. I know from my tests that he is capable of speech and understands language.

"There is a widespread theory that selectively mute people often unconsciously choose to be silent. People with selective mutism often experience a severe emotional trauma, which causes them to remain silent. Despite their physical ability to speak, they seem unable to form sounds. There have been reported cases of selective mutism in people who have experienced untreated, intense, emotional trauma and pain. From your description of the circumstances surrounding your brother's disappearance, and your father's subsequent irrational behavior toward family and friends, it's my opinion that your father is suffering from selective mutism."

Barbara was surprised by such an unusual diagnosis. "But, doctor, how can a trauma cause a person who knows how to speak suddenly be unable to speak?"

"The human body often unconsciously compensates for the experience of long-standing emotional trauma," said Dr. Gorman. "I believe there are two factors at play with your father. First, after the misery and anguish he felt from cutting family and friends out of his life, his subconscious might have protected him from further pain by not speaking. If he could no longer speak, he could no longer destroy further relationships. Now please understand that it's very possible these untreated feelings, after so many years, have turned to rage that is so internally strong that subconsciously your father dreads any verbal expression.

"Second, you must realize that feelings of guilt and anger are very harmful emotions. If unexpressed emotions are allowed to build and accumulate, it is common for the body to compensate in some way as a means of self survival. These mental compensations—when left untreated and unresolved for many years—could have contributed to your father's mutism."

Fortunately, Doctor Gorman suggested a solution. "Mrs. Rives, don't think of selective mutism as merely a reaction to the 'sorrows of life' or feeling sad or depressed. This is a very precise medical problem that can be cured with the proper treatment. I would urge you to have your father immediately start long-term psychological treatment with a competent therapist."

Barbara was pleased that someone had suggested a possible diagnosis with a solution. She thanked the doctor, but she did not mention how difficult she knew it would be to convince her father of the benefits of psychiatric treatment.

Barbara was correct. Pete refused to see a psychiatrist. After badgering him for six months, the three children gave up on their efforts to have their father seek treatment. Pete's mutism did not improve, and with each passing year, he continued to physically deteriorate.

CHAPTER XV

$\mathcal{D}$ANIEL'S $\mathcal{O}$PI

$\mathcal{F}$AMILY

The weather in Opi was ideal from late spring to September. The air was especially clean and always seemed to have a mild, sweet scent. The days were clear and bright. Daniel found the weather in the valley from spring to autumn to be an unexpected source of pleasure, almost captivating. However, the town always paid a price for the glorious spring and summer, and that price was winter! The winter months were brutality cold, windy, and shrouded by thick snow that fell two to three times a week.

Daniel and the other captives always felt weary, but never totally exhausted. The wood-burning stove kept his room warm, and Daniel's outward physical needs were well met. His emotional needs were a different matter—this was an ongoing problem throughout his stay in Opi.

Daniel's winter weekends were spent helping with rotating the cheese, making wine, working with the small animals, chopping wood, and doing other tasks that helped pass the time. He was much happier when he was busy. If he sat alone in his room on Saturdays, his thoughts would always be of his home in America, and soon an overwhelming feeling of total loneliness would take over and absorb him for the remainder of the day.

Saturday afternoons after his bath were spent helping Gelsomina prepare the bread she would make the following day, for the coming week. She used a portion of the bread starter she had stored for many years dissolved in warm water, to which Daniel would then add flour and beat it to make a soft batter. The bowl was then covered, and the starter, water, and flour was allowed to ferment until the following day. Gelsomina would not consider making her weekly bread without this mixture, which she called a *biga*.

Sunday morning after Mass, Gelsomina and Daniel were always alone making bread, and she was openly friendly and relaxed during this time. Gelsomina was no longer able to beat and knead the bread dough because of her painful swollen fingers, so she used Daniel for this purpose. During the first year, Daniel often wondered why Gelsomina did not have her daughters help her make the fresh bread daily. It is quite unusual for Italian women not to prepare fresh food every day, including bread.

Daniel didn't know that their weekly bread baking was Gelsomina's excuse to have private time with Daniel. After the first year, he allowed himself to enjoy his time with her and soon found it pleasant and rewarding. In a few years, he came to accept Gelsomina as a replacement for his mother. It made no sense, but he learned to be grateful for their relationship. The confused dynamics of his feelings were not strong enough to destroy the positive relationship he had mysteriously found in the Sgammotta home. He eventually realized he needed her as much as she needed him.

Gelsomina refused to tell Daniel her age, but she looked to be in her mid-sixties. Her eyes were sad and heavy, but deeply sensitive, and they immediately gave away her mood. She had a round face that could not hide her once youthful and beautiful features, which now showed the wear of many years of hard labor and grave tragedy. She wore her straight hair pulled back and tied in an intricate bun. She always wore long, black dresses with black, low-heeled shoes.

Working alone with her briefly on Saturday and then on Sunday morning, Daniel was able to observe Gelsomina's dual personality. In the company of Vincenzo, she completely deferred to him in all matters. She tended to be quiet and displayed a seriousness that bordered on sadness. But during her time alone with Daniel, her eyes, face, posture, and language would become lighter and refreshed with smiles. With Daniel, she felt free to express imaginative thoughts and creative ideas. Daniel found Gelsomina to be a friendly listener, interested in his feelings, his family, and his life in America.

One Sunday morning in the early 1950s, Daniel, who was then sixteen years of age, was making bread with her, when he said, "Gelsomina, can I speak with you about my feelings of being a hostage in Opi?"

"Well, of course, I want you to think of me as your Mamma. I think of you as a son, so yes, speak with me about anything."

"It makes me angry to know you won't accept the fact that being held in Opi against my will is the cause of terrible loneliness and sadness in my life."

Gelsomina smiled, as though Daniel had made an immature, child-like statement. "Oh, my Donato, you must realize you came to us as a young boy. All young children growing into adults have such feelings, no matter where they are. You will see—soon your sadness will pass."

"See, that's exactly what makes me angry," responded Daniel. "You won't admit the cause of my sadness is that I'm a prisoner in your home."

"Donato, please don't say such things! You are here with me, and we have such a good time together. We do everything in our power to make you happy. We are your loving family now. Let us love you."

"No, you don't do everything in your power. You won't let me go home to America!"

"Trust me when I say that the time will come when you will see how foolish these feelings are. Someday, you will choose to become one of us, find a nice Opi girl, marry, have children, and live out your years with us in happiness."

"If I'm becoming so happy, tell me why I have the same stupid, upsetting dream almost every night," said Daniel, who felt frustrated and defiant.

"Tell me of this thing you call an upsetting dream."

"What difference will it make? You won't understand."

Daniel was now vigorously kneading the *ciabatta* bread while Gelsomina watched him. "Donato, why are you harsh with me? I am only trying to be kind."

Daniel, feeling guilty, thought to himself. *Why does she always do this to me?* He continued, "Okay, here's my dumb dream. About three or four times a week, I wake up startled by the same scary dream. In the dream, Vincenzo lets me go home for the weekend, but all the time I'm with my America family, I'm worried about not getting back in time for work on Monday morning. Then I wake up sweating. It makes no sense—I told you it was a dumb dream. Are you happy now?"

233

Gelsomina, raising both hands, tilting her head to the right with a slight grin and expressing a sigh of complete understanding, responded immediately to Daniel's riddle. "See, Donato, my prayers are being answered! Your dream is telling you that your home is now with us in Opi. Listen to Gelsomina when I say you will soon find much pleasure with us."

Daniel rolled his eyes and mumbled to himself, "What's the use?" He continued to knead the dough, punishing every strand of gluten.

Being able to share his feelings with Gelsomina, although often frustrating, eventually helped relieve some of his tension. Gelsomina, for all her stubbornness and apparent unwillingness to accept his feelings, still remained a motherly comfort. But Daniel was not surprised that he was unable to penetrate her wall of denial. Gelsomina was able to block Daniel's true emotions out of her reality.

She also possessed the uncanny skill of being able to deflect his feelings. Knowing his interest in her war experiences, she would often cleverly change the topic of Daniel's unhappiness by recounting her experiences during World War II. Daniel had come to understand her clever tactics but decided it was fruitless to dissuade her.

Gelsomina often talked about her time in the caves, when she and her girls sought refuge from the expected bombing by the Americans. With newfound anger in her voice, she told him, "When the Germans made their headquarters in our little town, all the women and children packed whatever warm clothes they were allowed to take and went to the caves to protect themselves from the bombing. There was little money available at that time, and Vincenzo gave me everything of value to trade for food. My two daughters and my mother came with me."

Daniel knew this had been the most difficult time in her life, but he was more interested in the details.

"We were miserable. I had no money to buy food for my children, so what could I do? I sold my trousseau, the little gold I had, and my wedding band, but through it all I was strong and I kept my wedding vows."

"Where'd you get food when you had nothing else to trade?" said Daniel.

"We went to the mountains in the fall. The farmers in the area had already harvested their crops. So with sticks we would move the earth where the farmers grew their potatoes, looking for small potatoes left in the soil. Using these potatoes mixed with greens and herbs that grew wild in the mountains, we made a daily soup for our evening meal. We also went to farms in the area that had harvested their wheat crop. We would look for wheat berries that had fallen to the ground during the harvest. Using two stones, we would crush the berries into coarse flour, add water, and make flat bread in a skillet. Each day was spent looking for food for that evening. We lived like animals."

"Why did the caves cause the death of so many people?" Daniel had no knowledge of caves and didn't understand the conditions.

Gelsomina took a small cloth from her sleeve and blew her nose, wiped her moist eyes, and sat down, as though the question had suddenly caused great fatigue. "Donato, my words can never make you truly understand. There was little food, no medicine, not enough warm clothes, and the caves were always damp and cold. If a child or adult started to cough, there was no way to make the sickness go away. When sickness came, you waited and prayed that the dreaded typhus fever would not follow; it was the typhus that killed so many of our children and even some adults."

"What's typhus fever?" asked Daniel. "Why did it happen in the caves?"

"Water was hard to find, and it had to be saved for drinking and cooking. Typhus fever spreads easily when people who eat, sleep, and live together are unable to wash and clean themselves. A person would see the reddish spots caused by lice and fleas on their skin, and wait for the dreaded fever. If the fever came, death always followed. Mothers wailed for their children. Adults with the fever went to a corner of the cave, away from others, and waited for their death. When you are constantly freezing, the body stops working even as the mind keeps going."

"Why didn't you and your family get the typhus fever?"

"When the typhus fever started to spread, we moved to another mountain that also had caves. This mountain was close to an aqueduct that supplied water to the towns at the base of the mountain. There, we had all the water we needed for cleaning and drinking, but food was harder to find. We were very hungry during that time in hiding."

Gelsomina described the solid rock caves. "Besides the dampness and hunger, there was also the darkness. Never have I known such darkness. There were no candles, so just before sunset, we'd get our family together and gather everything we owned, because we were 'fraid of the other people also living in the caves. We'd get under our few blankets, because once the darkness came you couldn't see your own hand in front of your face. We slept next to each other for warmth. We put our girls in the middle between myself and my mother, and tried to sleep."

"How long did you have to live in the caves?"

"Five months in that damp hell. When the battle of the Sangro Line was over, the women were told to return to their homes. Vincenzo was happy we'd survived. Even my old mother had lived. The only thing we could do that winter was pray and try to stay warm. Even those who had never prayed before became devout and started praying."

Daniel's feelings for Gelsomina would always remain a mystery. He found himself becoming closer to her, in spite of the part she played in the hell that was his life in Opi. He would often think, *How is it possible to feel so close to this woman? How can I feel toward her as I do my own mother?* Daniel would always remember a saying Gelsomina frequently used: *"La ironia é il modo del per a rimanere anonimo* (Irony is God's way of remaining anonymous)." He wondered if there was some truth to this saying.

Vincenzo—the person Daniel understood the least—was the one with whom he spent the most time. Vincenzo looked to be in his forties when Daniel was first brought to Opi. His skin was a leathery olive brown. His full, thick head of black hair had become spotted with grey streaks over the years, and his black, bushy mustache eventually became solid white. His long, thin nose changed very little and the geometry of his jaw softened, but his intense eyes did not— they remained glaring and challenging. Vincenzo was not a tall man; he had thick broad shoulders and arms demonstrating both power and delicacy. His hips were as wide as his shoulders; his stomach was flat and muscular; and his thighs and legs were equally large and wide. Even as he aged, he was a powerful man with unusual stamina. Vincenzo had a raspy voice and a frequent cough.

As talkative and pleasant as Gelsomina was, Vincenzo was the exact opposite. Like so many others in Opi, he had gone to school for only a few years—enough to learn to read and write. Once that was accomplished, he was made to work to support his family. Daniel noticed that Vincenzo read papers and documents, but he never saw him reading a book. He saw him write his name and other common words but never a document or lengthy letter. He rarely spoke to Daniel in a social context. When he did speak, it was usually for instruction, direction, or clarification of a work task. They worked together farming the fertile valley land five and a half days a week for over twenty years, yet Daniel knew very little about his jailor. Daniel often wondered if Vincenzo would have made the decision to kidnap other human beings in order to save his people if he had lived in a more urban area and had the advantage of a full education.

Vincenzo was never harsh or vindictive without reason, except at the very end of his life, nor did he seem shy in any way. He was demanding, but never once did he expect Daniel to work while he rested. Even as Vincenzo grew older, he still managed to work alongside Daniel without slowing his tempo.

Once Daniel was able to speak the language, he frequently questioned Vincenzo about why he was being held hostage and when he would be released. During Daniel's early years in Opi, Vincenzo chose not to answer Daniel's constant questions. He would take a puff on his cigar and simply not respond. After a period of time of Daniel persisting in his questioning, Vincenzo would irritably reply, "Young man, I am not here to answer questions. I am here to provide for my neighbors, and you are here to assist me in that duty."

Then one day in 1954, Vincenzo became frustrated and relented, and very much in character he told Daniel in short, quick sentences, "You think we are bad people, but we are not. After the war, the people of Opi were unable to survive. Our existence had been stolen from us by the Germans. I watched my neighbors and friends slowly dying. We took the only option available to us. I received no pleasure by bringing you to Opi, but I had no choice."

In time, Vincenzo was more accommodating of Daniel's frequently repeated question. "When do you intend to release me so I can return to my family in America?"

"Yes, I have disturbed your life, but only until our children and grandchildren can once again become responsible for the next generation, as I am now being responsible for my generation," said Vincenzo.

Daniel had been in Opi for four years when Vincenzo arranged a marriage between his daughter Angelina and the son of a man he met selling produce at the market in Pescasseroli. Vincenzo was in favor of such an arrangement only if Angelina and her husband lived in Opi.

The main objective of the Opi social order was to replace, through marriage and children, the males that had been lost during World War II. Angelina's husband agreed to live in Opi and be trained by and assist Patrizio in caring for the sheep as the flock began to grow.

When the price structure of wool drastically changed in the 1950s because of the importing of New Zealand wool and the introduction of synthetic fabrics, Opi and many other European towns turned from their dependence on sheep to farming for their existence. Vincenzo expected Angelina's husband to shift his work to farming. He refused, no longer feeling bound by the marriage agreement because of the change in his work status. Vincenzo felt betrayed when Angelina moved with her husband to Pescasseroli so he could work in a small machine factory. For Vincenzo, the line of succession of the Opi communal structure had been broken by a member of his own family. This was a shameful, shattering blow to Vincenzo and his great pride.

Daniel had expected Maria Antonia to marry and also move out of the house, but she never did. Daniel and Maria Antonia's relationship became an evolving story. She was an attractive, personable woman. Her appearance was very much like her father's—she had smooth, appealing olive skin, a thin nose that made her look stately, and long, light brown hair, which was always tied back. Her build was like her mother's—short and thin.

Although Daniel was never permitted to be alone with Maria Antonia, there was something about her manner that told him she had empathy for his situation. Their nonverbal relationship, which started after Daniel had been in Opi for two years, was one he came to value and from which he gained a great deal of satisfaction. Daniel was sure these feelings were hormonally driven. He could think of no other explanation.

He was pleased that Maria Antonia had never moved away from the Sgammotta house. His cloudy sensual feeling for her—which he experienced only from a distance—was just another mystery. By 1951, Daniel had become sexually mature, and he assumed his attraction for Maria Antonia was part of that process. Unable to have any personal interaction with her, Daniel was unable to verify whether these feelings were something more than his maturing sexual urges.

The fleeting, frequent touching of his face and temples by Maria Antonia when she trimmed his beard and hair became more frequent by the mid-1950s. Her warm hand holding his chin as she slowly trimmed his beard aroused a strong sexual urge in him. Daniel would stare at her lovely, olive face, unable to tell her what was happening inside his body. Maria Antonia would shyly grin when she noticed Daniel staring at her face with his desperate, yearning eyes.

One day, as Maria Antonia was trimming his beard, he could stand it no longer. He reached up and touched her hand. Maria Antonia stopped breathing for a moment and turned to see if her parents had noticed. When Maria Antonia saw Vincenzo's eyes covered by his newspaper, she once again began to breathe and returned her gaze to Daniel, looking at him with equally passionate eyes. These few moments of shared passion ended abruptly when Maria Antonia removed her hand from Daniel's, glancing once again toward the dining room.

This brief sensual touching without words continued throughout Daniel's time in Opi. He would lie in his bed at night recreating the feeling of Maria Antonia's hands on his face. He fantasized these same hands stroking his entire body. The time between haircuts became abbreviated, using the excuse that he wanted a shorter beard. Daniel waited anxiously for his beard and hair to grow.

With a comb in her left hand and scissors in her right, Maria Antonia would glance in the direction of the dining room before moving her left hand past Daniel's lips and holding it there momentarily, pretending to be using the scissors. Daniel would feel the rush of energy to his loins. Maria Antonia would glance toward the dining room as her hand remained against his lips, and Daniel's hand gently touched hers as he pressed it against his lips. If her hand remained in place, Daniel knew Vincenzo and Gelsomina were unaware of what was transpiring between the pair of sensually thrilled young adults. If she removed her hand quickly, Daniel understood that one of her parents had moved to a position where they might notice.

In the summer of 1967, Danny, the oldest Ciarletta brother at seventy-one years of age and now retired, was admitted to a Miami hospital with congestive heart failure. He survived for two days and then died on the third. His wife Kate had his body shipped to New York for burial services. Years earlier, they had purchased a double burial plot in St. Raymond's cemetery in the Bronx. The one-day wake was scheduled to be held in a funeral home on Soundview Avenue.

The receiving line at the wake included Kate and her sisters Suzy, Anna and the twins Margaret and Grace, and her brother Frank, and Danny's four brothers, Pete, Al, Bob, and Phil. The three brothers, who had not seen or spoken to Pete for years, greeted him politely and respectfully, shaking hands, inquiring about his obviously deteriorating health, and asking about his children and grandchildren. They had heard that Pete was having problems talking, but they did not know he was no longer speaking. They interpreted the nodding of his head and his silence as continuing hard feelings, and the atmosphere remained cold.

The next morning, the immediate family gathered at the funeral parlor for the final viewing before the casket was closed, and then driven a short distance to Holy Cross church for the Funeral Mass.

Phil, the youngest Ciarletta brother, had always felt indebted to Pete for the way Pete supported him when he first arrived in America, and he approached Pete as the family was chatting while waiting for the casket to be moved.

Phil shook Pete's hand warmly, and said, "I wanted to let you know we're going to retire in a year and turn the business over to Bob's oldest boy, Leopoldo and my two sons, Carl and Leopoldo. I think Pàtete is in heaven smiling, knowing two of his grandchildren named Leopoldo will be running the business."

Pete nodded and managed a brief smile.

Pleased and encouraged by even this brief but positive response from his oldest living brother, Phil said with anguish in his voice, "Pete, Pete, what happened to us? I still don't understand how things went so wrong when we were so close."

Pete looked at Phil with older, sadder eyes and simply shrugged his shoulders. Phil interpreted Pete's response as meaning indifference and decided to leave the subject and move to less emotional topics. He told Pete about his brothers. "Bob and Gerasina are living on Long Island. Diana and I live in Yonkers in a nice little house off McClain Avenue. Al got divorced from his second wife about eight years ago, and with no children to keep him here, he's decided that when we turn the business over to the kids he is going to return to Castellamare di Stabia and live in Pàtete's empty apartment." Phil shook Pete's hand warmly, as the family began moving out to the cars for travel to the church services.

After the Funeral Mass, the motor procession arrived at Saint Raymond's Cemetery for the burial. There was a final brief prayer service at the cemetery chapel after the burial. The family members were standing on the steps of the chapel saying goodbye to each other, when Kate suddenly and publicly confronted Pete with fire in her eyes.

"Pete, the night before your brother died, he asked me to tell you he understood your deep pain. His words to me that evening were, 'Tell Pete I love him.' Now that I've told you what I promised my dying husband, you must also hear from me. Danny and I loved Daniel as though he was our own child. When he disappeared, our hearts were also broken. We finally accepted his death and mourned his loss. We went on with our lives. But not you—you decided to hate everyone who loved you. Danny was not able to live with your anger, so we moved and were forced to separate from our family. Because of you, Danny was denied his four brothers and my sister Suzy by his bedside so he could say goodbye—and for all those years in Miami, I was deprived of the companionship of my sisters and brother. Pete, Danny may have forgiven you, but I am unable to find it in my heart to forgive you. I know the Almighty will punish me for this failure. I will say to God, 'Lord, I honestly tried to forgive Pete, but I failed.' Pete, I ask you one question. What are *you* prepared to say to your Lord?"

Kate quickly turned, walked down the chapel steps, and proceeded to Emile's car. The other family members were stunned at Kate's defiant outburst in such an inopportune, questionable setting, and they were slow to follow her lead by moving to their individual cars. Pete remained immobile, nostrils flaring, face red, eyes glaring. Frances went to her father, took him by the arm, and helped him down the stairs and into her husband's car.

CHAPTER XVI

ℛELEASE ℱROM ℭAPTIVITY

As the spring of 1969 approached, the captives were back in the valley for their twenty-second year of farming. The unhappiness and loneliness of their life was a burden they had learned to balance, until the time when they were no longer needed in Opi and finally disposed of. They no longer enjoyed any zest for life. Attempting to escape was an activity that had become a distant memory. Their listless, quiet Sundays together, and the bitterness they felt toward the people of Opi, now extended to the few Opi females who were their age. Interestingly, all that remained for the six hostages was the curiously, quirky satisfaction that came from the skill and competence they had attained in their routine farming chores.

All six men believed they would never be freed by the people of Opi. They had concluded years earlier that when their usefulness to the people was over, they would be killed. This conclusion was no longer an assumption kept secret by each captive—their inescapable anxiety had been shared years ago.

Klein remained positive only with Giovanna, not wanting to destroy the hope that only she continued to affirm. In the privacy of his room and with his brothers, Klein expected that he and Giovanna would never experience married life in Austria, even though Giovanna's father continued to assure her that marriage to the Austrian boy would someday become a reality.

Daniel was confronted with a new problem. Vincenzo had significantly changed. He was moody and short-tempered, and incidents of him losing his temper were increasing. Simple chores that had been acceptable in the past were now unsatisfactory. One day, after all the peas had been planted, Daniel and Vincenzo began planting lettuce and beets. Vincenzo was distributing the lettuce and escarole seeds in narrow trenches, and Daniel was planting the beet seeds. Vincenzo suddenly became concerned that the furrow Daniel had made for the beet seeds was too deep and ordered him to correct the problem. Daniel elected to ignore the criticism and follow whatever new directions Vincenzo had decided on for that day. He simply did not have the energy to challenge Vincenzo for another unfounded criticism. He changed the depth of the furrow and proceeded to plant the beet seeds in a trench he knew was too shallow.

The following day, after their midday rest period, Daniel and Vincenzo were preparing a new planting area by removing dead plant vegetation. After placing the dead vegetation on the large *mucchio di spazzatura* (waste or mulch pile), Vincenzo surprised Daniel by telling him to stop work because they were leaving the valley early. It was rare for Vincenzo to leave work early. This occurred only if there was an important town meeting or a special family event.

"Why are we going in early. Is there an occasion today?"

"No occasion," said a raspy-voiced Vincenzo.

Their wagon began to move on the dirt road parallel to the hill town. Vincenzo's usual cough seemed harder and more frequent. Halfway up the road, Daniel noticed he was having difficulty holding onto the reins.

"Would it help if I took the reins?" said Daniel.

"No, I'm capable of controlling my wagon,"

As they approached the two men in the wagon at the bottom of the dirt road, Daniel could see that Vincenzo was in a great deal of discomfort. He noticed what looked like blood coming from the side of Vincenzo's mouth.

Daniel pressed Vincenzo one more time. "Stop being stubborn, Vincenzo. Let me take the reins! Don't worry—the protectors won't let me get away."

"Controlling this wagon is not your responsibility."

By now, Vincenzo was barely able to hold the reins, and the horse—which was no longer a slave to the bit in its mouth—began to veer off the road.

Daniel pulled on the reins and raised his voice. "Vincenzo, the horse is moving off the road! Give me the reins until we reach the protectors."

With the last ounce of strength left in his body, Vincenzo pulled the reins out of Daniel's hands. Daniel stood and waved to the men in the wagon about twenty yards away and shouted, "*Puo venire qua?* (Can you come here?)" In the time it took the men to get to the wagon, Vincenzo had lost his grip on the reins. The protectors stopped the horse. One of the men grasped Daniel by the arm and brought him to his wagon. The other protector took the reins of Vincenzo's wagon and struck the back of the horse, which galloped toward town.

When they arrived at 25 Via San Giovanni de Battista, Vincenzo was helped to his apartment and Daniel was placed in his room and the door locked.

About three hours later, Maria Antonia entered Daniel's room with his evening meal. "Maria Antonia, why are you here. Why are you alone?" A wave of excitement rushed through his body. For the first time in twenty-two years, the unspoken rule had been broken. Daniel found it difficult to concentrate on anything but the image of holding Maria Antonia in his arms. Once the sensual image had passed, Daniel noticed she was distraught and shaken—and she had not come to his room thinking of falling into his arms, but rather because she was in terrible turmoil.

"I'm afraid Papa's condition is very serious. He's been taken to a hospital in Pescasseroli." Maria Antonia placed his meal on the table.

"Do you have to leave?" asked Daniel.

"Oh, Daniel, please understand. I cannot remain here alone. Mamma is expecting me to return." She hurried to the rear door, looked back at Daniel for a moment, and left, closing the door behind her. As Daniel was eating his bread and bean soup, he became quite angry. He wondered, as he always did after disappointments, what caused him to feel such intense rage, a fury so intense that it frightened him.

The following morning, Gelsomina's hands were shaking as she handed Daniel his breakfast. "Vincenzo is in the hospital in Pescasseroli," she said. "And there will be no work at the farm today."

Two days passed without any work. On the third day, Daniel was invited to spend time with Gelsomina and her daughters. They spent part of the morning in the new small piazza that had recently replaced the empty lot where the captives gathered on Sundays.

Angelina, who was living with her husband in Pescasseroli, had traveled to Opi to spend the morning with her mother and sister.

Around eleven o'clock, Maria Antonia went into the house to begin preparations for the afternoon main meal.

Gelsomina began to reminisce about Vincenzo. "Angelina, how am I to continue without my husband? He has been my strength and the strength of Opi. If God takes Vincenzo, I will have only my two girls."

Angelina, in her usual brusque manner said, "Mamma, you always let Papa make the decisions, but now it must be your turn. You are a very smart woman. Papa held you back. You do not need to rely on others."

"Oh, Angelina, if that was only true," said Gelsomina, her mind filled with doubt.

At *pranzo*, they talked about the arrangements being made for Gelsomina and her daughters to visit Vincenzo in the hospital. Immediately after the meal, the three women cleaned the dishes, placing the extra food in their small refrigerator. Nicoangelo Leone arrived with a small car to take the women to the hospital. When he entered the dining room, he spoke directly to Daniel.

"Stand, I'm taking you to your room. When I return from Pescasseroli, I'll explain what will be expected of you." Nicoangelo placed Daniel in his room and locked the door.

Daniel had been in his room for approximately ten minutes, when he heard the front door being unlocked. It was Nicoangelo once again, this time carrying two plates covered by a cloth.

"Gelsomina will be returning late this evening from the hospital, and she wanted you to have food for your evening meal."

The following day his usual breakfast was not delivered. In the late afternoon he heard the front door being opened; it was Nicoangelo again. "I have been placed in charge of you while Vincenzo is in the hospital. I will be responsible for your meals."

"What's wrong with Vincenzo?" inquired Daniel.

"He has *cancro della gola* (cancer of the throat and lungs), and the doctors have given him only days to live."

Daniel was surprised to hear the news, but he was determined not to express any words of concern, even though he was curious. "How could this have happened so suddenly?"

"The doctors said Vincenzo had this problem for a long period. They were surprised when they learned he was able to work with his disease." Nicoangelo added nothing further and left Daniel's room.

The days passed slowly as Daniel remained isolated in his room. One afternoon, Daniel heard his name being called from the back of his room. It was the other captives. *Today must be Sunday,* he thought.

"Dan, have you heard? Vincenzo is dead," said Gabriel.

"Dead? Nobody told me."

"It's not surprising that you would be the last to know," said George. The captives had become accustomed to the confusing relationships the people of Opi had with their hostages.

The following morning, Daniel heard his front door being unlocked. He was surprised once again to see Maria Antonia enter his room. He had not seen her, Angelina, or Gelsomina since the morning at the piazza. She brought his breakfast and midday meal. Maria Antonia was visibly distracted. Daniel's first inclination was to attribute her unusual nervous behavior to the fact that her father had recently died.

"Maria Antonia, I have never seen you so nervous. Are you okay?"

"Yes, Donato. I'm fine. It's just that I must leave town, and I don't want to be late. I have come to tell you that papa died eight days ago, the evening after mamma and I went to the hospital. I'm very sad, but it was for the best. He was suffering. We knew he had chest pains and a sore throat for the past year, but he kept saying it was simply his age. He refused to go to the hospital."

Daniel confronted Maria Antonia. "I'm upset that nobody thought to tell me your papa died. I worked with the man for over twenty years, and no one told me...."

Maria Antonia interrupted Daniel, "Donato, we wanted to say something to you, but Nicoangelo told us not to speak of papa's death or allow you out of your room until the governing council had met and made their decisions about the future. That is all I am allowed to say."

"Well, I guess I shouldn't have expected anything different, but I thought by now Gelsomina or you..., well, never mind, I just should've known better."

"Donato, please don't be angry. All I ask is that you wait a few more hours."

"Wait a few more hours? Wait for what? I have been waiting twenty-two years!"

"Donato, please, I'm sorry. I can't talk further." Maria Antonia hesitated and then said, "I will say this to you, but you must promise not to tell anyone that I told you. Do you promise?"

Daniel was still irritated, and not knowing what he was promising, said smugly, "Yeah, I promise."

"Donato, I know you are upset, but please try to understand there are many things I have no control over."

Looking at the shaken woman before him, Daniel suddenly realized that perhaps he had been unfair in taking out his frustration on her for being locked in his dour, windowless room for almost two weeks.

"You're right. I'm sorry. You're not the one I should be angry with. I know it's not your fault. What were you going to say," he said, feeling unusually apologetic.

"There will be a meeting of the governing council tonight, and all six Angels will be brought to the meeting. Please, Donato, no more questions. I've already said too much. I am leaving town now, remember your promise." With that Maria Antonia rushed for the front door. Before leaving, she turned to Daniel and said, "Mamma is in mourning and will not be coming out of the house or seeing anyone for at least a few weeks." She left and locked the door behind her.

Considering Vincenzo's death, Daniel didn't think it particularly strange that the entire town would gather to elect a new head of the council. What was curious was the fact that the captives were going to be taken to a town meeting. This had never happened before.

Daniel kept thinking about Maria Antonia's behavior. He had never seen her in such a shaken state. She seemed more anxious than sad. Then he thought, *Ah, this is it—going to the council meeting might be the first step in getting rid of us.*

Even with this fatal thought, he found it difficult to get Maria Antonia out of his mind. Daniel thought it strange that she would be leaving town—especially today, when the entire town was to meet with the governing council—but he was also curious about where she was going and how she would get there. *Was she going to ride a horse or wagon. Was someone taking her in a car?*

He suddenly stopped asking himself questions, when an alarming thought entered his mind. *They're going to kill us tonight. Maria Antonia left town because she doesn't want to be here when it happens. That's why she was acting so strange.* A sense of calm came over Daniel. He was not frightened, and he gave no thought as to how he would be killed. He simply spent the next few hours recalling his youth in the Bronx and his time in Opi. He felt prepared to die, but he was also content. Daniel was not angry, only sad about the past twenty-two years. He was ready for his Opi life to be over. He thought about Omar's words just before he was killed and believed he, too, would be welcomed by his God.

Later that afternoon, Daniel began thinking about his years with Vincenzo and the ambivalent feelings he had toward him. He had been working with Vincenzo for more than twenty years, yet he knew very little about the man. He knew most of his characteristics and how he worked, but beyond that Daniel had no clear picture of Vincenzo's personality or emotional make-up. He wondered how a person could keep himself so private, so insulated for so many years.

As the afternoon drifted into early evening, Daniel's thoughts of Vincenzo were replaced with the expectation of leaving his room and what awaited him and his brothers.

Daniel heard his door being unlocked. A familiar-looking, large man entered the room and ordered him to move outside. Daniel was pleased for the chance to leave his room, yet he saw an opportunity to exert control. Daniel and the others had learned many years ago to grab at any opportunity that might give them even fleeting moments of power and control. This concept was so important that even though Daniel's mind had been focused on his death for most of the day, he couldn't let this opportunity pass. He decided to be obstinate and experience one final moment of control.

"Follow you. Why should I follow you? I don't even know you. How do I know what you are planning? I won't leave my room until you tell me where I'm going."

The big man was annoyed and surprised at Daniel's response. "Come peacefully, or I'll drag you by the hair of your head. Now get moving."

Having had his moment of satisfaction, Daniel abandoned his "tough guy" role, shrugged his shoulders, and proudly walked with the man to the church.

As they entered the crowded building, he saw people sitting in pews, in the choir loft, and standing in the back and along the sidewalls. Daniel was escorted to the front pew. Jem, George, and Gabe were already seated. Eight men were seated in chairs on the chancel at one side of the altar—four of whom Daniel recognized as being from the families of the other captives. Father Mascia was also seated on the chancel.

Klein and David arrived and were seated with the others in the front pew. The room was buzzing with muted talking. The six men asked each other if they knew why they had been brought to the church.

Daniel whispered to his friends, "Maria Antonia told me this morning we were going to be brought to the meeting and had me promise not to say that she told me, but that was all she said.

None of his brothers had received any advance notice of being brought to the meeting.

When Nicoangelo, the father of Omar's Opi family, stood and approached the front of the chancel, the talking quickly subsided into silence. Nicoangelo addressed the people.

"Welcome to this important meeting. Father Mascia will open tonight's meeting with a prayer."

Father Mascia moved to the lectern and announced that he would open the meeting by reading from Luke, Chapter 6, verses 27 to 29 and verses 35 and 36:

"But I say to you who are listening: love your enemies, do good to those who hate you. Bless those who curse you, pray for those who mistreat you. To him who strikes thee on the one cheek, offer the other also. But love your enemies and do good, and lend not hoping for any return, and your reward shall be great, and you shall be children of the Most High, for he is kind toward the ungrateful and evil. Be merciful, therefore, even as your Father is merciful."

When Father Mascia finished, Nicoangelo arose again and spoke to the people. He mentioned Vincenzo's recent death and how important he had been to the town over the years. He paused, looked toward the ceiling, and then continued. "Now that Vincenzo is gone, I've been elected to take over the leadership position of the council."

Daniel was surprised the people didn't have a chance to vote for their leader. He was seeing firsthand how communism functioned.

"First, let me review the events that have brought us to this evening." Nicoangelo proceeded to give a verbal summary of the events leading to the seven young boys being brought to Opi.

Nicoangelo then switched topics by talking about Opi, "With our country now able to pay a meager pension to its older citizens, we no longer have to worry about our existence. Our young people over the past few years have left Opi seeking employment opportunities in the larger cities and towns, and although many of us are not pleased with this fact, we have learned to be realistic and accept this new chapter in the history of our town. Our young people do not seem interested in our past struggles or our sad history with the Germans. Perhaps this is best. Finally, our population has also decreased because of the death of many of our older neighbors and there have been fewer children born. Because of these factors, we expect in the near future we will no longer have the necessary manpower to provide the proper security at the entrance to our town, which has been our custom."

The six hostages exchanged glances. Daniel was convinced that his eerie assumption about the six hostages being killed was correct. The other five captives had similar thoughts.

Nicoangelo continued, "That brings me to the topic of tonight's meeting. As many of you know, the governing council has been debating the fate of our six Angels for almost a year. Vincenzo, God rest his soul, and the others on the council were unsure as to the best time to implement our plan for returning the Angels to their homelands. However, the governing council is united in its decision that *now* is the time."

Daniel was sure he had heard the last statement correctly, yet he was unwilling to change his belief that he was going to die tonight. The six men had been listening very carefully to every word, but they were not yet ready to believe the words, "returning the six Angels to their homelands."

"Furthermore, we will end this chapter in the history of Opi with my full guarantee that everyone will be able to move forward with confidence that our people and our town will remain peaceful. No one will be disturbed in any way by outsiders."

A low chatter began among the people gathered in the church. The six hostages were surprised, wide-eyed, and gaping at each other. George began to mentally speculate. *How could this be? They must know the first thing we will do is report them to the authorities. How are they going to explain Omar's death? They're not going to let us go home. He's just saying that so we won't be scared. They're going to kill us; they have no other option.*

David was also sure they would never be released, and his thoughts were similar to the thoughts of the other hostages. *I'm not surprised they are keeping the truth from the people. They'll take us out of town after telling the people they are letting us leave for home. Then they will probably take us to the forest, shoot us, and bury us there.*

Nicoangelo asked for attention. The chattering stopped, and he continued, "Please, please, let me explain. We've planned every detail of this matter and have taken the steps necessary to ensure its complete success. If you let me explain, I'm sure you will agree."

He moved his position on the chancel and stood in front of the six captives, talking directly to them. "Opi Angels, we owe you a great deal. We want you to know that through the years we have made every effort to make your stay here in Opi as comfortable and peaceful as possible. Our plan was always to make you feel like part of our families. We understood this would not be a perfect situation for you, but I want you to know that we did everything in our power to make you—as boys and now as men—feel that Opi was your home. Please know that we were heartbroken at the death of our Omar. This was a terrible tragedy for my family. As you know, the protectors pleaded with him...."

At this point David stood and spoke directly to Nicoangelo in a firm but respectful manner. "Sir, may I interrupt you and speak?"

"Yes, of course," said Nicoangelo.

"You have complete control of us, and we have learned to accept this. However, I must, with all respect to your position as leader, ask you not to speak of Omar in any way. I believe I speak for my brothers when I say we feel that speaking of him by a representative of the town of Opi is not acceptable to us or to Omar's memory."

Without any cue or look of recognition, the five seated men arose from their pew and stood with David. There was a still tension and absolute silence in the church.

Nicoangelo hesitated a moment and then quietly responded, "As you wish."

The six men sat down, proud of David. At that moment, David's successful confrontation suddenly empowered the six men with their first sense of meaningful potency since being brought to Opi. They were invigorated by David's assertiveness, and pleased that he was able to prevent Nicoangelo's attempt at manipulating Omar's memory.

Jem thought, *What a great way to go out—telling Nicoangelo to shut up!*

Nicoangelo continued speaking to the people. "Allow me to explain the plan that will give these six men their freedom."

The enormity of the word *freedom*—which Nicoangelo had just said—still did not fully penetrate their years of fear, doubt, and confusion.

Freedom, he said freedom. Maybe we won't die, thought George.

They're planning something; they're not gonna let us go; they can't let us go, thought Gabriel.

For a moment, Daniel felt a glimmer of hope when he heard the word freedom. Then he returned to his expected reality. *Freedom— he said that to fool the people into thinking we are not going to be killed.*

Nicoangelo continued his explanation, "The governing council has carefully taken the steps that will enable our friends to leave Opi and allow us to continue our lives undisturbed."

The hushed mumbling of the townspeople could now be heard throughout the church.

Nicoangelo, who was standing in the center of the chancel, raised his voice and spoke to them, attempting to reassure them. "Please, please, my friends, allow me to explain." The audience soon fell silent, and Nicoangelo confidently began to elaborate. "We have had false Italian passports made for our six Angels. We used the individual pictures we took of them at last June's San Giovanni de Battista festival. The members of the governing council—along with Alberto, Paulus, Emilio, and Loreto—will take the six men by car tomorrow to the port city of Mazara del Vallo in Sicily. There, we have hired a boat to transport all of us to Carthage, in Tunisia. We have arranged for cars to meet our boat in Carthage and drive us to the Tunisian airport."

The six hostages had similar thoughts. *So that's their plan. They don't intend telling the people we are to be killed. They will tell the others in town that we were sent home, and that will be the end of the Opi Angels.*

Nicoangelo walked over to a pile of papers lying on his seat, held them up to the audience, and said, "I have here in my hand airplane tickets for each of our Angels, which will enable them to return to their home countries."

Once again, there was uneasy stirring and quiet talking among the people in the church. Nicoangelo regained their attention by raising his voice for the second time. "At the Tunisian airport, we will give each Angel his plane ticket, his false Italian passport, and forged entry documents. Since Tunisia does not interfere with Italian internal affairs, if any of the Angels are foolish enough to tell the authorities about their stay in Opi, Tunisian authorities will naturally investigate and immediately determine that the six men entered Tunisia with false documents. Having no proof of personal identity other than the forged documents, they will immediately be placed in prison. So, as you can see, at the Tunisia airport when they receive their entry documents and plane tickets and are allowed to go free, they will have no choice but to use these documents to board their planes and return to their home countries."

Nicoangelo then looked at the six men. "I can assure you that you do not want to spend any time in the Tunisian prison system. If you do, you most likely will be lost forever."

Hearing this last statement, the six hostages wondered if perhaps they didn't plan to kill them after all. The plan Nicoangelo had just described would insulate the people of Opi from prosecution for kidnapping and false imprisonment. The six men began to relax somewhat, and they listened with a different mindset. Yet, they were still a bit hesitant to accept the idea that their lives might be spared.

Turning his attention back to the citizens of Opi, Nicoangelo continued. "Once they are home, it is highly unlikely they will be able to convince their local authorities of such a tale. However, if by chance the authorities in their countries inquire about the accuracy of their charge, there will be no trace that they were ever in our town. Therefore, it will be impossible for any of them to prove they have ever been in Opi. Our united fellowship regarding this matter would surely be in opposition to the claims of six foreigners. So, my neighbors, I can assure you there is nothing to fear. The governing council has made plans to thoroughly scrub each man's room and prepare it as living quarters for family members once the Angels are on their way. We also plan to dig up Omar's grave and respectfully bury his bones in the cemetery with a fictitious Italian headstone and dispose of the rock with his name carved on it."

Each captive made a mental note of this last statement. They remembered the promise they had made to Omar about returning his body to his family once they were freed. How would they be able to keep their promise to Omar if his grave were moved?

Damn! They've thought of everything, thought David.

Nicoangelo asked if anyone wanted to speak before the meeting ended. From the rear of the church came a familiar voice.

"Yes, I have something I wish to say." Walking up the center aisle was Maria Antonia. The people again began to buzz in low tones. When she reached the chancel, she climbed the two stairs, turned, and faced the people, waiting for them to be quiet.

She began by talking about her father, "Vincenzo, my father, worked for years to protect the people of our humble town. He devoted his life to continuing Opi's rich history after the Germans stole our men. Those of us here tonight lived through that terrible time. We cried, but my papa, with great pain in his heart from the loss of his two sons, my brothers, acted to save our town. Like many of you, I also loved and respected my papa. If I am to be honest—as I stand before you tonight—I have to say my beloved papa was wrong to imprison seven strangers to save Opi."

The people stirred uncomfortably. Nicoangelo arose from his chair and moved toward Maria Antonia. He gently took her arm, trying to move her back toward the altar. She broke away from his grasp and moved to the front of the chancel platform. The low whispering of the people, when blended together, caused Maria Antonia to raise her voice in order to be heard.

"Please, my sisters and brothers, listen to what I have to say!"

The attention of the people once more focused on Maria Antonia. "Father Mascia, who is a good and holy man, told us that history and our personal experience was justice enough for what we did, and he honestly believed he was right. We listened to his counsel. My sisters and brothers, please think carefully of what we have done. Can we honestly continue to live in silence with our secret sin? Who will take away the guilt we feel from knowing we have stolen another mamma's son? People of Opi, we stole seven lives so our lives could go on. Yes, we said we would be kind and generous to our Angels, and we told ourselves they would someday come to thank us. If we truly believed this, why did we continue to post guards at the entrance to our town? Why did we have our people watch them on their Sunday holiday from work?"

The eight men seated next to the altar moved toward Maria Antonia and completely surrounded her. She struggled as they began to move her toward the rear of the chancel.

Suddenly, a booming voice from the rear of the church shouted, "Gentlemen, leave that woman alone!"

Moving swiftly down the center aisle, a large man dressed in a dark suit, white shirt, and necktie continued his verbal order. "Remove your hands from that woman!"

The council members, seemingly caught off-guard by such an unexpected and booming challenge, stopped and turned. By the time they had recovered from the surprise, the man was standing on the chancel next to the altar. The people were dumbfounded at the sight of such a formally dressed stranger at the front of their church. He then brought Maria Antonia to the front of chancel. During the brief melodrama being played out in front of them, few people noticed that another well dressed stranger had moved inside the church through the front entrance with two uniformed officers, who positioned themselves beside the jacketed man at the door. The stranger on the chancel called for and received the full attention of the people.

He calmly addressed the audience. "People of Opi, I am detective Ricardo Fontana of the Roma Police Department." There was immediate silence. Detective Fontana continued, "There are detectives and uniformed police officers positioned at each door of the church and two police officers outside the church in a police van, which is blocking the road." Detective Fontana could sense movement and murmuring at his back. He quickly turned, and in a firm manner ordered the governing council to return to their chairs.

Nicoangelo protested, "Detective Fontana, I demand that you and your men leave this peaceful meeting and our town. You have no jurisdiction in our community. Your presence here is illegal."

Father Mascia supported Nicoangelo. "Detective, you have desecrated this consecrated house of the Lord. As pastor of this church, I demand that you and your men leave this holy building immediately. You have no authority past the doors of this church. In God's name, I demand that you leave immediately."

Detective Fontana handed Father Mascia a form that had been officially stamped. He stated loudly for all in the church to hear, "Padre, may I remind you that police officers in Italy are permitted to enter religious consecrated areas in the execution of their duty with the properly stamped approval of a judge. My judicial notification limits me only in that I am not permitted to physically disturb religious property within this holy building."

Detective Fontana then removed other papers, folded in thirds, from the inside pocket of his jacket and asked Nicoangelo, "Sir, are you the elected leader of Opi?"

Nicoangelo replied, "Detective, I have been legally installed as the chairman of our governing council, which has authority over the operations of our town."

"Then you, Sir, are the person to receive this judicial authorization, which governs the L'Aguila province of the region of Abruzzo, of which the town of Opi is a part. As you can see, this stamped document not only authorizes our presence in Opi, it also requires us to investigate this matter. Therefore, as of this moment, I have judicial authority over whatever occurs in this community—and may I remind you, Sir, I have been listening with interest to the detailed description of the plans you had for these six men."

Nicoangelo returned to his seat, and he and two other members of the governing council reviewed the papers given to Nicoangelo.

Detective Fontana returned his attention to the noisy crowd and called for silence. After a few moments, the people complied. "Thank you, citizens of Opi. Your cooperation is most appreciated," said the detective. "I will ask you to remain calm and allow Ms. Sgammotta to finish her comments." Detective Fontana, reaching out toward Maria Antonia, took her hand and moved her back to the center of the chancel. "When Ms. Sgammotta has finished her remarks, I will instruct everyone as to our next procedure."

The six hostages only now allowed themselves to be receptive to the word *freedom*. However, even though this official looking man seemed to be from the police, they were still not sure he would be able to make them free men. The people of Opi would surely, somehow, find a way to block their freedom.

The people in the church were absolutely silent and focused on Maria Antonia as she continued to speak. She started slowly, a bit shaken by what had just occurred, but in a matter of seconds she had regained her composure. "I made arrangements early this morning to be taken to the train station. I boarded the train for Roma, and there I explained to the capital city police what we've done over these many years."

The assembled crowd began to protest, but she raised her voice to be heard. "My sisters and brothers, please hear me before you judge me. I've not betrayed you. Rather, I've freed us all from the heavy burden that we've been carrying these many years. In 1947, my papa, Vincenzo Sgammotta, believed that the course of action taken by Opi was the only option we had available—and we all agreed to bring seven Angels to Opi to save our people from starvation. We believed we needed to do this in order to preserve the long history of our town. My papa is now with the Almighty, and I believe in my heart that

God understands that my father, although he was wrong, believed with all his will that his actions on our behalf were morally correct, given our circumstances. For this reason, I'm sure our compassionate Lord has welcomed Vincenzo Sgammotta to his eternal reward.

"I, and I hope others in Opi, believe it's time for someone to speak the truth on this matter. I, like you, remained silent, and cooperated. I, like you, told myself we were doing this for Opi and that there was no other way. In truth, my neighbors, we who disagreed and were quiet. We were the villains. We were the cowards, afraid to challenge our parents, our leaders, and our priest. Along with the other people of Opi, we will not be forgiven by the Lord unless we begin, this day, to take responsibility for what we have hidden for so long. It's not easy to tell the truth when we know family and friends will look at us as betrayers. It's time for us to stop thinking of only today and begin to accept that when we die and ask the Almighty for entrance into his kingdom, he'll first ask, 'Did you ever admit you were wrong in this matter with your hostages? Did you ever ask for forgiveness for what you did to those seven boys? Did you do everything in your power to heal, as best as you could, those you wronged? If we say, 'Dear God, we secretly sent the men we injured to Tunisia so we could protect our own selfish interests, then, like wolves, we'll have to hide in our dens from the hunters and be sorry for all eternity.'"

As she was speaking, Maria Antonia had slowly moved down the two steps from the chancel and was now standing in the center aisle with her right hand on the front pew across the aisle from the six hostages.

She continued, "But if we have the courage to shout, 'Yes, Lord! At the end, we tried to do all that was humanly possible to heal those we wronged!' If we can tell God we took responsibility for what we did; if we say we are sorry and ask His forgiveness, surely our merciful Father will welcome us to eternal happiness. I plead with you: Let us now, with good and open hearts, tell the truth, no matter how much pain and humiliation it will bring to us and our town. If we send these six men to Tunisia and then pride ourselves on our cunning, our souls will never heal, and I fear we'll soon come to regret what we have done and quickly begin to hate ourselves.

"It may be that many of you here tonight are saying, 'I did no wrong! I was not the one who brought these young men to our land.' Yes, that may be true. But we were all quiet and accepted the benefits of their labors. For this reason, we must also accept equal responsibility if we are ever to heal ourselves and our town."

The six hostages looked at each other with a hint of joy in their eyes. At that moment, the captives were able to internalize what had been troubling them for twenty-two years. *Finally, we have heard the words spoken, the words that the people of Opi have been denying for all these years.* Suddenly they felt confident that they were going to be freed, free after all these years!

Maria Antonia, with arms raised, perspiration building on her brow, and now speaking to a deadly silent audience, said, "There's one final thing I wish to say before Detective Fontana addresses you. Let us not forget that as painful as it might be to explain to our children that mamma and papa are not perfect and have made mistakes, explaining our complete history, the good and the bad, will help our children to understand that it's human to be weak, and that only the truth can help us find eternal happiness."

Maria Antonia slowly moved back up the steps, onto the chancel, and stood behind Detective Fontana. The governing council remained seated and silent. The people in the church were alarmed but remained silent. Detective Fontana stepped forward and spoke to them in an authoritative tone. "My countrymen, I want to assure you there will be a fair investigation into this matter."

He looked at the eight members of the governing council and instructed them to stay seated so his assistant could obtain some personal information. Detective Fontana then spoke directly to the people with final instructions.

"Officers from my squad will be taking the six men to the Roma police headquarters this evening. I encourage you all to go home and attend to your normal activities. An investigative unit will be formed and return to Opi the day after tomorrow. They will be responsible for a thorough investigation, which may include interviews with some of you. Two officers will remain in Opi until the investigative unit arrives. Their duty will be to obtain a census of all residents. That will be all for this evening. You are now free to return to your homes, but do not leave this town until you have been interviewed by members of the investigative unit, who will complete their work within two to three days after they arrive."

Detective Fontana then instructed the six hostages to remain seated. He asked one of the uniformed officers to escort Maria Antonia to her home and wait there with her until given further orders.

As the people were quietly leaving the church, Detective Fontana gave instructions to the six hostages. "An officer will escort you to your houses to collect your personal effects. You'll be taken immediately to Roma in the police van, and at that time you'll be given further instructions."

The police officer assigned to escort the six men to their rooms told the hostages to follow him. As he started to the door, he stopped, realizing the captives had remained in the pew unable to move. Time seemed to have stopped. They were not sure what to do. The police officer stepped back to the pew and grasped the arm of Klein who was seated at the end of the pew and stood him up. Then he gave a second, more forceful command for the hostages to follow him. The five other men stood and followed Klein and the police officer toward the church door. They silently moved in single file, walking behind the officer who held Klein by the arm. They entered the police van, still incapable of communicating. The comprehension that their twenty-two year imprisonment was about to end did not seem real.

Jem broke out of his trance-like state as the police officer was moving him into the van. "No, my room is there." Pointing to the house next to the church, he yelled to the others, "I won't be long— I've a sack to pick up and want to say goodbye to Caterina."

The other five, jarred by Jem's directions, suddenly seemed to return to reality. They were bewildered and silently staring at each other.

When Jem returned to the van, the officer drove to the next house. Gabriel gathered his few possessions and went to the first floor to say goodbye to Theresa. The front door was locked. He knocked loudly, but no one answered. He could see lights in the dining room so he continued to bang on the door. He was about to strike the wooden door again when it opened. Standing in the doorway was Theresa's mother.

"I'd like to say goodbye to Theresa," said Gabriel, feeling impatient.

"Theresa has locked herself in her room and told me that she does not want to speak with you. She wants nothing further to do with you."

Gabriel was surprised. He turned, looked at the van, and then back at Theresa's mother. He hesitated and then said, "Goodbye, Mrs. Vecelli." He hurried down the stone stairs to the police van.

Next the van made brief stops at the Opi homes of David and George so they could also pick up their few things.

Klein was the fifth man to stop at his room. He swiftly gathered his belongings in a cloth sack and went up the back stairs to speak with Giovanna. Klein knocked on the door, and it opened immediately. There stood Giovanna. She closed the door behind her and extended her arms to Klein. They said nothing, simply looking into each other's eyes. Then their bodies were tangled in a warm embrace. Giovanna was crying.

Klein whispered, "When the investigation is over, I'll come back to Opi. We'll be married in the church and then have our happy life in Austria."

"Oh yes, yes, my love. I'll be waiting for your return."

"Giovanna, you are the love of my life," whispered Klein.

Giovanna, still crying, kissed Klein passionately and then pulled away, saying, "You must go. I'll wait for your return. Hurry back."

They kissed one more time, and Klein hurriedly descended the back steps. When he reached the bottom, he turned and shouted, "I'll be back soon!"

Daniel's room was the last stop, and there was only one thing he wanted to take with him—the winter coat he was wearing when he first arrived in Opi. He had worn this coat for the first eight months, until he grew out of it. When Vincenzo gave him a replacement coat, he vowed that he would one day walk out of Opi with this coat under his arm as a symbol of his freedom. Twenty-one years ago, he had folded the coat and tied the arms into a knot, placing the compact bundle under his bed. Rarely, if ever, did he have occasion to move his bed, and although he remembered where he had placed the bundle, he wondered if it was still where he had left it. Daniel planned to take his jacket and a few other items, and then go upstairs to say goodbye to Gelsomina and Maria Antonia. He knew Gelsomina was in mourning, but he hoped she would see him one last time.

The door to his room was open. He went directly to the bed, moved it away from the wall, knelt down, and began to reach for his coat. He suddenly stopped, frozen by the charcoal words written on the lower part of the stone wall, smudged but still readable: *Monte Cassino, Renault, black car, license plate CA 261, mountain road, Opi,* and the number 25. These were the words he had written with burnt wood charcoal on that first night, thinking that somehow they would be helpful in his rescue. The memory of those words, long forgotten, caused a sudden flood of emotion.

He whispered to himself, "So many stolen years....Damn these people." He slumped to the floor, sitting between the stone wall and the pulled-out bed, his knees bent up against his chest, his arms wrapped around his bent legs, and his hands clasped at the wrists. Tears began to flow, and soon he was sobbing. At some point, he felt a hand on his shoulder. Still crying, he quickly turned to see Gelsomina, dressed in black and looking weak and drawn, sitting on the bed next to him.

Without thinking what he was doing, he placed his head in her lap and continued to cry.

Gelsomina gently stroked the back of his head. Finally, she spoke, "My Donato, often at night I'd wonder if you were here in your bed thinking of your mamma and crying. I'm sorry to see I was right. Allow me to say one thing: You, Donato, healed my heart when my two sons did not return. I don't know if I would have been strong enough to survive the loss of my boys if God had not given you to me. After you came to our home, I was not strong enough to give you up. You became for me what I had lost. You not only helped put food on our table, you also gave me back my life. You replaced the sons I had lost."

Gelsomina lifted Daniel's head, looked into his wet eyes, and said, "I know you must leave. I will continue to pray each day that you will someday lose the bitterness you must have in your heart toward the Sgammotta family."

Daniel stopped crying. His shoulders and head continued with final shuddering movements as he suppressed his last sob, and then he said in a quiet tone, "No, Gelsomina, I never once cried—and I often wondered why, because there were so many nights of sadness. At night, in my bed, I often wondered why I became so fond of you. Gelsomina, I have no bitterness toward you. Somehow I came to love you. I don't understand how or why, but instead of hating you for your part in my horror, I made you a replacement for my mother. You were both my captor and my family. Saturday afternoons and Sunday mornings were happy times for me in my unhappy life."

Gelsomina, who was now crying, kissed the back of Daniel's hand and placed his open palms to her cheeks. She asked if he would do her one last favor. "Maria Antonia is upstairs and would like very much to say goodbye to you. Could you find it in your heart to grant her this wish?"

Daniel arose to his feet, looked into Gelsomina's sad eyes, and kissed her on the forehead. While her face was in his hands, he simply said, "Goodbye, Gelsomina."

With his bundled coat under his arm and his cloth bag, Daniel quickly went out past the animal stall—the tall gate was closed but unlocked. He climbed the back stairs, and as he entered the upstairs room, Maria Antonia arose from her chair. She seemed very unsure of herself. As she spoke, she was looking down, unwilling to make eye contact with Daniel. In her soft voice she said, "Thank you for coming to see me. I will not keep you long. I wanted the opportunity to explain something to you."

Nervously playing with her hands, she continued, "My papa dedicated his entire life to his family and Opi. As I grew older, I understood that it was wrong to bring you and the other boys to Opi. My papa, I loved him so. I didn't have the strength to tell him how I truly felt, because I knew it would break his heart. So I remained silent these many years. In that time, I fell in love with you, not as a brother but as a man. After what we have done to you, I know you can never love me as a woman. To never know your love will be my punishment for remaining silent. I don't expect you to fully understand how difficult it was to love both you and my papa, and then have to make a choice. I'm not asking for your forgiveness. I know that would be too much to ask. All I ask is that you try to understand."

Daniel was silent for a moment. The feeling of Maria Antonia's hand on his cheek and lips while she was trimming his hair and beard was all that passed through his mind.

Maria Antonia, misinterpreting his silence, said, "Donato, it is better if you do not speak. I accept your silence."

Her words brought Daniel's mind back to the present. Daniel tried to reply, "Maria Antonia...." He was unable to speak the next word—his tongue seemed too heavy to lift off the floor of his mouth.

Maria Antonia, once again misinterpreting Daniel's silence, said, "No need to speak, Donato. You owe me no words. You have been through too many years of forced labor at the hands of my family. I have no reason to expect anything from you but contempt."

Finally, Daniel gained enough composure to respond. He reached out and touched the smooth, olive colored skin of her hand and said, "Maria Antonia, I longed to hold you in my arms all these years, while only being allowed to feel this hand on my face and lips."

Maria Antonia interrupted, "Please, Donato, don't speak of us. It's too painful to hear your words."

"In these few minutes, how can I say what I've wanted to say to you for the past twenty-two years? After I am back in America, and have time to think about my time in Italy, I will write you a letter."

Maria Antonia was still unable to look into Daniel's eyes. "That would be wonderful. I would be very pleased if you found it in your heart to write to me. Take as much time as you need. And, Donato, if you change your mind and choose not to write, I will also understand and accept that decision as well. You owe nothing to me or the Sgammotta family."

Daniel's mind was on both Maria Antonia and the van waiting outside. "Over the years," he said. "You have shown me great kindness, and, more importantly, you gave me a great deal of comfort. No, I do owe you. I promise I'll write after I am back in America."

She offered her hand in a gesture to shake Daniel's hand. He was about to take her hand, but instead he continued his right hand past her outstretched arm and held her waist, his left arm gently placed on her right shoulder, their bodies finally touching. The thrill of holding Maria Antonia after so many years of desiring her was exhilarating. He rested his head on her shoulder, the warm, velvet skin of her cheek pressing against his beard, the gentle touch of her breasts and hips tantalizing his every nerve. They held each other for a few moments. She was crying, and she impulsively moved back, but now for the first time she was able to look lovingly into Daniel's eyes. He moved his face slowly toward her mouth and their lips met and remained locked for a thrilling moment.

But, once again, Maria Antonia abruptly separated from Daniel. "Donato, please, you must go." He composed himself, squeezed her hand, and turned to leave. Suddenly he stopped, looked back at her, and said, "You were the one who made it possible for us to be free. We all know the sacrifice you made today. We will never forget you for what you did for us. Maybe the people of Opi will someday understand."

As he entered the van and closed the door behind him, George, who was sitting in front of Daniel, turned and softly said, "It was surprisingly difficult for all of us." As George turned to face forward, the van began to move down Via San Giovanni de Battista on its way out of Opi. Tonight, there were no men in a wagon with rifles to block the police van from leaving.

CHAPTER XVII

$\mathcal{D}$EBRIEFING IN

$\mathcal{R}$OME

The van arrived at police headquarters around two in the morning. The police asked a few basic questions: their full names, the dates when they were kidnapped (as best they could remember), where they were kidnapped, and information they thought would be helpful in finding their missing person reports from 1947. Due to the late hour, the former captives were to sleep on cots at the police station. Before they went to their room, the police explained that there would be an inquiry and what the police referred to as a *debriefing* would take at least five days. The six men were disappointed, but the police insisted this time was needed to obtain the necessary information, to complete the paperwork, and — most importantly — the men needed to spend time with the police psychiatrist and generally get acclimated to their new environment.

After breakfast the following morning, the former hostages were presented with clean underwear, shirts, and pants, stockings, and sneakers. The men marveled at the interesting sneakers, surprised that they were not made from canvas material. They requested scissors, shaving cream, and shaving razors. They were determined to remove the last remaining visible reminder of Opi — their beards.

After a glorious warm shower, the cleanly shaven men dressed in their new clothes and sneakers, and met with the police interviewer. He asked specific questions, which forced the former hostages to explain their captivity in a chronological format rather than by random facts. By noon they were exhausted. The police assured them they were making good progress on collecting the necessary missing person reports. The police expected to be able to contact their families during the day, and the men could begin making phone calls to their families the following day. They had lunch and were taken to another building, which would be their living quarters for the remainder of their time at police headquarters.

They were brought back to the main building at four in the afternoon. Their missing person files, including Omar's, had been located, and one officer was in the process of making the initial contact with each family. The hostages had earlier explained in detail what had happened to Omar, and the police were able to pass that sad information along to his family.

It was decided that Daniel, who spoke English, would ask permission to speak with Omar's family as soon as possible. The men knew Omar's sister spoke English, and they decided they would travel to Egypt to attend Omar's burial service, which they were sure his family would be conducting.

Daniel spoke to Omar's sister that evening. He explained her brother's relationship with other hostages, and emphasized how close they had become during their captivity. Daniel talked in detail about Omar's decision and his mood on that final Sunday afternoon.

Omar's sister was unable to contain her emotions after hearing about the relationship her brother had with the other captives. Through her tears, she expressed relief at knowing the details of Omar's state of mind on the day he died. She told Daniel her parents would take great comfort in knowing Omar was with friends during his time in Opi. Omar's sister said they were planning to move Omar's body to Egypt and hold a burial service. Arrangements were made for Daniel to contact her when he arrived home in America. He would then contact the other five men to coordinate their trip to attend Omar's burial services.

That next morning, they were scheduled to report for individual physical examinations. Having blood drawn from the veins in their arms for the purpose of performing various medical tests was a new experience. When the individual physical examinations were completed, the doctors were quite surprised at their excellent health. Each man exceeded the health standards for their age group. The only problem was tooth decay, which would be treated when they arrived home.

The two examining doctors were intrigued by the excellent health of the former hostages, and requested to meet with the six men as a group. The doctors had many questions about their living environment, eating, sleeping, work, leisure activities, and the type of medical attention they received during their time in Opi.

David, who had an interest in medicine, had been allowed time with *Dattore* Tatti to learn from him. During their early years of captivity, the people of Opi had expected that David would one day assume the functions of *Dattore* Tatti. David explained that a man by the name of Beniamino Tatti was the doctor for all the people of Opi. "Everyone simply called him *Dattore*. The front room of his house was used as the town *ambulatorio* (doctor's office). He told me he had been schooled in Naples, but he would not say whether he had a license to practice medicine."

With a surprised smile, one of the doctors commented, "Considering the excellent state of your health, I'm very curious to know the methods he used when you or others became ill. In twenty plus years, some of you must have become seriously ill, broken a bone, had an accident, or come down with an infectious disease."

David explained how Klein's broken ankle and Gabriel's broken arm had been treated. He described what had been done to heal George's and his bullet wounds. Primarily, *Dottore* Tatti used herbs to treat infections and other common illnesses.

"Herbs?" questioned one of the doctors. "What kind of herbs?"

"He used a book called *De Materia Medica*, written by a Greek person named Dioscorides. *Dottore* Tatti told me Dioscorides lived in the first century A.D. and traveled with the Roman Legions, identifying, illustrating, and using the medicinal plants of the Mediterranean area."

David was able to talk at length about the various herbs *Dottore* Tatti used to treat a wide variety of ailments. When he was finished, the doctors expressed their gratitude and the men were taken back to their rooms.

On the third day, Daniel asked if he could contact his relatives in Castellamare di Stabia. The police were able to determine that Daniel's Aunt Pia and her husband Rodolfo were the only direct relatives of his father still living in Italy. The police contacted Rodolfo, informing him that Daniel had been found alive and arrangements would be made for him to call them the following morning. The officer made it clear to Rodolfo that he was not to inform local newspapers or mention to anyone that Daniel had been found. An official statement would be made by the police after the men were out of the country.

When Daniel called the following morning, his Aunt Pia answered the phone. When she heard Daniel's voice, she began to cry. After a few moments, he asked about his mother and father. Zia Pia told Daniel she believed they were still alive, but she had not seen or spoken with Daniel's father since he last visited Italy in 1951. Daniel thought it strange that his father would have lost contact with his sister.

Zia Pia told Daniel that Nonno Leopoldo died in 1949 and her mother, Nonna Francesca, died in 1954. Her sister, Alessandrina, had passed away in 1965, and Leonida had passed away last winter. She explained that almost all the children of his father's sisters were living in Italy, but only two still remained in Castellamare di Stabia: Uncle Iseo's son, Emilio, who now operated the bakery, and her daughter, Angelina, who married a local man. She further mentioned that Uncle Iseo, Leonida's husband the baker, was still alive and was now living with his oldest son.

Daniel asked Zia Pia, "Does Ruffino live in Italy?"

"Ah, Ruffino has made everyone in Castellamare di Stabia very proud." She told Daniel that Ruffino was a very important world scientist, now working in Vienna, Switzerland. "Ruffino is the boss of something called the International Atomic Energy Agency, and his position requires him to travel the entire world." Zia Pia mentioned that he was often in America visiting the United Nations. She told Daniel that she would contact Ruffino and let him know Daniel had been found.

Daniel asked Zia Pia, "When you speak with Ruffino, give him my father's American address and ask him to contact me when he gets to America."

Daniel promised to write to Zia Pia when he got home, and he asked her not to forget to contact Ruffino.

When Daniel finished speaking with his aunt, the police informed him they had spoken with his older brother. They told him to stay by the phone while they dialed his brother in America.

Daniel was waiting excitedly to hear his brother's voice. The phone rang twice, and then he heard, "Dan, Dan, is that you?"

"Lee, it's me, Dan." They talked briefly, and toward the end of the conversation, Leopoldo told Daniel that he and Barbara planned to be at Kennedy Airport when he landed. They would take him to see Frances and his mother and father. Daniel felt a spine-tingling rush of elation as he realized he was finally going home. "I can't wait to see you and the rest of the family!" he said to his brother.

Although the hostages were disappointed that they were not allowed to leave for home immediately after arriving in Rome, they understood the wisdom of spending what turned out to be seven days at the Rome police headquarters. There was a great deal of information and emotions to process, and these days gave them the needed time and space prior to their return home.

Daniel felt uneasy when he was told that he was scheduled to meet with Dr. Amabilia Luciani, a psychiatrist, the following morning.

Dr. Luciani welcomed Daniel into her office. She started the session by saying, "Studies have shown that victims of kidnapping display high levels of distress immediately after release and a high frequency of traumatic symptoms for an extended period of time after they are free." She explained the feelings associated with trauma and distress, and ended on a positive note by telling Daniel that in time these negative feelings would pass.

Dr. Luciani then asked Daniel to talk about his experience as it affected his feelings. Daniel started by talking about his overwhelming loneliness and sadness, and how these feelings were with him constantly while he was in Opi. "Most of the time my chest and stomach felt so hollow that I often wondered if there was something wrong with my body. I felt relieved when the doctor examined me and said my chest and stomach were fine."

Doctor Luciani was pleased that Daniel was willing to share his intense feelings so quickly.

"I'm glad you mentioned your feelings of loneliness and sadness. First, I'm not at all surprised to hear you experienced these feelings, and second, your chest and stomach symptoms would be quite normal for the loneliness and sadness you felt for such an extended period."

Daniel was relieved to hear the doctor's assurance that his feelings were normal.

Doctor Luciani continued with her fascinating analysis, saying it would have also been normal if Daniel had experienced feelings of shame, helplessness, abandonment, guilt, depression, loss of confidence, and perhaps even the loss of self-control.

Daniel and the doctor discussed his relationship with the Sgammotta family—especially his fondness for Gelsomina and how illogical and troubling this relationship was for him, especially during the early years of his captivity. The discussion moved smoothly from Gelsomina to his unconventional relationship and feelings for Maria Antonia. Dr. Luciani encouraged him to keep his promise to write to Maria Antonia. She explained how this correspondence could be very useful in helping him interpret and comprehend their emotional connection.

Daniel told the psychiatrist about his recurring, confusing dream. "The same dream used to wake me up many nights of the week. "Why do you think I had such a crazy dream...over and over, the same dream?"

Dr. Luciani gave Daniel a warm grin of recognition. "Don't be alarmed at the content of your dream. Actually, it would be more accurate if I referred to it as a nightmare." Dr. Luciani described a rather interesting theory, recently developed, that not only addressed Daniel's nightmare, but also many of his actions and feelings while he was in Opi.

The psychiatrist introduced Daniel to what she called the *Stockholm Syndrome.* "This syndrome is thought to be an unconscious emotional response to the traumatic experience of being kidnapped and held for a long period of time. The positive emotional bond that often develops between the victim and captor is a defense mechanism of the captive's ego to cope with stress. Feelings such as rage, blame, disgrace, castigation, and accusation can all be displaced in the mind of the kidnapped person, because it might be too risky to express these feelings directly against the kidnapper. The premise behind the Stockholm syndrome is that it's a life-saving defense mechanism for the victim. It is also believed that this unconscious mental process helps the captive avoid violent reactions, and in some cases, foolish escape attempts that could lead to death. After an initial period of shock, disbelief, and denial, it is common for victims of kidnappings to gradually accept their situation and experience feelings of imminent release alternating with disillusion, discouragement, and despair."

The doctor explained that when victims experience traumatic shock, isolation from normal surroundings, hearing repeatedly only what the kidnappers want them to know, not being killed by their captors, and being treated with unexpected kindness, they can easily fall into a certain pattern of positive behavior toward their captor. She assured Daniel that when a person is held prisoner, it is quite normal for the individual to eventually think their captor is kind, simply because they have not killed them. Victims often display a series of feelings that range from outrage to fear to passivity and, finally, friendship. The person who is kidnapped may begin to believe that the kidnapper is a good person simply because of their kindness. Many hostages eventually feel they owe their lives to their captors.

"But why did I have these nightmares every week? Daniel asked. "And why would I be so worried about getting back to Opi on Monday? If I was dreaming about being home, shouldn't my family be the most important part of my dream? But they weren't—Opi and Vincenzo were a bigger part of my dream."

Dr. Luciani responded, "I suspect the content of your nightmare went back to the fact that you were replacing your deep, intense angry feelings against Vincenzo for kidnapping you, in an attempt to prevent you from confronting and fighting with him. You might have been unconsciously afraid that if you continually confronted Vincenzo he would have eventually killed you."

This explanation helped Daniel understand some of the reactions that he found so confusing while he was a hostage in Opi.

Dr. Luciani also speculated, "You probably tried to take control of your emotions, but were unable to think clearly for the first week or so. It would have been perfectly normal for you to experience hope of survival and freedom, when at the same time you were having overwhelming fear that you were about to die. It is not unusual for people who have been held in captivity to feel this way for long periods after being captured."

Dr. Luciani then changed the subject. "When I spoke with the other men, they described symptoms of a diagnosis we call *stress*. Dr. Hans Selye, a Czechoslovakian Biochemist at the University of Montreal, recently introduced this term to describe the way trauma can cause over-activity of the adrenal gland, and with it a disruption of bodily equilibrium. So I feel confident, that a diagnosis of stress can be applied to the six of you in the context of how you behaved.

It's important to understand that some of your daily behaviors were quite normal for people who experience the stress caused by long isolation. These feelings usually bring on physical symptoms, such as teeth clenching, pacing back and forth, being anxious or having anxious thoughts, being unable to focus and concentrate, always feeling threatened even when the threat is nonexistent, nail biting, dry mouth, rapid heart beat, nervously rubbing your hands together, and what we call a nervous stomach, but what I learned you men called 'butterflies' in your stomach."

Daniel smiled and nodded his head. He knew these feelings well.

Doctor Luciani made one last point. "There is one final symptomatic stress behavior that's important: believing you are the only one experiencing these symptoms." Dr. Luciani paused and asked Daniel if he had any questions.

Daniel had been listening intently with his mouth open and a look of amazement on his face, as though he had just seen the greatest magic trick in his life. "How can you possibly know all those things? What you are saying is exactly what I felt while in I was Opi. How is it possible that you know how I felt?"

Dr. Luciani smiled. "I wish I could say I am that brilliant, but the truth is after Dr. Selye's work on stress, these behaviors have been researched by talking with hundreds and hundreds of people to find out what symptoms they experienced when they were held captive.

"As a matter of fact, Daniel, by talking with you and the other five men, I believe I have learned something new, a trait that I can share with other psychiatrists, my colleagues. It is rare for someone to be held captive for as long as you men were held, and other doctors have not had the opportunity to talk with victims of such long-term captivity. I have learned from the others, and now from you, that around your eighteenth year of captivity all of you lost interest in living, and during that time you were convinced that the people of Opi were going to kill you. Thanks to you and the other hostages I will be able to share this important information with my colleagues."

"So you think even feeling that we were going to be killed was normal?"

"Oh yes, Daniel. I now feel this might be quite normal."

Daniel smiled and slid down in his chair. "Boy, you don't know how relieved that makes me feel!" he said.

"Do you remember having an unusual number of headaches, or if you had the need to urinate excessively during the first year?"

Daniel thought for a moment. "I recall many days with headaches, but I don't remember having the need to frequently urinate."

Doctor Luciani moved on to other subjects. "Since you were not tortured, you were probably able to adapt to your surroundings and your situation sooner than what is considered normal. Another aspect of your long captivity is that all six of you must have had a strong will to survive until about the twentieth year. You probably made an internal decision to live within weeks of being kidnapped."

Dr. Luciani then made reference to Omar. "When Omar decided to walk out of town, I suspect he had made a conscious decision that he no longer wanted to live as a hostage."

Dr. Luciani continued by asking about the effect Omar's loss had on the remaining hostages. "After his death, did you feel as though your group unity and bond had somehow been broken?"

"No, I don't think so," said Daniel. "After Omar's death, I felt like a part of *me* had been killed, but I didn't feel our group changed. We believed he was okay with his decision. We knew he was a smart, mature guy, and he convinced us he was ready. I think Omar was even happy to die so he could be with Allah."

That afternoon, Daniel was more relaxed with the doctor's questions and analysis. He asked her a question, which the six captives had constantly discussed: "Do you know how we were able to continue living our sad, lonely lives for so many years without losing our minds? We were always afraid that someday one of us would go crazy, especially after the incident with George. Did he tell you about what happened?"

"Yes, George and I spent a good deal of time discussing that incident."

Doctor Luciani leaned back in her chair, put her pencil down on her note pad, and looked at Daniel for a moment. "That question has been on my mind since I was assigned this case. Daniel, you are the fifth hostage I have spoken with, and I have come to the conclusion that your free Saturday afternoons, and especially Sundays together, were the reason you all remained as stable as you did for so many years. The little we do know about isolation for long periods of time is that it can cause insanity. It's my guess that the crucial support and communication you had with your fellow captives—and, perhaps, the faith and loyalty you had in each other—enabled the six of you to get through this ordeal with your mental processes intact. It's my belief that without your Sunday socializing, and for some of you, Saturday afternoons with your Opi families, the six of you probably would not have been able to survive your ordeal. Someone in Opi had a good understanding of human nature or an intuitive sense that socializing with other people was necessary for maintaining your sanity and survival. I can't come up with any other explanation."

Daniel enthusiastically agreed. "You know, I'll betcha you're right. We really enjoyed being together on Sundays."

The doctor returned to the subject of Daniel's relationship with the Sgammotta family. She explained to Daniel that it was not surprising that each captive was able to establish some type of a friendly, or in his case, a loving relationship with a member of his captor's family.

"I was not surprised to hear similar stories from the other hostages. In addition to the relationships you established with each other, it was probably very important that each of you was able to develop some type of personal relationship with other individuals. I can't possibly imagine the six of you surviving for over twenty years without establishing these relationships.

"Daniel, the first and most important thing you must do when you return to America is consult with someone in the mental health field for the purpose of continuing the healing process we have started today. Think of our talk today as puncturing a can to let some of the air out so it won't explode. You still need someone to help you go into the can to examine the contents and try to make sense of what you find there. I believe the doctor you speak with in America will be extremely helpful to you as you adjust to returning home to your family, friends, and a new life.

The doctor finished her session by saying, "The police are not going to release the facts of your case until the six of you are out of Italy. They are concerned the publicity might interfere with their debriefing and perhaps delay your departure."

Dr. Luciani then added one last caution. "When you are with friends and other people, you might experience a change in their behavior. For example, if you join a group of people who are conversing and perhaps laughing, don't be surprised if you see them stop laughing or change their mood when you join them. It is nothing you have done. You have to expect to be treated differently when you are returned to your family and friends."

Dr. Luciani told Daniel that unless he had anything further to add, she was satisfied that the session was complete. Daniel looked at the floor for a moment, sighed and hesitantly said, "Uh... No, no, not really."

Dr. Luciani could easily tell there was something more on Daniel's mind. "If there is something still bothering you, I would like to hear what it is. Even if you think it's foolish, I promise to take it seriously."

"It's not that I think it's foolish," said Daniel. "It's just something I think I should talk to a priest about."

"Of course, Daniel, I completely understand, especially if it is something more appropriate for the confessional."

"Oh no, it has nothing to do with sin," said Daniel, his frustration plainly evident. Then, more forcefully, he added, "I..., I can't understand why God allowed this to happen to me! Why did God allow this to go on for such a long time? My mother always said, 'God wouldn't give anyone a burden they couldn't carry.' Well, this burden was too difficult to carry, and I don't understand why God made it last so long."

Dr. Luciani was sympathetic, but she agreed this was something that he should discuss with a priest. Daniel stood, thanked Dr. Luciani, and left the room.

On the day before he was scheduled to leave for America, Daniel was resting in his room after the midday meal, when he received a call to report to the main office immediately. Arriving at the main office, he informed the officer at the desk that he was Daniel Ciarletta.

"The captain gave us standing orders that none of you were to speak to anyone from the outside, but he found it necessary to make an exception in your case. Go to room number two and pick up the phone. The caller is holding for you."

As Daniel walked down the corridor toward room two, his head was filled with fearful thoughts. *Damn it! I knew something was going to go wrong! They're making an exception for this important call. It has to mean someone is going to stop me from going home. I knew this was all too good to be true.* He cautiously picked up the receiver and said meekly, "Hello?"

He was greeted by an excited voice. "Donato, this is Ruffino. Do you remember me, your cousin, Alessandrina's son?"

Almost yelling into the phone, Daniel said, "Ruffino, yeah, I remember! How are you doing. Oh, I'm so glad to hear your voice!"

"Donato, what a wonderful surprise to hear you are alive. Zia Pia called me yesterday. It's a miracle! The agency I work for was able to convince the police to let me speak with you. I just wanted to call and hear your voice, and let you know I have not forgotten you."

Daniel was overwhelmed with joy. "Ruffino, I'm so happy you called. I thought of you often over the years. Zia Pia told me you are an important scientist. How great that your dreams came true."

Daniel told Ruffino he still remembered the day when they went to the *calcio* game, and how Ruffino was so despondent about his chances of going on to a university.

"Donato, you remembered that? I'm ashamed to say I haven't thought of it since we last saw each other."

Daniel was so excited, and he asked Ruffino to explain what had happened to him since their days in Castellamare di Stabia.

"No, no, not now. The police will only let me speak with you for a few minutes. My job often requires me to visit the United Nations. Do you remember, twenty years ago, you promised to show me around New York City? Well, I am going to hold you to that promise the next time I'm at the United Nations." Ruffino gave Daniel his address and phone number, and made Daniel promise to send his phone number and address to him.

"I won't take any more of your time. I know you must be exhausted, and also excited about going home. I just wanted to hear your voice and let you know I had not forgotten our wonderful few weeks together many years ago. Remember, send me your American address and phone number—we must get together when I'm in the United States."

Daniel thanked Ruffino for calling and especially for remembering him.

Finally, the time came when all six men were scheduled to go to their home countries the following morning. That night, they talked about how important it was for them to maintain contact, not only in their reunions but also by writing frequently and talking by phone.

Before they left the next day, Dr. Luciani visited briefly with the men and wished them well. She made a point of telling them that no matter how loving, caring, and understanding their families were, it would be impossible for them to fully understand what the captives had experienced. "So, remember to be patient with them." Her last comment to the men was that they would need each other more often than they could imagine.

CHAPTER XVIII

ℛETURNING TO

𝒶MERICA

Seven hours had passed since Daniel's plane left the Rome airport, and he was feeling restful, almost sleepy. His intense excitement, inability to focus, and muscle twitching had subsided. He was now thinking of his house on Beach Avenue. He could see himself in the various rooms, picturing the joyous Sunday afternoon meals with his big family, his aunts, uncles, and cousins. He was old enough now to join his father and uncles in the card game Boss and Underboss. His racing imagination made the final two hours of the trip pass quickly.

His wandering mind was interrupted by a male voice speaking over the plane's intercom announcing the plane's descent to Kennedy International Airport in New York.

"All passengers please return to your seats and fasten your seat belts." With this announcement, Daniel's excitement once again began to rise. He was no longer thinking about his future life, but now only that the plane was about to land and soon he would be able to see New York City from his small, oblong window. Looking out the window, Daniel could still see only clouds.

Suddenly, the wing on the right side dipped downward for a short time and then leveled off—the same maneuver happened three more times. The clouds no longer seemed puffy and round. They became thinner and seemed to be passing by the window faster and faster. Daniel could now see water through the streaking clouds. It was evening, and he wondered when he would be able to see land from the sky at night. Within a few minutes, he began to notice little dots of light. *That must be land,* he thought. *Could that be New York City? No it can't be, there would be many more lights.* The ground seemed to be getting closer and closer as the plane wings continued their dipping and leveling movement. Daniel was becoming impatient. *This is taking so long. Why haven't we landed?* The plane was now completely over land; the water was still visible, but off in the distance. He could see actual houses, roads, and cars. He thought, *Those are American roads and American houses, but where is New York City?*

Daniel was sure the plane would be landing any moment now. Looking out the window, he was fascinated by how everything on the ground looked from his window. Then, suddenly, the plane was very close to the ground and flying over big buildings. He could see black, flat roofs with box-like structures on their surfaces. These buildings quickly disappeared, and now all he could see was grass and concrete, which was almost close enough to touch. He felt a bump, a thump, a skid, and then an unusual loud noise like a great wind passing by. He was overjoyed. *I'm on the ground in New York. I'm home!*

The plane continued to move for a few minutes, and each passing moment brought more and more excitement. His brain was whirling; his body wanted to move; he was ready to burst out of his chair.

Then, in an instant, all his emotions were frozen as though someone had pushed an "off" button. He heard an announcement over the intercom: "Will Mr. Daniel Ciarletta please report to one of the stewardesses before leaving the plane? Mr. Daniel Ciarletta, please see a stewardess before disembarking."

They said my name. Oh God, something's wrong. What does disembarking mean?

The plane eventually came to a stop and everyone seemed to rise at the same time. They were busily collecting their bags and luggage from the enclosed shelves over their seats. Daniel had one bag under the seat in front of him. He was terribly annoyed—the plane had stopped, but the people weren't moving. He waited nervously, standing like the other passengers. Soon the line began to slowly move toward the front of the plane. Daniel was moving, too, with his head down and still feeling frightened about the announcement of his name.

As he moved down the crowded aisle, he thought, *Maybe this is not America. What if I got on the wrong plane and Barbara and Lee are in New York and I'm in another country? That's why I couldn't see New York City from my window. Oh no! How am I gonna get to New York? I should have known something bad was going to happen! What'll I do now?*

Daniel approached the uniformed woman standing opposite the exit door of the plane. "I'm Daniel Ciarletta," he said cautiously.

The woman smiled and asked him to follow her out of the plane. Now he was sure something was wrong. He immediately asked the woman, "Did I get on the wrong plane? Am I in trouble? Have I done something wrong?"

The stewardess seemed sympathetic and was quick to assure Daniel that nothing was wrong. "I'm taking you directly to an airline representative, and I'll give him your entry papers so he can walk you through customs. Everything is fine. You will be home soon."

Thank you, Lord, thought Daniel, and he smiled once again. As they left the plane and entered a hallway, the stewardess brought Daniel to a man in a blue jump-suit. She handed an envelope to the man and introduced Daniel. Then she turned to Daniel and said, "He'll escort you to the proper gate."

Daniel followed the man closely. Although he had been told there was no problem, Daniel immediately asked his escort, "Will I be allowed to go home tonight?" The uniformed man grinned and promised that his papers were in order and he would be on his way soon.

"These documents are notification from the Italian government that will be used in place of your passport," explained the man. His escort made a point of telling Daniel everything was fine and not to be concerned. "I will make sure your entry into the United States goes smoothly."

Daniel was relieved when he heard "entry into the United States." They walked through various hallways, making right and left turns, and then entered a large room. There were seven or eight lines of people who appeared to be showing papers to uniformed people at counters. The man took Daniel past the various lines and directly to a side office. He showed Daniel's papers to a man in the office. After a brief discussion, they both smiled and said Daniel could pass through. The man in the blue jumpsuit pointed to an opening with the word *Exit* over it, and he told Daniel to follow the other people who were going through the opening and out of the terminal. The man shook Daniel's hand and said, "Good luck to you, Sir."

Daniel was caught off-guard for a few wistful moments. His escort had called him Sir. *I've never been called Sir before,* he said to himself. The man in the blue jumpsuit had turned away and blended into the crowd. Daniel strained to find his blue uniform, but it was nowhere to be seen. Daniel had expected the man was going to take him to his brother, but now he was gone.

Daniel stood frozen, looking at the opening in the wall where he had been told to go. Many people were rushing toward it. *That's probably where I should be going, but what if I'm wrong and get lost? I have no phone number. The police in Rome called my brother and I never asked them for my American phone number. How am I going to get to Clason Point if I can't find Lee or Barbara?* He was now perspiring, and his shirt clung to his damp chest. He knew he had to do something, so he decided to return to the man in the side office.

He politely excused himself and said, "I'm sorry to bother you again, but I don't know which way I should go to meet my brother."

The uniformed man behind the desk looked annoyed, which made Daniel even more uneasy. He pointed toward the opening Daniel had been looking at. "Like I told you before, go through that opening, down the hallway until you come to a big room, and then just follow the sign that says 'luggage pickup.'"

The man abruptly turned away to continue his conversation with another passenger.

Nervously, Daniel blurted out, "But I don't have luggage. I only have this bag." The man at the desk looked angry. "That's great mister; now please just leave."

"But I can't leave. I have to meet my brother."

"Look, fella, are you deliberately trying to be a pain in the ass? God, enough from you, meet your brother, meet whoever you want. I can't help you anymore; now please just go and don't come back."

Confused and uncertain, Daniel slowly moved toward the opening. Halfway there, he stopped and wiped the perspiration from his forehead. His legs seemed to be locked. He mumbled to himself, "The man said go and leave, but leave for where? How am I going to find Lee and Barbara? They won't know me after all these years, and what if I don't recognize them?"

Alone in the crowded, noisy room, frozen by terror, perspiring heavily, not knowing what to do, or where to go, he felt as isolated as when he was in Opi. His immobility only seemed to make his terror more intense. *I must move. I must do something. I can't just stand here.* He forced himself to move one foot forward, followed slowly by the other. He began to inch his way forward toward the large opening and the long hallway beyond. Fear and anxiety still consumed his every step, but he forced himself to continue, unsure of what waited for him at the end of the long hallway. Once he was in the hallway, he stayed close to the side wall keeping his hand on the wall as he walked. People were rushing past him. Finally, he reached an opening at the end of the hallway.

There were many people and the noise was deafening. He stepped out into the room, but immediately moved a step to the left, his back against the wall. *Should I walk forward into the crowd? No, there are too many people. What if my sister and brother aren't here? S'pose I'm lost; what will I do?*

There was so much noise and confusion—people greeting each other, hugging and laughing; the lights were so bright; everyone was moving so fast. Daniel's head was beginning to throb. He wished the blaring noise would stop, and the bright lights seemed to be burning his eyes. He felt his arm being pulled. Startled, he turned to see the smiling face of his brother Lee.

"Dan, didn't you hear us? We were calling you!"

Fear and anxiety had invaded every cell in his body. His face was drawn, and he was unable to move or respond.

"Dan, what's wrong? Your shirt is soaked!" Lee put his arms around him and held him tightly. The physical contact with his brother relaxed his muscles, and his fear and isolation flowed from him.

Finally able to speak, Daniel said, "Lee... Lee it's really you, it's really you." Daniel held on tight, refusing to separate his clammy body from his brother.

Lee murmured, "Its okay, Dan, I've got you now. Take your time, whenever you're ready."

Daniel finally pulled back from Lee, and stammered, "I'm okay now. Just don't leave me."

With his arm around Daniel, Lee led him toward the center of the passenger waiting area. He kept repeating softly, "You're home! You're home! We were calling you. I guess you couldn't hear us." With his arm still around his brother's shoulders, Lee led Daniel in the direction of their sister. Daniel recognized Barbara immediately. She was still very pretty, but her eyes looked tired.

Barbara was crying as she embraced her brother, and she kept repeating through her tears, "We thought you were dead. I can't believe you're alive! Oh, you're alive. All this time and you're alive. "

The end of the tears and disbelief brought smiles of joy. Lee and Barbara were both surprised at how well and healthy Daniel looked.

There seemed to be people circled around the three of them. Their faces were smiling and watching Daniel. He was very uncomfortable due to their proximity.

Barbara abruptly said, "Well, Dan, aren't you gonna say hello?"

"Whaddya you mean, 'say hello?'" asked Daniel.

One of the smiling faces then spoke to Daniel. "I came to see you. I'll betcha you don't remember me; I'm Skelly." That single name acted as a mental trip wire, bringing Daniel back twenty-two years in time. Immediately all the smiling faces were familiar—his friends from Clason Point. The tall man named Skelly embraced Daniel, and now Daniel was smiling with all of them: Francis (Skelly) Donahue, James (Tiny) Koehler, Jack (Dutch) Schultz, John (Jack) Jaeger, Pete (Mitz) Sicilian, Louie (Giggy) Ferintino, and Joseph (Sal) Salvato.

They were patting his shoulders, messing up his hair, and laughing. All Daniel could do was laugh and cry at the same time. He knew they understood his tears were a display of happiness. His initial feelings were right—he would not able to make them understand the important role they had played during his years in Italy. For now, he simply expressed how much he appreciated them for coming to welcome him. How could they possibly understand? Perhaps at another time and under different circumstances he would be able to find the proper words to explain the important role they played during his captivity over the past twenty-two years.

They walked together through the terminal to a place where many cars were parked. His friends told him they were going to arrange an evening later with a few more guys and the wives for a real celebration. Daniel simply stood and watched their smiling faces and waving hands as they scattered to their cars. He still felt so alone, incapable of expressing himself to men so important and close to him, but yet so remote. At that moment, Daniel understood how difficult returning to life in America was going to be.

"Dan if you're ready, let's go and see Frances," said his concerned brother. There were so many questions as Lee drove to the Bronx that the conversation became an overload of information.

Suddenly Daniel noticed how his brother was dressed. "Are you allowed to dress like that? Aren't you supposed to wear a priest collar and black suit?"

"Oh, that's right, you don't know. I left the seminary just before ordination. I had some doubts. I felt maybe I wanted a family of my own. I left to have time to think, and eventually I decided that I didn't want the priesthood as a vocation."

This was quite a surprise to Daniel. "You mean you're not a priest? How did Mom take it when you left the Franciscans?"

"Not too good. We'll talk about that later."

"Are you married?"

"I married a girl named Joan. We have three children and we live in New Jersey."

"I have five children and live on Long Island," said Barbara.

"Frances has us all beat," Lee added. She has six kids and lives on White Plains Road, very close to Clason Point."

"Wow, I've... let's see, how many... fourteen nieces and nephews? Boy, that makes me feel old," said Daniel with a big grin.

Daniel asked about his mother and father. Barbara said they were fine and quickly changed the subject. "We're going to pick up Frances now."

A long bridge led directly to Bruckner Boulevard, which was a maze of concrete roadways that eventually led to Frances's house. Lee parked in front of a row of brick houses on White Plains Road. Daniel entered his sister's home and began walking down a long hallway. At its end, standing in the open doorway, was his sister Frances. She had gained weight, but there was no confusing that beautiful Ingrid Bergman face. Frances yelled out Daniel's name, and they embraced and smiled at each other. Daniel was out of tears at this point, but he was very happy to be with Frances, his big sister, who had pampered him as her baby brother.

Daniel was introduced to France's husband and their six children while Frances served coffee and pie. They sat at the kitchen table— Daniel, his two sisters, and his brother. How long he had waited for this moment. He was completely exhausted but he felt warm, happy, and truly loved.

Frances began to speak cautiously. "Before we take you to see Mom and Dad, you need to know the years have not been kind to them." Before Daniel could ask what was wrong, Frances said, "Your disappearance has had an impact on their health."

"Please tell me what's wrong," said Daniel. He put down his coffee cup and sat up, giving them his full attention. "C'mon level with me. What's wrong with them?"

"When you were taken," said Barbara. "Dad stayed in Italy for a coupl'a months, filing police reports and hiring a detective agency from Naples to find you. He thought gypsies had kidnapped you for money, but that turned out to be a false lead. When he came home, he felt terrible. He couldn't concentrate, and he was moody and hard to live with. In the meantime, Mom was also a wreck. First she blamed Dad for letting you get taken, and then she began to believe that your disappearance was God's way of punishing her for her sins."

Lee interjected, "Then I left the seminary, and she saw that as another sign that she was being punished by God."

Barbara continued, "Father Lewis talked to both of them many times, but nothing helped. After about a year Dad sold the house on Beach Avenue."

"What? We don't own the house anymore? Why did Dad sell the house? Where do they live?" This was shocking news for Daniel.

Lee joined the conversation. "Dad and Uncle Danny moved to a two-story apartment house on Bolton Avenue near the old Patterson baseball field."

"But I dreamed of living in the Beach Avenue house again," said Daniel. He was obviously disappointed.

Barbara reached over and placed her hand on his. "We're sorry, Dan. I know this is not gonna be easy, but we felt you needed to hear the truth."

Frances finished the explanation. "Dad sold the house. With this money, he went back to Italy, hired two detective agencies, and stayed in Castellamare di Stabia with Grandma and Grandpa for two or three months. He came home when the money was gone. When he returned from Italy, there was a misunderstanding over the conversion of the business from ice and coal delivery to oil delivery. The brothers had a fight and Dad left the business."

"He left the business? How could that happen when he was the leader?"

Lee responded to Daniel's surprised questions. "Dan, we were here when the break-up happened, and we're still not sure how or what happened. Let it go—it's ancient history."

"Is this too much? said Frances. "We can talk about it some other day."

"No, no," replied Daniel. "Go on, what else has happened?"

Frances continued, "Well, Dad began to act very strange. He was no longer talking to his brothers except for Uncle Danny. Then one Sunday, from out of the blue—I remember it was Easter—he told Aunt

Grace he didn't want her in his house any longer. That ended the Sunday family dinners. Gradually Dad got worse—making enemies with everyone in the family, arguing with friends, and getting angry with us for foolish reasons. It was like he was pushing everyone he loved away from him. One doctor called it self-destruction. Then Dad fainted one night at work and went to the hospital. They found out he had low blood pressure, and they wanted him to get something called a pacemaker, but he refused and signed himself out."

"That figures," said Daniel.

Barbara explained, "He was always exhausted. It was his low blood pressure, but he refused no matter how much we hounded him about the pacemaker. Then he started to stutter, and eventually he couldn't talk at all. The doctors could find nothing wrong. One specialist eventually decided he had something they called selective mutism."

"Selective mutism, what's that?" asked Daniel. "Are you saying Dad can't talk?" Daniel was still unable to comprehend so many sudden revelations. "How could he just stop talking if nothing was wrong? Are you telling me he won't be able to speak to me?"

Lee tried to explain. "No, Dan, he is no longer able to speak. The doctor felt there were two reasons: one was that dad subconsciously stopped talking so he would stop hurting everyone. The other was that your disappearance caused him intense guilt and anger, and because he refused to get help, it built up. Over the years, it became something the doctor called trauma.

Daniel was overwhelmed by these medical concepts. "And this trauma thing—it made him stop talking? How could that happen?"

"Well, that's what the doctor told us," answered Lee.

Daniel was visibly shaken by the information about his father. Barbara put her arm around his shoulder, trying to provide some comfort. "Now don't go blaming yourself. The doctor told us he could've been cured if he had gone to a psychiatrist. We were after him for months to get help, but he refused. He could've gotten better. It's his fault, not yours."

"Oh, don't worry. I'm not gonna start blaming myself. It's those damn people from Opi. That's whose fault this is, those damn Italians!"

Lee, seeing Daniel's anger, decided to change the subject. "Uncle Danny could no longer watch the conflict surrounding Dad, so he moved to Florida. He died four years later."

A surprised Daniel cried out, "Uncle Danny is dead! Who else is dead?"

"Aunt Kate died about a year later, but everyone else is still living," said Lee.

Daniel placed his elbow on the table and moved his open palm to his temple. "Uncle Danny and Aunt Kate dead, no house on Beach Avenue, no business, no more Sunday dinners—those lousy Opi people have stolen my life. I hope they burn in hell for what they've done.

There was a pause. The others could see the fury in their brother's eyes, his clenched fists were being held so tight his knuckles were white, his back pressed against the upper portion of his chair, his lips pressed firmly together.

Barbara once again placed her hand on her brother's shoulder.

"Go on. What happened after he died?" asked Daniel.

Lee continued, "After Uncle Danny's funeral, Aunt Kate was really mad at Dad and let him have it in front of the family. It was hard to watch, but that's what happened. Then Aunt Kate died a year later. Cousin Rita believes that without Uncle Danny, Aunt Kate no longer wanted to go on living."

"Mom, what about Mom?" asked Daniel, his voice lowering with anxiety.

"I'm sorry to tell you that Mom has also changed, said Frances. "She no longer looks or acts like the robust, take-charge woman you knew in 1947. The strange thing about your disappearance is that Mom was the only one who believed you were still alive. No matter how hard we tried to convince her that it would be best for her to accept the fact that you were dead, she just wouldn't listen. She would sit in her upholstered chair by the window next to the front door in the apartment on Bolton Avenue praying her rosary. She would always tell us "Someday I'm going to see my Daniel walking toward the house coming home to me."

Frances finished by saying, "Things have become very strained between Mom and Dad. After your disappearance, their relationship slowly went downhill, and now, although they live in the same apartment, they might as well be apart. There is no longer any happiness or laughter in their lives, only silence and anger."

"Take me to Mom and Dad now," said Daniel.

Lee's car entered Bruckner Boulevard, which took them to Soundview Avenue. Traveling east on the main thoroughfare in Clason Point, Daniel was surprised at the changes that had taken place in his old neighborhood. There were no longer empty lots along Soundview Avenue where he used to play ball. These once-empty pieces of land now held stores and row houses. Holy Cross Church and School had been torn down, and a new contemporary church stood in its place with a separate school building. The car stopped at a red light on the corner of Randal and Soundview Avenue, across from the church. Daniel spontaneously asked his brother to make a right and take him to their old house on Beach Avenue. They passed the Beach Theater, which was now an Evangelical church. Bain's candy store had become a walk-in health clinic.

His brother stopped in front of their former house. Daniel got out of the car and walked up to the front stairs and stopped. Standing on the sidewalk, he thought, *How funny, I never thought of a house as something you sell. I always thought a house was part of a family. I wonder how people decide how much a house is worth. How can other people move into another family's house?*

Daniel moved a few feet to the left so he could see the window of the bedroom he used to sleep in with his brother. Daniel's distress grew more intense. He was confused and angry that others were living in what he still thought of as *his* house. It was not a longing for the past or even anger at all the lost years. His unease came from a feeling of betrayal. *My house is still here—the trees are bigger, but the patch of grass in the front is exactly the same; the stoop is still made from brick; the color of the house and shutters are different, but it's the same house, the same shutters. Someone else is sleeping in my bed. All those nights alone in my room in Opi, Imagining sleeping in my bed on Beach Avenue, believing that some day I would be back in my bedroom in Clason Point. Each night, I fell asleep with this thought. What will happen to all those memories? Are they lost forever, where will they go? Will they just disappear?*

Daniel felt a silent numbness, as if he was frozen for a moment, and then the same sadness and hollow feeling in his chest and stomach that he so often felt in Opi began to overtake him once again.

Daniel immediately returned to the car and asked his brother to take him to his mother and father.

It was a short ride to the apartment on Bolton Avenue. Frances had a key to the front door, but she also rang the bell. Daniel was first to walk into the hallway. He was having mixed emotions based on what he had heard from his sisters and brother. He passed a door on the left, which was the entrance to the lower apartment. At the end of a short hallway, there was a steep stairway going to a second floor apartment. He started to climb the stairs, his brother and sisters behind him. On his third step, Daniel heard the squeaky door open a few inches and then stop. He bolted up the stairs two steps at a time and threw open the door to see his mother. They stared at each other for just a moment, and then Suzy extended her arms to him and drew him close to her.

She said nothing as Daniel whispered in her ear, "Mom, it's me. I'm home." Suzy began to cry. Daniel sensed his mother's weak grasp was all she could possibly manage. Finally, they separated. She stared at her son, moving her eyes up and down, closely examining him from head to foot. Still holding his hands, Suzy stepped back, examining him a second time, again looking at Daniel from head to foot.

She raised her eyes to the hallway ceiling and cried out in a loud, anguished voice, "Almighty, forgiving Lord, You did not forsake me. You have answered the prayers offered for Daniel!"

She looked deeply into her son's eyes once again. "Oh, Daniel, I was so afraid that when I saw you, you would be weak and worn from years of abuse and punishment. But look at you, strong and healthy. God has finally forgiven me!" She strained to kneel in front of Daniel. She made the sign of the cross and said, "Thank you, Lord. I will never again abandon you!" With assistance from Daniel, she arose to her feet. Daniel leaned forward and kissed his mother on the cheek and embraced her once again. As he was holding her in his arms, she whispered, "I knew you were alive. I knew you were alive. No one would believe me, but I knew."

Holding onto her son, she seemed to gain more strength in her frail arms. They parted for a second time. As they looked at each other with tear-filled eyes, Daniel was able to see what his brother and sisters had described. His mother's deep, hollow, recessed eye sockets were worn smooth like stones rounded from years of flowing tears. Her brown eyes, those eyes that used to twinkle when he was thirteen, now only expressed suffering.

Suzy took her son's hand and led him toward another room. As they entered what looked like the living room, with the kitchen beyond, Daniel saw his father seated on a sofa. His heart momentarily stopped at what he saw. His once big, strong, vibrant father had become a thin, gaunt shell of a man with sunken cheeks, thin neck, and vacant, expressionless eyes. His father's eyes were completely deserted—they showed no pain, no sadness, no feelings, only emptiness.

Pete was wearing a dark blue suit, pressed pants, white shirt, a tie, and highly shined shoes. His shirt collar, now much too large for his neck, was misshapen from his necktie knot pressing tightly against his throat. His father's suit and tie brought Daniel back twenty-two years in time to Castellamare di Stabia, when he first saw Nonno Leopoldo in bed dressed in his finest clothes and beret.

Daniel moved quickly toward his father. He knelt at his feet, tenderly clutched his father's thin, cold hands, kissed them, and for a few moments rested his head on them. Daniel did not speak, knowing his father would be unable to answer. Pete tried to move, and Daniel leaned back as his father made an effort to struggle out of the sofa. Daniel tried to help by holding his father's arm, but Pete removed his arm from Daniel's grasp. Pete continued struggling, but eventually was able to stand on his own. Reaching out, he took Daniel's face in both his hands—those same fleshy, warm, powerful hands that would often enclose Daniel's cheeks as a child were now scrawny, angular, and bony. The thick flesh, which had provided warmth to Daniel's face on the coldest day, was now wrinkled and no longer able to radiate heat.

Looking at Daniel with his forsaken eyes, Pete quietly and with great hesitation tried to speak. "Fffor… gggggive… mmmee." Daniel leaned forward, took his father's frail, thin body into his strong arms, their bodies touched in a warm embrace.

Pete let out a slight sob—finally, some sign of emotion. Daniel held his father tightly as their heads rested on each other's shoulders. Daniel said softly, "I'm home, Dad. It's all over. I love you dad. There is nothing to forgive. You did everything a father could do to protect his son. You must no longer blame yourself for the evil acts of others."

Pete would not allow his body to be separated from his son. Slowly his sobs increased in intensity until they became a torrent of uncontrollable tears, along with his quaking body. Daniel was forced to grasp his father tightly because Pete was no longer able to hold on to his son. Daniel feared that if he let go, his father would collapse. Pete's crying became more and more intense. Daniel continued to hold his father, as his brother and sisters helped Daniel lower him back down onto the sofa. With Lee and Frances on either side of their father, they began to gently massage Pete's shoulders. Daniel knelt at his father's feet and rested his head on his lap. Pete's uncontrollable crying continued. Daniel gently embraced his father's waist, as Frances and Lee continued to massage their father's shoulders.

Suzy seemed to have gathered strength from the reunion with her son. She raised her voice and said, "This has been twenty years in the making. Maybe now my husband will return from his private hell and come back to his family."

It was difficult to keep track of time in this highly emotional situation, but at some point Pete's agitation gradually reduced to a level at which Daniel's brother and sisters felt they could sit next to him on the sofa. Although tears continued to roll down his cheeks, his entire body was now completely limp, and he rested his head on the back of the sofa. Eventually his tears stopped, but he seemed unable to move. Suzy suggested that Pete be taken to his bed. With help from his sisters and brother, Daniel brought his father to the bedroom at the front of the apartment. Daniel told them he wanted to be alone with his father. After removing his father's outer clothes, Daniel helped him to bed and placed the covers over his shoulders.

As Daniel stroked his father's forehead, he said, "There will be no more blame. The blame belongs to the evil people in Opi."

Pete stared into his son's face with eyes that now seemed to express a tinge of solace. Pete removed his right arm from under the covers and clasped Daniel's left hand in his. With the little strength left in his body, he tried to squeeze Daniel's hand. Daniel, sitting next to his father, placed his right hand over the top of his father's cold hand. Pete, once again began to quietly sob, and he gave short, hesitant gasps as his shoulders and chest moved in unison with his sobbing.

Daniel talked quietly to his father, telling him how much he had missed him while he was a prisoner in Italy, and how he thought of him each night. "That's all in the past. All that matters now is that I am home and we are together again."

Pete soon closed his eyes and his sobbing subsided. Daniel held his father's hand until his deep breathing suggested he had fallen to sleep. Daniel gently began to slide his hands out of his father's grasp, but Pete—with his eyes still closed—gripped his son's hand again, moving it closer to him. Daniel thought angrily about how the acts of the Sgammotta family had not only affected him, but had reached across the Atlantic and devastated his parents. Daniel was beginning to understand that along with his own healing he would have to help his parents through their healing process.

Daniel kissed the back of his father's hand and rested his head next to his father's hip. Soon, Daniel could tell by his father's deep breathing that he was in a deep sleep. Daniel gently raised his head, removed his hand, and quietly left the room.

EPILOGUE

Klein returned to Opi five weeks after being released and married Giovanna. The Wedding Mass was performed by a new priest, who had been assigned to Opi three weeks after the captives were freed. Klein told the others that his parents were initially unwilling to go to Opi to meet Giovanna and her parents, and attend the Opi wedding, but Klein was adamant about them joining him for the special event. He knew how important their presence would be for Giovanna. They eventually consented, not wanting to disappoint their recently returned son. There was a brief, awkward reception consisting only of Giovanna's and Klein's families immediately after the Mass. The following day Klein, Giovanna, and Klein's parents left Opi and returned to Austria for a second wedding ceremony and the beginning of their new life.

After Daniel had been home for ten weeks, he traveled to Egypt to attend the funeral services of his fellow captive Omar. The six men spent a great deal of time discussing the difficulty of reconnecting to their former lives.

Daniel was now living with his parents on Bolton Avenue and was attending night school to earn his General Educational Development high school diploma. Eight months after being freed, Daniel received a call from Ruffino, who was in New York attending a conference at the United Nations headquarters in Manhattan. Ruffino invited Daniel to visit with him at the United Nations building. They had a happy reunion and lunched in the United Nations delegates' dining room. That night, Daniel and Ruffino walked in Times Square eating ice cream, laughing, and thinking about the gelato they had enjoyed so many years before in Castellamare di Stabia.

Ruffino knew someone from the United Nations who was friendly with Dr. Roscoe Brown, President of Bronx Community College. Ruffino arranged for Daniel to meet Dr. Brown to determine if he might be eligible to register as a student. Ruffino once again was motivating Daniel intellectually. In addition to his role in supporting his parents, Daniel's main achievement was his education. He became a proud junior college student at Bronx Community College. Daniel soon earned the nickname "Pops," an affectionate name given to him by his African-American and Hispanic classmates. When Daniel finished his schooling, he became a judicial court stenographer in Manhattan.

Pete died in his sleep three years after Daniel returned. During this time, Pete began to slowly regain his ability to speak, first in simple greetings, then groups of words that eventually led to short sentences. In time, he was able to express thoughts and simple feelings. Daniel was gratified that his return had such a positive effect on his father. He was especially pleased to see the smile on his father's face when Daniel interacted with Pete's fourteen grandchildren, teasing them and laughing with them, and the pleasure Pete felt when he was able to say, "I love you," as his grandchildren gave him a goodbye hug and kiss.

However, Pete was unable to completely resolve some of his family relationships. His unwillingness to reconcile with his younger brothers remained a frustration for Daniel. Bob and Phil paid their respects at his funeral. Suzy received a Mass card from Al and Pia two weeks after the funeral with a brief note telling her of the many people who attended the Funeral Mass in Castellamare de Stabia for Leopoldo's son.

Suzy passed away five years after Daniel's return. She died peacefully, fully confident that she had been forgiven by her God.

Daniel heard that John Owens, an old elementary school friend, was now living in Woodmere, Long Island, New York. He was able to make contact with John, and soon thereafter the two men met for lunch and a long afternoon of conversation. They reminisced about their days at Holy Cross School. John rummaged through some old boxes in his basement and found the 1947 graduation picture from Holy Cross School, a picture Daniel should have been in. It was great fun seeing all those familiar faces and trying to put names to each face.

As usual, whenever Catholic grammar school friends meet, the conversation invariably turns to the teaching nuns. In March of 1947, while visiting Nonno Leopoldo, when Daniel's dad suggested that he tell his mother about his newfound resolve to work hard in school, there was one other person Daniel had planned on telling, Sister Clara. She had been his seventh grade teacher, and she had constantly tried to motivate Daniel to improve his study habits. Sister Clara was a member of the Franciscan order that made up the Holy Cross School faculty. The nuns wore a dark brown, flowing garment from neck to ankles, black shoes, a stiff, white bib called a *guimpe* secured tightly at the neck, a headpiece that had a stiff, heavily starched white front that sharply pressed into the skin of their foreheads, and a black veil that covered the back of their necks and shoulders. They wore a double white rope around their waist with two descending knotted rope strands on their right side.

The church and school were in the same building. The Franciscan priests lived in a brick semi-cloistered rectory to the right of the church, and the nuns lived on the second floor of a two-story, wooden building to the left of the church. The lower level of the wooden building was a large room with a stage. This open area was used for recreational and church activities, fife and drum corps practice, basketball games, play rehearsals, and adult and student meetings.

Attending school with the nuns had not been a pleasant experience for Daniel, but he often felt sorry for his teachers. They wore what looked to be the most uncomfortable garment that could be designed and they lived over a hall where a fife and drum corps practiced in the evening. Considering the religious garment they were required to wear and their living arrangements, one should not have been surprised at their lack of patience.

At lunch that afternoon, John told Daniel a very moving story about one of the teachers at Holy Cross School. John's younger sister had become a Franciscan nun, and she worked in a home for the retired sisters of her province. One of John's former teachers at Holy Cross School, Sister Dolerine, was now living at the facility, and John was interested in visiting her. He was thrilled she had remembered him. After an enjoyable conversation, John was preparing to leave when Sister Dolerine became quite serious and said, "John, I hope you can forgive me for the way I taught you and the other students. I was very young when I became a nun, and we were taught to be harsh and strict with children. I never enjoyed teaching that way, but I was bound by a vow of obedience. I can now see that our methods were often cruel, and in many ways harmful to children."

John embraced his frail, old teacher, assuring her that there was nothing to forgive and that he was sure his classmates—now that they were older and had families of their own—certainly understood and appreciated her efforts.

John was a very spiritual man, who saw God as a constant presence in his daily life. He went on to explain to Daniel that he was sure God brought him to New Jersey that day to bring healing to a good woman whom he suspected wanted desperately to say to one of her former students that she was sorry.

This simple story of Sister Dolerine helped Daniel think more seriously about how he was adapting to his freedom and the unique way he looked at life since his release. Daniel had been home for almost six years, enjoyed his time at school, spending time with family and friends, and earning a decent salary. He had taken five special trips to visit with his five brothers from Opi. However, he continually found himself categorizing people, events, and social and educational experiences in the context of his hostage experience.

Daniel often thought about Sister Dolerine. Did her obedience to her superiors cause her deep conflict about her duties and perhaps her life? Daniel wondered if Sister Dolerine also experienced the feeling of being held hostage to methods she might have intuitively felt was inconsistent with her beliefs. Did she also experience the anguish of being *forced* to work each day knowing she was not free?

Daniel's parents, in a very real way, had made themselves hostages for twenty-two years. They bound themselves—through the punishment of guilt and false beliefs—to a form of captivity that had a devastating effect on their lives and the lives of their family members.

What about Maria Antonia, Gelsomina, Father Mascia, and the others in Opi? Were they not held hostage in their own homes—not by the precipice the town was built on, the forest, the bears, the distant mountain range, or the men in the wagons—but by their own consciences, which constantly reminded them of the evil they had perpetrated on seven young boys and their families?

Daniel was beginning to understand that this narrow way of processing life's events was not helpful to his adjustment. He held on to the hope that in the future he would one day be able to lose his sad way of observing people and events, and learn to accept his life in a more satisfying and natural way.

POSTSCRIPT

I have taken the liberty of using the actual names of some of the current residents of Opi in this story. Maria Antonia Sgammotta, the author's first cousin and the daughter of his Aunt Alessandria, lives in a modest house in Opi close to the town church. Nicoangelo Leone, the author's second cousin and the son of his grandfather's brother, also lives in Opi. Petrizio Ursitti lives in Opi and tends to his small herd of sheep. The author's Aunt Pia's husband, Rudolpho Mascia, lives in Opi with his two daughters, Furina and Angelina. Uncle Rudolpho is in his late 90s and in relatively good health. Ruffino Sgammotta, the son of the author's Aunt Alessandrina is retired and lives in Opi with his wife and son.

Gelsomina Boccia Cimini, a beloved aunt of the author, was born, married, and raised two young children in Opi. She immigrated to the United States in the mid 1950s to join her husband, who had been living in America and had served in the American Army during World War II. In this novel, the author describes various World War II experiences of Gelsomina. Many of the war tales in this novel were adapted from the actual experiences of the author's Aunt Gelsomina, who passed away in October of 2004 at the age of 93.

The Battle of the Sangro Line was a major World War II battle that began in November, 1943, in and around the town of Opi, and lasted until the spring of 1944. The Allied force during this battle was comprised the British 8th Army, led by General, Sir Bernard L. Montgomery, and the American 5th Army, led by General Mark W. Clark.

One final note of interest: *The Independent*, a British newspaper, reported on April 21, 2004, that three former Nazis SS officers were put on trial for their involvement in the massacre of 560 Italian citizens in the Tuscan hill town of Sant'Anna di Stazzema. The defendants— Gerhard Sommer, Alfred Schoneberg, and Ludwig Sonnntag—now live in Germany. During 2004, they were the subjects of a parallel German investigation into this alleged atrocity.

Using the author's personal family experiences to write the early part of this novel helped reconnect him to his deceased parents. The opportunity to recall their actions and behaviors not only helped the author to write the second and third chapters, it also restored them to his memory, giving him unexpected joy he had not anticipated.

ABOUT THE AUTHOR

Peter D. Cimini is an educator, inventor, and writer. He holds two United States patents: one for a device called The Expand-a-Binder, and a second for a Flossing Mouthpiece. He obtained his undergraduate and graduate degrees from New York University. Peter served two years in the military and taught in the New York City Public Schools for three years, where he met his wife, Virginia.

Peter moved to Connecticut in 1970 and served as a curriculum specialist for the Newington Public Schools for twenty-two years. He retired from his administrative position in Newington to write full-time. He wrote magazine and newspaper articles, and completed his first novel, *The Secret Sin of Opi*, using his love of Italian culture as the backdrop for this unique story of long-term captivity and exploitation.

ABOUT THE COVER ARTIST

Stephen Linde is a Signature Member as well as the Vice President of the Connecticut Pastel Society. His work has been exhibited at Connecticut Pastel Society shows and various galleries in Connecticut and New York. Steve is a graduate of Central Connecticut State College, where he obtained a Bachelor of Art Degree as well as a Masters in Art Education. He has been a teacher of art in the Newington, Connecticut school system for the past thirty-two years and resides in East Granby, Connecticut with his wife, Pat. Light, shadows, and the passing of the seasons provide an unending source of material for his paintings.

ABOUT THE EDITOR

Jessica Bryan is a freelance book editor and author. In 2005, three of the books she edited for the American Academy of Neurology's patient series were nominated for the Foreword Award. In addition to specializing in health-related books for laypersons, she edits self-help, spiritual, and metaphysical books, including three published by Beyond Words Publishing of Portland, Oregon: *Cell-Level Healing*; *JOHN OF GOD: The Brazilian Healer Who's Touched the Lives of Millions*; and *Animals in Spirit*.

Jessica is the author of *PSYCHIC SURGERY AND FAITH HEALING: An Exploration of Multi-Dimensional Realities, Indigenous Healing, and Medical Miracles in the Philippine Lowlands* (Red Wheel/ Weiser/Conari, 2008). She is also the author of *Love is Ageless: Stories About Alzheimer's Disease* (Lompico Creek Press, 2002).

Jessica lives in Southern Oregon with Tom Clunie D.C. and can be reached by e-mail to editor@mind.net or telephone: 541-535-6044.